ASHREALM: Book I

A Blue Horizon

M.R. Darling

Dedicated to those who said I couldn't.

Prologue

The morning was cold, dark, and wet as Jerich trudged his way to the train station. Despite the clear skies that had been forecasted from his unrelenting clock radio, life had taught him to expect the worst. Expect it from people, expect it from life, expect it from everything really. With an umbrella and the shame of years in a dead-end job as his only companions, he marched on as his thoughts drifted towards escaping. Daydreaming about pulling himself out of his self-imposed confinement, he imagined scenarios filled with vindication; quitting and leaving his employers with such a concise and calculated piece of his mind that his exit would long be recounted.

He was fooling himself of course. The spiraling economy had made jobs few and far between with full-time jobs rarer still. His freedom would likely come in the form of termination, and there would be no whispers of his leaving. He would simply be another ripple in the great stream of consumerism that rushed inextricably onward towards insolvency. Jerich instead concentrated on happier deceptions such as Lottery winnings and other get rich quick schemes that helped stem the tide of depression. Headlights beamed beneath the drizzle as the rush of steel roared past him towards, presumably, better paying jobs and lazy latte conversations with people not ready to eat the barrel of a shotgun to escape their lives. He was a lone, wandering soul stuck beneath the drenching canopy he held listlessly, unable to afford more than the fraying canvas and crooked pole keeping him from complete saturation.

The lights of the train station in the distance cut through the fog of moisture in the air as Jerich skillfully dodged and jumped the various pits of mud and despair. He could hear the approach of the train and knew, once again, that he would miss the immediate departure that had forever eluded him. Eternally ten seconds too late and ten feet too short, he had long realized that running only made you tired as you watched your ride leave without you. At least he would have an empty place to sit as he waited for the next arrival.

The water cascaded down the glass of the station, blurring out the view of houses with big back yards, patio furniture and expensive barbecues waiting to entertain those who could afford them. Dim and musty, the platform was empty save for a few Mockingbirds hiding from the downpour. The track light was green in the distance announcing that no train would be arriving soon. His mind drifted to old habits. Long ago Jerich had ceased to bring music with him on his travels, despite the small comfort it granted. His life was full of distraction and he needed to concentrate on getting himself out of this pit of low-wage existence. Success would not present itself to him if he didn't bother to listen.

Thunder rolled in the distance as the rain increased its assault on the city. Three years ago, a flood had washed his boss's car away along with enough debris to cost the city millions in damages, and in the lowlands, entire villages and small towns had almost been completely destroyed by the calamity. The area was still reeling from the devastation, and any rain that lasted longer than a few hours tended to make people nervous.

Jerich on the other hand silently willed it on, hoping it to mean a few days off. It was selfish, but he wished for it all the same. Not that time off did him much good, he spent his hours doing literally that, spending. Spending time on nothing, money on the unnecessary, and thought on the inescapable return to drudgery. His girlfriend of five years had left him and Jerich could hardly blame her. His life was a rotation of survival, small hopes, and resignation.

The light down the track switched to red indicating an approaching train. Jerich stood and shook his umbrella of the excess water. Getting too comfy would only make exercise of any kind more difficult than it had to be, and he had an entire day of it to look forward to. Looking down the track, he searched for the approaching light. The caw of a crow overhead caught his attention and he turned instinctively towards the noise. The bird sounded as though it was inside the station, just overhead. He searched for it. Unable to locate anything moving he stretched to listen.

The rain had stopped.

'That was sudden.' Jerich thought, it seemed unnatural. Looking around the station, he realized that everything was silent. Not a horn or even the sound of wind through the station could be heard.

A definite build up of tension could be felt in the air though. A silent pounding that seemed to press against his eardrums like barometric pressure. Jerich opened his mouth to relieve the tension then swallowed hard. The faint popping in his ears restored the sounds of the world around him, and he silently thanked the powers that be for not striking him deaf. He noticed the approaching train was almost upon him, and following its usual screech and wine, the train stopped with a hiss and the doors opened in front of him.

Strangely, no one exited the train. The doors were not automatic, and he had not pressed the button to open them. Stranger still was that no one seemed to be aboard. At this time of the morning the cars were usually brimming with jostling passengers barely clutching to consciousness. Jerich stepped in and found a seat next to the window. The doors closed, then opened and finally closed again. With a lurch, the train began to travel back the way it came instead of continuing onwards.

"What the hell?" Jerich said out loud as he stood up, "We're going the wrong way, assholes!"

Stepping over to the emergency stop lever, Jerich wondered if he should pull it. If he did and something wasn't catastrophically wrong he would likely be fined, something he couldn't afford.

Instead, he looked out the window through the streaming water that passed by. Nothing seemed out of the ordinary except that they were traveling in the wrong direction. Perhaps he had missed an announcement, perhaps there was a problem up the track, and the train was being re-routed.

The lights flickered above him with a faint buzz and the train seemed to sputter and slow down beneath his feet. Through the window he noticed the headlights of another train approaching on the opposite rail. Wondering if these problems were restricted to his train alone, Jerich pressed closer. Outside he could see the remains of an engine slowly pass by. The front of the engine was pristine but as it passed by the car seemed to melt into the ground. A puddle of black mass seeping into the steel and stone beneath, the cause completely invisible.

Suddenly, the car lurched forward and sputtered again, coming to life and accelerating quickly. Jerich grabbed the pole overhead as he began to tumble with momentum. The speed of the train seemed to continue well past what he considered normal or even acceptable. In a panic, Jerich searched for anything he could brace himself with in case they derailed. At the front, he had missed a small girl huddled in the corner. No more than a ball of clothing and limbs hugging itself, Jerich could see the quick motions of panicked breaths, though she made not a sound.

"Hey!" Jerich yelled out to the small figure. "Hey, are you alright?"

The ball made no attempt to answer, but instead managed to curl up even smaller.

"Look," Jerich continued, "we have to get off this train. It's unsafe!" Again no reply was forthcoming. "I'm going to pull the emergency stop switch, you'd better hang on to something!"

Jerich hoped she would have the common sense to brace herself as he leaned out to pull the switch.

Nothing happened.

Jerich pulled it again fruitlessly.

"Shit!" he yelled, and hammered on it with the side of his fist. Frantically he looked around for something to smash open a window, but nothing was readily available. Moving to the front of the speeding car he wondered if he could kick open one of the side doors. He remembered reading something like that for emergency purposes, somewhere, but he wasn't sure if it was on a train.

Tentatively he gave a small kick at the center of the door, not much happened. Again he kicked, this time with more force, but the door wouldn't budge. Consuming fear grabbed ahold of him, and Jerich backed up as far as he could to get a running start. As he took flight, the train stuttered. Slamming into a post instead, his head bounced off of the metal. Staggered, he fell to the floor in a white flash of pain.

His head throbbing, Jerich tried to sit up, but the train was weaving back and forth in spurts. Reaching for his forehead, he felt blood, and the taste of copper was flooding his mouth. Spitting, he clawed for a handhold of something to help him get to his feet. The exertion almost rendered him unconscious, as another pang passed through his skull. The train had begun its climb to full speed again, and Jerich could barely stay vertical as it gained momentum.

The pounding in his head was getting worse, and he could feel another build up. The same kind that had assailed him in the station. It pressed into in his ears like deep water, all sound around him disappeared as the compression worsened. Just when he thought his head would explode, Jerich saw a flash of intense blue light appear at the back of the train car.

Despite the pressure, he could hear a hissing sound. Turning to look at the source, he was nearly blinded by the brilliant illumination facing him. Shielding his eyes, Jerich tried to see through to the cause. It looked as if the rear of the train was on fire, but bright and blue. Turning away he found renewed strength in the stark fear that overtook him. Focusing once again on the door and his escape from whatever was fast approaching, Jerich hurled himself at the exit.

One side of the gate gave way and bent outwards as his shoulder grew instantly numb from the impact. The adrenaline coursing through him had dulled the pain he would be feeling later, if he managed to escape. Grabbing one door with both hands, he pulled inwards while using his foot to push out on the other, trying to further separate the two halves. There was no give from either. Instead, Jerich grabbed the bar above his head and began to kick full force at the hole he had managed to create. The security glass cracked, and the door began to pry open in excruciatingly small increments.

After several solid hits, one side of the bar he clung to gave way, and Jerich fell back to the floor of the car. His chest cramped as the wind was partially knocked out of him, but his fear allowed him to recover quickly. Sitting up, he dared to steal another look at the rear of the train. The light was almost bearable to peer into now, and he could see that it wasn't a fire consuming the rear of the car. It appeared more like some kind of smoke, billowing out from something that was smoldering. Through the smoke, he could see bright blue flecks, like coals burning away, there were traces of white ash floating in the air all around it.

The smoke began to clear a little, and Jerich got a better look at what was creating the chaos.

A ball took up the width of the aisle, seething away at the rear. It blistered with blue light as smoke escaped from cracks on its surface. Jerich was awestruck, searching for understanding when the surface of the ball began to move. Sliding away, his back hit the doorway as he tried to distance himself from what he was witnessing.

At first, it looked as if the ball was crumbling and falling to dust. Then it began to expand, uncoiling itself. Slowly, it moved, rising. Jerich could clearly see legs beneath it, and he watched as arms extended outward towards the walls of the train. Finally, it raised its head and Jerich felt his heart stop as he stared into what was clearly a face. A halo of light and smoke surrounded the head while the eyes and mouth were only dark holes within.

The creature opened its mouth in a silent scream as it was consumed once again in a blinding light. Jerich turned his head from the flash. He could feel it move, the pressure increasing as it advanced. Glancing back, he could see tendrils of smoke emanating from the sides of the creature. They stretched out to the walls of the train and began to eat through everything in their path, burning and melting the very steel. An intense phosphorus smell filled the air, but instead of an intense heat, Jerich felt bone cold. A hopelessness came over him, and he thought he should just lay here, give up, and be done with it.

A harsh cough from behind brought him back from his stupor. Glancing to the front of the train, Jerich suddenly remembered the girl cowering there. The thought of another life depending on him reignited his fight or flight mechanic, and he found the power to stand up. Reaching above, Jerich grabbed the half-broken bar that had failed him and pulled. Wrenching from side to side, it quickly came loose in his hands. Turning back to the doors, he jammed the bar In the opening and began to pry them apart.

He was making good headway, a human-sized hole was almost accessible, enough for the girl to get through. Jerich called out to her, "Hey! You can get out through here, come on."

The girl sat motionless.

"Move it, we've got to go!" he yelled out once again.

She only huddled down farther.

Jerich turned back towards the approaching menace. It was slow but constant. There was precious little time left. He returned to expanding their way of escape. If it came down to it, he would grab her and push her through.

The rear of the train car suddenly dropped. Jerich lost his balance and bounced off the seats, the bar slipped from his hands. It tumbled down the inclined floor towards the blue glow that seemed unaffected by the sudden shift. The back of the car was completely missing, he could now see outside and into the gloom. Sparks sprayed from the metal as it dragged behind, but the train continued to move forward. Jerich quickly looked back to where the girl had been, but she was nowhere to be found. Afraid she had somehow slipped into the approaching doom, he pulled himself towards the front grabbing pole and seat where he could.

Hiding beneath a bench, the girl was clinging on to the posts for dear life. Jerich reached out and tried to pull her towards him but she held fast. "Let go!" he screamed. "I've got you!"

The girl yanked away and buried herself farther under the bench. Jerich looked towards the rear of the train, the creature was almost upon them. Once again he grabbed for her but she refused to let go. It would be him alone or nobody would be leaving. Going against all the preconceived notions he'd had about himself, his instinct for self-preservation won out, and he ran for the door. Starting head-first, he squeezed through and started pulling himself clear using anything he could grab. Looking at the ground passing quickly beneath him, he hesitated and worried about the landing. Inside the train, his leg suddenly became ice cold. Shocking him into action, he pulled himself the rest of the way through and braced for impact.

The stony ground came up hard and fast and Jerich heard his shoulder break. Tumbling with the momentum, he felt wet rocks scratch at his exposed areas, and dig into his skin. His body windmilled a few times and finally he came to rest on his back. The rain poured down on his face, washing blood into his eyes. Turning his head away from the onslaught of rain, he watched the sparks fly from the undercarriage of the train as it continued down the tracks. What remained of the car finally slid off the rails and tumbled, buckling as it rolled over. The consequences of what he had done came down on him with brunt understanding.

He had left her. She was dead now. Because of him.

Rolling his head back into the falling rain, he let it wash away his tears.

1

This Way Cometh

B ill looked out into the beautiful view he had from the back porch of his home away from the city. He had picked this spot specifically for many reasons, but this view was in the top three. Sipping his fresh espresso, he peered once again at the tablet in front of him. On it was a document that he had read five times now and he still wasn't sure it was real. The email responsible for its delivery to him was from a source he trusted, but he still just couldn't process the information yet.

In the distance, he could hear the staccato of a helicopter echoing off the mountain tops. Glancing at his watch, he suddenly realized how much time had passed in his pondering of the facts. Looking back at the small screen, Bill wanted to thank his source but that would acknowledge receipt, a definite faux pas. Instead, he poured some more coffee and added his customary color and sweetness into the steaming dark. The embargo with Cuba made it hard to get good coffee these days for some people. Bill was thankful as he sipped, that he was not some people.

It had been years since Bill was the head of an organization affectionately known as *The Shop*. On paper it was a Private Military Contractor, its real face - a highly funded and deep black arm of the government. Some country leaders came and went without ever knowing of its existence, others were trusted because they understood the necessity. The Shop specialized in informational warfare, but weren't above getting their hands dirty, and sometimes things just had to be done off the books. Bill had his hand in a few of the great but silent triumphs in world peace. He also had a hand in some equally silent but horrific atrocities committed to preserve our way of life. He was ruthless when provoked: it's what made him a force to be reckoned with and remembered. It's also what made him quit; that, and the toll it took on his life.

"Mister Wyburn," asked a small but rotund woman with a Mexican accent. "Shall I set another place at the table?"

"Thanks Rosalita, bring out some fruit and those fresh muffins as well," Bill responded as he flipped the cover of his tablet closed and slid it aside.

Reaching over to his small radio, Bill turned it on and flipped to one of his presets. Jazz began to flow from the small speakers as he sat back in his chair and looked skywards. Small wisps of clouds were floating overhead but otherwise, it was a perfect day.

"Hello Bill," said a voice from behind.

"Frank," Bill responded, still staring upwards. "Have a seat."

Frank took the adjacent chair as Rosalita placed an empty mug and a plate of muffins and fruit on the table.

"You wish I pour?" Rosalita asked Frank in broken English.

Frank raised his hand and shook his head, Rosalita smiled in response and returned inside the house.

Glancing first at the radio, then at the muffins Frank shook his head, "Bran and Jazz? Some things never change."

Bill disregarded the comment, "What's up Frank? You didn't come for coffee."

Frank smiled, "Oh, I don't know about that. It smells like Cuban you've got brewing there, embargoed isn't it?

"It is indeed," Bill smiled and took a healthy sip from his mug.

Frank poured himself a cup, added nothing to it and brought it up to his nose.

"Ahh," Frank smiled and took a small sip. "You've always got the best coffee Bill, even if you have to break international laws to get it."

Bill set the mug down and stared out at the scenery, "Nasty business up North Frank, seems almost implausible. I'm still having a hard time believing half of what I've heard."

Frank's frown was almost invisible, "I won't ask how you've come by your info, but here's the scoop Bill; it's bad. Worse than that, it's bizarre. We've got the entire research team on it now, but so far they've come up with nothing."

"What do we know?" asked Bill, falling into old habits.

"Beyond the information you probably already have?" Frank looked into his coffee, "Nothing."

It was Bill's turn to frown, "Now that's bullshit, and you know it Frank."

"You're not Shop anymore Bill," Frank pointed out, "You know the rules, same as I."

"How about I tell you what I know and you smile where I'm right?" Bill asked, wearing a lopsided grin.

Frank smirked, "I'd ask how secure your place is, but it took my team a week to find you."

"It's deliberate Frank," Bill said more somberly, "I shouldn't have to remind you why."

Frank sighed and looked out across the countryside, "Okay Bill, shoot."

"First, we have a containment situation, something so viral that nothing survives its touch." Bill pressed his finger onto the table in front of him, counting. "Second, it's something we don't even have a name for. We don't know where it came from or who's responsible."

Frank smiled and stared into his coffee.

Bill continued, "Third we have nothing to combat it, nor can we seem to get a sample because it can't survive outside of its own ecosystem. Which begs the question: why are we not just killing it? If it requires its own environment to live, the solution is pretty obvious."

"Bill," Frank chastened, "it's not that simple. We can't just change the environment in a tightly focused spot now can we?

"Now that's just more bullshit Frank," Bill sat back in his chair, "you're holding out in case it's useful."

Frank frowned again, more obviously this time. "That's just paranoia talking Bill, you don't have all of the facts, and you're speculating."

Bill was undeterred, "A possibly new virus that no one knows anything about in an environment ripe with natural experimentation on fauna, flora, animals and even humans. Costing the shop nothing to create, ask permission for, or assume any responsibility in founding." He stared at Frank, "It's almost too perfect."

Frank set his coffee down so hard it almost tipped, "Bill, you're talking nonsense! You've been up here alone for too long, and it's deteriorating your state of mind. We're the good guys here, remember?" He leaned back, "You have to let go of the past; it's killing you."

Bill narrowly regarded Frank, "Your concern for my well being is made of the same bullshit you've been handing me since you got here Frank. You want free advice on how to capitalize on this so you can go back to Keating and pawn it off as your own."

Frank looked away and sat back in his chair.

"That bastard is the reason behind my state of mind!" Bill paused and glared, "His manipulation, his insistence, and especially his lack of security to ensure plausible deniability all cost me dearly, and both he and you can go fuck yourselves!" Bill threw his coffee cup over the railing, into the ravine below and stared out into the blue.

Frank looked stone faced at his shoes, "You know Bill, there's been a lot of talk about security lately. Loose ends to put a finer point on it."

Bill looked back at Frank, anger and suspicion in his eyes.

"Some people think you're a danger to the organization." Frank met Bill's stare. "You know more about The Shop than any one person associated with it. Your capture or dissension could spell not only its end, but a risk to this entire country."

"Spare me the threats," Bill looked back at Frank, "and the patriarchal facade. If The Shop really believed I was a danger, I'd be dead right now. Your sharpshooter on that hill over there would have put a bullet through my head already."

Frank looked amused, "That's that paranoia talking again."

Bill grabbed for an apple, "I heard him coming in at six this morning. He must be a rookie, a pro would have hiked it instead of using a motorbike. Noise echoes off everything out here." Looking up at Frank, Bill took a bite.

Frank frowned and stared down into his cup.

"You better hope he's a good shot, the wind picks up quick in this ravine and from this angle," Bill sat back in his chair, "he's got an even chance of hitting you instead."

Frank looked back at Bill and shook his head, "Bill, you need to get out of this place for a while. Clear your head, and reconnect with the world again. You're seeing ghosts that aren't there."

Pausing to look out across the hills, Frank continued "I can't even begin to understand what you've gone through, and I won't pretend to, but The Shop, Keating, are worried about how you are handling things. They want assurances that you haven't gone off the reservation."

Standing up, Frank walked over behind Bill, "How about I bring you in as a consultant on this? It would do you some good to get working again, and get your mind off of the past. Set The Shop at ease about risk."

Bill looked out into the distance, but said nothing.

"I'll set it up, and I promise to keep Keating at a distance." Frank patted Bill's shoulder, "Strictly advisory, and you can get first hand knowledge instead of relying on week old intel from excommunicated agents hiding on foreign soil."

Smiling, Frank headed for the door to leave. "I'll send someone for you tomorrow, oh six hundred. Trust me old friend, after a week or so on campus you'll feel like yourself again."

"Frank," Bill finally said, "tell your rookie to bring some coverage next time. The light glinting from his scope is almost blinding."

––––––––––

The bathroom was awash in mist as the shower was turned off. Stepping out, Nick toweled dry and approached the shaving mirror. With a quick wipe, the glass cleared and reflected the unshaven and disheveled man in front of it. He was forty, and had nothing to show for it. He looked deep into the face before him: crevasses and lines that accentuated smiles he couldn't remember wearing stared back. He sighed and grabbed for his razor. Nick preferred a disposable over electric or those fancy triple-headed monstrosities: all those years in field he supposed.

The military base he lived on was cushy in comparison to the swamps, jungle, and sand he was used to living in. It always made him feel a little guilty and pampered when he returned from abroad, knowing how many soldiers were still out there slugging through the thick of it. His superiors had tried to promote him so many times he had lost count. When they had finally had enough and forced it on him, he punched the messenger and got himself time in the brig instead. They busted him down to Captain but his commanders had finally left him alone.

The call had come early morning. A new assignment, and he had to get his ass in gear to make it to the briefing on time. It was a good thing he did his uniform upkeep before bed, something he'd learned to do after getting calls like this in the past. It would be a quick dress then off across the base without any breakfast, but he'd be fine.

A knock at the door came just as he was lacing up his boots. Nick did a quick finish, and answered.

"Captain Miller," a decked out Lieutenant saluted, "please follow me."

Nick closed the door behind him, and followed the very stiff and well-pressed man. Obviously he'd never seen action in his time or he wouldn't be wasting effort on office politics. It's not how real advancement worked here, it's how you kept yourself chained to a desk. Nick kept his thoughts to himself like a good soldier, and was led to the master briefing room. This was clearly important, or the meeting would have been relegated to an office. He stepped through the doors to a vast room with only a few people in it, all seated and eating.

"Sit down Captain," said a balding and bearded man on the left, "have some breakfast."

Nick continued to stand at attention until Colonel Blackburn spoke up, "Take a seat Miller, get some food into you."

'Never miss a chance to eat, you never know when the next chance will arrive.' It was an old military concept, and it held true. Nick filled a plate with bacon and eggs and sat down. A few bites in, Nick could tell that both the bacon and eggs were fresh. All thanks to the company in the room no doubt. The only military personnel here was himself, the Colonel and a few ranks off to the side for show. The rest were civilians, so that meant civilian problems and, civilian attitude. Nick couldn't abide by it, the thought of some bleeding heart liberal calling him 'sir' made him cringe. They always wanted results, and never considered the actions it took to achieve them. Publicly condemning those actions later when things came out in the wash. Losing his appetite, he instead swallowed down some black and very stiff coffee, hoping this would be over soon.

Nick appraised the people before him. The bald guy was obviously in charge. The one sitting next to him definitely had a military background, his posture and demeanor were a dead giveaway. The last guy was an egghead, you could see the air of superiority surrounding his smug face. This was going to be anything but quick and easy, they would draw it out and over-explain everything so this poor jarhead could understand. He changed his mind and went back to eating, it would give him an excuse for a few minutes of bathroom break.

The civilian with the military background was the first to speak, "Captain, I heard you were in Sudan for the revolt a few years back."

"I'm not at liberty to discuss..." Nick began.

"These are our special guests Captain," Blackburn cut short Nick's response, "you will answer any questions they have."

Nick looked over their new friends again, 'Okay,' he thought to himself, 'not civilians - spooks.'

"Sudan was on my watch." Nick replied curtly.

"Alex, Nick. My name is Alex." he replied.

"As you say." Nick deliberately refused to use his name.

Alex continued, "Do you remember Colonel Coleman? He acquired the information your group needed to break the spine of the resistance."

"I recall the Colonel," Nick answered without admission.

"He was my father," Alex said and looked into Nick's eyes.

Nick played his poker face, and said nothing.

Alex continued, "His men died getting you that intel, every last one. Did you know that Nick?"

Taking a sip of his coffee instead of replying, Nick thought about using his bathroom card before long.

"What did you do with that intel?" Alex pressed.

Nick paused then looked up at Alex, "It's as you said, we broke their spine." The implication obvious in his voice.

"Perhaps we should start the briefing," Blackburn broke the tension, "You two can catch up later."

"Of course," the bald man spoke up. "Everything you are about to hear is strictly Special Access Program. Colonel Blackburn has already given you SAP approval so I don't need to go over the rules." He paused to look directly at Nick, "Suffice to say, it's treason to leak any of this information. You already know the consequences."

Nick sat motionless and stared.

"My name is Keating, Gerald if it matters, but Keating will be fine. Alex has already introduced himself, and the man on the end is Doctor Strieber," Keating gestured towards the Doctor. "We are going to have to dispense with a full briefing, and keep to the facts today."

Nick almost sighed with relief.

Keating stood up and walked over to the whiteboard, "You may have heard about some peculiar happenings up north, there were sporadic public reports that escaped our lock down. Either way, whatever information you have will either be absent of facts or folklore."

Blackburn cleared his throat loudly.

Keating took the hint and continued, "At about 5am today, two public trains derailed just outside of their station. The cause of this derailment seems to be the work of, or in conjunction with, a biological agent of some kind. One we have never encountered and can't ascertain at this time. We currently have no death toll but it is estimated at about two dozen based on daily patterns. There are no infection reports currently."

Nick spoke up, "If there are no infected and the bodies have no signs of anything we have encountered, how do you know it's biological?"

"The reason there is no death toll is because we have no bodies." Keating answered, looking uncomfortable, "I will let Doctor Strieber explain further."

The Doctor stood up and walked over to Keating, "Thank you Gerald." Keating sat back down, and the Doctor continued, "The agent in question leaves no bodies, they are turned to ash." There were traces of German in Strieber's voice, but it was distant, "If extreme radiation exposure could be a virus, this result would be similar. Any toxicological studies made in this state will provide us practically nothing."

"What about the indigenous plant life surrounding the area?" It was Blackburn's turn to ask questions.

"Concentration seems to be centered on the train cars," Keating offered from his seat, "We feel it must have been a focused attack or maybe a trial run."

"And the train cars?" Blackburn continued.

"They were also mostly ash," Strieber interjected, "again, there is very little to examine at this point."

Nick felt the answer was simpler, "Everything you've explained points to a bomb, not a virus. A small nuclear device of some kind would have these results."

"Captain," Strieber said patiently, "this is not our last rodeo."

"First," Nick offered.

Strieber looked confused, "What?"

"First rodeo, the saying is 'not our first rodeo'," continued Nick.

"I don't want it to be our last either," Keating stepped in, "This goes beyond a couple of destroyed trains. The source of the infection seems to be only a few miles away from the scene."

Blackburn looked pained, "How do you know that?"

"Satellite photos show a section of land scorched to ash," Keating answered. "We suspect a breach in a holding area for the virus, it got away from its keepers and began to spread."

"You said plant life was unaffected," Blackburn prompted in reply.

"In the case of the trains Colonel," Strieber retorted, "the scorched area is obviously the concentrated source. A small building owned by the rail company is within the affected area, it's even money that the virus was being stored within it."

"How big of an area has been affected?" Blackburn directed to Keating.

Keating looked grave, "Better than a square mile initially, but it's growing."

"Growing?" Nick asked with apparent concern in his voice.

"It's at a snail's pace last we checked, perhaps centimeters an hour, but there seems to be no decay," Keating stared at Strieber.

Taking the cue from Keating, Strieber continued, "Nothing appears to move within its borders and a spectrograph shows no variance in density within. It's a solid, dead mass."

Nick could see this coming, "And you want us to go in to get a sample?"

"We've tried samples from the edges Captain, beyond ash there is nothing to be found." Strieber sounded perturbed, "What we need is a sample from the source."

Nick thought about telling them to get it for themselves. "And how are we to do that?" he asked. "You know nothing about it, stands to reason that you also don't know how to protect us from it."

Strieber shook his head, "Captain, we are used to dealing with the most dangerous pathogens in existence. We are well educated in keeping our people safe."

"In a lab environment," Nick responded tersely. "The field is not a safe or sterile place. The smallest branch could rupture those fragile suits without any warning."

"You've been on several operations of this type Captain, I've read your file," Keating interrupted. "This will be no different."

Nick shook his head. Having no intel got someone killed every time. So far, he'd been lucky enough not to be that someone. There was no point in continuing the debate, he would lose and be seen as difficult to deal with. A stigma he was already up to his neck in. Best to let the Colonel ask the questions and hope for some proper reassurances.

"Also," continued Keating, "despite appearances, enemy combatants could still be in the area."

"So we are classifying this as terrorism?" Blackburn questioned. "Send in Homeland, this is exactly their kind of situation."

Keating winced, "We can't be sure it's terrorism at this point. We can't even be sure what it is we're dealing with. If Homeland gets involved," he paused to look directly at Blackburn, "that information will simply disappear. Along with all of our research so far."

Blackburn was unamused, "So what you're telling me, is that you don't want to share?"

"Colonel." Keating waved away Blackburn's jab, "Homeland would quarantine the entire city, currently a financial backbone. The effect it would have on the already unsteady economy is incalculable. Would you bankrupt a country over what could turn out to be nothing?"

Blackburn looked hard at Keating.

Keating quickly added, "We on the other hand would be more than happy to share our findings with those who helped us to achieve them. I have no doubt that there is a branch at this very base that would benefit from such intelligence."

Blackburn finally smiled.

————

Beau Bradley stood in his boss's office at the local TV station KLLTV. Kill TV was how everyone referred to it when not on the air or in earshot of this room. It was an oxymoron as the station was anything but racy. The letters KLL meant nothing, they were simply available at the time the station was founded by its seemingly oblivious owner. The same man who sat in front of Beau and told him for the fifth time that his story wasn't running.

"I didn't even want to do this damn story!" Beau shouted. "End of the hour, small-time bullshit, and now you won't even let it run?"

Jason Greaves, chief and final say at KLL was unperturbed, "It's not running: the end. I don't report to you Beau, you report to me."

Beau wanted to jump across the desk and strangle the fat cretin. Instead, he smiled, "I'm going to edit my story while you think about how important I am to this little station of yours, Jay. Then you are going to apologize and run it in the first quarter, and not as some small footnote."

Greaves looked at Beau unconcerned, "Beau, I'll let you tell yourself whatever you want to hear, but it stays off the air."

Beau continued to smile as he turned to leave, "I'll be in the editing room when you're ready." Instead of waiting for a response, he simply left the office.

Beau clenched his fists in frustration. Greaves had lucked into the money he bought this station with, and he ran it like local access. Beau wished, once again, that Greaves would count his beans from home and leave someone with experience in charge. Continuing on to the editing room, he would make his story ready for broadcast despite what his boss would do in the end. It would go into his portfolio if it didn't get aired. It's best to have an abundance of resources to choose from when courting a new job: you never knew what they may be looking for.

He passed David Kingsly on the way through. The look on Beau's face gave away what had just happened.

"Pulled your story did he?" David offered with a knowing look on his face.

"Not Pulitzer material anyway, Dee," Beau said half smiling, "I just hate wasting my precious time."

"It could have been worse," David suggested, "he could have sent you on the cat of the week shoot."

Beau rolled his eyes and continued on to the editing room.

The station had its own editors, but Beau believed a good journalist could do it all; it also made sure the broadcast always got his best side. The hard drive from today's shoot was already waiting in the desk's inbox. Plugging it in, he loaded the raw footage into the workstation and scrubbed through, looking for possible edits. He'd threatened every camera man the station had with hell and brimstone for catching him in a bad light, and it was finally paying off. There were a few spots of bad lighting, but nothing that couldn't be massaged back to pretty.

Sliding back and forth across the timeline, he took in the bigger picture. It was nothing more than an accident, an electronic malfunction at best. No bodies, no carnage, no shock factor. In short, nothing top of the hour. Greaves was making a good call, there wasn't anything newsworthy by today's Reality TV standards. Frustrated more at his boss's triumph then his wasted time, he let it play out and scrutinized his delivery instead.

Right at the end he noticed an ambulance in the far side of the frame. He hadn't remember seeing it on the scene, but here, clearly, was someone being loaded into the back. How had he missed that? Maybe it was nothing but he'd take a look into the local Hospitals in case there was something he could use. More importantly, to make Greaves eat his words. Pulling the drive, he subconsciously slipped it into his jacket and headed back into the bullpen.

Bullying past everyone in his path, Beau was heading for the door when Greaves stepped out of his office.

"Bradley!" Greaves called, "Where are you off to? We need to have a quick chat."

Beau's instinct was to tell Greaves what he and his horse could do, instead he answered with: "Out to get you a better story big guy. Want a bear claw while I'm out?" Silently adding, 'You fat prick!'

Greaves didn't answer, apparently confused at the response, so Beau made it out the door before his boss could reply. Down the stairs, into his sports car, and off before someone came after him.

Reaching into his pocket, he put his cell on vibrate and blasted off to his favorite coffee spot. Hospitals had the worst coffee, a step down from a police station, and that's saying something. He'd die from caffeine withdrawal before placing that swill anywhere near his lips.

A short trip and a triple espresso later, Beau headed towards the Hospital nearest to the crash site. It would be tricky getting any real information from the front desk. He had no relationship to the victim and reporters got the brush off. Best to hit the emergency entrance and play the sympathetic friend, slash father, slash brother looking for someone. He had an even chance to guess gender so he would be vague as long as he could.

The emergency room seemed pretty crowded for such an early hour, it would be a lot harder to avoid specifics in his query. Instead, he sat down and observed. Listening and looking like a good reporter should. Hopefully he could avoid direct questions until he had more information to use. Across from him sat a father and daughter looking very distraught, this was not a good place to avoid conversation.

Beau got up to move when the father spoke up, "Did you lose someone at that station as well?" He asked.

Beau put on his serious face, "I... Uhh... I don't know yet." He tried to sound confused and pained.

"We heard about the accident this morning," the father continued, "my wife takes the train for work."

Beau had caught his fish, "Did they bring her here?"

"I don't know." the father's grief deepened, "We've heard nothing since we arrived."

That was strange, Beau thought, Hospitals contacted next of kin and rarely did anything without insurance information. "The hospital didn't call you to come down?"

"No," he replied, "we just heard about the accident, but she always leaves from that station so we rushed down." Pausing, he took a closer look at Beau, "Wait. You're that guy from the news, I know you."

Beau flashed his million dollar grin.

"You're a reporter, a celebrity." the father suggested, "With your clout, they'd have to give you more information."

"There may have been nothing to tell you when you asked," Beau said trying to sound reassuring. "I'll check in at reception for you, maybe they have more information now."

Excusing himself, Beau headed for the desk. There was a lineup waiting, it could take all morning at this rate. Bolstered by the adrenalin rush of being recognized, he decided to play his reporter card and jump ahead of the queue.

"Hi, Beau Bradley of KLL News," his practiced smile once again on his face. He pressed his card against the glass separating the receptionist and himself.

The receptionist was startled. She was in the process of talking to some concerned soul when Beau intruded. "Sir, you will have to wait your turn."

"KLL News," Beau insisted, warding it like a talisman.

"I don't care who you are or where you're from," the receptionist replied. "You'll wait your turn just like everyone else."

Beau's smile folded into a sarcastic parody. It was going to be a long morning.

2

The Briefing

Nick sat in the small cargo plane as it plodded on to their destination. It had been decided that they wouldn't take military aircraft in order to maintain a low profile. A group of soldiers he had never met sat beside him along with a few eggheads who were concentrating on their equipment. The heavy drone of the plane was lulling him to sleep when Alex Coleman, who had been silently put in charge, approached him.

"You feel this is a waste of your time," Coleman said smiling. "I can understand that. The chances of opposition is slim at best, but you are looking at this the wrong way."

Nick said nothing, but stared into Coleman's face.

"This keeps you in the loop." Coleman continued, still smiling. "Even if we find exactly what we're looking for, an answer to this attack will be required."

Nick continued to stare.

"I know you better than you think Nick." Coleman paused for a reaction, but got nothing. "You're a career soldier. You don't want desks or promotions or even retirement. The battlefield is your life."

Anyone who had read his record could have told you that and Nick was annoyed that this pretend soldier had done so. He knew Coleman was just trying to break the ice, but fuck him. He was a pencil-pushing moron looking to play armchair general on this little mission, and Nick would be stuck answering to him soon enough. He wouldn't be goaded into doing it any sooner than necessary, so he simply sat there in silence.

"If we have to extricate something or someone, we will be picking from existing stock. That means you." Coleman nodded at Nick. "This will give you more time before they push that pension on you." He leaned in towards Nick, "You really should be thanking me."

The urge to punch Coleman in the face was almost intoxicating, his smug look shattering against Nick's fist was an image that finally made him smile. "You know Coleman," Nick finally broke his silence, "that intel you were so hot about back at HQ was completely bullshit."

Coleman was taken aback, "What do you mean?" he questioned.

"Wrong, weeks old at the time, and utterly worthless." Nick took joy in catching him off-guard.

Coleman's eyes narrowed, "Then explain how you 'Broke their spine' as you put it."

Nick continued. "HQ already had all the intel before we even left, it was laid out before the final push. The leader of the resistance was the target, and there was exactly two places he could have been. A heavily guarded base, or a smaller outpost that could easily be taken. The plan was simple; take the lighter defended outpost out and capture the target if he was there. If he wasn't, there would be an assault on the main base that would almost certainly kill him in the process."

Confusion crept across Coleman's face.

"Those men were sent to the main base in hopes that they would capture the target, not gather information. Someone wanted a trophy for his mantle, wanted to be the hero." Nick paused. "Your father's pride killed those men, they died for nothing."

Confusion was turning to anger as Coleman continued to listen.

"His history and his impending retirement were the only things keeping him from a court martial." Nick stated, looking into Coleman's eyes. "The intel was just a smokescreen to hide the facts."

Coleman clenched his fists.

Nick smiled, "Full disclosure, remember?"

An anger flared in Coleman, then a calm came over his eyes.

"Nick, my father was a hero. He lived a hero, he died a hero - fighting cancer. Neither you nor anyone else will belittle his accomplishments, and you would do well to avoid conversations like this in the future."

Nick felt his smile waver despite his feeling of triumph.

"It would be unhealthy for what's left of your career." Coleman gave a small smile in return.

The pilot called out, "We're approaching the border, we'll have to land for customs."

"We'll only be here long enough to fuel up." Coleman said loudly, returning to his seat. "Nobody leave the plane."

As the aircraft began to descend, Coleman went into his briefcase, sorted some papers and retrieved a manila envelope. After looking at his watch, he began to scribble something on one of the sheets, then another. These pages were placed in the envelope, and he pulled out a rubber stamp and pad. Inking and pressing the stamp on the envelope, Coleman then sealed it properly and set it down, placing the left over papers on top while he put everything else away. It was impossible to see what was on the envelope with the papers covering it but Nick had recognized the size and shape of everything involved. Stamps like that were kept in desks by high-ranking officers under lock and key. The envelope had the telltale security precautions used for high level communications. If Nick wasn't dubious enough of this whole mission, that topped it off perfectly.

Seemingly oblivious to his own observation, Coleman checked his watch again, and fumbled in his pocket to retrieve his cell phone. Ignoring the usual protocols against such things, he turned it on and began to thumb furiously. Stopping only occasionally to read. Before anyone could remind him of his indiscretion, the cell phone was turned off and slipped back into his pocket. The plane hadn't exploded once during Coleman's brief lapse of judgment.

'There goes that myth' Nick thought to himself.

———————

On the tarmac, the plane had come to a halt, and Coleman had exited promptly after collecting the hastily prepared envelope. A few security agents stepped inside after he left and took a perfunctory glance around. They spoke to no one, nor did they ask to look inside of anything. They simply left shortly after coming on board. That had to be the fastest search Nick had ever seen in his career. Unstrapping himself, he stood up to stretch his legs.

The other soldiers were talking among themselves, obviously they knew each other already so that put Nick on the outside. He was fine with that. Morale was one thing, but it's best not to fraternize too much; it made giving orders difficult. He walked passed them and on to the front cabin where the flight crew were talking to each other.

"Gentlemen." Nick said, trying to sound only semi-official.

The pilot turned to look at him, but said nothing. The co-pilot was undeterred though, and continued his conversation despite Nick standing there.

"It's just unprecedented is what I'm saying." the co-pilot continued. "When have you ever gotten through customs this fast?"

The pilot stared at Nick for a little longer before turning back to the co-pilot and answering, "Never. This guy's ability to part the sea of red tape is biblical."

The co-pilot looked at Nick, "How about you? You know what the deal is here?"

"Standard mushroom management," Nick replied with a shake of his head, "keep everyone in the dark and feed them shit."

"He looks more CIA than military." The co-pilot observed. "Why would he soil himself with grunts?"

"To keep us from the long wait obviously," the pilot answered, "this has to be something serious."

The co-pilot paused for a moment, "Terrorists you think?"

Nick knew how to keep his mouth shut, "How long until we hit our destination?" He'd let them draw their own conclusions on the who's and why's.

"Assuming the spook gets us out of here after we fuel up," the co-pilot answered, "at least three more hours."

"So long enough for a few hands of poker then?" Nick tried to lighten up the mood.

"What if it's another 9/11?" the co-pilot shot towards his companion.

Nick took his leave before more questions came his way, "I'd better get back there before our good friend returns." Thankfully, no one tried to press him for more info before he left. You could only play stupid for so long before they started to believe you.

In the rear, the conversations had fallen off to a trickle. A few were trying to get some sleep while the others were either reading or staring blankly into space. "Good,' thought Nick, 'they either know enough not to ask questions or they're afraid of me. I'll take either at this point.' He sat back down and pulled on the necklace he wore. A sturdy ring of metal that contained his dog tags and an engagement ring that had cost him months of salary to get. He looked at it once again, and remembered back to when he'd tried to give it away.

She wasn't pretty, she wasn't happy. She wasn't much of anything, and she had nothing going for her before Nick came along. The worst part was that he didn't even love her. It was just a last ditch effort to escape his belief that he would never have anyone special in his life. It had failed. He couldn't even remember her name at this point. He kept the ring as a memento, a keepsake to remind him that the military was his wife now and it was all he needed.

He placed it back into his shirt, and sat back to wait for Coleman's return.

————

Bill was sitting on the chopper looking out across the scenery below. He was sipping the fresh espresso he had brought along, savoring every drop, as it would be the last good cup of coffee he would have for a while. Once he was on campus he would be stuck there for the duration: a security precaution in case he should fall into the wrong hands. No one survived a serious interrogation for long; you give up everything once a professional sets to work on you.

He knew of his confinement coming in, but if the documents he had been sent were even half true, it merited any sacrifices to his comfort. This included stepping back into the very mess he'd walked away from years ago. Included Keating and all the two-faced bullshit he would have to endure, despite Frank's assurances. Included facing a past he was trying to hide from. Yes, hide. Returning to The Shop was sharpening the perspective he was trying to dull, pointing him to realizations he was trying to avoid. Opening wounds that he had only covered, not healed.

Taking another sip, he sat back and pushed his personal thoughts aside, and concentrated on what he knew. Another sip, 'Not much.' he thought. Dealing with Frank would be problematic, he would not be forthcoming no matter what he promised. Bill would be relying on old connections and old friends to get the big picture he needed. He just hoped that these people were still here, still loyal to him, still in the loop. At the very worst he would have a clear definition of how serious the situation was, and what he would have to do to stay out of its reach if necessary.

The helicopter was approaching familiar territory. Below, farmlands and buildings alike passed by. Now only slightly different from how they were a few years ago. The pilot turned to announce their imminent approach, but before he could say anything, Bill gave him a knowing thumbs up and smiled. The pilot nodded and returned to flying the chopper. Taking the last sip of his coffee, he looked into the silt at the bottom of the cup, 'Going to miss that,' he said to himself. He crushed the paper cup with his hands and placed it into his pocket to throw out when they arrived.

"That was quite the place you have." the pilot yelled over the noise of the chopper.

Bill wasn't wearing a headset to answer through so he simply gave another thumbs up.

"Must have been difficult to get a building permit there," the pilot continued, seemingly used to one way conversations.

Bill only nodded his head in agreement. He didn't really want to start a dialog over the noise inside the cabin.

"The wife and I are trying to get one about two miles north of where you are." Apparently he was completely missing the hint.

Bill tried no response this time, he knew where the pilot was going with this.

"Any idea of who I could talk to about that?" He aimed his best smile at Bill.

Bill leaned over, "Try Keating," he finally answered with a smile of his own.

The pilot stopped smiling and returned his concentration to the approaching base, Bill sighed with relief. Announcing their arrival to the ground, the pilot pitched the helicopter down towards the oncoming landing zone. Things below gained clarity as they descended. The base was awash with motion. Fueling and loading were in full swing, as the tarmac was crawling with people. He heard the pilot making assurances on their landing zone as they expertly glided in.

A small bump and Bill had arrived. Climbing out, he was met by a few unknown faces who waved him towards an entrance to the main building. He obliged them and followed through the door and into a small secured room with bulletproof glass. Precautionary measures were necessary of course, but Bill found this belittling. One soldier stood inside with his gun at the ready, he stared into Bill's eyes.

Bill refused to be intimidated. He took the one chair in the room and visibly relaxed with one arm over the back of the chair. His placed his elbow on the armrest and propped his chin up on his thumb. Bill stared back, stone faced at the armed soldier, and visibly appraised him. The soldier held his gaze for another minute before turning away, 'Pussy' thought Bill.

The door opened and someone stepped inside, the soldier stood at attention. "Bill," Frank said, "sorry I couldn't meet you at the chopper."

Bill only stared back at Frank.

"This is all standard procedure," Frank said dismissively, "you know how things work."

Bill stood up and turned towards the door.

"Not so fast Bill," Frank interrupted, "you need to sign some paperwork."

Bill knew what he had to do, he just resented doing it in this holding area meant for questionable visitors. "Of course," he answered, "how about your office?"

"Sorry Bill," Frank shook his head, "we have to do this here. It's onto a plane and up north to a black site."

'There goes the good-old boy network.' Bill thought. A black site guaranteed incubation from the outside world, information came in but rarely left. Any friends he had left at the shop would be too valuable to pull from main operations.

Taking the pen and papers from Frank, Bill signed them and handed them back.

Frank gave an amused smile, "Not going to bother reading them?"

"Already have," Bill smiled back, "the revision number hasn't changed since I was here last."

"File these," Frank said and handed the papers to the armed soldier. Turning around, he pulled the door open and began to explain, "We have assets up north now. Just a soft team, research only, but we have a point team incoming. Should be boots on the ground and in-mission by the time we get there. Hopefully they will have what we came for by the time we arrive."

Bill began his questioning, "Now that I've filled out my NDA, how about you give me the real story on what we're dealing with."

"Actually, I was being straightforward with you back at your place." Frank turned to look at Bill. "We really don't know anything about it at the moment. There has been no successful sample removal since we found it."

"And how long ago was that?" Bill continued, still hoping for honesty.

"Initially," Frank paused to think, "about ten days ago we picked up some chatter on the tinfoil hat network about a UFO landing. At first, it was the usual screwball stuff. Dead animals, missing people, all the usual cock and bull except for the mention of an explosion. That part coincided with local police reports."

"So, the aliens have landed?" Bill smiled wryly.

"Mock if you will, but that network was being used by terrorist organizations to pass information back and forth to one another," Frank continued. "A perfect cover; no one of reputation believes anything coming out of it. Ideal really. We just happened across it while taking out a cell in Chicago last year."

"I read about that one," Bill interjected, "an attack on the Sears tower."

"No one was supposed to read about that one," Frank frowned. "We need to have a talk about your sources sometime in the future, but for now we concentrate on up north."

Bill would worry about crossing that bridge when he had too.

"It took a few days to coordinate with officials up there. They were reluctant at first, but finally agreed to let us come up and investigate when their own team began to get ill and finally refused to go in altogether. We landed, and the soft team tried unsuccessfully to extract some usable data from the site."

"Why not just use rovers to collect the samples?" Bill asked.

"They tried. The remotes simply won't connect within the affected area. It could be radio interference or some kind of electromagnetic field causing problems. Either way, our team believes that there is a coordinated force within working against us, and the outer rim is just too diluted for meaningful examination. That's where the point team comes in. We're sending them to the heart to hopefully find the source."

"Assuming they make it out alive." Bill suggested.

"Our biological experts assure me the usual preventative measures will be adequate but there's no precedent to base that on." Frank looked out across the bustling preparation, "This is strictly provisional, prepping a response team for both combat and containment. The usual procedure, but we'll go in full force if the necessity arrives."

"And the media reaction?"

Frank shook his head, "We have assets already taking care of that."

Beau returned late to the office, having spent all morning at the hospital and a leisurely lunch afterwards. Greaves looked fit to be tied through his office window, but Beau decided it would be better just to get it over with. He stepped through the door with his best smile, "Afternoon boss! You look like you could use a stiff drink."

Greaves slammed the receiver down, Beau wasn't sure if someone was on the other end or not. "Where the fuck have you been?" Greaves yelled.

Beau had never heard his boss use the 'f' word since he'd been here, and was momentarily speechless.

"Where is that footage you shot this morning?"

"You said it wasn't running."

"Not the point, it's KLL property and it doesn't leave this office without authorization or publication. You know that!" Greaves was pointing his finger like a child's pretend pistol.

Beau had automatically put the drive in his pocket before he left, just force of habit. "I left it in the car, I'll go get it, and you can avoid having a coronary." he said sarcastically.

Greaves' face seem to regain some of its color, Beau turned and left the office.

David waved his arms frantically in the air, trying to get Beau's attention. Glancing back into the office, Beau saw Greaves on the phone. With his boss currently occupied, Beau felt it was safe enough, and went over to see what the fuss was about.

"What the living fuck is going on here Dee?"

"We had suits in here this morning," David said in hushed tones, "they were looking for you."

Beau felt a pang of anxiety flash over him, "Who were they? What the hell for?"

"Don't know, but they took every drive from the editing room." David looked pissed, "My footage was in there as well, what the hell am I going to run tonight?"

"This explains why Greaves was so hot for that footage we took this morning."

"Speaking of which, they had your cameraman Raul in the back office for an hour." David continued, looking around in paranoia, "He went home right after they let him out, didn't speak to anyone."

Clearly, there was something on this drive he had overlooked. Maybe it was best that it stays missing a bit longer. "Dee, you have an empty drive handy?" Beau asked.

"You're not thinking..."

"Sure am!" Beau smiled. "There is something big going on here, and I'm not giving away my only lead."

"Beau, this is government here. They don't forgive, or forget."

"They have to prove there was something there to begin with before they can accuse me of tampering. I never actually sign out my drives so there's no way they can know what drive I had." Beau knew he was not the only one to employ this practice and bet David was among the guilty.

"I'll know," David said.

"No Dee, you won't," Beau said earnestly. "You need to shut your mouth about the whole affair, and then I owe you one."

"The great Beau Bradley will owe me one?" David said mockingly "That's a get into heaven free card!"

"Seriously my friend, no one can know. I'll give you co-credit on the piece, and you won't have to do a damn thing for it."

"Except lie to the government and risk a lifetime in prison."

"Dee, did they even talk to you when they were here?"

"Well, no..."

"Then why the fuck would they care now?"

"You have a point," David said and reached into his desk.

Beau reached out for the drive but David pulled it back at the last second, "Do I get top credit?"

Beau stared with a look of bewilderment, "Of course not."

"Well, that's an honest answer anyway." David handed over the drive. "Here you go."

Beau took the drive, and headed out to his car. He could hide the original in his glove compartment while swapping it for the empty one. This also gave him a chance to rehearse the bullshit he would have to feed Greaves on why the drive was empty. Dropping it wouldn't erase it. A Magnetic field? Maybe, but where would he have been for that to have happened? Time was running out here.

He would just have to turn it over and have something cooked up for when Greaves confronted him about it.

Leaving the vehicle with the empty drive in hand, Beau returned to the boss's office and plunked it onto the desk. Greaves was still on the phone and waved Beau out the door.

'Well that was easy.' Beau thought.

————

Heading out across town, Beau was on route to a buddy's place he used to do a little 'fashion' work on his videos when the editor was busy. It was slower, but it got the job done, and he had the added benefit of a drink or two while he was there. Pressing the call button on his steering wheel, he recited Raul's name and the radio came to life with the ringing from his phone's earpiece. He needed to know what the authorities had asked so he could prepare a good defense. The call was cut short by Raul's answering machine, in Spanish no less. Beau didn't speak a word of it but he didn't need to, 'I'm not available' sounds fundamentally the same in any language. He hung up the phone before it could beep him for a message.

He arrived at a small house that was, thankfully, lit up. Through the side window, Beau could see Dennis watching some Japanese cartoon on a huge television. Beau approached and knocked. After a few moments, Dennis answered the door - in his underwear.

"Dude!" Beau said in disgust.

"Sorry man," Dennis answered, "just relaxing for a few hours before I have to go in."

Dennis worked for a local internet company slash cable service, and would have everyone believe he was single-handedly responsible for every byte of information that passed through the servers. Beau had never met a tech geek that didn't believe they were the master at whatever they worked on, but he let Dennis have his fantasy.

The two had met through a report Beau had done on net neutrality and what it meant to John Q. Public and their internet consumption habits. Specifically with regards to the toll booths that any provider could erect arbitrarily and charge you for with impunity. Beau may not be the most tech savvy, but he could read the writing on the wall. The future of entertainment would be internet-based, and if companies could stop you from shopping elsewhere, why wouldn't they? Thankfully, that was a battle that had been won by the masses instead of the conglomerates. Net neutrality was here to stay.

"Need the avid buddy," Beau said with a smile, "and a beer of course!"

"You know where they are man, help yourself." Dennis turned and left Beau to close the door behind him.

Beau went to the fridge, opened it up and almost gagged from the smell coming out. Various take-out leftovers were rotting away and birthing new forms of life on the top shelf. Covering his nose and mouth with his hand, he reached into the bottom drawer where Dennis kept his favorite Mexican beer. Closing the door, Beau reached for the nearest towel to wipe off the bottle when common sense kicked in: The towel would probably be just as dirty, or worse. Using the cuff of his coat, Beau wiped the top of the bottle off and then cracked it open using the cleanest edge of the counter. The cap fell to the floor and rolled out of sight, Beau shrugged and headed for the small room with the avid.

When Beau passed by the living room, the cartoon was still playing. On screen, some angry guy with a large chin was slicing through somebody in slow motion. Blood gushing slowly in the air, the body separated vertically, cleanly cut. If it wasn't extreme violence, it was doe-eyed waifs looking far too young to be dressed the way they were. Beau didn't get it and didn't want to.

Considering the state of rest of the house, the room with the computer was immaculate. One could almost call it a shrine except Dennis was an atheist. As Beau stepped through the door a wave of cold air hit him, Dennis kept it at a temperature that almost required a winter jacket. It was great in the summer but brutal in the winter, today was a half way mark, so he was more or less dressed for the occasion.

"Coaster man," Dennis called out from in front of his TV, "don't forget like last time."

'Geeze,' Beau thought, 'I set the damn bottle down once.' He glanced at the neat stack of coasters standing tall in their holder, adorned with a formal looking anime character pointing furiously in his direction. "Okay, I get it!" he said out loud, grabbed one and sat down in front of the keyboard. Placing the coaster deliberately on the desk followed by the beer, equally deliberately, he looked at the monster screen in front of him.

The computer was on, as always. A screensaver of some animated girl swayed side to side with her huge eyes closed and a big smile on her face. Beau waved her away with a flick of the mouse, and pulled up the editing software. Retrieving the drive from his pocket, he sunk it into the slot that Dennis had mounted just for him. A few seconds later the contents of the drive loaded up into the editor, and Beau began to scan for what all the fuss was about.

It was the same nothing he had watched earlier. Demolished trains, ash and very little else. A few spectators watched from the sidelines, but no one noteworthy. Just a few cops wandering about and a couple of EMT's with nothing to do. The very definition of 'not playing at six'. He was obviously missing something. Scroll to the beginning, scroll to the end, repeat. "There is fuck all here." he stated to the screen.

Retrieving the phone from his pocket, Beau thumbed Raul's number again. Not only would he have answers about what questions were being asked, but they would likely tell Beau what he was looking for on this video. Once again he heard the voicemail and hung up the phone, frustrated.

He leaned back in the chair, which was incredibly comfortable despite all the accessories hanging off of it. It had speakers, a subwoofer in the seat, headphones, a tablet tray and a heated vibrating pad to sit on for extended periods of time. Beau glanced up across the room in a vacant stare, running the morning through in his head. Cops were calling it nothing more than an expensive accident. City hall had sent someone from the public transport office, but he knew even less. Finally, the EMT's had nothing to say because there were no bodies.

Even his promising lead at the hospital involving a distraught husband and his daughter turned out to be a false alarm. The mother had felt sick and went home to bed. The ambulance he caught on video was some poor seizure victim who was currently in a coma. All he had here was bad wiring that turned two trains to mush. At best, maybe vandalism. Either way, he had an end of the hour, forgettable news story. Nothing worth the attention of government agents.

There was something big attached here, Beau just had to find the thread that tied it in. A return to the scene would definitely be in order but it would have to be covert. If the authorities were still looking for him, he would have a few more hours at best before it looked suspicious. He needed a disguise.

Going back to the living room, Beau found Dennis fully clothed and silently gave thanks. "Hey Dennis," Beau tried to sound nonchalant, "does your company have any cable in the ground down at the south train station?"

"Yeah," Dennis answered but continued to watch the television. "Why?"

"You have your old repair coveralls from when you were still physically keeping the internet gods happy?"

"Yeah," Dennis said again, this time turning his head to look at Beau. "Why?"

3

The Bridge Across

T rue to his word, Coleman had gotten them cleared through customs before the plane had even been refueled. He sat once again with his face in his briefcase, reading a dossier that looked fresh from the printer. No clearance stamp on the cover indicated it was a hastily thrown together bundle of intelligence. Nick had seen his share; it always meant 'Eyes Only', and unreliable information was inside. It also meant Coleman wouldn't share anything it contained without permission, as if he needed an excuse not to. Coleman was definitely a type A, control-over-everything person. To get any real information out him you would need time, and something sharp.

Nick had operated under dozens of people just like Coleman in the past, and his lack of patience for them had only grown with age. Perhaps it was time to just get out of this whole thing, take up something free of bureaucracy that he could feel positive about doing. Right. That was a complete bullshit thought that came to him repeatedly over his lifetime. He always arrived at the same conclusions: If he could fish or farm then he could fight, and he was good at that. It gave him purpose. People without purpose die quickly in their own misery and regret, something Nick refused to do. He would go out on his feet, not whimpering on his knees.

So fuck Coleman.

Nick looked at his watch, they would be landing soon. He gathered up his gear and began another check through its contents, more to pass the time than anything. Coleman took the opportunity to walk over and take another shot at conversation.

"We will have equipment waiting for us when we land. I want you to coordinate your troops on a map before you head in," Coleman said leaning against Nick's seat.

Nick looked up at Coleman in disbelief, there was insufficient data to plan ahead.

"There will be zero communication while you are in field, and we need to know where you will be in case there is trouble."

"This is a live op with no intel, possibly armed insurgents, and a biological agent to top it off. It's the textbook definition of 'dynamically changing mission parameters'," Nick said sternly. "I can do a paint-by-numbers for you before insertion, but you can throw it out the door once we're inside."

Coleman was about to retort.

"It's simple: if things go wrong, then we're fucked," Nick continued, "Don't send anyone else in, just get clear, and quarantine the place."

Coleman paused, but seem satisfied with that answer, and turned to sit down.

"You do have quarantine procedures ready I assume?"

Coleman turned to look at Nick, "Of course."

———

The ground team were pulling their equipment from the plane while Coleman was talking to someone in an expensive suit. A few armored land cruisers were waiting for them to pile in so they could be off. Nick had grabbed his gear, and was slowly making his way across to the vehicles. As he approached, Nick did a quick scan of the area for military presence, but none could be found. They had landed at a private airstrip that, presumably, belonged to the man talking to Coleman. Nick knew this op was strictly black bag, but he expected some kind of official welcome.

Coleman finished up and began to walk towards Nick, a smug look playing across his face. Nick waited for him to catch up then continued walking to their destination.

"We have the full cooperation of the authorities," Coleman said, almost reading Nick's mind. "Should be at the site in twenty minutes."

Nick knew better than to ask about their well-dressed benefactor. He was obviously not military, so clearly there were favors called in for their arrival. The suit waited until the cruisers had left the compound before beginning his own exit. Nick looked for a company name or logo, but there was nothing, it was built for discretion.

The heavy vehicles were surprisingly fast and agile, and an easy ride as well, considering they were armor plated. Clearly the luxury version, and probably very expensive. There was only silence inside the cabs, the drivers listening to earpieces, and focusing on the road. Outside was bustling with standard traffic, nothing seemed out of the ordinary for a city under the threat of biological warfare. It was clear that the situation had been kept under wraps, and meant that civilian interference would be null. It also meant that casualties would be high if something went wrong. Nick hoped the contingency plan was quick and concise.

They drove through traffic heading south east, and began to leave the city. Turning onto a service road, running along a railway heading south, they drove for another five minutes before reaching a roadblock. Multiple military vehicles lay across both road and tracks, behind them was a bridge that crossed a deep gorge. A company of soldiers jumped up as they approached and held their guns at the ready. The cruisers stopped and Coleman exited the vehicle, heading into the group. The front line aimed their weapons at both him and the land cruisers. Coleman seemed unfazed, and continued walking to an unarmed soldier standing front and center. Nick already knew from experience that he was the grunt in command, but was slightly surprised that Coleman had picked up on it.

Stopping in front of the soldier, they spoke for a brief moment before Coleman reached into his jacket. The soldiers did not move but continued pointing their weapons. Retrieving an envelope from his jacket, Coleman handed it over, and waited for the man to read it. Seemingly satisfied, the commander handed the envelope back to Coleman, and spoke to his soldiers. Each of them lowered their weapons, and returned to their various positions. Coleman turned around and waved everyone out of the vehicles.

Nick and the rest of his team exited, and began retrieving their gear. The drivers remained in the cruisers with the engines running, apparently they wouldn't be staying. Once the equipment was removed, the vehicles backed up, and left the way they had come. As Nick was walking up to Coleman, he noticed the on-site company of soldiers had begun to unpack various boxes of equipment of their own. It was mainly electronic equipment. Some of it, Nick had never seen before, but everything looked brand new.

Coleman noticed Nick staring at the equipment, "This is some privately funded equipment we have requisitioned directly from one of the biggest military contractors. This is their first live field test, you should be honored."

"Oh yeah?" Nick said unimpressed, "What does it do?"

"That's not important," Coleman waved his hand dismissively. "What is important is that it will keep you and your men safe."

Nick had his doubts about that.

The commanding officer approached the two talking men. "The map is up and ready," he said to no one in particular.

"Fine," Coleman answered, "Shall we?" he nodded to Nick.

There was obviously no arguing about the pointlessness of planning, Nick would just oblige and get it over with.

The small table had a large touchscreen computer laying on it with some cables running into the back of a troop transport. The entire team were gathered around it, and waiting for Nick. Two chairs were set up in front, but Nick decided to stand. He looked at the map displayed on the screen in front of him, this was far more advanced than the paper equivalent he was used to. Assuming it was like a cell phone Nick tried the usual touch gestures to move and zoom the map, it responded as he expected it to. Their position on the map was a red cross, while the location of the building believed to hold the biological was designated by a black cross. The map was complete with elevation and current wind direction and speed. It would be a handy device in the field if it didn't require an entire truck to power.

Nick touched the screen just below a ridge, and a red line connected it to their start position.

"You can move and bisect the line by dragging and tapping." The commander added helpfully.

Nick said nothing, but nodded his head. He continued to zoom and plot until a red line zigzagged from red to black. Seemingly satisfied he looked to Coleman, "That should give you the basics of what we'll be doing. As I've said, this will likely be completely thrown out once we hit the field."

"Well, break it down for me," Coleman chided. "It's all about keeping you safe from this point on."

Nick found Coleman's assurance just as hollow the second time.

Pointing to the first break in the line, Nick explained "Here, we should get an elevated look at the target." He traced his finger to the next point, "This, is where we'll deploy the first sniper. We have no radio contact as you have stated, so he needs a clear view of us and the target." Touching the other side of the black cross, he continued. "This, is where sniper two will be located, same function. And this," Nick continued, pointing below the cross, "is where we separate the remaining squad into teams. Team Alpha will take this side with their suppressed HK MP5's, while Team Bravo, will be approaching from this side with the heavier AR-15's." Nick Pressed on the black cross, "We'll close in just downwind with Alpha breaching first and pushing the combatants into Bravo." Pressing just north of the black cross, he added, "We pop green smoke here if everything goes according to plan."

"And if it doesn't?" the commanding officer asked.

"Assuming we're still alive?" Nick looked grave. "Purple. Containment and contingency - No hesitations."

———

The bridge crossed a small chasm, and was train support only. The team was gearing up in hazmat suits while Nick stared across into the forest beyond. This was not the first time Nick had been under the threat of a biological agent, but he'd never had the luxury of protection. He was worried about the weight and restriction of the suit more than the threat of contagion, but that was definitely not far behind. The entire team could drop dead five feet in or five months later. Nick pushed it from his mind, and put his faith in the eggheads. They had the training, they had the schooling. Surely that qualified them keep his team safe. The target wasn't a large building. His squad could take it easily assuming everyone followed orders - and they got lucky.

"You're up." Coleman said from behind Nick.

Lost in thought, it took Nick a moment to respond. "Yeah," was all he could muster. He set his gear down and unbuckled the equipment he would need close at hand, then turned and headed towards the prep tent. Stepping in, two men were at the ready, and handed him a breather and hood. He was told to put it on to test it for size, he did so. The other man handed him a bag of powder, and told him to pat down his clothes with it.

"What is this?" Nick asked through the breather, holding the bag up to inspect it.

"Talcum powder," the man answered. "It will help the suit move easier."

Nick shrugged and began to pat himself down with it.

"These suits are Level A hazmat," the man holding his suit offered. "Complete enclosure and breathing apparatus. It has a double undercoating for strength, but the cost is stiffer movement, hence the talcum."

Nick nodded under his hood. Thankfully, the breather and hood gave him a wide view. He was also relieved to see the suit was a gray camo instead of some bright color. Not that they could get close enough to anything to blend with, but it was better than nothing.

"How is the mask?" the man who gave him the talcum asked.

Nick gave a thumbs up in response.

He was handed his suit when he passed the bag of powder back. The two men helped Nick put it on. So far so good. The hazmat suit wasn't as restricting as he feared, but it would be hot. After strapping on his air tank, one man attached a meter to his left wrist.

"You have a half an hour to forty five minutes of breathable air." the man said, pointing at the meter. "I would avoid using it until absolutely necessary."

"And how am I supposed to know when that is?"

"We have attached a number of chemical reaction strips to your arm. If any of them begin to change color, you will want to turn this," he replied pointing to the manual valve next to the oxygen meter.

Nick's look of concern sparked additional explanation, "Your team will also be carrying gas as well as radiation detection, the strips are just additional. We don't know what this is, so we are covering all the bases."

Nick tried to take comfort in that, but somehow it did not ease his mind. Instead, he gave another thumbs up as he left the tent to strap on the business part of his gear.

Coleman was concentrating on a tablet when Nick rejoined the team. He glanced up with a slight look of concern on his face. "The spread rate is increasing, we need to finish this quickly. If you can completely contain the infection just do so, otherwise capture the sample with that container." Coleman said, pointing to the metal cylinder attached to the belt of a squad member. "Assume all contacts are hostile, you understand?"

Nick knew his job, and didn't need reminding. This included not assuming anything despite Coleman's assurances. He nodded, but said nothing, and instead walked over to his team. Seeing his approach, they began to gather up their loose equipment.

"Alright gentlemen, we don't know what we're in for," Nick stated, "but I have been assured we have the very best in protection." That was a slight exaggeration, but it's what the team needed to hear. "We should be in and out within the hour," he added. Also likely bullshit, but it was possible. "A round of the most expensive scotch we can find will be on me tonight."

The team all traded looks amongst themselves, hopefully that had some of the intended impact. Walking to the front, Nick began across the bridge with the rest of the squad in tow.

He was sweating already.

Bill had been reading the current reports when the plane had hit the tarmac. After stopping, Frank had left to shake hands with the local brass, and smooth any feathers that their arrival had ruffled. Sweeping up the paperwork, Bill neatly placed it back into the folder, and stretched the elastic around to keep it from falling out. Retrieving his luggage, he headed for the front of the plane to disembark.

It was cool but not cold, a crisp breeze brought the local smells and fresh air to Bill, and he inhaled deeply. It had a different smell than his hilltop home, but not unpleasant He could get used to it with a smile. Exiting the plane, he took the stairway down to where Frank was now standing, and they began to walk across to the awaiting vehicle.

"No problems I assume?" Bill asked.

"Some concern about removal, but that is to be expected." Frank answered. "We can operate here unmolested, and even have full cooperation a phone call away."

"They would have us believe they are desperate in agreeing so quickly," Bill offered, "but it's really a matter of expendable assets."

Frank smirked, "That and plausible deniability. Something goes wrong, and we're left holding the bag."

"Can they offer us anything we don't already have?"

"They're trying to avoid a panic, but are ready to evacuate the city if necessary. I don't think they appreciate the gravity of the situation - this is potentially an unknown virus. Their investigation team believes that no detected radiation or biological presence means no real threat." Frank shook his head.

"More likely they believe that the threat is over," Bill retorted.

"True enough," Frank allowed. "Also, undue panic would only provide terrorism a stage."

"Which brings up the most obvious questions: who are they, and why did they pick an almost empty train station?"

"Our best guess is that the two trains were carrying remote charges destined for the center of the city. Something went wrong, and they detonated prematurely."

They had arrived at the car. Frank reached out to open the rear door. "And the who?" Bill asked.

"That we don't know," Frank shrugged. "Radicals looking to make a name for themselves? A terrorist cell testing a new biological?" He gestured for Bill to enter the car. "We'll know more when the team takes the building."

Bill got in and sat down. Frank closed the door, walked around, and entered on the other side. The car began to move. The interior was tinted dark, but a comfortable temperature. Frank leaned forward to the minibar, opened it and grabbed a bottle of water. He offered it first to Bill, but it was declined, so Frank poured it into a small tumbler and added ice.

"Why aren't we using our own team for the recovery?" Bill asked after Frank had finished fixing his drink.

"Quite frankly Bill because we don't expect them to survive, even if they return."

"Then why send them?"

"For two reasons. One, there is still a chance for the return of some crucial information."

"And two," Bill interrupted, "you need martyrs to rally a cause." Frank Smiled.

————————

Nick's team headed out across the bridge. Beneath was a drop of five hundred feet or so with a small stream running by. The sun was already pumping up the heat inside his suit, as if it needed any more coaxing. He suddenly wished he had stripped down to his underwear before putting it on, but at least he didn't have to fend off insects as well.

Across the bridge, the trees began to thicken up and provide some shade which did much to cool things off inside his suit. Nick glanced at the compass he had strapped to his other wrist. Watching it waver back and forth, it indicating they were heading in the right direction. He navigated them around the denser foliage to avoid any possible tearing in their suits. This would make the trek even longer, but it had to be done.

They walked down a small dirt incline which brought them to a ledge overlooking the stream below. It was still a steep drop, so they would have to walk along its edge until they could find an easy place to get down. The stream ran directly to their first lookout point, and following it would help drown out any noise the team made. Although they were still some distance from their target, scouts or patrols could be anywhere.

"Where are the animals?" called a voice from behind.

Nick stopped and turned to look at the soldier.

"We haven't heard a single bird since we crossed," the soldier continued.

He was right. Not a gopher, groundhog, or even an insect had be seen around them. Nick quickly looked at the strips on his arm, they were just as they had been when they left.

"We're fine," Nick spoke up, "let's keep moving."

Despite his own assurances, Nick couldn't help but find it peculiar as well. He put it out of his mind and concentrated on the mission at hand. Up ahead, he spotted a place they could walk down safely.

Nick pointed, "There," he said.

They continued along and began down the zigzagging slope that would take them to the water below. The bottom of the hill was slimy with mud, the stream must have been higher only a short while ago. They would have to go through it, and get around an outcropping of rock to continue to their first destination. Nick tentatively stepped onto the mud and rock surface and put pressure on his foot, it slipped slightly but he kept from falling.

"Okay gentlemen," he spoke without turning around, "take this slowly."

Nick had plenty of experience climbing through worse environments, but back then slipping on his ass would have only hurt his pride - here it could get him killed. He expertly dispersed his weight to keep himself upright, and began moving along the slick surface towards the long bend they would have to get around. The soldiers followed suit, stepping carefully and avoiding the tiny pitfalls that would be insignificant any other time.

Ahead, the wall of rock jutted out over a makeshift path of large rocks that stood up out of the rushing stream. They would have to hug the wall for balance and navigate around it while keeping from puncturing their suits. Placing his gloved hand on the wall, Nick stepped out using the large rocks that had dried to keep his footing better. Sliding along the wall, he advanced around a corner and spotted a gap in his makeshift bridge. The rocks simply disappeared beneath the surface, reappearing meters later. It was too far to jump, they would have to wade through. Hopefully it wouldn't be too deep. He was sure their suits would be waterproof but the stream was muddy and it was impossible to tell what lay beneath.

Nick paused to make sure the team was behind him. All was good, so he carried on into the water. It was ankle deep at best - that was a relief. Nick felt more confident and began taking larger steps. Fortune smiled on the bold, and Nick emerged from the stream on the other side. He turned to watch his team make their way across. One by one they carefully waded though and waited behind him.

The last man to cross was carrying the Geiger counter. Partway, he decided to get cocky and jumped the last few feet. Landing one foot on a submerged rock, he fell forward and threw his hands out in front. Nick's instincts told him to reach out and catch the man, but the danger of doing so held him steadfast. He watched the soldier tumble onto the ground.

"Shit!" came a cry from both behind Nick and from the man on the ground in front of him. He watched their radiation counter smash off the ground and bounce. With one hand on the wall, he reached down he pulled the man up to his feet.

"What," Nick fumed, "were you fucking thinking!"

The man only panted as Nick examined his suit, turning him around and pulling on it, looking for tears. He found one just below his knee, he could see skin and blood beneath.

"You're done." Nick said to the soldier, "Head back to camp and be damn sure you tell them your suit is ripped before anyone gets close enough. You may have already infected yourself, don't take someone else with you."

The man looked at Nick, winced embarrassingly, and nodded his head. Nick bent down to grab the fallen device from the mud below. Wiping it off, he flicked the switch and was relieved to see it come to life. He turned it off and mentally assessed what damage had been done. They were one man down, but he would have been on Alpha team anyway. The snipers and heavy attack force was intact, the mission was still green.

The wounded soldier turned and began to limp his way across the water, one of the remaining team walked past Nick and over to him.

"Where the hell are you going soldier?" Nick demanded.

"Taking him back to camp, sir," the soldier answered, emphasizing the 'sir'. "I know the plan, I'll catch up before you get there."

Nick wanted to reprimand the soldier, and would have if they were his men; however, he knew that would solve nothing and only cause additional tension. He looked at his watch, "You have fifteen minutes. If you can't get back to us by then just return to camp."

It wasn't imperative that the soldiers return by then, but Nick knew he had to assert his authority after the obvious defiance. It may cost him another man, but losing control would cost him the whole team. He turned around and continued on to their first checkpoint.

Bill had returned to the reports he was reading on the plane when Frank cleared his throat to get his attention. Bill glanced up at Frank and nodded. Putting the reports back into their container, he prepped what little he had brought into the vehicle. His bags from home would be escorted without him to his new and, hopefully, spacious room. The years had bestowed upon Bill the need for peace and quiet, something a cramped and shared room would not provide. It was a new requirement in his life, but one he would be damn clear he needed.

The vehicle stopped, and a stiff man in dark clothes opened the door, first for Frank then for Bill. A large man in a tight black shirt stood off to the side with an unlit cigar in his mouth and aviators on his face. Good old fashioned military experience with a stiff jaw and wearing a grin. Bill didn't recognize him, but he knew the type; ex-special forces, loyal and perpetually bullheaded. Every toolbox needed a hammer, and this had to be Frank's. He stepped out, still smiling as he was introduced.

"This is Lawrence Murphy, my acting director here," Frank said with a wave. "Anything you need, this man will get it for you."

Murphy put out his hand, "You must be Bill Wyburn," he said around the cigar in his mouth.

Bill reached out and shook the man's hand.

"Sorry we didn't get a chance to work together," Murphy continued after taking the cigar from his lips. "Heard you were a ruthless bastard. We need more of those," he said with a smile.

Bill nodded, but said nothing in return. Murphy was wearing his psychology on his sleeve. Bill knew exactly how this man worked, and how to get what he needed out of him. A satisfaction came over Bill as he felt his edge return, nowhere near as dull as he might have imagined.

"We'll get him set up in one of the VIP areas," Frank said to Murphy. "Send his bags up when they arrive. He and I are heading to the war room, contact us the moment any of the ground team return."

Murphy nodded, bit down on his cigar, and headed inside. Frank and Bill began to walk in the same direction.

"He's a little stiff, but he gets the job done," Frank said nodding in Murphy's direction. "They gave him his walking papers when he went too far with a prisoner interrogation."

Bill was not the least bit surprised, but said nothing.

"He still believes in all the gung ho bullshit, but he's smart enough to leave it to someone else." Frank continued. "He's a morale magnet in the field, and appeals to the more hardened bad asses we get in this company."

"Offensive forces have their place," Bill finally answered, "but is this situation really where we want a blunt tool like that?"

"Bill," Frank smiled, "the natives here expect a certain bravado from their soldiers. Murphy is almost a comic book character in that regard. Yes, this is exactly where I want him."

They stepped inside and began a crisscross walk through the complex to their destination. Bill noted the purple flower symbol everywhere in plain view. It was something they used as a company logo, but generally only on letterheads.

"We're labeling ourselves so blatantly now?" Bill asked.

"We've become more public since you left," Frank answered, "adopting the name as well as the logo. Calling ourselves Orchid was problematic though. We had to split the name into an acronym due to other businesses using variations of the name."

Bill waited for the explanation, "And that is what now?"

"Outer Reach Communications & Human International Division," Frank said with a smile.

"Perfect," Bill shook his head smiling, "it says practically nothing but sounds officious."

"Indeed," Frank nodded his head.

They arrived at the war room in short time. Despite the dubious name, it was simply the main communications and planning hub. On one wall was an array of monitors containing continually updated information and satellite imagery. Seated behind various desks were the custodians of that data as well as radio and internet communications.

Bill noted the monitor with what was obviously the infected area cycling through standard view, thermal, and infrared. Stepping forward, he pointing at it and spoke with a practiced authority, "Has anything shown up in that gray cloud at all?"

A few of the people in the room turned to see who was talking, but stayed silent. Frank turned and looked at his people for an answer. Seeing this, one man who Bill assumed must be responsible for that data, replied to the negative.

Frank cleared his throat loudly enough to turn more heads, "This is our special guest and adviser, Bill Wyburn." he spoke forcefully and pointed. "You will answer any questions he asks of you." There was an awkward silence.

"Is our team on the ground yet?" Bill broke the tension.

One of the operators, glad to get things back to normal, replied. "Yes, they are almost at the edge of the anomaly as we speak."

4
Into the Gray

Nick and his dwindling team stood near the first lookout point. Glancing at his arm, he checked the strips there for the tenth time in five minutes. According to their color, everything was still normal. He had ordered the first sniper to the top of the hill for a quick look and then to double back. The soldier had taken far longer than Nick would have expected but now, after the long wait, he had returned.

The sniper looked alarmed, Nick stared at him for a moment before stating the obvious, "Well?"

"The area is dead," the sniper replied, still looking distraught. "Burned to ash."

"Can you get a clear view of the building?" Nick asked trying to keep the man focused.

"There is no building," he said. "It's nothing but silt and rubble."

This changed nothing, they would still have to go in and try to secure a sample from whatever was left.

"I want you back up there anyway," Nick told him. "We're not in the clear yet."

The man nodded, and began his trek back up the hill while Nick and the team continued on to their second sniper position.

Several hundred feet later, the ground beneath changed very distinctly from green grass to gray ash. It was a line that extended in both directions as far as the eye could see. This was the proverbial 'it'. Beyond here, they would be enveloped in something never before encountered. With his next step, Nick could fall to the ground and never get back up again.

Turning to face the team, Nick twisted the valve on his wrist that activated the oxygen tank on his back and sealed his suit. Around him, the squad began doing the same. He turned back and stared at the ominous dividing line for a moment. If he focused, he felt he could almost see it moving towards him. Shaking his head, he took a breath and stepped across.

Nick's foot sunk into the ash with a squish and small plumes sprayed out from the force of the impact. Beyond that small phenomenon, nothing else happened. Nick continued to walk, the rest of the team slowly caught up behind him. No one said anything for fear of jinxing the situation. After a few hundred feet, Nick's thoughts returned from the suspension they were locked in.

The soldier who had taken the wounded back to camp hadn't returned, and Nick contemplated deviating from the plan. They really wouldn't need a second sniper given the circumstances, and their assault team was two men down as it was. Perhaps just use him as coverage while the team approached.

Nick turned to the second sniper when they had reached his perch. "You are going to cover the team on approach. When we have arrived safely, I want you to move up if I give you the signal."

The sniper nodded and scurried up the hill. It was steep and slower moving due to the ash but he made it without tumbling back down. Nick moved the team out to their next position where he would split the team up. The ground was spongy and soft under foot, and only partial trunks of the largest trees were left standing anywhere. Everything else had been reduced to ash.

"What could have done this?" Asked the soldier that Nick had entrusted with the Geiger counter. He was closely monitored it for spikes.

"That's what we're here to find out," Nick answered.

"It looks like Chernobyl," another soldier offered, "I can tell you that first hand."

"Keep it down," Nick commanded. "We're not in the clear yet."

They arrived at the designated separation point. Nick halted everyone and hunkered down to draw in the ash.

"Okay, small deviation," Nick said after drawing a small box. "We are splitting into four groups. I want all four corners of that rubble pile covered." He began to draw lines around the four corners. "If we break up and follow these paths to cover the building, we will stay out of everyone's line of fire."

His orders were based on common breaching procedures but Nick wanted to be clear - he had zero experience with this crew.

"Questions?" Nick asked.

No one had anything to say. It was either a good sign, or a really bad one.

The teams separated and each found their way around the hill to approach the building. The ash crushed beneath their feet with almost the same sound as new fallen snow. Nick entered the clearing and caught glimpse of the building for the first time. It was demolished, there was little to no chance of there being anyone alive in that rubble. His first instinct was for the teams to fall back and change the strategy, but between themselves and the snipers, they had a clear view of the surroundings. An ambush would be almost impossible, so Nick decided to stick to the plan.

Like clockwork, all teams coordinated with precision. Each corner was covered and cleared without incident. The ramshackle building in front of them had stubs of walls still standing while everything in between was mounded with ash. Nothing moved, not even the wind. It was as silent as a church during the playoffs. There would be nothing to find here.

Nick turned to the soldier with the Geiger counter, "Has that needle moved at all?"

The soldier shook his head, "A television puts out more rads than this whole place."

"Is it even working?" Nick wanted assurances.

"Of course it..." The soldier stopped talking, and looked at the counter. "Well, it was."

"Uh-huh," Nick responded.

"It just died." The soldier smacked it on the side and shook it a few times. "It was at full charge when you gave it to me."

"Do we have a spare battery?" asked Nick.

"No," replied the soldier. "A single charge should last days."

Nick cursed under his breath, but said nothing further.

The soldier shrugged, and let the Geiger counter drop to hang from his belt.

There wasn't enough air for them to do a thorough investigation of the debris, especially with the threat of rupturing their suits. He would have to hope that a sample from what was left would do.

Nick turned to the soldier with the canister, "Dig into that ash pile with the butt of your gun and scoop up a sample from underneath for that container."

The soldier looked down at the pile, flipped his gun around and began digging through the ash.

"Sir!" Came a voice from the other side of the broken building, clearly alarmed.

Nick looked up towards the noise and hurried over to investigate. A few of the soldiers followed, leaving the rest behind. They rounded the corner of the building to see the man staring into the center of the rubble.

"What is it soldier?" Nick asked when he got close enough.

The soldier pointed and Nick turned around to see what he was missing. The center of the building contained a small crater, dug deep into the ash. Leftover boards and a partial wall had obscured it from the other side. While definitely strange, that clearly wasn't the center of attention.

It was the large footprints leading out of it.

———

Beau had the borrowed coveralls in the back seat of his car, thankfully they had been washed and even hung neatly. He was heading back down to the train station in hopes that a disguise might secure him some more info, people tend to exaggerate the truth when they think it will be on TV. As just another grunt in the cog of maintenance and clean up, the camaraderie may get him something more accurate. At the very least, some good gossip. He would have to avoid asking any names. When you ask, they ask, and Beau wanted to be as anonymous as possible.

Showing up in his sports car was clearly out of the question, he would have to park it and walk the last few blocks. When he had been here this morning, there hadn't been a spot to get a coffee for blocks. Being well acquainted with the trust a small gift can buy, Beau had stopped for an entire tray - complete with creamer and sugar. The only thing that could top fresh coffee would be cold beer, but that was obviously out of the question.

———

Now in costume, Beau and his tray rounded the last corner before he could clearly see the station. It had been cordoned off as expected, and crews were hard at work cleaning up the mess. He had no understanding whatsoever of the role he was playing, but that didn't matter: he was the best liar he knew. Walking up to the tape that restricted the public from access, he flashed his patented Beau Bradley smile at the cop on the other side.

Leaning the tray in his direction, Beau said "Thought we could use some."

The cop smiled, took a cup, and drank it straight black. Beau could feel his stomach turn as his mind imagined the taste, but he continued smiling all the same. The cop lifted the tape so Beau could easily get under it with his tray, he was in without so much as a question. The area was a flurry of activity as the refuse was cleaned up. The train cars had been loaded on flatbeds by a crane, and the ash was being shoveled into a dump truck. Beau looked over to a man staring at a clipboard. Clearly someone here to talk, not work.

Beau leaned the coffee tray in his direction, "Hey, here to take a look at the lines." He said hoping he wouldn't be asked anything specific.

The man looked up from his clipboard, "Oh, sweet!" he said. "I've been needing one of these for an hour now." He grabbed a coffee from the tray and added some cream and sugar.

This would be a breeze thought Beau.

"I'm new to town and they sent me down here without a map," Beau hoped the lie was sufficient. "Has anyone pulled up any cable from underground?"

"Not that I've seen, but with all this mess there may be yards of it buried beneath," the man with the clipboard answered. "I didn't think they had installed it down this far yet."

'Whoops,' thought Beau, 'could Dennis have been wrong?' "Oh, well, maybe this is some kind of prank on the new guy then," he smiled and shook his head. "Who are you with now?"

"City Hall," the man answered taking a sip of his coffee. "Though I don't see any reason for me to be here. There's nothing for me to do."

'Perfect,' thought Beau, 'you'll have every reason to talk to me then.'

"So what the hell happened here?" Beau asked trying to look curious.

"Some kind of wiring malfunction," the man said, "melted two trains to ash."

"Wow," Beau replied with practiced surprise, "how many people were hurt?" Beau knew the answer already but Joe Repairman didn't.

"We have a count of over twenty," answered the man, looking grim.

'What?' thought Beau. "Are you sure of that?" he asked.

"That's our best estimate," the man answered, "we have CRT footage of the passengers in the terminal before the accident."

Beau was here this morning, and there was no account of fatalities. He was told specifically that the station was empty. Multiple deaths and no reports? "How long have you been down here?" Beau probed, looking for possible gaps in information.

"I just relieved another guy who's been here since the first call," the man answered. "Problem at home so he left in a hurry."

'And perhaps forgot to tell you to keep your mouth shut?' Beau thought. "How is this not all over the news? There should be reporters and cameras everywhere."

The man shrugged his shoulders, "I assumed they were here and gone already."

'We were.' Beau answered in his head. "They take the bodies away already? I'd hate to uncover one while I'm sifting through looking for cable."

"You may be sifting through them," the man said shaking his head. "The bodies were completely ash, there's not even teeth left behind for dental records. We'll have to use the video to identify the victims."

'Twenty-plus dead bodies, turned to ash.' Beau's mind raced. The evidence was on video right in front of him, he just couldn't see it, wouldn't have imagined it. How could anyone expect to hide something like that? Those families would want answers. This explains the what, now who was suppressing it and why?

"So who is running the show here?" Beau asked. "Do I have to check in with someone?"

"There was a few government officials here earlier," the man answered taking another sip of his coffee. "Concerned about the environmental impact this would have. That's who people have been reporting to."

'Environmental impact?' Beau wondered. "But they've left now?" he asked.

"Yeah," the man looked down the tracks and pointed, "they went on down the line to the closest power station looking for a possible cause."

"So I guess you are the man in charge now then?" Beau tried to sound nonchalant. "Do I need to sign in or something before I get to work?"

"No," the man answered. "I'll just pencil in that the cable company was here, though I will need an account of any problems you find though."

"Of course," Beau smiled and said to himself, 'But I think you're neck deep in them already.'

––––––––––

Nick stared at the footprints in the ash. They were inhumanly large, and carried a stride that would place whatever made them at fifteen to twenty feet tall. The prints headed back towards the bridge, and camp. With the objective completed, they could follow the tracks and return to base without unnecessarily depleting their oxygen much further. The snipers had just arrived after being signaled to move up and regroup. They were currently taking in the spectacle with commentary from the other soldiers.

Nick turned to his team, "Is that sample secure?"

"Yes," came the reply.

"We will not be signaling the base. Doing so will only put them at ease and give away our position." Nick explained. "Instead, we're going to split up." Nick commanded. "Half of the team will go back the way we came with the sample, and the other half will come with me. One sniper per team."

"You want to follow those tracks? Into where exactly?" this came from the soldier with the Geiger counter. "We have no way of testing for radiation now."

"This was ground zero, you're last rad count showed nothing," Nick replied. "Clearly radiation is not a concern here. Those tracks, however, are leading back to base."

"The only thing clear here is whatever made those tracks, is fucking huge!" another soldier pointed out.

"The only thing clear here is that there is a possible threat to our camp!" Nick raised his voice and cut the soldiers panic short. "Now," he paused to calm himself, "whatever made those tracks doesn't matter. We are going to find out what it is, and stop it if necessary."

That statement seemed to halt any further quandaries the team had. Nick checked the oxygen gauge on his arm, they still had over half their supply, but that would dwindle quickly. He dispatched the team with the sample, putting the soldier with the questions in charge of them. They had all shown competency and worked well as a team, but someone had to have the final say.

Nick turned to the rest of the soldiers, "Time is not on our side gentlemen, we will have to hurry. I want two small teams twenty feet on each side of the trail, our sniper will cover us from the rear. Are we clear?"

"Sir, yes sir," a chorus of replies.

"Then let's move out people."

The teams split off naturally and began to follow the prints in the ash. Ahead was nothing but gray; hills and tree stumps protruding like jagged teeth from the ground. If not for the terrain, Nick was sure they would have a clear view straight back to camp. Not even a breeze seemed to stir in this wasteland as they jogged across its surface.

Nick noticed a pressure building up in his ears. He swallowed hard and shook his head, but nothing changed, his loss of hearing was mounting. The heat inside the suit suddenly seemed unbearable, he felt sweat run down his face and into his collar. Up ahead, through the fogging visor in the hood, a black and gray mass was jutting out from the top of a hill.

Nick raised his hand to halt the men, he turned to the soldier behind him and signaled for him to scout ahead. The rest of the team crouched down as Nick gave them the signal to stay put. Meanwhile, he slowly advanced on the object in front of them with his gun ready, the scout already almost upon it.

A few painfully long seconds later, the scout waved the all clear. Nick wasn't so sure though, he signaled the men to maintain their position, and advanced by himself to the awaiting object. As he drew nearer, he began to recognize its features. The tension in him eased, the suit became more breathable and his hearing had returned.

The scout stood beside a mangled jeep, its body and frame a mass of twisted black. It looked burned but with a heat so intense that the very frame warped and melted. The scout reached out to test its strength when Nick grabbed his hand and shook his head. He immediately looked to the strips attached to his arm, they had mostly peeled off and what was left was turning white. That sharp observation momentarily froze Nick in his place, and he barely had time to hide them from view before the scout could notice.

"All good sir?" The scout asked.

Nick turned to the team and signaled for them to move up. Telling them about the strips could cause a panic, it would be best to keep them concentrated on getting back as quickly as possible.

Nick avoided the question, "Has anyone seen damage like this before?" He asked the team when they had arrived.

"Again," said a soldier, "Chernobyl."

Coleman stood at the edge of the bridge with binoculars, he could just see the infected zone in the distance. It would have looked like a snow capped mountain if not for the blackened stumps. Despite the relatively clear view, there had been no smoke to indicate success or failure. The team had been out for over half of the expected mission time now with two members already back, one in the infirmary. They had nothing to report beyond the hasty outburst from their officer in the field that had left both men heated. Coleman had cut the explanation short once he realized it was a personality conflict. Despite what he may think of Nick personally, he had no doubts about his ability to command a squad.

Turning to the screen on the command center, Coleman looked at an estimated location of the team. They should have secured the sample, popped smoke and be on their way back by now. Assuming they had not run into trouble of course. There had been no reports of gunfire, but that meant nothing at this distance. The screen bloomed before him in a cascade of colors, but nothing happened within that gray cloud. It was a wall of silence.

"Eagle eye has arrived," the radioman said to Coleman. It simply meant that the head of Orchid had arrived at the black site. Presumably, so had this 'consultant' he was so desperate to acquire. Coleman couldn't see the need for an extra set of eyes in this sensitive operation, but clearly his opinion was falling on deaf ears. There was nothing to call in and report at this point, so he returned to his manual surveillance.

Coleman heard someone approach and clear their throat, he continued to look out across the landscape. "How are our test subjects, Doctor Strieber?"

"Neither were exposed to anything of interest." The doctor explained. "One has a sprained ankle and one has a bad attitude."

"They are both still in quarantine I trust?" Coleman asked.

"Of course," Strieber replied.

"Keep them occupied until the rest return," Coleman turned and looked at Strieber, "they may come in handy later."

The Doctor gave a small bow, and walked away, leaving Coleman to return to the view.

"Have we picked up anything at all on sonic?" Coleman asked one of the techs.

"That area is a complete dead zone," one man replied, "it seems to swallow up every sound emitted within."

Coleman mulled over the strategic value something like that would have if it could be replicated, or at least bottled. The unknowns brought so many possibilities with it that he openly grinned at the thought. An organization could become a world power with a weapon like this, and he was at the forefront.

"Sir."

The noise brought Coleman from his thoughts, and he turned to the tech responsible.

"We have something exiting the zone, it's heading in our direction."

"Is it our team?" Coleman asked and brought the binoculars to his face.

"I can't be sure, Sir," the tech replied. "It's the first blip we've had since they entered the area."

Coleman searched, but could find nothing. "What direction are they coming from?" he asked.

"They're following the tracks, Sir," came the answer. "They seem to be moving slowly though."

"Get a flying drone in there," commanded Coleman. "I want eyes on."

A small commotion began, and a buzzing echoed through the camp. A drone lifted off and plodded its way over the bridge and followed the tracks. Coleman stood in front of the monitor that mirrored the camera mounted on the front of the drone. The image was shaky despite the advanced stabilization techniques employed, and the image froze and cut out regularly. With all the money spent on this technology, Coleman had expected better results. At least the range had been extended dramatically.

The image continued to shake and move, grass and trees passed by the small window as it followed the tracks below. Coleman looked back to the map and watched the small dots slowly move away from the zone and along the tracks. They were bunched too closely together to tell how many individual blips there were. Then from the right of the screen, another group of dots appeared roughly where the team had made initial contact.

"Another contact sir!" someone shouted out.

Coleman didn't hesitate. "Stations people!" he yelled aloud, "we may have incoming!"

The camp jumped to high alert. People scrambled in and out of the various tents and vehicles, arming themselves. Two vehicles with M60s mounted to their tails roared to life and swung their asses around to meet the opposition. Three more drones sprang into the air, their camera feeds appearing at the bottom of the monitor containing the existing drones view.

Coleman looked back to the camera monitor, it had stopped and was hovering. "What happened to the drone?" he called out.

"That's the signals limit," the tech called out, "any farther and we may lose control."

"Goddammit!" Coleman cursed. "Okay. Send one of the three drones on an intercept course with the other group, leave the other two on our forward flanks."

"Yes Sir!" the Tech replied.

Coleman used the monitor in front of him to maximize the hovering drones view. He tried zooming in as far as he could while maintaining a clear picture, all he could see was tracks and stone.

"Can we get any higher?" Coleman asked, zooming the image back out.

"A little," came the reply.

Coleman watched the image change as the drone flew higher. He could now see farther ahead but it still wasn't enough.

"Higher!" Coleman commanded.

The image changed again and Coleman caught a glimpse of something at the top of the monitor just before the screen turned black.

"We lost the drone!" Shouted the tech.

"Shit!' Coleman shouted. "Send the closest replacement, we should be able to get a clear view now."

Coleman brought up the feed from the new replacement and maximized it. He watched impatiently as the drone slowly made its way up the tracks.

"Do we have a visual on the second group of contacts yet?" Coleman asked.

"Almost there," returned the tech.

The first group would arrive long before the second, and Coleman wouldn't take his eyes off the screen. The image that had appeared just as the drone had lost signal was a flash, but it was imprinted on Coleman's mind. He didn't know what he'd saw, but it wasn't the team; he couldn't be sure it was even human. Staring impatiently, he could feel his heart slow to a crawl. Time seemed to stand still.

Then, there it was. The image that was still fresh in his mind. A bright blue flare, burning intensely followed closely by another. Coleman tried to zoom in closer for a better view, but it made the camera shake even worse.

"Get that drone lower!" Coleman yelled at the tech.

The image began to expand and Coleman quickly zoomed back out for a wider view. Below, the two blue lights continued to burn brightly and move slowly towards them. Was this some kind of side effect from being exposed to whatever was in the infected area, Coleman wondered to himself. Were they carrying some kind of weapon that was causing the flare? The drone continued to drop altitude, the image grew and sharpened.

A white line started at the center of the screen and expanded to fill the image. The screen went completely black.

"We lost the feed!" a tech shouted.

Coleman didn't need another look; they would have to assume the worst. "Hostiles coming in from the bridge, cleared for engagement!" he shouted.

"Video of the second contacts now visible!" shouted a tech.

Coleman stared down at the screen and switched to the drone in question. Below he could see some of the team members moving back towards the bridge. They would be in a perfect position to flank the enemy, if they arrived here soon enough. This was good, the camp just needed to keep the enemy suppressed until the rest of the team arrived to help.

"Move up to the bridge!" commanded Coleman. "Erect the portable cover!"

A group of four men ran to the bridge and expanded a wall of metal for the soldiers to hide behind. It was Kevlar coated and would keep most small arms fire from penetrating, for a while at least. A solid mass of chest-high cover lay at the bridge's entrance when they were done, and the soldiers took no time in positioning themselves behind it.

Coleman brought up his binoculars, and searched down the tracks which followed a small hill that dipped out of sight. This gave his men the high ground, but at the expense of a clear view of the enemy, tactically it would still be to their advantage.

Pulling his eyes away from the binoculars, Coleman looked back down to the screen at the flanking soldiers. It would be close, but when the squad arrived, they would make short work of the enemy.

"Sir!" a tech shouted, "a third contact has appeared on the radar!"

Coleman quickly switched to the radar view on the screen in front of him. Clearly he could see another group exiting the zone a short distance away from the tracks. There was no point in sending another drone, time would tell if it was the rest of the team or not.

Glancing back to the closest blips on the radar, he could see the enemy were almost to the bridge now. He pulled up his binoculars and looked across.

On the other side, Coleman could see a bright light starting to crest the hill. He zoomed the binoculars closer, and tried to steady the view. When he'd finally managed to get a stable shot of the hill, a blinding light cut through the lenses and Coleman jerked back.

Rubbing his eyes he shook it off, then turned and brought the binoculars up for another look.

Again, the intense light made him wince and snap his head back in shock. This time he tried blinking the pain away from behind his eyes. He quickly realized that everything was going dark around him. He first thought it was some kind of weapon, then he understood.

"Strieber!" Coleman shouted to the surprise of everyone around him.

The front row of soldiers had begun to fire their weapons. Coleman could hear the chugging of the M60s roaring to life as someone grabbed him and pulled him down to the ground.

"What is it?" Dr. Strieber shouted over the noise.

"I'm blind!" Coleman shouted back.

5

The Return

Nick and his team had been following the footprints in the ash when he noticed they were down to their last five minutes of air. The longer route had eaten through it faster than he had anticipated. They couldn't afford to follow any longer, and he rushed the team straight out of the zone instead. They had been running non-stop until finally stepping out of the infected area. He looked down at his oxygen meter, it was about three minutes from expiring.

Turning to the team, Nick shouted, "Let's hike another minute away from here before we turn off our supply."

There were no objections. They continued to jog away from the zone in the direction of the camp. Nick could feel his skin burning from exertion, the sweat rolling down his back and face. His chest was beginning sting and itch like something hot was pressed against it. Passing a few large green trees seemed to ease Nick's mind and he stopped the team, turning to face them as he switched his oxygen off.

The soldiers seemed reluctant to follow his lead, but Nick was at the threshold of his tolerance to the cramped and hot uniform. Bolstered by the surrounding greenery, he first removed the hood and then the breathing mask. The cool air was almost magic. His eyes closed, he tilted his head skyward and took a deep breath. At first he coughed, the heat within his throat mixed with the cooler air caused some condensation. After hacking a few more times, his breathing returned to normal. He opened his eyes.

The team were watching intently. Nick smiled and pulled a glove off to wipe the sweat from his brow. "All good gentlemen." He said finally.

One by one the team pulled off their masks, each taking a tentative breath before filling their lungs. After which, not one face could be seen wearing a frown. Nick would have called the atmosphere giddy if asked.

"We'll head directly to camp," Nick said after a moment, "the second team should arrive shortly after us."

Nick turned and began to walk towards camp when he heard the discharge of a weapon in the distance. He dropped instinctively, the team took his lead and ducked as well. Another shot, then the air was filled with the sound of gunfire. Within, Nick could hear the unmistakable bark of M60s. A serious threat was advancing on the camp.

"Move!" Nick shouted, "we're on a direct path with the camp, get out of the line of fire!"

Nick took the team on a jagged path that he hoped would keep them from harm's way. Placing hills and rocks between them and echoing gunfire, Nick tried to lead them to the ravine beneath the bridge. There, a flanking position could be set up to help keep the forces from crossing. The occasional bullet could be heard ricocheting off of stone or embedding into a tree as they made their way across the land.

The gunfire was suddenly interrupted by an explosion, another followed closely behind it. Nick signaled for the soldiers to hold, and crawled up the side of a hill for a better look. Before he reached the top, he could see smoke billowing up into the air. It was clearly coming from the camp. That gave them precious little time to get there and provide support. Without bothering to continue up for a better look, Nick slid back down to the team below.

"That's the camp," Nick said to the soldiers. "We have to hustle our asses over there before it's too late."

"Sir!" a soldier yelled out and pointed.

Nick turned to see the second team running alongside a small hill. Rather than yell, Nick brought his finger and thumb to his mouth and produced a very loud and shrill whistle. The second team dropped to the ground, looking over to the source of the noise. Seeing it was not the enemy, they got back up and ran across to the other team as low to the ground as they could manage.

Once they had arrived, Nick asked, "Is the sample still secure?"

The soldier charged with it patted the side of his belt where it was fastened.

"Fantastic!" Nick said, not without merit. "We are going to get to a flanking position and slow those bastards down from getting across." Pointing to the two snipers, Nick said "I trust you two know your jobs by now."

Both snipers nodded and Nick waved them ahead, the rest of the team was waiting anxiously. Nick pointed, "Our goal is that ravine," he said, "they will have the high ground but they won't see us coming."

Nick looked at the soldier with the sample, "You are staying right here until this is over. We can't afford a stray shot hitting that container." The soldier nodded. "The rest of you, move out!"

———

Beau had left the train station behind and was following the tracks down to, presumably, where this power station was. It was clear these government officials were here for more than environmental issues with two dozen dead bodies. This was about mitigating or obscuring the cause, and Beau would have little time to find the truth before it was erased. He sped up his pace and the strain momentarily made him think about lowering his latte intake, but only momentarily.

Up ahead he could see a small building at the side of the tracks. Wires extended from it, upwards and into the ground. The door at the side was wide open but there was no one in sight. His repairman routine would seem pretty flimsy out this far, but Beau wouldn't let that stop him, the best conmen could dig gold out of bullshit.

Approaching the building, Beau kept alert, but there was nothing to see or hear. He walked up to the opened door and peered inside, the glow of a light could be seen coming from deeper within.

"Hello?" Beau shouted into the building. "I think I'm lost."

No reply came. The inside was silent but for the humming of electricity. Beau hadn't brought anything with him other than a few common repair items like a hammer and a few screwdrivers for looks. Items like a flashlight didn't seem necessary for the disguise, that wouldn't happen again.

Beau stepped inside and looked for the source of the light. It came from a bulb that was suspended by a single wire from the ceiling, exposing another open door. Looking back outside a final time, Beau went in.

Further down, against the far wall, Beau could see the machinery creating the hum covered in dimly lit lights and dials. The door was a dingy yellow, spotted with dirt and grime. It was opened towards him and blocked his view of what was inside. He would have to walk around and expose himself to whoever may be within. Stepping around the door, Beau chanced it.

A small control room with a desk and a single seat stood barely illuminated within. The desk had papers scattered all over it, a small ashtray and an old radio were amidst the mess. Other than that, there was nothing of note inside. Beau turned around to leave.

A man in a suit and overcoat stood in front of him, causing Beau to jump and yelp involuntarily in surprise. Grabbing him strongly by one arm, the man muscled him out of the building where a second suit and overcoat waited.

"Mister Bradley," said the second overcoat, "I thought that was you."

So much for gold mining.

"Sorry we missed you earlier," he continued "I guess we can talk now instead."

"I don't have it," Beau said, trying to look neutral.

"Don't have what?" the first overcoat asked.

"The video," Beau shook his head, "I don't have it."

"That's inconsequential at the moment Mister Bradley," second overcoat said while pulling out a pack of cigarettes. He lit one and continued, "We just need a few minutes of your time."

'Here it comes,' thought Beau.

In the distance, an explosion could be heard, followed closely by a second. The overcoat who had Beau by the arm pushed him down to the ground and ducked himself. The second man dropped his cigarette and reached his hand into his coat, leaving it there. Slowly he walked in the direction of the noise while the first man stood up and took a few steps towards him.

"That came from the direction of the camp," second overcoat said to the first.

"Things couldn't have escalated this fast," first overcoat answered.

"We need to make a call, get some bearing on the timetable," second overcoat continued.

"So we take the reporter with us?" asked overcoat one.

They both turned to see Beau standing behind them, smiling.

"Where are we off to gentlemen?" said Beau.

———————

Nick and his team had arrived at the ravine, they were using it as a guide to bring them to the bridge. In the distance he could still see the smoke billowing up into the air, but the gunfire had stopped completely. Judging by the thick cloud, the next turn should bring them within firing distance. Rounding an outcropping of rock, Nick stared in surprise at what lay before him.

The bridge was a shattered mess at the bottom of the gorge. It was melted and covered in ash, rather like the jeep they had found recently. Panic caught Nick by the throat, and he was momentarily unable to speak.

"What the hell happened?" a soldier asked from behind.

Nick continued to stare into the devastation, his mouth agape. That bridge was solid iron, it would have taken a tank shell to cause this kind of destruction. Yet here it lay, smoldering in front of them. Along the wall of the ravine, Nick noticed a path they could use to get up to the camp. It may put them directly in harm's way but it was the only path available as far as the eye could see.

"We need to get up there," Nick said pointing in the path's direction, "now."

Behind him came no reply, Nick took that to be silent affirmation. He began to jog towards the path, behind him came the sound of footsteps. Slowly they made their way up the steep hill. Nick listened intently for any further activity, but aside from his own breathing, there was nothing to be heard.

As they got closer to the top, Nick could see the remnants of the rails jutting out, melted like a candle with small trails of smoke still wafting from what remained. From up here, the bridge seemed in an even worse state than it had below: warped and almost fused with the rocks and ground. Now, only a short distance from the top, he could hear the sounds of fire burning, but nothing else. Fueled by concern, he doubled his speed and covered the remaining distance as quickly and quietly as he could.

Cresting the peak, Nick looked into the direction of the camp. Nearby were two vehicles burning away on their sides. A melted mess of another two or more lay next to the bridge, and everywhere he looked were huge smoking holes cratered into the ground.

Slowly taking the last few steps into the open, Nick was able to see more of the devastation. Tents, tables, and chairs were strewn around the area. A mess of melted electronic equipment puddled just beside a burning truck. A closer examination brought a shock with it, there was an arm jutting out from the melted equipment.

Nick steeled himself and continued to the first overturned truck. In the air was the tell-tale smell of burning flesh, something he was uncomfortably familiar with. Peering around the trucks remains, he got a better view of the carnage that lay beyond.

Bodies were burnt half to ash and scattered around the area like dolls. Some were in various pieces while others seem completely intact, but all were burnt black and smoldering. Nick felt his stomach lurch, and bile burned the back of his throat. He coughed and spit out the offending substance. Behind him, he could hear a few of the soldiers throw up. Nick spun around and signaled for them to be quiet. He realized the hypocrisy of this, but hopefully it would quell the cascade effect that such acts cause.

Turning back, Nick stepped slowly around with his weapon raised. Scanning the area for targets, he continued towards the largest collection of bodies. Part of him hoped to find someone alive, but looking at the damage the attack had left, perhaps death would be preferable. Worse still, there seem to be nothing but friendlies amongst the carnage before him. The current state of things made it impossible to tell though.

Continuing to search, Nick found his way towards the rear where the entrance to this whole mess had been. The cars they had arrived in were mostly undamaged, the main tent they had suited up in before leaving seem to suffer only minor tears and smoke damage. The best chance for either survivors or enemies would be there. Nick waved for the team to move up and headed in its direction. Slowly they made their way across the ruins. Nick signaled for the team to break up and take the sides of the tent while he continued on to its entrance.

The flap was unzipped and waving in the breeze, no sound came from within. Nick used the tip of his barrel to open the tent and peered inside. The front section of the massive tent was empty. Nick crouched to lower the noise he would make and slipped in quietly. The lights were all dead and it took his eyes a moment to adjust. Listening, he thought he could hear labored breathing coming from the next area in the tent. Cautiously, he slowly stepped towards the flap that would take him there. His eyes hadn't become completely adjusted to the darkness, but a rip in the tent was letting light into the next room. Lying completely on the ground, Nick slowly let the barrel of his weapon open the flap, and he looked inside.

The click of a pistol with no ammunition went off in repeated succession. Nick jumped up and rushed in pointing his weapon. Training his sights on the person in front of him, he yelled "Don't move!"

Doctor Strieber was aiming the weapon at Nick, still fruitlessly pulling the trigger. In a rage, Nick slapped the gun from Strieber's hand and pulled him roughly to his feet.

"What the fuck is wrong with you?" Nick yelled into Strieber's face.

Strieber was in a state of shock, his mouth wide open and muttering nonsense.

"You have clearly never been in the field before!" Nick continued his tirade. "If I ever see you on the same one as me again I'll shoot your ass dead!" Nick shook Strieber by his lapel, "Do you fucking hear me?"

"Captain!" came a voice from a corner of the tent.

Nick pushed Strieber backwards and turned, recognizing the voice.

"You'll have to forgive him," Coleman said from the darkness, "he was trying to defend me."

"Why the hell wouldn't you defend yourself," Nick shot out, still angry. "Why would you leave it to someone with no experience?"

"Because he's blind," Strieber finally found his voice.

Nick looked at Strieber in disbelief. From behind, members of the team had entered the tent after hearing the vocal exchange. Coleman tried to stand up, Strieber came to his aid and steadied him. Together they walked the few paces between him and Nick. The light from the rip in the tent illuminated Coleman's face, bandages were wrapped around his head, covering his eyes.

"What the hell happened here?" Nick asked to both of them.

From outside Nick heard a car pull up, he motioned for the team to get outside and followed them. The two snipers, who had arrived while the team was in the tent, had their sidearms trained on the vehicle as it stopped. Inside, the two men raised their hands in the air, but remained seated.

"Out of the car!" Nick shouted.

Both men slowly opened their doors and exited the vehicle, hands still raised.

"Who are you?" Nick asked the two men.

"They're with me," came Coleman's voice from behind Nick, "according to the good Doctor here. Let them through."

With the guns trained on them lowered, the two men dropped their hands and slowly walked up to Coleman.

"We found the reporter," said one of them to Coleman, "he's in the back of the car."

"Has he demanded a lawyer or started yelling about the fourth amendment yet?" Coleman asked.

"No," said the other man. "He seemed happy to come."

"Excellent!" said Coleman with a smile.

Beau sat in the back seat, his phone had been taken away from him. Outside the car door was an armed soldier guarding him from escape. In front of him he could clearly see the devastation of an upturned vehicle, smoke billowing skywards, but little else. In the time he had been sitting here, he'd witnessed the arrival of a clean up team. They had immediately set to work on the other side of the vehicle, enticingly out of sight. He had rolled down the window in an attempt to converse with the guard, and also hoping to catch any conversation close enough to eavesdrop upon. The guard had been completely unresponsive, but said nothing about the open window.

In the distance, there was muted sounds and some sporadic conversation, but both were unintelligible from the back seat. The clean up crew, their uniforms, and their vehicles were all completely nondescript. Not even a company logo to go on.

Beau had begun to regret his decision to come. He had hoped for some piece of the puzzle he could add to the confusing mosaic of clues. He wasn't expecting complete understanding, just a scrap of useful information that would begin to stitch things together. His freedom wasn't really a concern to him. The video should give him a bargaining chip as it was obviously important to someone, regardless of what the overcoats had to say. Besides, a government agency showing up at the station asking for a reporter who suddenly disappears without a trace would seem suspicious even to his moron boss.

This brought Raul back to mind, where had his little Latino camera man got off to? Beau would have to try him again when he got his phone back.

A soldier came into view at the front of the car, he waved at the guard who opened the door and motioned for Beau to get out. His legs cramping, Beau rolled out of the car and stood up to face the armed soldier. He waved for Beau to move into the clean up area, Beau smiled tauntingly and did so.

Around the truck, Beau could see bags and tarps covering what he assumed to be bodies. Other destroyed vehicles were scattered about as well as machinery that looked to be in the same state as the train cars he had seen only this morning. Beau felt a hand at his back prodding him along, and he turned to see a slightly damaged tent in front of him. Obviously, his destination. He continued to take in as much as he could from the periphery of his vision, but it was a short walk.

Just before they arrived at the opening of the tent, a stretcher was being removed from inside by two soldiers. On it lay some poor soul covered in a tarp, an arm hung out from the side. The escorting soldier had grabbed Beau to halt him so they could pass, and Beau got a good look as they did so.

The arm had strange burn marks on it, like a pattern of thick crisscrossed lines. Beau would have guessed it for a tribal tattoo if not for the fact that this was the second time today he had seen such a burn.

———————

Jerich was on the couch of a living room. In front of him was the blue light of the television, tuned to a wrong channel. It shone intensely in the darkness. He looked around the room, unsure of where he was. It seemed familiar, like a place he had been to in the distant past but completely forgotten about. The room was black, save for the television, and the blinds on the windows were drawn. It was obviously night as there was no light peeking in from around the dark shades.

The walls contained pictures of some kind, but they were obscured by the utter blackness around him. A book shelf of some kind jutted out of the one wall, its contents also hidden. A small coffee table was in front of the couch. On it was a remote with a single, large, lighted blue button on it. Picking up the remote, Jerich tried to read the single word that was written beneath it. The letters seemed to swim in his head, blurring and convoluting in front of him. His best guess at what he was reading was the word 'Incipere'.

Looking back to the television, Jerich pointed the remote at it, his thumb hovering over the bright blue button. It seemed so ominous in its singular unknown purpose, yet he was compelled to find out what it did.

He pressed it.

The television in front of him came to life. On screen was a dark image marred by static and distortion. Jerich focused on picking the image out of the noise. The camera was on a slant, close to the floor, a corner of some kind was in the distance. The camera moved drunkenly, coming up from the floor. The scene revealed an oblong black object lying there. Static filled the screen momentarily then focused in closer to the dark mass, it moved slightly.

The screen illuminated an intense blue, the object on the screen now clearly visible. It was immediately familiar and the pain of remembrance shot through him. A head with long hair lifted out of the pile, the face completely blank of features. It starred out of the screen at Jerich; eyeless, but watching, searching for him. The screen grew white with static again, when it returned the face completely filled up the screen.

Slowly, bright blue tendrils began to escape from the back of the television and crawled along the wall behind it. Crisscrossing as they slowly made their way skyward, the room light up from their intensity, their width expanding greatly as they climbed.

The centers of the tendrils began to darken, then turn white. Small pieces began to break off and float upwards to the ceiling. Slowly the bright light dimmed, and where it was darkest, Jerich could see the outside creeping in. The wall slowly disintegrated, taking with it the windows and blinds. The pieces turning white and floating up out of sight.

The sky above was dark and starless, oppressive and foreboding as it stood vacantly looming. In the distance, the horizon was a bright blue. Jerich could barely see buildings and bridges in its luminance. A jagged fissure of light was rolling across the land, chasing the horizon. Ripping everything it touched into pieces that floated skywards and into the inky blackness above. The world becoming absolute darkness in its wake, he watched as the last of the light faded into black.

The television was still on in front of him, seemingly the only source of light in the entire world. On it, the blank face still stared outwards. Jerich looked into its empty expression. The world around him was silent and still, the very air seemed a vacuum that pushed on his skull and lungs.

The image disappeared and the blue screen returned, slow and ethereal it began seeping out and floated in front of the television. Swirling slightly and shifting, it began to take shape. A sphere, a line, dark holes, a face.

A scream, a ghostly echo reverberating, it rushed out at Jerich who was suddenly unable to breathe.

Jerich shot up and screamed into the darkness. He could hear the sounds of footsteps coming towards him as he tried to catch his breath. Bright light ripped through his eyes and he quickly covered them with his arm.

"Mr. Larsen," came a woman's voice near him, "I'm Doctor Brandt."

Jerich tried to escape the noise in front of him and fell to the hard floor below, he could hear the crash of metal and plastic around him.

"Mr. Larsen!" the Doctor said again, "Mr. Larsen, everything is alright. Calm down!"

Jerich tried to open his eyes, then immediately closed them again in pain. He could feel his heart racing and his breathing shallow and empty, he was suffocating. He tried to stand up, get more air into his lungs. He almost made it, but fell again.

More footsteps came towards him and he felt hands on him. He initially fought back, but they were far too strong for him to push away. He instinctively curled up to fend off any violence, but instead he felt himself placed on something soft, he relaxed a little.

"Mr. Larsen," a man's voice this time, "you've been in an accident."

"You're in a hospital," The Doctor's voice again, "do you understand?"

Jerich coughed, tried to swallow, but found his throat so dry that he gagged.

"Easy Mr. Larsen," the man's voice returned, "I'll give you some water, but you'll have to drink it slowly."

Jerich felt an arm raise him up, and a paper cup pressed on his lips, he sipped and coughed again. The arms brought him to sit upright, and, avoid choking, he coughed a few more times and relaxed. Trying to open his eyes again, Jerich managed this time, but could barely keep them ajar. The light was still painful, but he could finally see.

The man in front of him must be an orderly; he was tall, broad and smiling. The woman behind him was obviously the Doctor, her hand was on her hip, and she was wearing the complete opposite of a smile.

Jerich decided to speak to the friendlier of the two. "What happened?" he asked looking at the tall orderly.

"You were brought in this morning," the Doctor said with a scowl. "You have been here for most of the day."

"You don't remember how you got here?" the orderly asked in a friendly tone, seemingly to counterpoint the woman behind him.

"I..." Jerich started, then it came back in a flood. His dream, the girl on the television was the same girl from the train. He remembered leaving her behind to save his own ass from that, ...thing. That bright, blue, burning thing that had managed to grab ahold of him just before he jumped. He couldn't say anything about that, they would think he was crazy. He was questioning it himself.

"I don't... remember." Jerich finally finished.

"You don't remember that burn you have on your leg?" the Doctor asked. "It seems like it would have been very painful."

Confused, Jerich pulled his gown up to get a look at his legs beneath him. One had a long burn, etched in his skin very strangely. He reached down and touched it, it felt rough to his fingers, but it didn't seem to cause him any pain.

"How about your shoulder?" the orderly asked. "Can you tell us what happened to your shoulder?"

Jerich remembered clearly the pain and the loud crack of bone when he had hit the ground and tumbled, but now he felt nothing.

"I think I broke it." was all Jerich would allow.

"Yes," the Doctor said, "but that would have been a while ago. We're asking about the disfigurement you have."

"Disfigurement?" Jerich said perplexed.

"Yes Mister Larsen." The Doctor continued. "Your shoulder has sustained an injury, leaving an area of the skin hard and discolored. Do you remember where you got it from?"

Jerich shook his head in confusion.

"I took a biopsy to test for necrosis," the Doctor explained. "What we found was high levels of granite, ferrite and quartz."

"I don't understand," Jerich managed to say.

"We don't understand," the Doctor replied tersely. "Tell us how you received that injury."

Jerich had no answers, but he knew the questions would keep coming if he didn't get out of here.

"How much is all of this costing?" Jerich asked.

"Excuse me?" the Doctor asked taken aback.

"I only have basic health insurance," Jerich said, "I can't pay for all these tests you are doing, I can barely pay rent."

"I just told you that you have an unknown health condition," the Doctor said surprised. "Is money really what you should be worrying about?"

"I feel fine," Jerich replied, "and I can't afford to stay here any longer."

"Mr. Larsen," the Doctor softened her tone, "Jerich, it may be terminal for all we know."

"Is it contagious?" Jerich asked, already knowing the answer.

"Well, no," answered the Doctor, "it's not viral."

"Then I have to leave," Jerich said decisively. "I have to get back to work. If I get fired..."

"Surely wherever you work has provisions for..." the Doctor cut him off.

"You just don't live in the real world lady!" Jerich suddenly erupted. "Provisions is a concept that companies tell stockholders so they think the poor working wretches have options. The reality is that you'll get fired for pretty much anything because some poor schmuck right behind you is willing to work for less money."

The Doctor stared in disbelief.

Jerich wasn't finished, "It's great that your biggest concern is where you'll fly to on your next vacation while you drive to work in a car that costs more than I'll make in ten years," he took a breath, "but I have to walk to work because a bus ticket is all I can afford, and my idea of a vacation is two consecutive days off."

"Look..." the Doctor began.

"So don't talk to me about provisions," Jerich cut her off. "I'm leaving."

6
...to Devastation

The soldier pushed Beau through the flaps, inside was the musty smell that every tent accumulated. It was partially lit by rips in the fabric and lanterns that were scattered about. Beau was walked through this small first room and into a secondary larger one.

Two men were talking in hushed tones while three others were standing at guard. There was no sign of the two overcoats who had brought him here.

"Sir," the soldier escorting Beau announced.

One man turned with some effort, he was wearing a bandage around his head and covering his eyes.

"Mr. Bradley," the man said, smiling slightly. "We've been trying to have this conversation with you since this morning."

"I already told the other two," Beau started with his strong card, "I don't have the footage."

"I understand," said the man, "but we need to talk all the same."

So much for that strong card.

Someone helped him to sit down on a nearby chair.

"Thank you Doctor," the man smiled and situated himself. "I need a word alone with Mr. Bradley." he spoke loudly so everyone in the room would hear.

The Doctor nodded despite the man being unable to see it. The few people within began to file out with the doctor being the last to leave.

"My name is Alex Coleman, Mr. Bradley," said Coleman after the noise died down and he was relatively sure they were alone.

"What agency are you part of?" Beau asked, not giving the upper hand.

Coleman would have none of it, "That's not important. What is important is that you understand the bigger picture here."

Beau was all for that, "I'm listening."

"We are in the midst of a situation, one that is tied to the events of this morning," Coleman began. "It requires a level of diplomacy, especially in terms of the media."

"Such as covering up twenty or so dead bodies?" Beau asked with obvious sarcasm in his voice.

Coleman didn't miss a beat, "Things are much more complicated than that Mr. Bradley. There is a question not only of public safety, but of national security."

"All the more reason to publicize the details," Beau shot back.

"I couldn't agree more Mister Bradley," Coleman returned.

That caught Beau off guard, "So, you want me to go public with what I have?"

"No Mister Bradley," Coleman answered, "I want you to go public with the truth."

"Please," Beau said with a smile, "call me Beau."

———

Bill stared intently at the large monitor on the wall, it was repeating the same ten minutes of satellite view in fast forward. He watched again as two signatures appeared from the edge of the anomaly and plodded towards the base camp below. Behind them followed a trail of the gray impenetrable cloud, right into the heart of their fortification. The entire camp was almost consumed by it until, all at once, it disappeared. Taking every blip the cloud touched with it.

Beside it was a freeze frame of the one good shot they had of what had attacked the camp. In the center of the frame was a large and faceless gray mass, human-shaped but much larger and bulkier.

Bill pointed to the screen, "Can we get the last few minutes of footage on repeat there as well?" asking no one in particular.

The image shifted and began playing back in real time. The bridge was now in plain view with the ground team firing across, but the angle made it unclear what it was they were firing at. Bill watched muzzle flashes of the M60s and the small arms fire of the soldiers. The narrow bridge was a kill box where advancement of any kind would be suicide with nothing to take cover behind. Yet, there it was. Something advancing slowly across, despite the barrage of bullets. A bright light slowly marched into view, every step growing brighter until it blanked out the screen. The image remained there for several seconds, and nothing could be seen within the intense brightness until a parting at the center emerged.

The scene began to reappear slowly, and the bridge was visible again. It had changed; the bridge was now covered with ash, the rails beneath were glowing white as the men continued to fire. Then, there it was. A juggernaut of immense proportions running at an incredible speed across the bridge. Its image a blur of motion as it slammed into the two trucks firing the M60s, sending them into the air. The image froze there for a moment longer and then went blank, the scene began to repeat.

Bill was still awestruck after watching it for the umpteenth time. He tried to wrap his head around what it was he was looking at.

"Could it be a drone of some type?" Bill asked looking at Frank who was similarly enrapt in the playback.

Frank shook his head, "If it is, it's technology well beyond anything we have ever seen."

"What's the alternative?" Bill asked rhetorically. "Extraterrestrial intelligence?"

"Maybe it's both," Frank answered. "Either way, we need more data."

"And the local copy on site?" Bill returned his gaze to the carnage on display.

"We'll have to wait for it to arrive," Frank said from beside him. "The clean up crew is already there, someone will be on their way with it momentarily."

Bill looked back up to the map on the monitor, the team looked relatively intact by rough estimation. Not bad for a group that was expected to fail completely. Their testimony and the sample may just shed some light on everything.

A man in a white jumpsuit and a baseball hat entered the room with a bag beneath his arm. From behind a desk, one technician stood up and approached him. The two exchanged a few words and the white jumpsuit handed the tech the bag.

"The raw footage has arrived, sir," the tech spoke in Frank's direction.

"Good," said Frank, "hopefully this adds some pieces to the puzzle before us."

The tech went through the process of transferring the data into the computer in front of him. Small video thumbnails appeared on the large screen at the front of the room. Many appeared to be blank or very dark. The tech began to arrange them into categories as Frank waited patiently.

"Sir," said the tech doing the work.

Frank turned in his direction.

"There doesn't seem to be much usable video here," the tech continued, moving the thumbnails around on the main screen.

"Show me anything we haven't already watched," Frank said, pointing to the largest screen.

The monitor went blank, then a few images sprang to life. It was from a camera lying on its side, it showed the ground and a burning vehicle. The image disappeared, came back, disappeared again and finally returned to show a soldier's face fall directly in front of it - he was screaming. Thankfully there was no sound, but the pain on the man's face told you everything. His arm moved into view as he tried to crawl away from something, his body shifted slowly off screen to the left. As the body moved, it began to turn black in color and grow thin. By the time his waist had moved into camera there was smoke pouring from it, his body was bubbling and melting away onto the ground. His legs were completely gone except for a small protrusion of bone, his pants were smoldering rags dragging behind.

The silence was interrupted by a technician throwing up into his waste pail, followed quickly by another. Retching from others continued as the video on the monitor went blank again.

"Jesus," Bill whispered.

"I want everyone out of the room now," Frank shouted to his crew, "get yourselves cleaned up and go to the break room."

Technicians all began to get up and lumber to the door, still gagging or muttering quietly amongst themselves.

"You," Frank said to the tech who was in charge of the video, "do you have the stomach to continue?"

The tech nodded and returned to his seat, he was one of the few who had not reacted to the footage.

"Give me something else," Frank said to the tech.

The screen was black again, then there were trees. This was obviously footage from an aerial drone, the image shook slightly as it moved across the greenery below. Railway tracks appeared and the drone began to follow them, sliding from top to bottom. The image stayed there for a few seconds, then a flash and the video went blank.

"Lets come back to that," Frank pointed at the screen, "give me the next one."

Another video from a drone, this one over the ravine that the bridge crossed. It seemed to just hover there for several seconds until it started to drift to the right. Slowly, it followed along until the bridge came into view, smoking and sputtering sparks in every direction. The screen went white for a few seconds, then came back for another view of the strange event below. The tracks were glowing white as they trailed off of the screen, the bridge continued to spray white sparks intermittently as bullets ricocheted off the iron.

The camp began to swing into view from the bottom of the screen. There were two distinct, brightly burning spots at the camp's entrance to the bridge. Each slowly moved away from the tracks and hovered there, the view lazily spun in a circle for a moment. The trucks below crept into view, the M60s continued to belch ammo into the invaders. Then, another view of the juggernaut dashing across the bridge and into the camp. The two trucks were tossed into the air as the unnamed thing slammed into them, both landing on their sides. The gray shape began to pummel the trucks, each exploding into a bright blaze of fire that momentarily blanked out the screen.

The heat and force of the explosion sent the drone drifting away from the view below, it slowly circled back across the bridge. The rails below continued to burn brightly and the bridge was now following suit, growing brighter as sparks continued to spray from the iron. The drone was still drifting from the action, they would lose visibility before long.

In a bright flash, the bridge lit up, and the screen went blank again. A few seconds later the image returned, now showing the bridge lying at the bottom of the ravine, still burning. The rails leading away from the camp were losing their intensity, slowly returning to dull gray. The scene drifted for a few more seconds before the video stopped and the screen went black.

There was complete silence in the room as people contemplated what they had just witnesses.

"We have to safeguard the city here, Frank," Bill said, glancing in his direction. "It's too close for containment."

"Yes," Frank replied, "arrangements are already in motion but we'll have to accelerate our timeline."

Nick stood at the perimeter of the devastation on display. The clean up crew was busy at work reclaiming what they could, and bagging the rest. All were in the same heavy protective suit he still wore. He watched as two of them took a sample from a mass of ash that lay in the middle of the tracks. Heavy machinery had been brought in to remove the smoldering vehicles, and a personnel carrier had arrived to evacuate those who could still leave on their feet. His team had boarded to decontaminate and collect their thoughts on the past few hours. A debriefing would be forthcoming, and a clear head would be required.

Nick continued to stare at the remnants of a battle he had neither taken part in, nor witnessed. He knew nothing of what had happened here, but he knew two things for certain: it was the first of its kind, and it wouldn't be the last. He had seen everything from nukes to napalm to nerve gas, and this scene had just jumped to the number one spot in atrocities he would like to forget.

The tent flap opened and a civilian wearing a repair jumpsuit exited with two soldiers, he seemed completely out of place here, and he smiled like it was Christmas. Nick's temper flared momentarily until he realized the civilian could see precious little from his vantage point, oblivious to the surrounding carnage. Nick felt a small pang of jealously over his blissful ignorance as he watched the two soldiers pack him up into a vehicle before it drove away.

Coleman exited the tent next. Nick was a little surprised to see him alive. He wore a gauze bandage around his head that covered his eyes and Dr. Strieber was helping him navigate. Nick walked over to the two.

"It's the Captain," Strieber spoke to Coleman as Nick approached.

"Nick," Coleman said staring off into the wrong direction, "you and the doctor are heading to a local base for debriefing."

Strieber objected, "Alex, you need medical attention..."

"I'll be fine," Coleman reassured, "you will take any surviving data back, and explain everything you've told me. I need to make some arrangements before I go back, but this information needs to be conveyed immediately."

Strieber opened his mouth to object a second time, but changed his mind.

"Nick, this is clearly far more complicated than some terrorist cell and a biological agent." Coleman said, unknowingly staring at Nick's chest. "Don't be tight lipped about your opinions or any past experiences in the debriefing, anything you have to contribute will be valuable."

Coleman's pseudo-compliment took Nick off-guard, and he stared at Coleman for a moment before speaking, "Understood," he said finally, and turned to leave.

"Dr. Strieber," Coleman spoke loudly, being sure to catch him before he left.

"Right here, Alex," came the doctor's reply.

Coleman raised his finger into the air and waited for a moment, "Are we alone?"

The doctor looked around and replied hesitantly, "Yes."

Coleman leaned in towards the direction of Strieber's voice, "Prep a secure examination room, we'll need to do a full work up along with some specialized testing."

Strieber furrowed his brow in confusion, "Alex, I've told you already. There is..." he paused and swallowed hard, "nothing left to examine."

Coleman gave a small smile, "Our new friend the reporter has just informed me that we may have a direct contact survivor."

Jerich was unconsciously speed-walking down the street towards the bus stop, feeling guilty about snapping at the Doctor back at the hospital. Surely she dealt with dozens of patients a day, but there was no reason to be unpleasant. He had to deal with a dozen an hour at work, and he managed to keep even tempered, even with the worst of them. That's not what had set him off though, it was her implication that he was hiding something from her. He was of course, but she could have never known that.

Reaching for his shoulder, Jerich rubbed tentatively and probed it for pain. There was nothing. No pain, no soreness and suddenly he realized, no sensation. It was like the skin was frozen. He knew for certain it had broke in the fall from the train, he had heard the snap clearly in his ears. He tried extending his arm and rotating it in a complete circle - nothing. It was as if he had never hurt it.

Continuing to walk towards the bus station, Jerich wondered if he still had a job to go to tomorrow. He hadn't called from the hospital, and he was sure no one else had either. He couldn't afford crazy luxuries like a cell phone, so he would have to call from home right away and hope that his reason would be sufficient. There would be nothing said if it wasn't. He would just be called into the manager's office and told his services would no longer be required. It was that easy to get rid of someone in this day and age, the laws protected the businesses not the employees.

His mind drifted to the events of this morning. Jerich still couldn't be sure he had not imagined the whole thing. He wondered if it could have all been a bad dream. The girl, the train, the... creature. Thinking back to the mark on his leg where he remembered it touching him brought the whole fantasy crashing down. He was there, it had happened, that girl was dead, and it was his fault.

Shaking it off, Jerich pushed his thoughts to other interests. He turned and looked into the store windows as he passed by, trying to find something of interest. Instead, what he saw was his own reflection, and the ghost of a little girl behind him. Faceless, ageless, but clearly in pain. She wasn't there, he knew that: it was his guilt following him. He turned and ran the rest of the way to the station.

Jerich had made it home while managing to keep his thoughts preoccupied. The random people at the station coupled with the noise of all the chatter had kept his mind in neutral. He had arrived at his stop, disembarked, and walked the half block it took to get home. Now he stood in front of his apartment building. It towered above him like a thin granite mountain. He lived on one of the upper floors, but the view was crap, nothing but more buildings. His neighborhood was not the safest, but he couldn't afford to live someplace nicer. Instead, he kept a metal guitar slide he'd found on the bus one day in his pocket for protection. Telling himself that it was better than a roll of quarters. Jerich hadn't been in a fight since high school, but hoped if it came down to it, that might give him the edge to get away.

Entering the front door, Jerich first checked his mail. It was loaded with fliers and the usual crap. He separated the coupons and dropped the rest directly into the recycling bin that was kept beside the door. There was usually a local paper on the floor that he could borrow to skim the want ads before putting it back, but it was far too late in the day for that now. Instead, he began the trek upstairs. The elevator had been down for months now, and he doubted it would be fixed anytime soon.

His steps echoed off the stairwell as he trudged his way up. He could hear the sounds of television and people arguing from behind closed doors. He couldn't make out what was being said, but he didn't care to anyway. For him, other people's business was just that, and they could keep it. Passing the last turn before his front door, he could smell the usual french fry aroma coming from the apartment just down from him. Whoever lived in there had precious little care for their own health, but that didn't stop the smell from making Jerich hungry all the same.

Pulling the keys from his pocket, he unlocked his apartment and went inside. The coat rack beside the door rattled as it was slammed into for the umpteenth time. Closing the door behind him, Jerich took off his coat and threw it in the racks general direction. He tossed the coupons into a shoe box he kept on the ledge to go through later. Making a beeline for the fridge, he pulled out the last can of cheap no-name beer that he'd bought a year or so ago and popped the top. It was swill, but for all he drank, it didn't matter to him. Finishing half of the can, Jerich belched and wandered into the living area. It was a one bedroom apartment, so everything just blended into one another. His bedroom was big enough for the single bed and the used chest of drawers he put his clothes in, and that was about it. Sitting down on the green tattered couch that had been here when he moved in, Jerich threw his legs up on the cardboard box that served as a coffee table.

The small tube television on an equally small table against the wall in front of him was more for show than use. He couldn't afford cable, and UHF pulled in nothing these days. On the floor beneath it was an honest-to-goodness VCR that worked. He could still pick up movies at garage sales and flea markets for practically nothing. Granted they were older, but he preferred the practical effects over the computer generated one's anyway, they just seemed more real to him. Tilting his head back he stared absently at the stucco ceiling, unconsciously tracing its bumps and ridges as he waited for the alcohol to do its magic. He still had to make that phone call, but he wanted some cushion for any confrontation. He downed the second half of the beer and stood up.

Walking over to the phone on the wall, he recalled his work's phone number from memory and punched it into the yellowing aged buttons of the ancient black monstrosity. The phone went blank and then the familiar voice mail recording kicked in. Jerich waited and punched in the extension number when prompted. Muzak, then silence, then more ringing.

The phone picked up, there was silence on the other end.

"Hello?" Jerich said into the phone.

Distant static phased in and out, then nothing.

"Hello?" Jerich said a second time, much louder.

More static, heavier this time but he could hear nothing else on the other end. The equipment in the office was practically new, so it must be a bad connection. Jerich was about to hang up.

"... I am," a voice on the other end was small and quiet.

"Hello?" Jerich tried again.

More static, then a crackling sound. Jerich thought he could hear metal being dragged across metal, but it was faint. He plugged his other ear in an attempt to block out the background noise.

"You ..." the voice trailed off again into more static.

"I can't hear you," Jerich said loudly, "you'll have to speak up."

"... in the ... with ..." the voice cut in and out.

More metal sounds. Jerich thought he could hear voices in the background, they were obscured as if behind something. Unconsciously pressing the phone harder against his ear, he thought he could hear the dripping of water. The voices continued, at least two, maybe three people talking. Then silence.

"You can't..." the voice returned and then stopped.

Silence again, then a shrill scream almost split Jerich's eardrum as he yanked the phone away from his face. Goosebumps rippled down his arms as he stared at the phone with his jaw open.

"Hello?" came a voice from the black receiver in his hand.

Jerich continued to stare at it in shock.

"Hello?" the voice said again, louder and clearly angry this time.

It woke Jerich from his stupor, he returned the phone to his ear. "Hello?" he murmured into it.

"Hello?" the voice returned. "Who were you looking for?"

Jerich looked down into the receiver and then hung up the phone, staring at it like some alien object.

———

The transport that was ferrying Nick, the team, and the doctor to their unknown destination was clearly designed to move the infected. Everything was plastic, multiple compartments were sectioned off with sealed barriers designed to be airtight. Nick had experience with quarantine procedures, but this was much more advanced than some airtight portable housing. There were electronics and screens filled with data he didn't understand. Some of which could be guessed at, but identifying and understanding was beyond his education.

There were people already suited up and on board when everyone loaded up from the bridge. They had immediately begun a series of tests starting with Dr. Strieber. Apparently he was fine, as he had suited up and began to administer tests among the rest of the team. Each member was pulled, two at a time, into an airtight section for examination. Nick couldn't see inside, but past examinations had always been invasive. He didn't look forward to the prodding.

Nick knew that each of the members would be shuttled into a third holding area, designated as a clean room. The routine was always the same, the examination being the only thing that changed. His turn was quickly coming up and he mustered his courage, hoping he could still piss on command. A suited man stepped through the barrier between rooms and came towards him, Nick stood up to follow.

"Captain," Strieber said from beneath the hood and motioned with his hand to follow, "you are least but not last."

"Last but not least," Nick corrected.

"Of course," Strieber replied and let Nick walk past him to the examination chamber.

Nick entered the enclosed area to see two men in suits standing there, illuminated by a very bright light. To the immediate right was a chemical shower stall. Nick turned and walked into it, stretching his arms out to his sides.

"You are familiar with these procedures I see," Strieber said, sounding slightly muffled in his suit.

Strieber turned and picked up a Geiger meter from a small desk, and tested Nick first for radiation. Running the meter around his body, asking him to rotate as necessary, Strieber seemed satisfied with the readings. He stepped back and waved his assistants forward.

The other two began to remove the hazmat suit from him, carefully removing each piece, and placing them in a heavy container. His boots were the last thing to go, and he was now wearing only the clothes he had arrived in, still white with talcum powder. Underneath, Nick could feel his body still sweating. His shirt was making him itch, but he knew from experience never to scratch until the shower was complete. Irritated skin burned worse beneath the chemicals.

"I hope you aren't fond of those clothes, Captain," Strieber said pointing to his shirt. "They will have to be destroyed."

Nick shook his head and began to disrobe, pulling off everything down to his t-shirt and boxers. He handed them to the waiting crew. The final indignation had arrived, Nick had never grown accustomed to being naked in front of others. He wasn't ashamed of his body, it was the vulnerability that left him feeling helpless. It was an interrogation method that worked even on those who understood its design. Nick started with the t-shirt. With a quick and practiced flip it flew over his head. Turning, he held it out to be taken.

The three suited men just stood there and stared.

Nick narrowed his eyes and looked down to see what it was that had caught their attention. He first looked at his legs, they would be a likely candidate for a suit breach but he saw nothing unusual. His arms were next, examining the unders and overs, again nothing. His belly, his sides, his chest - there it was.

The chain and ring he had kept around his neck had been partially eaten away. He wondered why it had not fallen off altogether until he realized that it had grafted itself into his skin. Panic began to take ahold of Nick, and he slowly reached up to touch the offending area.

"Stop!" Strieber shouted. "Do not touch it, we will have to remove it later. For now, we will cover it so we can continue with the decontamination."

One of the other men stepped off to the side and returned with a plastic sheet and some gauze tape. He began to construct a waterproof bandage from the two, sealing the wound from possible chemical contact. Once it was securely in place, he stepped back so Nick could remove his boxers. The usual discomfort seemed to be nullified by the new situation he was now in. Instead of feeling intrusion, Nick felt he was being aided by the men in front of him. They had suddenly become doctors instead of invaders. The two began to scrub Nick down with hand brushes, being careful around his neck.

Strieber had picked up a clipboard and pen, his gloved worked with practiced precision as he hastily wrote. Continuing to stare at the clipboard he spoke to Nick, "If you had to guess when that happened to you, when would it be?"

"If I had to guess," Nick replayed the mission in his head, "I'd say on the way back."

"Did something significant occur?" asked Strieber.

"Not really," said Nick, thinking. "It would be just before we came across the remains of a demolished jeep."

"What makes you think it was then?"

"There was this build up in my head, like the pressure of altitude when on a plane," Nick began. "Then it felt like my body was on fire, like I had run a marathon."

Strieber stood silently for a moment, staring absently through Nick. "And then?" he asked in barely a whisper.

"Nothing," Nick answered. "It went away."

Strieber continued to stare for a few seconds, then looked back down to his clipboard. He quickly wrote something, but said nothing further. The two other men had finished scrubbing and were now carefully rinsing. Strieber began to mutter to himself and pace, waving his finger around absently as he did so. The rinse completed, Nick was handed a blue polyester jumpsuit to put on.

Nick stepped out of the shower area and carefully dressed, the jumpsuit material was uncomfortable, but it fit well enough. He had taken special care to avoid touching his plastic bandage. Thankfully the jumpsuit had a wide neck but beneath the plastic, he could feel nothing.

Strieber finally stopped pacing and turned to Nick, "I'm afraid you will have to endure your malady a little while longer, Captain."

Nick's face turned grim, "Because you'll want to run some tests first," he said bitterly.

"Correct." Strieber answered.

7

Collating Correlations

Sitting in the back of a jeep, Beau was being driven to his vehicle by a stiff and silent soldier. The two overcoats had disappeared without a trace, but his new friends offered him a ride. Beau's understanding of them was tenuous at this point, his benefactors giving him precious little information about themselves. That would come later. He was busy mulling over the information he had just been given. It was, he was assured, just the tip of the iceberg.

Despite his initial enthusiasm, he had expected to be fed a pile of bullshit. Beau was familiar with bullshit, it was the paint for his canvas of social engineering. He was practically a bullshit detector, and this information was mostly bullshit-free, it had to be. There was just no way to spin a story like this in a good light, and it would have far reaching implications.

An unknown weapon had been used, presumably by terrorists, on those trains from this morning. The camp he had just come from was also attacked, but he couldn't use any of that - yet. Tomorrow morning would arrive with an emergency broadcast that would evacuate a south-eastern part of the city. An emergency broadcast that he would have a front row seat for, and first broadcast rights as well. KLL would beat out CNN for the first time in history, and possibly not the last.

Beau assumed he had lucked into exclusivity due the footage of the trains he had in his possession, but this Coleman fellow told him that he simply had the right attitude. Beau took that to mean he was susceptible to bribery, which in this case, he was. Money was just a tool to Beau, but fame, that was priceless.

Beau grinned to himself as he looked out the window into the sky, it was clouding over and getting dark. Beau didn't care, an act of God couldn't keep him from that broadcast tomorrow. He would have to get ahold of Greaves at the station, and get everything prepared for the morning, but right now he was basking in his bright future.

The jeep hit the city limits and zigzagged across the intertwining streets towards his waiting sports car. The soldier behind the wheel clearly knew exactly where he was going without any help from Beau. Two short turns later, the jeep stopped and Beau exited without either man uttering a word. Beau shut the door, and the jeep sped off back in the direction it came from.

His vehicle was only a few yards away, if nothing else this group was efficient.

Walking over to his car, Beau hit his key fob, and it chirped in response. Opening the passenger door, he pulled off the bits and pieces of his disguise and threw them on the seat. He had worn it over a t-shirt and jeans that he had borrowed as well, so the first objective would be to recover his belongings. Feeling a lot cooler now, he closed the door and jumped in the driver's side to fire up his baby.

Normally, he would stop for coffee, but he was in a more celebratory mood. Dennis would have some beer at the house, but he would be gone to work by now. Beau knew where Dennis kept his spare key and they had a verbal agreement about this kind of thing. Beau would grab some premium brew and head over, it was the least he could do. The disguise may have provided little, but the outcome was pure gold.

After this event had run its course, Greaves and KLL may just have to fall by the wayside on his path to greatness, but he was getting ahead of himself. Best to sit down and plan a strategy for his journey to the big league, and a cold beer was a good place to start. Arrangements for tomorrow had to be made and that included getting ahold of his missing cameraman Raul.

Throwing the car in gear, Beau headed across town.

———————

The war room was empty save for Bill and Frank, they were alone now that all the footage had been reviewed. Nothing more of value awaited within the remaining files from the camp. What wasn't corrupted or blank was mostly audio or pre-attack footage.

Bill was scribbling on a piece of paper while Frank was talking on his cell phone. The paper in front of him contained a bullet list of priorities he was building from habit. Bill looked back up to the screen on the wall containing the map with the anomaly, a faded blue outline indicated any growth it had made. Jotting down some ballpark calculations, Bill began plotting infection radius versus time.

Frank thumbed his phone off and slipped it into his pocket, "The ground team is almost here, Murphy will be bringing them down shortly."

Bill nodded and continued to scribble.

Frank looked back up to the monitor containing the footage of the creature attacking the camp, "Just look at that thing, M60s didn't even slow it down."

Frank took a few steps forward, marveling.

"Notice the movement of the anomaly," Frank said looking at the screen, "the creature stays within it at all times. It obviously contains something required for that thing to function."

"The question is," Bill asked without looking up, "what caused the anomaly to move and focus on the camp?"

Frank glanced at Bill, then looked back towards the monitor. "Clearly it was seen as a threat," he finally said.

Bill was silent for a moment, "What about this morning?"

"What about this morning?" Frank asked.

"Were two train cars full of civilians also seen as a threat?" Bill said looking at his paper.

Frank was silent.

"Were we monitoring the anomaly then as well?" Bill broke the silence again.

"No," Frank answered, "it was an hourly audit until this morning's events. Why?"

Bill looked up from his paper, "What do both events have in common here?" he asked.

Frank looked back, thought for a moment, "Railway tracks?"

"Exactly," Bill answered.

The door to the war room opened, and Murphy strode in, his ever present cigar hanging from his lips. "Dogs are back from the hunt," he said with a smile. "The doctor and the captain are outside, the rest of the team are in the debriefing room as you requested."

"Thank you, Lawrence," Frank said and turned to power off the overhead monitors, "show them in."

Murphy opened the doors and waved the doctor and the captain inside. Strieber was a little ragged and dirty, while Nick was wearing a decontamination gown as a shirt over some jeans.

"Alright, Nick," Frank said leaning back against a table, "let's start with you. Take it from the beginning."

Nick laid out the events of the mission to the room, in practiced detail. He kept it as succinct as possible, leaving out any speculation on his part. He ended his report before their arrival at the camp, he had no wish to go into detail about that unless he was asked.

"So, your team encountered nothing the entire time you were inside?" Frank said in disbelief.

Nick fought off the desire to reply with a 'yes sir', "That's correct," he said instead.

"And you failed to retrieve the sample?" Frank continued.

"As I said," Nick replied, "the entire building was rubble and ash. We took a sample from what remained."

"These footprints you mentioned," Frank said, "could you describe them to me."

Nick had glossed over that little detail, "Imprints in the ash, though they were clearly much larger than a man's."

"And you say they came from the center of this ruined building?" Frank continued questioning.

"It would appear so, yes," Nick answered.

"I noticed you have been bandaged," Bill said from his chair, "how did that come about?"

Strieber stepped in, "It seems to be a reaction to exposure, I'm not sure yet how it happened."

Frank glanced at Bill then back to Strieber, "What about..."

"There is no threat of contagion," Strieber cut him off, knowing what he was about to say. "It is a physical injury."

Frank seemed visibly relieved.

Strieber continued, "I want to run some tests before I try to remove it, but the Captain says there is no pain."

Bill and Frank exchanged looks at hearing this information.

Returning his view to Nick, Frank continued, "What happened when you arrived back at the bridge?"

Nick mentally clinched, he was anticipating being asked, but hoped to avoid it all the same. "The battle had clearly already been fought and lost," he said with a morose look. "There was nothing left to do but pick up the pieces." Nick hoped he would not have to go into details.

Frank looked pensive for a moment, "Thank you, Captain," he said finally. "Lawrence, would you please escort him to the infirmary until I am finished with the doctor here?"

Murphy nodded and rolled the cigar from one side of his mouth to the other. Nick turned and headed out the door, Murphy followed and closed the door behind him as he left.

"Now," Frank said staring at Strieber, "tell me what really happened."

Nick waited and then fell in line behind the solid, cigar-chomping man as they proceeded to the infirmary through the pristine hallways that lead everywhere in this building. The man was bulkier and slightly taller than Nick was. He also had a few years on him, but Nick recognized the person in front of him by name. Lawrence Murphy had been a legend among the troops some years ago, but like all legends, it had faded with time.

"Lawrence 'The Law' Murphy," Nick stated.

Murphy gave Nick a sideways glance, "Not anymore," he said around his cigar.

"Kuwait, Afghanistan, Mozambique, you were a fucking force of nature," Nick said, not without esteem. "What are you doing here?"

Murphy pulled his cigar out of his mouth and looked in Nick's direction. "Uncle Sam and I had a falling out," he said mirthlessly.

Nick waited for the rest of the story, Murphy walked on for a few moments before continuing.

"Seems I push too hard when it comes to keeping the wolf from the door," Murphy finally said, the sarcasm in his voice clear. "He thinks, just because someone burns babies alive doesn't give you just cause to violate their rights. They should get a fair trial and spend the rest of their lives in a nice quiet cell."

Nick stayed silent.

"I know a salty dog when I see one, Miller, and from one salty dog to the other," Murphy said pointing his cigar in Nick's direction, "we both know that's bullshit." Returning the cigar to his mouth, he continued, "Uncle Sam has gotten too soft on the terrors out there, and all of western civilization is paying for it."

"So 'The Law' has become a mercenary," Nick said wryly.

Murphy gave Nick a stern look. "Don't kid yourself, Miller," he spoke, shaking his head, "I'm doing the exact same thing now that I was doing for Uncle Sam. I just don't answer to liberals. The pay's a hell of a lot better, and at the end of the day, no one is going to chain me to a desk because I did a good job."

"Is this your recruitment speech?" Nick asked sarcastically.

Murphy stopped, pulled the cigar from his mouth and turned to face Nick. "No, Miller," he said staring into Nick's eyes, "that's the simple truth. This team doesn't work for the highest bidder, it works for the god-fearing western world, and that includes Uncle Sam."

"Call yourselves a Private Military Contractor if you want to," Nick said keeping Murphy's gaze, "in the end it's always about the money."

"You have no idea what you're talking about, Miller," Murphy retorted. "You're just spitting out the same pablum-puking bullshit that uncles Sam has been spoon feeding you since boot camp."

"So I guess you just wised up," Nick said in an ironic tone.

"No, Miller," Murphy replied, "I never bought into it in the first place. It's what made me... How did you put it," he paused, mockingly lifting his cigar in thought and then pointed it into Nick's face, "a fucking force of nature."

Murphy jammed the cigar back into his mouth, turned, and resumed walking. Nick watched him trailing away, his anger flaring for the moment, then reluctantly followed.

"So we lost the entire camp, millions of dollars in equipment, and our diplomatic liaison is now blind." Frank said when Strieber paused, "Why the hell do you seem happy about this?"

"First, I am sure that Alex's blindness is only temporary," Strieber began.

"Doctor," Frank cut him off, "there's more..."

"Please," Strieber said loudly, breaking Frank's intrusion, "allow me to continue."

Frank shook his head, but was silent.

"After the beast had smashed everything in its path," Strieber paused and then gave a slight smile, "something interesting happened."

"Before or after the bridge collapsed?" Bill asked.

"After," answered Strieber. Reaching into his pocket, he retrieved a cell phone, "It will be easier to show you," he said holding it up.

"You took video?" Frank asked. Bill walked over to stand beside him.

"Alex asked me to capture what I could with his cell phone camera," Strieber answered and began to thumb through the phone.

A few flicks later, a video appeared on the small screen. The quality was the usual shaky image that cell phone video provided. First was a shot of the ground. It held there for a moment while the background was loud with noise. A quick pan up, low to the ground, revealed a truck in the near distance. Then an explosion erupted in front of the camera, and it jerked upwards as its user fell backwards. There was a close up of the ground. It stayed there for a moment, then a quick blur of movement revealed the truck now on its side, engulfed in flames. Strieber's voice could be heard cursing in German in the background.

Pointing back towards the ground, the imaged moved as its operator ran to an unknown destination. Another blur followed, and onscreen was the behemoth from the overhead monitors, it was pummeling a soldier into the powder white ground with its fist. Another soldier advanced, firing his SPAS-12 shotgun into the monster's torso. Shot after shot, it had no effect until the creature reached out and grabbed the soldier with its large hand. Turning, the gray giant threw the soldier like a rag doll into the iron scaffolding of the bridge where it folded in half and slumped to the ground. A quick zoom of the camera showed the soldier bent backwards, his spine sticking through his waist.

Another blur of motion and the video showed a table on its side with some equipment sprawled out in front of it. A soldier stood up from behind and fired his M4A1 Carbine at something off-screen to the left. Emptying a clip of ammo he reached for another, slotted it and continued to fire. A bright light began at the corner of the screen and slowly traveled its way across. The image went completely white, but you could hear the gun continue to fire until a shrill scream erupted and the firing stopped. The image cleared up revealing a black, melted mass where the soldier and equipment had been. It was smoldering and bubbling, streams of smoke trailed away into the air.

The image swung to the right and a blur of white and black flashed by. It stopped and focused on a shot of the bridge. The metal was white and glowing, sparks were shooting off from various places, then a loud creaking was heard. The camera swung sickly to the left, and the image went a bright white. It stayed there for a moment while the cell phone adapted to the brightness. A shape began to form in the middle, the outside of the image growing darker. It looked first like a tall bonfire, smoke was extending from its every side. Then the image grew clearer and it took on a more familiar shape.

Bill believed he was watching a man burn to death, his face grimaced as the video cleared up. The shape was moving slowly away, purposefully in a direction instead of panicked. It stopped and slowly turned around. The head looked back at the camera. A face suddenly visible in all the white, black holes for eyes, and a jagged tear for a mouth. Bill could feel his stomach clench and his teeth clamped down in reaction to what he was looking at.

A loud noise caused the camera to be jerked away and focused on the bridge once again. The image zoomed out to give a wider view. The creature was now visible again, its arm was stretched upwards holding a vehicle door. A long moan echoed loudly. Behind the creature, the bridge could be seen bending in the middle. Dropping the door to the ground, the creature turned to look. It stood there motionless and for a moment, there was complete silence.

Suddenly the bridge gave way and fell out of sight, a white flash spread across the image and blanked out the video again. When it returned, the creature was still standing there in front of the gaping hole where the bridge had been, its arm extended over its head. The railway tracks hung over the edge on the far side, faintly glowing. The light slowly faded, leaving the gray bulk standing there like a statue chiseled from granite. The camera zoomed in to focus on it, and the scene froze there for a moment. Then its arm moved slightly.

All at once the creature toppled to ash on the ground, a puff of dust emitting in all directions as it hit.

"Mein Gott," Strieber's voice emanated from the phone, barely a whisper.

The video stayed on the pile of dust for a moment longer, then it ended. There was complete silence in the room.

Bill was first to speak up, "What was that white flash at the end?"

"It's actually blue," Strieber answered, "the intensity gives the appearance of white on the video."

It was Frank's turn, "So what caused the flash."

"It happened when the bridge collapsed." Strieber answered. "The burst came from combustion of some kind."

"Coming from the bridge." Bill suggested.

"No," Strieber paused, "from the smoldering creature you saw earlier. There were two of them. The moment the bridge collapsed, both simply ignited with a flash and disintegrated."

The room was silent in thought.

Strieber continued, "Based on both occurrences, I would have to postulate that the railway is somehow providing a path for this anomaly to reach out."

Frank and Bill exchanged looks.

"It could be an element within the rails itself that attracts these creatures," Strieber seemed to be speaking to himself more than anyone else, "or it could contain something the anomaly requires to sustain itself."

"Did you get a sample from the remains?" Frank asked, trying to break the Doctor from his monologue.

Strieber's eyes leveled at Frank's, "Of course I did," he said in indignation. "I had them both sent here immediately for proper storage until I could examine them."

"And the sample from the mission?" Bill asked.

"That will be worthless by comparison, it was never expected to return anyway." Strieber waved his hand dismissively. "However," he paused in thought, "the good captain's injury may have provided us with something after all."

Nick was on a doctor's table. He had taken off the bandage and the blue gown he was using as a shirt, and now sat half naked in the industrial lighting. The room was a full service shop, it contained more apparatus than Nick had ever seen in a med-bay. Most of the equipment was visually familiar to him, but their purposes were unknown, the rest looked more like science fiction. He tried to look down at the chain around his neck, but its position was not ideal, so he stood up and walked to the single mirror in the room.

The face in front of him had seemed to age another ten years since this morning. His eyes were dark and sunk in, giving him a haunted look. Glancing down at his chest, he got his first good look at what had happened to him. The marriage ring he had never used was now partially embedded into his skin, the top protruding out at an angle. The chain he wore was not military issue, he had opted to get something stronger so it wouldn't break while in the field. It held his dog tags, which swung freely from a section but other parts of the chain were weaving in and out of his skin. He stared unbelieving, there was still no sensation at all. Instinctively he reached his hand up to touch the dangling mess.

"I wouldn't," Murphy said from across the room, he had obviously been told to guard him until the doctor arrived.

Nick lowered his hand, but continued to stare in disbelief.

"Something tells me that's a discharge injury there soldier." Murphy said around his cigar. "That close to your windpipe and arteries, I don't know how they'll be able to remove it."

Nick looked across at Murphy through the mirror, but said nothing.

"But don't worry about it, Miller," Murphy pulled the cigar from his mouth and smiled, "I'm sure they'll find a place for a good soldier like you."

Nick's eyes returned to himself in the mirror, Murphy's implication echoing his very fear. There would be no way to convince the military to keep him in the field now. He would be a desk jockey or, if he pushed hard enough, be busted down to training instructor. His career in the military was over, it just didn't know it yet. Either way, he wasn't going to give Murphy the satisfaction.

Nick turned around to stare directly at Murphy, "Roosevelt was paralyzed from the waist down, and he commanded an entire country," he said, stone-faced.

Murphy shrugged his shoulders in response and jammed the cigar back into its place.

The door opened and Dr. Strieber walked in carrying a clipboard. "Captain," he said staring at Nick's unique wound, "please sit back down on the table."

Nick turned and did as he was told. Murphy took the cue to leave, "He's all yours doc," he said around his cigar. "I'll be outside if you need me." Smiling and giving Nick a condescending nod, he left the way Strieber had entered.

"Now, Captain," Strieber said, staring intently at the ring around his neck, "you and I are going to have an all night stand."

Nick was going to correct him, but then he realized, that was probably more accurate.

———

Coleman's arrival had triggered a message to Frank's cell, and he and Bill were now heading down to the man's office. Despite his blindness, Coleman had demanded to be taken there so he could finish making phone calls. The base seemed serene to Bill as they speed walked through its halls. You would never know humanity had just encountered its first unclassified and possibly extraterrestrial biological entity.

Bill had been binge-planning since he'd first laid eyes on that creature. Up to that point, he believed they were dealing with an unknown pathogen of some type. Perhaps some new kind of irradiated weapon. This new evidence was unquestionably something far more severe and biological. It was virtually impossible that those creatures could have occurred naturally through some kind of evolution gone wrong. It was also equally improbable that they could have been vat-grown by a foreign government. Genetics had come far, but that level of mutation was decades away. They were exotic to our biological hierarchy, the question was how did they get here, and how many more were there?

A million possibilities entered Bill's head as he continued to follow Frank in auto-pilot. Outlandish theories such as worm holes, dimensional travel, multiple planes of existence, and plain old science fiction ideas like teleportation to name a few. They would seem like fantasy to anyone who had not just watched those twenty or so minutes of video, but reality on this planet had just changed irrevocably.

"I think we need to contact NASA and SETI to ask a few questions," Bill said to Frank as they turned a corner.

"Yes," Frank answered, "Alex has a few contacts that could help discreetly."

"We're past the point of discretion here, Frank," Bill stated plainly, "this is going to require a concerted effort."

"We've planned for that," Frank replied.

———

When Bill and Frank arrived at Coleman's office he was still on the phone. A gauze bandage wrap lay on his desk in front of him while he sat back in his chair, talking. Bill and Coleman had never met. Diplomatic Liaison was a new job that opened after Bill's self-imposed retirement. Bill could see the red around Coleman's eyes from the door, he had probably been rubbing them trying to clear the blackness. Coleman looked into their direction when Frank rapped on the open door, but he gave no indication he knew who it was.

Cupping the receiver, Coleman spoke out, "Frank, that you?"

"Yes, Alex," Frank answered, "Bill is here as well."

"I'll be with you in a moment," Coleman said and returned the phone to his ear.

Coleman's conversation had a practiced volume and timber that made it impossible to hear from a distance, he was definitely a practiced politician. His office was nondescript, purposefully so to the trained eye. Bill appreciated that level of attention to the details, useful versus ordinary was a hard balance to maintain. The only descriptive item in his whole area was the ostentatious writing pen on his desk. Ridiculous and over the top, it gave away the high self-opinion he obviously had. Everyone has their shortcomings, Coleman's was clearly vanity.

The conversation came to a close, and Coleman fumbled for the cradle to return the handset.

"Here," Frank said, and walked over to hang the phone up for him.

Coleman looked into Frank's direction, "Well it's not all bad, at least I don't have to look at that ugly tie you were wearing this morning Frank."

"You're the one who bought it for me, Alex," Frank said with a slight smile.

"Exactly," Coleman returned. "How did you not see that coming?" he also seemed in light spirit.

Frank's grin faded, "The good doctor said he believes it's temporary."

"I'm starting to believe him," Coleman answered. "I can tell the difference between a dark room and light room now."

"So, Alex," Bill began. "Strieber said looking at one these things with binoculars burned your retinas?"

"I may as well have stared at the sun with them," Coleman said, shaking his head. "One minute it was there, then the image just faded away into darkness."

"The cell phone video was a smart move," Frank said, "the rest of our footage was barely useful."

Coleman nodded his head, "I expected as much when I heard the destruction going on. Hundreds of thousands on surveillance, and an off-the-shelf cell phone saves the day."

An awkward silence fell on the room.

"Alex," Frank began, "Bill and I believe this whole thing could be..." he trailed off.

"Other-worldly?" Coleman offered. "Yes, the thought had come to me the moment I set eyes on that thing across the bridge. I've placed a few calls to some people who can give us more info, but they haven't returned my messages yet."

Coleman sat up from his chair and placed his hands on the desk. "I've made the arrangements for a press conference tomorrow morning at nine sharp."

"How much are we going to quarantine?" Bill asked.

"The south end for sure, the downtown core may follow," Coleman said moving his hand across an imaginary map in front of him. "We can't shut down the industrial area without causing serious panic." He looked up in Frank's direction, "We'll have to keep attention away for as long as possible so we can collect more information. Shutting down a city of this size will require considerable evidence."

118

Bill shook his head, "An encounter with one of the creatures would be all the evidence needed."

"We can't afford that kind of exposure," Coleman stated firmly. "The effect that would have on the public would be catastrophic. It would be War of the Worlds all over again."

"Times have changed," Bill offered.

"Xenophobia hasn't," Coleman returned. "Faith and fear still rule most of this planet."

Bill had to give him that.

"Gentlemen," Coleman said and rapped the desk with his knuckles, "I would like to see the good doctor while I have a moment. Bill, could you go put your thoughts on this matter to paper so I can review it later. By Frank's admission, your experience will be invaluable."

"Of course," Bill said.

"I'll need Frank here to help me to the infirmary," Coleman said waving his hand in Frank's direction.

"You can use your old office Bill, it hasn't been touched since you left," offered Frank. "How you found room to change your mind in that closet is a mystery to me."

"No distractions, Frank," Bill replied, "always the key."

Turning around, Bill opened the door and left, his footsteps echoing in the distance.

Coleman turned to Frank, "Your research paid off, we have a new friend in the media."

Frank nodded, "He was an easy mark. Young, eager, and greedy."

"And already paying dividends," Coleman said with a grin. "He's given us our patient zero."

8

Eroding Realities

Beau hung up the phone with his boss. Greaves was surprisingly accommodating considering how little information Beau had given him. There would be a van and a cameraman waiting for him by six in the morning. At ten to seven they would cut live, giving Beau ten minutes of lead up. He would spend the next few hours mentally writing and rewriting things he could say in that small amount of time. First though, he would have another beer.

Dennis had not returned home yet. Beau could only assume there was some big problem with the network that he wouldn't understand no matter how many times Dennis explained. It was all good though, the huge seventy inch television that sat in front of Beau had every channel on the planet available. Currently it was playing a courtroom scene from an old movie; the judge was leaning over with his gavel and giving someone what for. Beau had muted the volume while on the phone, and somehow lost the remote during the proceedings. He gave searching for it a pass momentarily so he could get that beer.

Heading into the kitchen, Beau opened the refrigerator door, remembering once again to hold his breath. Pulling another of the expensive custom local brews from the wooden box it came in, he shut the door and breathed in relief. The beer was wrapped in a golden foil, meant to be left on to help keep the beer cold. Beau believed it was more for show than anything, so he pulled it off, scrunched it up, and threw it into the recycling bin. The silent marketing for the beer was clearly directed at the hipster crowd;

locally made, the container was reclaimed wood and the label beneath the foil was ridiculously understated. Beau didn't care for any of that, it was just good beer.

Instead of heading back into the den, Beau grabbed the pad of paper from the top of the fridge and pulled a pen out of the little anime figure holder it was sitting in. Searching for the cleanest seat at the kitchen table, he sat down, dropping the pad and pen in front of him. After taking a healthy sip of his beer, he set it down and grabbed the pen, immediately giving it a quick squiggle test in the top corner of the paper. Taking a deep breath, he exhaled through his nose and scratched his chin in thought.

Ten minutes wasn't much, and he couldn't say anything about what was being addressed, he wasn't supposed to know yet. He had convinced Greaves that he got a tip from a secretary from city hall he was seeing off and on, that seemed to clinch any doubts that Greaves may have had. In reality, Beau had been handed a scoop that would make his station a national name, at least for a day or two, and Greaves had damn well better appreciate that.

He stared at the blank paper in front of him, Beau was never much for scripting his live reports. He preferred using broad strokes and just letting it flow off the cuff. He was a gifted gabber, and the thrill of making it up as he went along was one of the jobs perks as far as he was concerned. Greaves would probably faint dead away if he knew that. Lifting the pen, Beau began to make bullet points:

- Emergency announcement concerning the south end of the city.
- National attention will be required.
- The accident with the trains is related.
- Quick highlight video of the trains from the footage he had.
- CNN will be scooped.
- Beau will be famous.

He grinned as he wrote the last two points, he realized there wasn't really any reason to prepare too much, it would be best to seem unsure. He would have to cut together that highlight video though, and soon, three beers was his limit. It was a good thing he didn't need sleep.

———————

Jerich was lying on his couch, once again staring up at the ceiling and now contemplating his sanity. The events of today had created large doubts in his own state of mind. He wondered if he had finally succumbed to some sort of breakdown. The stress levels in his life were great, he didn't need a doctor to tell him that, but he believed things were under control. Subconsciously reaching down to the strange scar on his leg, he rubbed it and felt no sensation whatsoever. Frowning, he shook the lie from his head, deluding himself could not explain things away.

Trying to avoid thinking about it, Jerich got up and went to the fridge. Inside was precious little; condiments, a jug of water and a box of baking soda that had been there since he moved in. He closed the fridge and went to the cupboards over the counter that served as his entire food area. The main room of the apartment was barely big enough to fit the few bits of furniture he had, and things like a kitchen table were a luxury he didn't have room for. Opening the stained and well-used doors hiding what little food he had, Jerich looked inside for something quick and easy. What awaited him was just as depressing as his day had been - ramen and tea.

Making a bowl of the tasteless noodles, Jerich threw in some black pepper and a packet of soy sauce from his stash of pilfered sundries. Doing his best to mix it into the long and starchy noodles, he returned to the couch to eat. Staring out the single window in the room, he could almost see the sky past the gray brick building that took up the rest of the view. It was the ending of a red sunset, the light almost completely gone. Finishing his noodles, Jerich washed up the few dishes he owned, and leaned against the counter in thought.

Tomorrow could bring unemployment, he had not called in to explain what had happened, nor had he purchased a note from the doctor. It was a sad reality that you had to purchase proof that you were sick or in a hospital. Years of people looking for a free ride had made it so. Jerich would hope against hope that his perfect attendance would give him a pass in the morning, and he could get on with eking out the meager living he had.

Returning to the couch, Jerich looked across at the old television, but he wasn't in the mood to watch anything. He could retrieve the book he had been working through from his small bedroom, but that seemed too far to go at the moment. Instead, he reached to his shoulder and gave it some preliminary prodding, looking for any signs of pain or even feeling, but it was dead to the touch.

He stood up and took off his shirt. Walking to the bathroom, he turned on the light and looked in the mirror over the sink. His shoulder looked bruised, a slight but dark purple. He turned in the mirror to get a better look at it. The back of his shoulder was the same. Hardly a disfigurement to Jerich's untrained eyes. Pressing with his fingers, he found sensation on his skin everywhere around the injury, but the bruise itself was completely numb. He pressed harder on it to invoke a reaction, but nothing came of it.

Glancing over to the tiny shower, Jerich thought about jumping in to wash the day off. A few minutes under some hot running water sounded good right about now, and would probably help him sleep. Stripping off the rest of his clothes, he pulled back the pale blue curtain and turned on the faucet to get the water going. Looking down, the black mark on his leg caught his attention.

It was a bizarre thing to behold, crisscrossed lines that bulged out from the skin. Reaching down, he gently rubbed his fingers across the surface. It was rough and bumpy to the touch. Like his shoulder, the black areas had no feeling in them while the skin around felt normal. Experimenting, Jerich tried picking at it, but there was still no sensation. Picking harder, he could feel something giving away under his fingernail. A piece of the scar had separated and was sticking up. Using his fingers, Jerich clamped around the small fragment and pulled.

The piece came free in his fingers, and a black liquid began to pour out. Jerich quickly reached over for some toilet paper and began wiping at it, the paper quickly became black in the process. The seeping was not slowing down so Jerich applied pressure but the liquid seemed to keep flowing.

Throwing the paper into the toilet, Jerich jumped into the shower and closed the curtain behind him. The water was too cold, so he reached down to adjust it, he could see the black liquid oozing down his leg and being washed away into the drain. Turning his leg into the stream of water, it continued to weep for a few more minutes then stopped. Waiting for a while longer, Jerich was convinced it had finished and began washing himself, careful to avoid the irritated area. Jumping back out, he toweled off and carefully dried the hole he had made. Opening his medicine cabinet behind the mirror, Jerich pulled out a bandage and applied it lightly over the spot on his leg. It was still numb despite the ordeal, but no more liquid came from it.

Collecting his discarded clothes, Jerich went into his bedroom and threw them into the hamper at the foot of his bed. Collapsing onto the sheets, the air around him was cool but comfortable. He looked over at the alarm clock, its green numbers illuminating the small bedroom from the other corner. He would get a decent nights sleep and be early tomorrow morning to catch the store manager and explain what happened. He just hoped he still had a job come this time tomorrow.

Jerich was taking a breather in the quiet room at work. Most called it the family bathroom, but to Jerich it was a small safe haven from the noise and intrusion. He stood, arms wrapped around himself, staring at the floor trying to calm himself and empty his mind of frustration and anger. The door was locked, giving him a further sense of separation as he breathed deeply and counted the tiles he stood on. The noise from outside the door was still audible but muffled, the only words he could hear clearly were the pages over the announcement system. This wasn't slacking off in Jerich's mind, this was a sanity check. Many retail businesses had quiet rooms for their employees, but this establishment had no such concerns. Losing his cool would be bad for business, so really, this was more for them he rationalized.

The hum from the fluorescent lights above him were almost calming in a way, like white noise to help him drown out frustration. Jerich clenched and unclenched his teeth, trying to reduce his stress level. At this point he wasn't sure what had set him off, and that meant it was working. The dull noise continued from outside, and he thought he heard his name over the PA. He froze for a moment and listened for the second page, but it didn't come. It was best he got back out to the floor anyway, he wasn't sure how long he had been in here. Bending over, he arced his head upwards to stretch his back, waiting for the tell-tale cracking. They finally appeared with the usual relief, Jerich smiled and stood back up. Turning around, he washed his hands compulsively, and did a quick check in the mirror.

The face in front of him looked different somehow, it was older and thinner. Jerich passed it off as stress, he was not eating properly, and this is what happens. Looking back down to his hands, he noticed they were covered in sores and weeping black into the drain. Jerich quickly put his hands back under the water and rubbed furiously. The sink quickly became stained dark, then pitch. His hands stayed the same color, still oozing the substance thickly. Pumping more soap into his palms, he went back to scrubbing.

Glancing up into the mirror, Jerich noticed a black line creeping up from under his collar. It was slowly zigzagging its way up his chin and across his cheek. He instinctive pulled his hand up to touch it, and covered his white shirt in the black liquid coming from his hands. Pulling his hand away, he looked down at the stain. It was covering the entire front of his body. Ramming his hands back under the water, Jerich returned his gaze to the mirror. Now the line had spread out across his face. Its surface was bulging, cracking and peeling his skin.

He heard his name paged for sure this time, and Jerich turned his head in the direction of the door, someone began knocking and mumbled something.

"Just a minute," Jerich managed and turned back to the mirror.

His face was perfectly normal, he leaned in to get a closer look, but it appeared exactly as it always had. Looking down at his hands, they were red from the hot water and the scrubbing, but otherwise they looked normal as well. His shirt was slightly wet, but not stained. The sink was completely clean.

Dumbfounded, but unwilling to deal with the situation, Jerich dried his hands with paper towel, and wiped the sweat from his face. He gave his hair a quick fix, and did a fast inspection to be sure he looked natural. Adjusting his shirt, he turned and walked towards the door. The banging had stopped by then. Reaching out, he unlocked the door and slowly pulled it open.

A bright light and a gust of wind hit him in the face. Snow was blowing and Jerich raised his hand instinctively to block it, he squinted to let his eyes adjust to the brightness. The calm returned almost immediately, he could feel the snow landing on his exposed skin. Opening his eyes wider, he took a closer look at his hand. It wasn't snow.

Peering out from the doorway, Jerich stared at mounds of white ash and broken walls. The entire store was gone, along with everyone in it. The sky was pitch black, and a bright blue sun beamed at him from the distance. Bits of ash fluttered down from above, passing through the bright light in front of him. He took a few steps out of the bathroom and stared. In the distance was blackness. Flat and shapeless, the earth stretched out and disappeared into the horizon.

Jerich gaped at the scene in front of him. Looking around, the only thing that wasn't completely devastated was the room he had just come from. Glancing behind him revealed the bathroom still there, the light and fan still running. Returning his eyes forward, he suddenly spied a dark shape in the distance. Jerich tried blocking the light from his eyes for a better look, but it wasn't there anymore. Searching around, he tried to spot it once again. There, in the corner of his eye, a dark object. Squinting, he stared across, and, once again, it vanished.

Stepping farther out into the falling ash, Jerich tried shouting "Hello! Over here!"

A slight wind was the only response. Again he looked out into the darkness for any signs of life, the blue sun beamed relentlessly into his eyes. Minutes passed, but Jerich could find nothing in the bleakness that lay before him. He turned to head back into the bathroom, perhaps if he closed and opened the door a second time everything would return to normal.

From behind, he heard a noise. It sounded like people muttering quietly in the distance. Jerich turned back around and looked, this time the dark shape remained there. It looked like a tall, black stone. Unmoving and featureless. More muttering came from his left, he turned to look in response. Another shape stood frozen in the distance, this one closer, but still indistinguishable. Jerich returned his gaze forward, the single shape was no longer alone. Now four more surrounded it at various distances, the muttering had become louder.

In his peripheral, Jerich noticed something. He glanced in its direction to see more had arrived. Jerich's eyes darted left and right, searching the horizon. Each time his eyes stopped, more of the black objects materialized in the distance. The muttering became louder, but it was still incomprehensible. Everywhere he looked, the black forms were slowly closing in on him without moving. Instinctively, Jerich began to step backwards, away from the noise, but it only grew in intensity. Feeling overwhelmed, he turned to run back into the relative safely of the lighted room behind him.

The bathroom was no longer there.

Instead, Jerich found more ash and an encroaching sea of the nondescript black things stretching off into the horizon. The muttering was now a roar of white noise coming at him in deafening intensity. He covered his ears, trying to drown it out but it made no difference.

"Shut up!" Jerich screamed.

There was silence.

Jerich removed his hands from his ears and looked around, but the tide of black had only gotten closer. He slowly backed away, trying to distance himself from the oncoming wave. Jerich felt he was being watched, his every move, his every thought, scrutinized. He turned away, hoping the feeling would subside.

Jerich stopped dead, a small figure stood in front of him clothed in gray rags. He immediately recognized the girl from his dream, her long hair framed a face with no features. She stood still as a statue, the world around had completely stopped. Before Jerich could say anything, a blue line appeared at her feet. He watched it grow and split, traveling up her legs. Growing brighter, it quickly made its way up to her neck. Two bright blue slits appeared where her eyes should be, and a jagged crack became her mouth.

Suddenly the mouth burst open, a blinding light hitting Jerich in the face. An intense, high-pitched squeal accompanied the light, and Jerich tried to shield himself from the onslaught. He felt himself falling, down, below the ground beneath him, and into a void of cold black.

Jerich sat straight up in his bed, his eyes frantically searching around him for traces of what had just happened. He was in his room, covered in sweat. The alarm clock was bleating its harsh tones into the morning air. Throwing the wet sheets from himself, he staggered out of bed and walked over to shut the alarm off. Jerich looked outside the window in his bedroom. It was a gray morning from what he could tell, but nothing from his nightmare confronted him there. The cold from the window, coupled with the memory of his dream were making him shiver. Jerich grabbed his housecoat from the back of the bedroom door, and headed for another shot at washing away his anxiety.

Standing outside of his apartment building, Jerich waited for a taxi to arrive. After yesterday, he doubted he would ever take a train again, plus he wanted to arrive at work early. Hopefully the store manager wouldn't be too busy to give him a few minutes of explanation time. They weren't on a first name basis, but Jerich had established a rapport over the years. Perhaps it would be enough to avoid termination.

The taxi arrived a few short minutes later, inside an older man was at the wheel. He stopped the vehicle by the curb, picked up a clipboard and began scribbling something on it while Jerich walked to the car and got in. Jerich preferred the front seat in a cab, the rear seemed pretentious to him - he wasn't royalty. Sitting down, the old man smiled and set his clipboard back down.

"Where to?" he asked.

Jerich obliged and they were off. The vehicle was big, quiet and comfortable. It smelled of the same air freshener that every taxi seemed to employ. Outside, the day looked overcast at the moment, but it was still early. The weather could change on a whim. The radio played some old-time band music at an apologetically quiet level, but Jerich didn't mind. It reminded him of spending time with his grandparents as a child. The driver was wearing a cologne that Jerich was sure didn't exist anymore, he wondered if the old man had a stockpile from before its disappearance.

"Quiet morning," the driver offered.

"Yeah," Jerich replied, "not usually up this early."

"I love this shift," the old man continued, "it's the best time of the day."

Jerich looked out over the city as it passed by, it was definitely tranquil. He could appreciate the need for a respite from a long day of short tempers. An occasional jogger or dog walker passed by the window, but for the most part, the city seemed empty of people.

The cab turned onto what was usually a main artery of traffic, but there wasn't a single car to be seen.

"That's odd," said the driver.

Jerich looked over at him, but said nothing.

"There's always some traffic on this road," the old man said searching through the front window. "I've never seen it this empty since I've owned this cab."

Jerich wondered to himself how long that may have been.

The old man continued to drive, still keenly glancing left and right. He reached down and began to fumble with the radio, pressing presets until he located the one he was looking for. The news began to play from the tinny speakers and he turned it up a little.

"...today and possible showers for this evening. On the local front the mayor is once again trying to rally support towards his campaign for bike paths..."

"What a waste," the old man said, shaking his head. "When they're talking about blowing millions on bike paths, then city hall has too much money for its own good."

"I suppose," Jerich managed. He couldn't imagine thousands of dollars, much less millions. If there was any money left after paying his bills, he was lucky for it to be tens.

The old man continued, "If there is that much surplus cash, then they should just give us all a tax break instead of some damn bike paths. It snows for over half the year anyway, what use would it be?"

Tax breaks were great for people who actually made enough to use them, Jerich wouldn't benefit a dollar. The cab driver probably owned a small house somewhere with manicured hedges and a garden in the back yard. Yet, here he was upset about money he didn't even know about until he turned on that radio. Jerich found people just like to complain, especially when they had nothing to complain about. There would always be somebody who was better off, but people rarely gave a second thought to those who had it worse. Jerich wasn't homeless, didn't suffer from some debilitating disease, and wasn't addicted to some narcotic, but people had no idea how poor you could be and still manage to function in society.

Jerich said nothing of his thoughts on the subject, that would invite debate. It was best to let the old man blow himself out and keep the setting calm.

The old man darted his hand out and hit another preset, the big band music returned.

"Don't know why I bother listening to the news, it always works me up," the driver said and went back to concentrating on the road.

The final turn to the home stretch was upon them, the cab made it in a slow and practiced arc. A block ahead, there were barriers set up across the road. A police car and a city public service truck were on the other side. The cab glided in slowly and stopped before the barrier. An officer stepped out and walked over to the driver side window, the cab driver rolled it down in anticipation.

"What's going on?" the old man asked.

"I need you to turn around, this road has been closed until further notice," the officer said, his voice hard with insistence.

"I have to get to work," Jerich suddenly found himself saying, "can I just walk it?"

"No one is allowed through here until further notice" the cop continued in a stern tone. "Now please turn around."

Apparently finished with the conversation, the cop walked away. The old man rolled up the window, and proceeded to turn around and head back the other direction. Rolling a discreet distance away from the blockade, he stopped the vehicle.

"That's the only road in," the driver said and looked at Jerich, "you want to go somewhere else instead?"

Jerich gave it some thought, "Drop me off at the nearest phone booth."

"Phone booth?" the old man sounded surprised at the suggestion. "Haven't seen a phone booth in years, you don't have a cell phone?"

The irony of the situation was not lost on Jerich, "No, I've never wanted one." That was a lie, Jerich simply couldn't afford it on the best of terms.

"Me neither," the cabbie answered, "but I have no choice driving this cab. I'd let you borrow mine, but it's company property and they check for that sort of thing."

Jerich smiled bitterly, "Thanks anyway. Just drop me off at the nearest coffee shop."

The old man nodded and hit the accelerator, the cab was once again in motion. Jerich looked out the window, searching for something close. The driver seemed to already have a destination in mind, so Jerich sat back and trusted his choice. A few turns later, they pulled into a parking lot of an expensive looking cafe. Jerich was uneasy about the choice, but it was close as advertised. He paid the man and exited the cab, closing the door behind him.

This place was above his usual budget, but it was an unusual situation. He entered with what confidence he could muster. The cafe was almost empty, a few patrons were at the counter ordering expensive-looking coffee and sweets. Looking around, Jerich didn't see a public phone anywhere. He would order something and hope he could persuade the woman behind the counter to let him use theirs.

The wait was relatively short, and Jerich found himself ordering the cheapest coffee he could find on the menu, still twice what he would have paid on the best of days.

"Do you have a phone I could use?" Jerich tried to sound professional. "I left my cell on the counter at home, and I need to call the office." It was all bullshit and bluster, but if Jerich came across as a mouse, he would be treated as one.

"Yeah, I'm sorry," the lady said behind the counter in a tone that implied she was anything but, "we don't have a public phone here."

"Thanks anyway," Jerich gave his fake smile, "is there somewhere close that does?"

"I'm sure I would have no idea," the woman returned in a condescending tone.

Jerich grabbed his overpriced coffee from the counter and headed over to the condiment table for cream and sugar. For the price they were charging, one would think that actually making your coffee would be complementary. Putting in the most expensive options he could find, he gave the concoction a stir and tried a sip. It was coffee, plain and simple, nothing he would have gone anywhere to find. Unhappy with this whole morning so far, he turned around to find a seat and think about where to go next.

"Hey there," A well dressed man stood in front of Jerich with a smile. "I overheard your story at the counter, not very convincing."

Jerich smiled in spite of himself, "I tried," was all he could get out.

The man rummaged through his expensive looking coat and produced his cell phone. Tapping on the screen for a few moments he turned it over to Jerich.

"Local I assume?" the man said, still smiling.

"Yes," Jerich replied. "Thanks, I'll only be a moment."

Jerich began typing into the on-screen keypad, dialing his work number from memory. It was an expensive looking product, immediately bringing up the company name over the number he had just entered. The phone rang, but the automated voice system didn't pick up. Waiting for a half dozen more rings, he looked back at the screen, found the hang up button, and pressed it.

Handing the phone back, Jerich smiled and said, "Guess no one is in."

The man retrieved the phone and gave the screen a quick glance out of curiosity. His brow furrowed, and he looked back at Jerich.

"Is that the store up the street here?" he asked Jerich.

"Yes," Jerich replied, "they've blocked off the road for some reason. No one would tell me why."

"I can tell you why," the man said with a slight look of mischief on his face.

"You can?" Jerich asked quizzically. "Who are you?"

The man shot out his hand and gave a big smile, "Beau Bradley, KLLTV News."

9

The Announcement

Jerich and Beau sat at a table in the expensive cafe, patrons had began filing in steady since they sat down. Beau had bought a dozen doughnuts to go, they now sat in the middle of the table with each of them munching on a favorite.

"So the entire south end of the city is going to be closed off?" Jerich said between sips and bites. The coffee tasted much better when washing down these expensive pastries.

"It would appear so." Beau said, sounding a little unsure. "Of course, you didn't hear that from me." He paused, "At least not for," he looked down at his expensive watch, "another hour or so."

Jerich smiled, he couldn't help but like this guy. He had gone out of his way to help, and was now giving him some privileged information. Granted it would be common knowledge in that hour or so he just mentioned, but there was just something about Beau that you gravitated towards. Probably his confidence Jerich supposed, that and his easy manner.

"So you're heading down to city hall to cover this?" Jerich asked.

Beau finished a healthy sip from his cup, "Yes, and I need to head out soon." He looked once again at his watch.

"Well, thanks for the use of your phone," Jerich said and raised the last of his doughnut, "that and the munchies."

"No problem," Beau said and smiled. "Since you're clearly not going into work today anyway, you want to come down and watch first hand?"

Jerich paused mid-bite, "Um," he muttered, "I don't really have any way to get there."

Beau shook his head, "You can ride with me," he said glancing into his cup, "just let me grab some more coffee here."

Jerich felt uneasy, "I couldn't impose..." he started to say.

"Nonsense," Beau said and flashed a smile. "I'll even get you a ride back to wherever you need to be."

Jerich had never been to anything even remotely resembling a news broadcast, it would definitely beat out sitting at home worrying about his job all day. "Sure, if it wouldn't be a problem," he finally managed.

"No problem at all," Beau said heartily. "What are you drinking? I'll grab you another for the road."

"Um, I'm good," Jerich said weakly.

"My treat," Beau said. "Tell you what, I'll grab you a Beau Bradley special, and you can give me a second opinion."

Jerich couldn't deny the power of Beau's charisma, he was a positive force in the otherwise negative world Jerich lived in. "Sure," he finally said, this time with more confidence. "I'd like that."

Beau had pegged Jerich five seconds after seeing him - a loner with little in his life. He had known many like him over the years, Dennis was once the same. Beau had managed to get Dennis out of his shell, and he knew he could do that with this kid too. Beau had grown up rough, he would have been exactly the same as either Dennis of Jerich if he hadn't met 'The Great Calanoni'.

Rudy Calanoni, a.k.a 'The Great Calanoni', was a grifter, a shyster, charlatan, and all around good guy. Beau had met him one summer when a circus was passing through. Rudy was a crap magician, but that didn't matter, people liked him all the same. They came to watch the same old tricks night after night because of Rudy's banter and stage presence, he was a natural. He knew how far he could push a joke or a person instantly, on top of that he was just funny. You simply liked being around him, and Beau wanted to know the secret.

Spending two summers working the circuit with Rudy as his apprentice, Beau had studied him. Watched his every move, listened to everything he said, but the secret had eluded him. Finally after giving up, Beau had just asked him outright. 'The Great Calanoni', as always, knew exactly what to say.

"Beau my boy," Rudy said sipping on his favorite gin, "you already have the talent, I seen it the first day we met. The rest is simple; Make everyone your friend, especially your enemies."

It was a simple sentiment, but one that Beau would have never understood without all the time he had spent with the old magician. Once he had the answer, all of Rudy's behaviors and common sayings made perfect sense to him. He began utilizing this new philosophy at the start of the next school year. By the end, he was staring in school plays and editing the school paper when he wasn't reporting for it. He would never have accomplished any of it without Rudy, and it bothered Beau that he never got a chance to thank him for it. 'The Great Calanoni' died of liver failure years before Beau had the self-awareness to contact him.

Now Beau took it upon himself to take a new protege under his wing when he could to help them become more, in tribute to his dead mentor. Dennis was at least a partial success, he had been a quiet wallflower with no belief in himself whatsoever. Beau had taken him from his mother's basement to a successful job at a cable company doing the computer work he was already doing for free. Instead of hiding, he was doing something he liked, getting paid for it, and had the self esteem to stand up for himself when he was right. Sure, his housekeeping priorities needed work, and he spent an obscene amount of time watching cartoons, but everyone had their quirks. Beau was sure Jerich was just another low self-esteem sufferer, and some time with a winner could change all that.

Jerich was suitably awed by Beau's sports car, not saying much, but clearly reverent of it. He was careful sitting down not to drag himself across the expensive seats, or hold on to anything that might leave a mark. Buckling up, he used a napkin under his 'Beau Bradley Special' to be sure it didn't spill on anything while the car was in motion. Jerich had seemed to like the coffee, he felt it needed a little sugar was all he would allow when pressed. Beau was not utilizing his usual driving habits of accelerating with a roar at every chance, partially not to scare Jerich, but mostly because of his upholstery.

"So Jerich," Beau broke the silence, "I take it you don't watch the local news much."

Jerich looked slightly uncomfortable, "I just don't watch television much."

"What do you spend your free time on then?" Beau asked.

"I read now and again," Jerich replied, "but mostly I just keep to myself."

"Got a girl you spend time with?" Beau asked, already knowing the answer.

"Not anymore," Jerich shook his head. "Things..." he paused, "Things just didn't work out between us."

"How long ago was that?" Beau continued his questioning.

Jerich thought for a moment, then shrugged, "Guess it's been about a year now."

Beau nodded his head but said nothing. He made a right without even slowing down, he loved how his car handled - It turned like it was on rails. Jerich wasn't ready for the sudden shift, he scrambled for his coffee with both hands, and just managed from spilling it.

"Turns like a dream," Beau said smiling.

Jerich gave a small noncommittal laugh in response.

"So Jerich," Beau began, "how long have you worked at that place anyway?"

"Well," Jerich paused, "I've been there for about seven years now."

"You must be running the place then," Beau said with a grin, but he guessed what the answer would be.

"I'm just low-level management right now," Jerich answered, "but I'm working my way up the ladder."

Beau doubted that, "What does that place pay? It must be hard to make ends meet."

"It's..." Jerich started, "Tough sometimes, yes. Things could be worse though."

"Things could be better, too," Beau admonished. "Have you thought of doing something else?"

"Only every day," Jerich said with a slight smile.

"And what would you do," Beau said, summoning the spirit of his high school guidance counselor, "if you could do anything?"

Jerich sat in thought for a moment. "Be happy," he finally managed.

'And, bingo' Beau said to himself.

"I know that's not an answer," Jerich quickly added, "but right now... I'd settle for that."

"You know what buddy?" Beau said waving his finger, "I know exactly what you mean. When life has got you down, you would do just about anything to feel good - even for a day."

Jerich jumped ahead in the conversation, "No, I'm not into drugs." He paused to gather his thoughts, "It's a control issue, drugs help you lose control, and I have so little of it now. I'm not about to give what I have left to some narcotic."

Beau shook his head and smiled, "Well I wasn't going there, I'm not your mother but that's good to know."

"Sorry," Jerich apologized, "I just get the indoctrination speech from the pot-smokers cheering squad so often. A common hazard of working so low on the totem pole I suppose."

"You seem like a smart guy," Beau said. "Why are you wasting your life on a dead-end job like that?" he asked.

"Not a question I don't ask myself," Jerich answered. "I suppose it's because I have low self-esteem, and this is an environment I can dominate with little effort."

'Perceptive, too,' Beau thought. "What I was getting at," Beau said, "was wouldn't you rather be happy every day?"

"Of course," Jerich answered, "who wouldn't? It's just not a realistic goal."

"Everything is realistic," Beau chided, "it's your perspective that isn't."

Jerich turned away and looked out the side window.

"I'm here, right now, because I wanted to be here. Nobody handed me this life," Beau said, waving his finger randomly. "I made that happen by believing I could, and not taking no for an answer - especially from myself."

Jerich shook his head but said nothing.

The car fell silent, they were coming up fast on their destination, and Beau felt he hadn't made the impression he wanted.

Beau took a final stab, "What you need my friend is a change of scenery, some quality time with better people."

Jerich gave a slight smile in response.

"Look, Jer, I'd like us to be friends," Beau said glancing over. "Is that okay with you?"

"Sure," Jerich said after a small pause. "Just one thing though," he looked back into Beau's direction, "don't call me Jer."

"See," Beau said with a smile, "you're already making changes."

————

Bill was groggily going over his evaluations and observations for what he knew at the moment. He had spent a few hours last night making bullet points to flesh out this morning. Six in the AM came early, and he hadn't slept well. Mentally going over the possible implications this event could have for the city, and ultimately the world at large. Stemming the tide here would be optimal, but was growing less and less likely as a viable option. During the night, the anomaly had reached out in a direct line and struck a part of the city. Thankfully the path consisted mostly of storage facilities and one of the city dumps. Casualties had not been enumerated yet, but human losses seemed unlikely to negligible. Regardless, the incident toll was rising and would continue to do so. Worse still, the newly grown arm of the zone was not receding. It had stayed put, and there wasn't a railway track to be found, completely blowing a hole in his theory.

The pages were piling up in his trusted, but outdated, word processing program. Apparently Orchid had not bothered to update his terminal in any way. The operating system warned him it required pages of updates, but Bill didn't have the time, so he skipped them. The Shop was behind some of the best hardware firewalls money could buy, they also employed the brightest to maintain order across its many locations. Getting anything malicious through to his machine would require an act of God. He continued to punch through ideas and recommendations, some realistic, some fantastic. Bill was definitely of the mindset that global action would eventually be required to eradicate this, but he allowed for fringe success. A proper plan employed an array of contingencies; low, medium, high, and nuclear. The last was used as a metaphor, but in this case it could be literal.

It would take hours to properly make this look pretty, right now it was a stream of consciousness that crashed from one concept to the next. Bill wondered how official he had to be. His role here was only as a consultant, but that was no excuse to be sloppy. He would organize the ideas into their perspective priority, and separate them with simple objective statements. That should suffice, and considering the immediacy of the situation, brevity would be tantamount. Looking at the work left to be done, Bill was already missing a good cup of coffee.

The door to his office opened, and Frank stepped though. "You haven't been at this all night have you?" he asked, seemingly sure that he had.

"No," Bill replied with a tired smile, "my drive for all-nighters abandoned me years ago."

Frank smiled back, "I brought you a small gift."

Bill looked up from his keyboard to a large brown mug, steam was still billowing from its contents. Studying Frank in apprehension, Bill reached out with both hands to take it from him. Tentatively inhaling the aroma from the brown liquid inside, Bill immediately recognized it.

"You wonderful son-of-a-bitch!" Bill smiled wide and took a sip. "Even french press." Another sip. "You must have someone good in the kitchen because..." one more sip to be sure, "that is a magnificent cup of Cuban."

Frank nodded, "Well Bill, we both know how much you love your coffee. I couldn't expect you to function without proper fuel."

Taking a few healthy swallows, he set the mug down. "I was dreading the cafeteria coffee, waiting until I couldn't take it anymore to get some."

Frank shook his head, "It's not terrible but it's no french-pressed Cuban."

Bill picked the cup up again for another sip, "So how do I..." he began.

"Call down to the kitchen, extension 611, tell them you're coming down," Frank interrupted.

"Do you think someone would be offended if I made my own?" Bill asked with a smirk.

"Definitely," Frank answered. "Marceau would most probably quit at the mention of it."

"Well," Bill waved it away with his hand, "we can't have everything," he said still smirking.

"The broadcast is coming up soon here," Frank said looking at his watch, "we're gathering in the boardroom to watch it."

Bill saved his document, logged out, and finished off the last of his mug, his throat was still used to knocking back hot coffee when he had to. He started to put the mug onto the desk, then he stopped and turned to face Frank.

Lifting the mug into the air, Bill smiled and asked, "Do we have time to say thank you to Marceau?"

Bill sat in the boardroom, a fresh mug of Cuban in his hands, and a smile on his face. Next to him sat Frank who was thumbing through his tablet and reading. An entire wall was one big screen, focused in the center was a cropped image of blue with the words 'No Signal' at the top. Three technicians were connecting wires and shouting into cell phones as they tried to solve the problem.

Across from Bill sat Coleman, his eyes were no longer red, but obviously he was still not seeing things clearly. Strieber was next to him, speaking in hushed tones. Murphy was nowhere to be seen, either he didn't qualify as 'need to know', or was busy elsewhere. Other than the techs, it seemed to be just the four of them at the long and expensive table.

"No special guests?" Bill leaned over and half-whispered to Frank.

"As I promised Bill," Frank replied without looking up from his tablet, "you wouldn't see Keating unless there was no other choice."

"And I appreciate that, Frank," Bill responded, "but I was referring to our local contacts. They need direct answers, and so do we."

Frank nodded his head, "I've been on the phone all morning, Bill. After the broadcast we will go over everything."

Bill sat back and took another sip from his french press, "Assuming we can get the signal up," he said nodding in the direction of the screen.

"Apparently our uplink was severed over the evening, all of our sister sites are down as well." Frank tapped the tablet a few times, "No response from our central server, looks like it's satellite feed or nothing."

"Gentlemen," Frank said addressing the technicians, "we'll have to go unencrypted for now. It's only the news, we should be safe."

One technician nodded and began giving orders to the other two. The blue screen flickered to black, then after a few seconds KLLTV News came up. Currently a well-dressed man seemed to be going over the hockey scores, in silence. One technician began cursing and returned to the massive wall panel that housed the various outputs for the boardroom.

A few seconds later the sound returned. "...scored for the win." the reporter finished off his sentence. "Now for the weather," he continued. A technician brought over a remote control and set it down in front of Frank, then blended into the background.

"Why aren't we watching this on CNN?" Bill asked pointing to the screen.

"CNN doesn't know about it yet," Frank said and looked in Bill's direction, "but they will within the hour."

Bill pondered over what he wasn't being told.

The station went to a commercial, a smiling elderly man standing in front of a fireplace appeared. Before he had a chance to speak, the image switched to a 'KLLTV NEWS Special Report' graphic. Appropriately intense music played in the background while an announcer proclaimed the usual opening statements, apologizing for the interruption. An elegantly-framed shot of city hall appeared, complete with description in case you never left home. The image panned down to show a well-dressed man with a microphone and a poker face, seemingly unsure of why he was there. The name 'Beau Bradley' was emblazoned beneath him, couched in a tasteful blue banner.

Pausing for a moment, he began. "This is Beau Bradley down at city hall. Behind me, the mayor's office prepares for a public announcement that they say will quote, 'require the cities undivided support,' unquote. This comes on the heels of a disaster early yesterday morning where an incident involving public transit claimed the lives of two dozen people. KLL was on the scene, but were asked by officials to withhold the footage until today's upcoming announcement. Here now, we can show you the devastation that occurred only twenty-four hours ago."

The scene cut to video of the two destroyed trains, Beau's voice continued the commentary. A colorful description, full of metaphors that described everything but the cause. This was old news to the team sitting at the table, each of them absently looking for something to entertain themselves with while they waited. This was the first time Bill had seen any footage of the trains, but the damage was identical to the camp attack. Looking into his coffee cup, he noted with some concern how empty it was getting. Deciding cold coffee was worse than no coffee, Bill finished off the mug and set it down on the table.

"...but expected to have some answers soon." The voice over finished, and the scene returned to Beau standing in front of city hall again. He was now wearing a hard look, like the footage had made it difficult to continue. "Today we will hear the official report of what went wrong, plus the unspecified official announcement to affect the city. We wait for the appearance of the mayor, where we will go to a direct feed of the announcement, followed by a short Q&A period afterwards."

"Q&A?" Bill said looking at Frank.

"Seeded questions," Frank answered, "we need to keep confidence high and concern low. You know the drill," he smiled.

"Sure," Bill said, "until someone with intelligence has a question. It's live, you can't edit it out later." He shook his head, "This is an unnecessary risk Frank."

"Worth it to keep the public calm," Frank retorted, "we need them quiet and content that everything will be fine."

Bill found it hard to argue that point, and the damage was already done. It was best to plan for mitigating circumstances.

"It looks like the mayor and several city hall officials have exited the building, they are approaching the podium now," Beau stated and the report cut to the stage for the approach of the mayor. At the bottom of the screen in the same tasteful blue banner was 'City Hall Special Report', at the top right was the word 'LIVE' in bright yellow. A dapper-suited, slightly overweight man in a purple tie stepped up to the microphone and placed some papers down in front of him.

"Good morning ladies and gentlemen of this fine city," the mayor began. "I'm here today to address recent developments that will affect us all." He paused for dramatic effect. "Yesterday at approximately five o'clock in the morning, a terrorist attack destroyed two public transit trains. Ending the lives of two dozen of our fair citizens."

A gasp spread across the attending people. Someone close to the microphone could be heard cursing profanity, conservative citizens we're likely already writing letters of protest to everyone involved.

The mayor raised his hand to silence the crowd, "The system of attack is currently unknown and the area affected has been quarantined until its origin can be determined. To further aid in this investigation, and to be sure that no other citizen come to any harm, we are forced to close the south-eastern part of the city until further notice."

The crowd began to talk amongst itself in a much louder tone now, angered voices began shouting. From behind the mayor, a formally-dressed man approached and stood to his right. Bill guessed it to be the chief of police.

"Ladies and gentlemen," the mayor said into the microphone and raised his hands to quiet them down. "Ladies and gentlemen, please." He waited for the chatter to settle down before continuing, "Temporary lodging has been made available to those who will be inconvenienced, and no expense will be incurred to them. We believe this disruption will only last a short duration, and that citizens should be back in their own homes within the week."

Bill knew this last part was a lie, he wondered if the mayor knew this as well.

"We have sent a group of representatives to notify the areas affected. Members of the police force will be on scene with transportation for families," the Mayor continued. "We expect the transition to be completed before nightfall."

The crowd was once again loudly voicing their disapproval with the situation. Police officers in riot gear could be seen advancing from the corners of the broadcast. They were keeping their distance, but it was clear they were ready for action.

The mayor ignored the crowd, "A map of the affected areas is available from the table to my right, along with the locations of the temporary housing facilities for those wishing a specific neighborhood."

A few citizens began to approach the table in question, members of the police force moved in as casually as they could.

"I want to thank you all in advance for your cooperation in the matter," the mayor said extending his arms, "and I wish us a speedy recovery from this disturbance in our otherwise peaceful lives."

The crowd was clearly unhappy and made it known, vocally.

"Please," the mayor said and raised his hands, "I know you all have questions, and I would like to take this opportunity to answer some of them now."

A wall of noise thundered out of the crowd in front of the mayor, he raised his hand and pointed at someone off-screen. The crowd seemed to calm down a little as someone shouted out a question, it was not heard through the broadcast.

The mayor's finger was behind his ear as he listened, it then dropped and he replied. "The question was, are the terrorists still here in the city? Based on current reports it appears that something in their plan has backfired and they have fallen victim to their own device. We are unsure at this time what that device is and that is why we are moving citizens out of harm's way."

The crowd jumped into action again, yelling simultaneously. Again the mayor pointed and pressed his finger to the back of his ear. Again, the crowd seemed to die down enough for the question to be heard.

The mayor answered, "The question was, what about looting? I assure you that we will have the area patrolled regularly, by armed officials who will be instructed to arrest on site. This brings up a good point: citizens will not be allowed into the quarantine zone for any reason." The last part was elevated in tone to project importance. "I want to stress that this is for your own protection. Despite the hazard precautions available to them, our volunteers will be putting their lives at risk to protect your belongings. You can rest assured that your homes will be safe."

Instead of waiting for the crowd to jump back into action, the mayor pointed to another person off-screen immediately. A pause while the question was asked and the mayor answered, "The question was, what if it spreads? The answer is, we have no reason to believe that it is spreading at this time and the quarantined area will be more than sufficient to contain it."

Instead of waiting for another question, the mayor immediately went into his closing speech, "I want to thank you for your patience in this matter, and please take a copy of the literature we have prepared for you. It will answer further question you may have. Correspondence for this matter can be directed through social media and directly via the special email address we have prepared for this matter, available to my right and on the city's web page."

People began to shout out more questions. The mayor backed away from the podium, into the waiting contingent of officers behind him. Turning him around, they ushered him through the building's doors which were immediately shut while the crowd continued to yell out their displeasure.

The camera cut to Beau who turned to face the camera, "There you have it, a terrorist attack on the city. KLLTV News will be giving you up-to-the-minute coverage as the events unfold. We go now, live, to a panel of specialists who will be discussing..."

The volume disappeared and the word 'Mute' appeared at the top. Frank set the remote control down in front of him. "Thank you gentlemen," he said to the technicians, "that will be all for now."

The three technicians picked up their equipment, filed out the door, and shut it behind them.

Standing up, Frank walked to the front of the room. On-screen behind him was a group of men seated around a table, presumably discussing the announcement that had just occurred.

Frank leaned forward on the table, his fingers splayed to prop him up, "We have the green light to do whatever is necessary to regain control of the situation." He looked around the table. "The military is sending troops to the local base just outside of town, they should be here by nightfall. They are ours, should we need them, but I'm hoping to keep their involvement to a minimum. I've also spoken to Security Intelligence Service, and they are willing to let us take the risks for now. However, they have stated their intentions to have us removed from the situation should we falter," his slight frown indicated his feelings on the matter.

"Starting today, we are going to send in teams to perform a series of tests designed by Dr. Strieber." Frank waved his hand in the doctor's direction. "He believes, as do I, that the spread of the anomaly will be unavoidable, so we need to work quickly to determine a preventative measure. We need a fast solution to stopping or, at the very least, slowing the spread."

"Mr. Coleman has provided us with some leading edge technology that will be arriving within the next twenty-four hours. It's a rover that was meant for planetary exploration and examination, so it is designed to function in the worst of environments," Frank continued. "Hopefully it will operate within the anomaly, and yield the information we have so far been unable to get."

"Did we get anything from the sample the doctor retrieved from the camp?" Bill asked.

Frank looked to Strieber, who answered, "According to preliminary examinations, it contains sodium, calcium, potassium, trace minerals of chlorophyll..."

"In other words," Bill interrupted, "it's ash."

10

Premonitions

Jerich had been anticipating his look into the inside of broadcasting. He was allowed sit in front of the monitors inside the van that had been on scene when they arrived. Onscreen, he watched Beau deliver his opening monologue while a disheveled man sitting beside him gave orders through a headset to the local crew. Elated about the opportunity he was currently in the middle of, he had missed most of what Beau had said. Concentrating instead on the rhythm and dance involved behind the scenes of a standard broadcast. Everyone worked as a unit, sliding effortlessly from moment to moment like they were born to do it. It was a level of teamwork that Jerich had never witnessed first hand: a clock with perfect timing. He tried to imagine being part of such a perfectly-oiled machine, but it just seemed like a fantasy to him. He could never be this coordinated and fault-free.

Jerich heard the call to switch to tape, apparently they still used the term 'tape' despite everything being digital these days. A monitor sprang to life from black to color in an instant, onscreen was a familiar site to him. It was the devastation of yesterday, in full color and live on TV. Two transit trains in ruins and a crew of people hard at work cleaning it up. The image brought back the memories he had blissfully forgotten about since first meeting Beau. Now here on television, it seemed larger than life and somehow more real. The rush of emotion made Jerich feel lightheaded. He stood up to breath better, steadying himself on the wall of the van. No one seemed to notice him.

"Where's the closest bathroom?" Jerich asked a man standing near him, currently watching the feed.

He turned around as if in a stupor, it took a second before he registered Jerich's question, "Restaurant across the street," he said, and pointed behind Jerich.

Jerich turned and exited the van through the side door, shutting it lightly behind him. He paused for a few breaths of fresh air, staring absently at the ground in front of him. He knew the events of yesterday would have to be covered by the media at some point, he just wasn't expecting a front-row seat when it happened. His lifestyle naturally insulated him, he would have been lucky to spot it in the local newspaper. Having it so vividly displayed in front of him was jarring, like being woken from a dream.

Looking across to the restaurant, he noticed it was expensive. He guessed being across from city hall made it easy to charge whatever you wanted for food. Jerich doubted, dressed in his cheap slacks and dress shirt, that he would be mistaken for part of the news crew. Upon entering the establishment, he would most likely be ousted as rabble that clearly wasn't able to afford such luxury - and they would be right. Instead, he looked up and down the street for something that wouldn't notice or care about him. Something in the fast-food line. A block or so away, he noticed a pizza place that fit the bill. Walking in that direction, he heard the beginning of the mayor's speech play through the speakers behind him. Jerich suddenly felt no interest in what was about to be said.

The odor of onions permeated from his destination, but Jerich walked passed and continued on to the downtown core. Beau had promised a ride home, but re-witnessing yesterday's events brought on feelings of guilt and shame. Jerich wanted nothing more than to lose himself, hide in the stream of normal people doing normal things.

The events on the train came back vividly in a rush, his failure to help and his abandonment to save his own neck played heavily on him. Had Jerich stayed in the news van, he may have learned the name of that poor girl. Something he could address when he was apologizing over and over in his mind for his actions. He could come forward, explain what happened to the police, and maybe give some closure to her poor parents, but what could he say? Any attempt at a truthful explanation would land him in the loony bin with a steady supply of drool medication. No one would believe him, and he couldn't blame them.

The bustle of shoppers surrounding him did much to take his mind from things, and help him think more abstractly. His life was suddenly somebody else's that could be examined more analytically. What would be the benefit of telling others about what he saw on the train? Nothing, other than the relief of confession. It would help no one but himself. Her parents wouldn't believe him, and the police would think he was somehow involved. How would that benefit anyone? Besides, they had their hands full with this quarantine. They didn't need some crackpot trying to explain his fantasy to them.

Jerich knew he believed what he saw, it was just as real as the concrete he was walking on. The scar on his leg, the pain he remembered, all a testament to the truth. He also knew that crazy people said the exact same thing. At this point, all he could really trust in was that a girl was dead, and that he somehow contributed to it. Everything else could just be a figment of his imagination.

Picking a store randomly, Jerich entered. Inside was expensive antiques and pottery. The dusty and musty smell of old trinkets brought him out of his thoughts. He began to look around the store, it contained nothing that interested him, but he wanted to avoid questions. Passing by some gaudy looking, but expensive vases, he found the rear door that exited into the mall that sprawled across the entire downtown area. Elevated walkways and crosswalks zigzagged through the buildings and high-rises that occupied most of the core. One could spend the entire day walking though it's Escher-like construction that seemed to grow and intertwine organically in accordance to some mad God of consumerism. It could provide a zen-like state to those wishing to lose themselves to the art of discovery.

This artery of the monster of merchandising contained five floors. At the top, vegetation could be seen peeking out over the concrete handrails. There partly as color, but likely more to help with the carbon dioxide output provided by the constant flow of customers. Jerich decided it would be a great place to lose himself for an hour or so before heading back home to figure out his future.

Jerich looked into the windows and doors of shops as he passed by the faceless blur of shoppers. Expensive clothing stores and electronic shops were amply represented, along with the occasional retailer of obscure curios. Items built from metal, built from plastic, even built from garbage. How people could spend princely sums on reformed garbage was a mystery to Jerich. He supposed having more money than things to buy played a large part.

Slowly making his way to the top, Jerich crossed floors to use the stairs instead of employing the elevator. Immersing himself in the kinetic energy of shoppers and the bombastic sights and sounds of the passing retailers was drowning out the nagging voices in his head. He concentrated on nothing but the flurry of motion as it brushed passed him.

Reaching the indoor arboretum, Jerich was dismayed to notice the complete lack of smell. The lush, fresh air associated with such greenery was not present. His first thought was that they were plastic, there for looks and easy maintenance. However, reaching out and touching one of the large leaves encroaching on the walkway proved otherwise. Jerich wasn't sure how you could homogenize the wholesome out of nature, but this concrete garden had managed to do so. It was now as plastic and lifeless as everything being sold here.

Looking around for someplace to sit for a while, Jerich felt the need for something to drink. After the expensive coffee that Beau had provided for him this morning, he found he'd developed a taste for it. Across the walkway to the other side of the top floor was a small, standing cafe with some well-dressed people waiting in line. Jerich immediately understood it to be expensive and likely requiring some knowledge on his part to order correctly. Asking for a double-double would only get you a confused look or a wincing shake of the head. It would cost him some of his food budget to buy, but the day had demanded a change of routine for him.

Walking over to join the group of elite connoisseurs, Jerich looked up at the hand drawn menu over top of a busy kid likely working his way through college. Although young, he managed to appear regal with a slight air of condescension surrounding him. Jerich suspected that was exactly what had landed him the job. Reading through the various types of coffee available here, Jerich was amazed and lost at the selection. He remembered back to Beau mentioning that Cuban was the best coffee, when you could get it. At the top was something called 'Cuban Caracolillo Peaberry' and a hefty sum next to it. Jerich wasn't sure what a peaberry was, but he was willing to gamble the price of a meal based on this mornings sample of the good life.

Listening to the people in front of him, Jerich tried to piece together the jargon required to sound like a regular. Coupled with Beau's small lesson in the proper coffee experience, he decided he had a decent chance of pulling it off. With the well-pressed, blue suit in front of him walking away with his nondescript cup of expensive black stimulant, it was time for Jerich to put his guesswork to the test.

"Four minute, single-cup, pressed peaberry with room." Jerich said and attempted a slight smile.

Without hesitation the kid behind the counter set to work. Jerich's impromptu research had resulted in perfect infiltration, no one suspected he was a sheep in wolf's clothing. Satisfied with his success, and wishing not to botch it up now by saying anything else, Jerich tried to look casual. Slipping a hand into his pocket and nonchalantly glancing around at nothing in particular, he found a sudden grudging appreciation for the prestige and distraction a cell phone provided.

The kid turned around and handed Jerich his beverage, wrapped in a brown and thick ring of protective, recycled paper. Despite the added layer, the coffee was still scalding hot to the touch. Jerich barely made it to the small condiments rack before setting it down. After rubbing his hands together to dissipate the heat, he selected the items that Beau's lesson had taught him to look for. Stirring the finished concoction with a selected wooden stick instead of plastic, Jerich tested the cup again, and was relieved at the decrease in temperature.

Noticing a large picture window with a spacious view of the downtown area just meters away, Jerich lifted his novice attempt at a masterpiece, and walked over to look out on the city below. The sun was out, the sky was blue and almost cloudless. Outside, the sea of glass glinted like a sparkling brook on a hot summer's day. The cars and travelers following concrete routes on their way to destinations unknown. Jerich had a bird's eye view of the social cooperation that was humanity, looking directionless from up here yet implacably rigid from down there. Tentatively, he tried a sip of his pressed Cuban, and found his first attempt was a good one. Certainly not at a Beau Bradley level, but a start worth pursuing. He smiled and lost himself in the view before him, feeling like a different and somehow better person.

In the distance he could see the mountains, they were hazy even from this height. The slight cloud density made them appear to shimmer in the light. Jerich wondered what it would be like to be there, looking over here. Although only a few hours away, not having a vehicle or money to travel meant they might as well be on the other side of the planet. He stared off into the horizon, and tried to picture a better life for himself. One where the price of a coffee wouldn't mean he would have to split a meal over two days. One where he could tell the person standing here exactly what that mountain looked like. One in which he didn't dread getting up every day and having to deal with the absolute dregs of humanity looking to make their day better by ruining his.

The horizon seemed to sparkle brighter before him, almost pulsing with a life of its own. Jerich noticed the mountains start to fade into the blue sky. A bright line stretched out across the horizon, taking its place. The line expanded, the ground beneath began disappearing under a fog that rolled in. It started slowly then picked up speed, swallowing details as it moved towards the city. The fog grew brighter as it approached, the light reflecting blue off of its surface.

Sensing a mild pressure in his ears, Jerich felt a vibration through the floor and fear gripped him. He eyed the horizon intently, and watched in horror as the fog before him became wall of force. The debris within starting to take shape. He could now see the destruction it was causing as it ate its way towards the city. Entire buildings were swallowed up, their remains thrown skyward as it rolled over everything he could see.

Taking a step backwards, he watched as the wave of annihilation raced directly at him. The wreckage of its path swirling clearly within it now as skyscrapers shattered under its force. The floor beneath him was crumbling under the tremor as the world around him became intensely silent, crushing in on his senses.

Before him, the world was being eaten away by a bright cloud. His feet became rooted, and his muscles seem to lock in place as his jaw tensed in an effort to scream. The coffee cup in his hand slipped from his fingers, and he could feel it falling to the ground in slow motion. Every inch was an eternity as he watched his doom close in on him.

The cloud was now mere meters from the window. Inside, Jerich could see light barbs that pulsed among the giant chunks of wall. In the deep center, past the bits of ruined civilization, Jerich observed outlines of vaguely human shapes. Some balled up, while others were splitting apart and separating in a slow dance of death. A powerful blue light slowly arced its way through the veils interior, and the flash almost blinded him. Deep inside his head, Jerich could hear a low warbling that sounded like a dozen voices heard underwater. It was intense and manic, sounding pleading despite being incomprehensible. Reaching a crescendo, Jerich felt like his head would explode from the pressure and intensity.

His leg burst into pain, and the world around him abruptly exploded into life as a rush of sound. Jerich yelled out, and time returned to normal. He looked down at his feet to see the cup of coffee spilled on the floor, a hot splash of brown on his shin, burning the skin beneath. He looked up and out through the huge pane of glass to see the world perfectly intact and unmolested.

Glancing about, he noticed his shout had attracted the attention of those nearby. Most looking at him like a crazy person, some with genuine concern. The kid who had served his coffee up managed to have a surprised, yet demeaning look on his face - something that didn't seem possible to Jerich.

Trying to ignore the looks, Jerich went back to the condiments stand and retrieved a handful of napkins to wipe up the coffee. Walking back to the spill, he threw half of the flimsy brown paper on top to soak up the mess. The other half he used to wipe at the coffee on his leg, it was cooling down now and had begun to get sticky under his slacks. Sopping up the visible stain as best he could, he threw the used remains onto the puddle in front of him and began to wipe it in a circle with his shoe.

"I'll call maintenance," the kid from the coffee stand said, "just leave it." He was clearly perturbed by the mess or Jerich's outburst, likely both.

Wanting to leave the scene of the crime as quickly as possible, Jerich walked around to the restrooms that were conveniently nearby, and slipped inside. Thankfully they were empty. He walked over to the sink, and began pulling paper towel from the dispenser. Turning on the tap in front of him, he dipped the paper towel in water, and mopped at the coffee on his leg. The material of his pants now cold against his skin as he dabbed and wiped it away.

A few minutes later, Jerich was satisfied he had removed all he was going to for the moment. He wished he could remove his pants and wipe away the sticky feeling on his leg underneath, but he would wait until he got home. Throwing the paper towel in an arc towards the garbage can, he watched it bounce off the rim and hit the floor. Fighting against his nature, he left it right where it landed, and instead washed his hands in the sink.

Looking up into the mirror, Jerich noted the pale skin and sweat that covered his face. He looked sick, feverishly so, and his appearance drove home a stark reality - he was sick. What had just happened could not be put off as a dream. He was awake and cognizant, had even been happy for the moment, and yet he was assaulted by these terrible images. He must be suffering from hallucinations brought on by stress, or perhaps the scar on his leg was something more than charred flesh. It could be poisoning his body somehow, and that was bringing on these crazy visions. Maybe Dr. Brandt had been right after all.

———————

Nick's eyes opened. He was staring at the ceiling of the examination room that he had spent the night being poked and prodded in. Looking at the clock on the wall, he noticed it was after nine in the morning. Nick had been a five AM sharp man since his first day in the service, alarm clock be damned. Sick with malaria, he would rise in the morning despite the berating of the camp sawbones. Now, here it was after nine, and he felt like he hadn't slept at all.

A thin, blue sheet covered him on the gurney they had wheeled in here as a bed. It was stiff and uncomfortable, but Nick could sleep on worse. Rolling on his side, he attempted to sit up, and immediately regretted it. The world swung around him like he had spent the night in a cheap bar drinking cheap booze. He steadied himself with his hands and closed his eyes in an attempt to stop the spinning, it wasn't working. Opening them again, he concentrated on the clipboard hanging from the wall in front of him. He couldn't read it from here, but it was covered with scribbles of blue ink. He suspected it was about himself, and he would take a peek the moment the room slowed down enough to let him.

In his experience, doctors, especially company doctors, confided absolutely nothing in you unless you had a gun to their head, and his was nowhere to be found. For the moment he did a quick check on himself, looking for new scars or stitches. He felt the chain around his neck, the ring still protruding from his skin. Tentatively he touched it, wiggling it slightly with his finger, but everything was completely numb.

Holding on to the rails, Nick slid off the bed and onto his feet. The floor was cold, and his legs immediately tingled with the return of blood flow, the gurney was obviously not meant for extended stays. He tried a step forward and almost fell, his leg practically paralyzed from its lack of fluids. The grip on the railing had saved him, he held tight with both hands, and waited for his mobility to return.

The door to the examination room was shut, perhaps even locked, and there was no one in sight. Nick's flight mechanism kicked in, and he immediately needed to leave. He searched the room for his clothes, but they were absent. The blue and backless gown was all he would have to wear. Thinking better of his situation, he concentrated on retrieving any intel he could find instead. Despite the cooperative exterior, Nick simply didn't trust Strieber. He told himself it wasn't because of the doctors nationality, but secretly he suspected it was.

His legs were feeling functional again, so Nick walked over to the clipboard hanging from the wall. Picking it up, he was instantly angered by his own foolishness - everything was written in German. He could get it translated, but he would need to make a copy, and the means to do so were completely out of his reach. Putting it back, he walked over to the computer on the desk. It was turned on, a screensaver consisting of a complicated mathematical string rotating across a black background. The equation was just as incomprehensible to Nick as the German hanging on the wall. He touched the mouse to wake the computer, and was confronted by a password request.

"Goddammit!" he said in hushed frustration.

Simple information retrieval had suddenly become increasingly problematic. Looking around the desk for telltale signs of a password reminder, Nick realized that whatever it was would likely also be in German. He admitted defeat for the moment, but opportunity would present itself if he was patient. Walking instead over to the mirror, Nick loosened the gown's collar for another look at his latest battle scar.

Everything was exactly as it had been, nothing had been cut. The surrounding skin was lightly bruised, likely from being poked at. His face was pale and sweaty, another day's growth of beard protruding in its latest shade of salt and pepper. Nick didn't like beards to begin with, but the gray on his chin made him feel ancient. He looked instinctively around for something to shave with before admonishing himself for his vanity - he would survive a few hours of gray stubble.

Turning back, he walked over to the gurney to sit down again. He needed breakfast and coffee. His energy was extremely low and the lack of sleep, coupled with the loss of body heat was making him tired again. He hadn't tried the door, but even if it was unlocked, he wasn't about to wander the halls half-naked. Just as he was about to lie back down and wait, the door opened and Murphy walked in.

"Little late in the day to be in bed isn't it, soldier?" Murphy taunted, he was carrying a plastic tray filled with food.

Nick didn't rise to Murphy's jeer. Instead, he sat up and accepted the plate of food, immediately digging into its ample offerings.

"The doc will be in shortly," Murphy said, "he wants you to stay put for the time being."

Nick continued to say nothing, and instead gorged himself on the food, it was fresh and very flavorful. The last time he'd tasted anything like this was in Europe.

"We've got some French chef on base here making the chow," Murphy said, seeing Nick's obvious enjoyment. "Not the most pleasant individual, but he cooks some fantastic grub."

Nick had to agree. Finishing his meal, he swallowed down some of the coffee Murphy had brought him. It was an odd taste, and Murphy seemed to notice the look Nick was wearing.

"Coffee is a bit off," Murphy pointed at the mug Nick was holding, "but after your second cup you get a taste for it."

Setting the tray down, Nick finally addressed the man in front of him. "Where are my clothes?" he asked, clearly anticipating a problem.

Murphy shook his head, "We chucked them, but don't worry, we'll get you suited up after the doc has made his checkup."

"Am I a prisoner here now?" Nick asked, his jaw set for battle.

"Until the doc clears you," Murphy said and crossed his arms in front of him, "you are in quarantine."

Nick gave a small smile, knowing it was smokescreen. "Aren't you afraid of catching whatever I might have?" he asked.

Murphy waved his hand in dismissal, "I've had it all. If it's that bad then I'm dead already."

Nick heard the underlying conviction in Murphy's answer, he had to give him points for living up to his hard-ass reputation.

"So," Nick said and pointed to the chain around his neck, "does this mean I'm out of the game now?"

Murphy gave a noncommittal frown, "Up to the doc. If it was my choice then I'd leave that up to you, a good soldier knows his limits."

Nick gave Murphy's sentiment some thought. The fact that the chain was still there meant one of two things: one, they couldn't remove it, or two, they were waiting for something more interesting to happen. If it was the latter, he wasn't getting out of this room anytime soon.

The door opened and Dr. Strieber stepped in holding yet another clipboard. This one he was busy writing on as he entered. Without looking up he said, "Thank you Lawrence. I'm sure you have more pressing matters to attend to. We'll be fine."

Murphy signaled for Nick's tray with his finger. Nick doubted it was a nice gesture, likely more in concern that Strieber may get brained with it. Nick obliged and handed it to him. Swallowing the last of the coffee, he handed over the mug, as well. Nick attempted a demeaning grin as he did so, but Murphy seemed unfazed, he took it and left.

"Now, Captain," Strieber said, still concentrating on his clipboard, "let's go over what we know."

Nick stared into the top of Strieber's head until it finally tilted up and away from his writing.

"As you can see, we were unable to remove the ring or chain." Strieber began and pointed to the items in question. "They seem to have fused with your skin on a molecular level. Do you understand what I mean when I say that?" he asked, not entirely condescendingly.

"Yes," Nick replied in the same tone.

"Good," Strieber said, seemingly pleased not to have to explain it. "The chain is not standard military issue, is it, Captain?" he asked.

"No," Nick said, "I wanted something stronger so the chain wouldn't break."

"Yes," Strieber said looking at it, "it contains precious metals. Nickel or silver?"

"Both I believe," Nick answered.

"Of course," Strieber said, seemingly to himself. "It appears that precious metals are affected by the anomaly, this explains much of the troubles we have been having." Looking back up into Nick's face he continued, "You have provided an instrumental key to this project, Captain. I wish to thank you personally."

"I had nothing to do with it," Nick replied in a sarcastic tone.

"All the same, it has given us a much needed boost in our research," Strieber said, clearly pleased. "I wish to reward you in some way."

"I'm a soldier, not a dog," Nick spat back. "You want to reward me, let me out of this room."

"I have no intention of holding you here, Captain" Strieber said, furrowing his brow. "On the contrary, I want you back in the field as soon as possible."

Nick wasn't expecting that answer.

"In fact," Strieber continued, "I have requested that you head up our first team back in."

The suspicion on Nick's face was palpable.

"You have proved most resilient to the dangers there," Strieber said, pointing to the chain and ring. "I believe you are the perfect man for the job."

"Your idioms are getting better," Nick replied.

Strieber smiled, "Thank you, Captain. Practice creates perfect," he said.

"Never mind," Nick replied under his breath.

11

Cultivating Culmination

Beau had watched the mayor disappear into the guarded building beyond the stage. He had already been warned that further communication would be refused at this time, so there was no point in hanging around. Back at the broadcast van, his repeated requests for Jerich's whereabouts had returned nothing useful. Apparently, the kid left to use the bathroom, and had fallen off the planet. Beau had checked the restaurant that his crew had suggested, but no one of Jerich's description had entered. Perhaps the events had proved too much for him, but Beau though it more likely the kid just felt out of place.

Beau would hunt him down for another chat, but in the meantime he was sitting in the van, reveling in CNN's catch up 'Special Report'. They had been broadsided and scooped by a small, local TV station, and were now simply repeating what KLLTV had already broadcast. Much to Beau's dismay, they had used none of the footage with him in it, and had completely muted the train footage with his meticulous narration - such bastards. Worse still, they had their 'B' team reiterating the few facts they had available. Beau would soon have much more for them to play catch-up with, so long as his source kept their promise. That thought made the moment all the much sweeter.

On the other screen was KLLTV and its local panel round table, making predictions and trying their best to play down the events. Beau was warned about keeping a leash on the scare factor. A frightened public was a curious public, and that could be dangerous to everyone. The panel now talking on screen had already agreed to such, thanks to his new friend Alex Coleman. Beau wasn't actually listening to what was being said, he knew he could rely on their professionalism, or they wouldn't be there. Alex was clearly a zero-tolerance man, and Beau was someone who could appreciate that.

As an example, Coleman was intensely interested in the burn mark that Beau had seen at the hospital yesterday morning. Beau had some trouble remembering the name of the doctor that he had spoken to about the coma victim, he had made a bad mental association with her name. Coleman, in turn, was ready to call off the entire deal based on a detail that could be uncovered with a single phone call. Despite Beau's fear of that reality, he had to give him credit for not putting up with incompetence. The name had returned to him a few moments later, it wasn't Blunt it was Brandt. She was the one who had showed him the pictures of the burn, after he had completely lied about who he was of course. It seemed to sate Coleman, and everything fell into place after that small bump in the road. Now Beau had access to first-hand information, all he was required to do was not rock the boat.

Beau understood that, with a long-term plan, revealing your cards too soon could spell disaster. He wouldn't be covering up the news per-se, merely piecing it out so contingency plans could be established first. This was how big business worked, and if Beau wanted his shot at the brass ring, he would have to play along. Looking at the CNN news room through the monitor, he could picture himself on-set. Perhaps not the lead reporter, not yet anyway, but it sure looked posh compared to KLL's small stage.

In the middle of his daydream, Beau's cell vibrated in his pocket. Habitually he turned it off before going on the air, but always kept in on him, he felt naked without it. After the mayor had left the scene, and Beau did his sign-off, he had turned it back on - his connection to the world once again established. Looking at the caller i.d. before answering, as was his routine, he read 'Private Number' and paused. Normally, he would assume this was an ad, or some other marketing call, and just ignore it. Now that his new friends could be calling at any time, he would have to answer every one - especially private numbers.

"From KLLTV News, you've got the Beau!" he said in his best radio voice and smiling.

There was silence on the other end.

"Hello?" Beau said into the void.

"Mr. Bradley," came a voice that Beau didn't recognize, "In the future, please refrain from using names or places whenever you are unsure of the caller - it's safer for everyone."

The admonishment changed Beau's tone, and he frowned slightly. Although he didn't know who was on the other end, he assumed it was one of Coleman's team. "Of course," he said more somberly, "what can I do for you?"

"I'm sending a package for you," the voice said evenly, "it will arrive at your office in precisely one hour. Can you be there before it arrives?"

"Yes," Beau said, looking at his watch.

The other end of the phone was silent again.

Beau put his finger in his other ear to drown out the background noise, "Are you still there?" he asked.

Pulling the phone away, he looked at the screen - the call had ended. Slipping his phone back into his pocket, he told the crew he had to get back to the office right away. They were still in cleanup mode so there really wasn't much for Beau to do here anyway.

"If that kid comes back," Beau said before shutting the door on his way out, "tell him to use that number I gave him and call me."

Bill had went back to his cubbyhole after the broadcast had finished. His sense of urgency regarding paperwork assured as he was practically ejected from the briefing room. Bill suspected that Keating was on approach, or already waiting for a debriefing on the events, and Bill's efforts would be required shortly. He sat in front of the terminal, and finished off his preliminary projections as well as practical solutions.

Firing up the local network email client, Bill attached the completed report with a small note. He would be required to reiterate on his calculations as new data became available. Eventually though, his involvement would come to an end as his suggestions were utilized or disregarded. His job here at Orchid would be finished, and he wasn't sure how he felt about that. Frank had been correct; now that Bill had put time back in, he found it hard to imagine returning to his mountain getaway.

It had been building up over a while now, if Bill was going to honest with himself: he was no longer happily retired. The first communication had come about a year ago by way of a secure mail carrier that had been in disuse for at least twice that time. Bill had been reviewing old reports that were available around the time of his wife and daughter's untimely death. He already knew what they contained, this was just a reality check for him. Whenever he starting thinking about returning to work, these reports would remind him of what that cost him.

Inside his inbox had been a new communication in an older encryption cipher that Bill still had access to. It was from a previous agent, named Sviato Richter, that Bill had recruited. He had proven an able agent in the field, usually exceeding his goals. Richter had suddenly left Orchid under unexplained circumstances. After completing an assignment in the far east, Richter simply vanished, leaving Bill a single communication - 'I quit'.

Bill had always suspected that something more nefarious had happened, but this new email provided a good argument against that. Initially rejecting the whole notion, the information Bill was receiving had proved to be valid. He was never really sure if it was Richter, the emails could never be replied to. Bill's access to the server in question was federally actionable, answering, and thus providing proof of his trespassing, would be foolish. Instead, Bill read and verified as discreetly as possible. More for the mental exercise than anything else. He could do nothing with the information as a simple civilian.

As the months rolled by, Bill started anticipating each new packet of information. The examination and dissemination of it made him feel useful again, alive. It had culminated in the last email of a simple document containing a report on the anomaly, leaked from some redacted official source. When Frank had phoned, asking for a meeting, Bill knew it had to be one of two things. Either the Shop wanted him back in some capacity for this new threat, or his knowledge of it was about to land him in a shallow grave. Bill knew the risks when he first went poking about, and thankfully, his experience had proven more valuable.

Looking back at the screen, Bill hit send and stood up to stretch. The chair had been comfortable at one time, but there were a few more pounds of him since then. Now it was just hard and confining. With the first report sent, he found himself with some time to kill. Perhaps he should hit the cafeteria, put his feelers out, listen to conversations, and make some new friends. Maybe even find a reason for the Shop to keep him around a little longer. He didn't know how long he had here, but occasionally, one got lucky.

Powering down the system, Bill left his small office and headed to the lunchroom. It wouldn't be off-limits, or look suspicious, and everyone went there, eventually.

Jerich had left the mall after cleaning himself up. He didn't want to return home just yet, regardless of how nice a clean pair of pants would've been. Instead, he decided to go down to the waterfront. It had been some time since he'd been there, and it was only a short distance away. The shores were mostly populated by expensive hotels and casinos, but there were a few plots of undeveloped land as well as a small park used mostly by tourists. An hour or so of some fresh air would be a nice change to the reprocessed commercial equivalent.

Despite the years since he walked these paths last, everything seemed exactly where he had left them. A little greener, a little fuller and, unfortunately, a little busier. People were out in force, trying to get in some quality time with nature before the weather made the trip insufferable. Most were jogging or walking dogs, but some were clearly there to suck up the atmosphere. Jerich had wanted some alone time now, and all these people were making it difficult to locate. He passed by couples staring puppy-eyed into each others faces, old couples simply staring out into the blue, and a few artists either painting or busking for change. He was slowly running out of path to walk, and would have to turn around soon.

Jerich walked out on the pier, more to put in time until the crowd thinned out. At the end was a small lighthouse, more decorative than functional. Behind it, on the tip of the pier, he spotted two men fishing and conversing. He suspected there would be little to catch, and that fishing was just an excuse to gab for them. Jerich walked up and sat down on one side of the lighthouse, unseen by the two fishermen. He wasn't trying to listen in, he just wanted a place where he wouldn't have to see, or be seen, by another person.

Trying to ignore the low mumbling coming from the other side of the cosmetic facade he was leaning against, Jerich concentrated on the slow movement of water in front of him. It wasn't windy, but the river was big enough to never be in a state of tranquility. The air was pungent with moisture, and Jerich took a heavy and satisfying breath in into his lungs that weighed on his body. It was soothing in a way that nothing else was, and he closed his eyes in silent meditation.

The mumbling from around the corner slowly became words in Jerich's ear. As much as he wished he could ignore it, they coalesced into audible banter about the events of this morning - the very thing Jerich was trying to avoid.

"...and shut half the south end down," one man said to the other. "It's ridiculous, where the hell am I going to take my trash? The dump for the south end is closed now."

"It's not closed, it's gone," the other man said.

"Gone?" said the first in disbelief. "How the hell can a city dump disappear?"

"Drove by it this morning on my way into town before they barricaded things up," the second man explained. "There's nothing but broken pieces and powder there now. Like the entire thing burned to the ground."

Jerich's eyes widened, his mind racing.

The second man continued, "Didn't stop there either, the entire strip mall just north of that was in exactly the same state."

They were talking about the mall where Jerich worked.

"Now you're saying an entire mall is gone?" the first man said, clearly shaken. "How the hell can the city say that everything is fine?" He paused for a few breaths, "Fuck this, I'm taking the misses up north to the cabin. You'd be smart to get the hell out as well..."

The two men carried on their debate, but Jerich had stopped listening. He was gripped in the memory of his dream last night. The bathroom, the destruction, the girl. It had to be some kind of coincidence, a sick joke played out by fate. Precognition was something that Jerich placed directly into the 'bullshit' file, along with ghosts and demons. No one could know the future because the future is not set, it's simple dynamics - the butterfly effect.

Jerich stood back up and left the point, continuing on to the bus station where he boarded the first one going anywhere. On the bus he was in a daze, numb to the world around him as it continued in a mumbled silence. The city outside the window passed by, first in familiar, and then in unfamiliar locations. He didn't know where he was going, but right now, he didn't care. The momentum had become soothing, lulling him into a stupor that drown out the noises in his head. Malls, parks, and sky-rises all seemed to slip by in a blur until the bus came to a halt.

Looking around, Jerich watched a few passengers leave the bus. He was the last one sitting down when the driver stood up.

"End of the line buddy," he called back to Jerich. "You'll have to transfer if you want to go anywhere else."

Jerich looked up at him, but said nothing.

"You okay?" the driver asked. "You look pale, are you sick?"

Jerich could see a concern on the driver's face that went beyond good Samaritan, he was clearly worried Jerich may have something contagious. Jerich stood up and left the bus without so much as a second glance in the driver's direction. Stepping down, he tried to get his bearings and gauge where he was in the city. Clearly he was far up north, he could see the radio tower for the local station looming in the distance. That was about as far north as you could get and still be in the city. He had been here once before when he took a stray dog to the local shelter. For some reason they had their offices way out here, Jerich wondered if that was a deterrent of some kind.

Looking back towards downtown, Jerich spotted a strip mall a short distance away. The unfamiliar environment seemed to be doing much for distracting his mind, and he didn't want to leave just yet. He found himself suddenly famished. Perhaps they had a restaurant there that he could sit and have a bite to eat. Slipping across the busy street using the only crosswalk he could see for miles, he walked along the side of the road and down to the plaza.

Cars passed by in droves, many seemed to be leaving rather than returning to town. Perhaps the two men at the lighthouse had a very popular idea, that or many lived outside of town for the lower housing costs. Jerich couldn't fault either idea right now, he kept walking and tried not to think - about anything.

The mall came into view. It was a shoddy looking thing, and was clearly very low rent. Jerich sighed, the real world had dragged him back to the affordable. At least he wouldn't be paying a fortune for a meal here, this neighborhood couldn't afford it. Walking into the parking lot, Jerich had a full view of his options, and they were bleak. A dime store, a liquor store, a convenience store, and a head shop. Everything else was boarded up. Jerich was going to turn around and head back to the station, but his stomach wouldn't allow him to. Some junk food at the convenience store would be cheap, but not filling. It would be better than nothing at this point.

Walking in, he was assaulted by the smell of pot, sweat, and spice. The combination was not doing much for his nose, but his appetite was uncaring. Routing through their strangely huge selection of chips, Jerich picked up a bag of boring old plain. Selecting a chocolate bar and taking a drink from the cooler, Jerich walked up to the counter to pay. On the wall was an old tube TV, not unlike the one he had at home. It was playing the news as a foreign language scrolled by on the bottom. The man behind the counter appeared to be the same kind of foreign as the news broadcaster. He stepped up after a moment and rang Jerich's purchases through without looking at either. Jerich payed, and the man threw everything into a plastic bag, leaving it on the counter and continuing to silently watch the screen. Jerich shook his head at the stellar customer service he'd just received, picked up his bag and left.

Jerich had spent his entire employment history in the retail industry. As much as he sometimes hated it, he at least had the decency not to let the customer know that. A strange sense of pride in Jerich had been offended by this man and his shitty little store in this shitty little mall. He knew this was from all the brainwashing that the retail industry had pounded into his head over the years, but all the same, he felt it was an affront to the duty and respect of one human being to another.

"Give me your fucking money!" a voice pulled Jerich out of his thoughts.

Jerich turned around to see a kid with a gun pointed at his head. The kids bare arms were covered in tattoos, and he had piercings in random places on his body. The look on his face was one of someone who did this regularly and clearly wasn't worried about consequences.

Jerich shook his head, "I don't have any money on me." he said in protest, holding his hands up.

The kid took a step towards Jerich and pressed the gun into Jerich's forehead, "I said give me your fucking money!" he shouted, spitting into Jerich's face as he did so.

"I don't have any fucking money on me!" Jerich shouted back and closed his eyes.

"Walk!" the kid yelled and pushed the gun into Jerich's head to get him moving.

Jerich stepped backwards, not knowing where he was going. His arms still in the air as he did so. He could see they were going behind the strip mall by the way the buildings passed him by. Jerich was worried he would fall at any moment, causing the kid to fire off his gun, but instead he just felt a wall hit his back, and he stopped.

The kid grabbed the plastic bag from Jerich's hand and threw it aside, "Gimme your wallet!" he shouted.

Terror gripped Jerich, there was nothing in there this guy could use. Slowly he reached into his pocket and pulled out his wallet, handing it out to the kid. Snatching it from Jerich's hand, he took a few steps back and began going through it.

"You haven't even got a fucking credit card!" the kid said, shaking his head. "The way you are dressed and not even a fucking credit card!"

Jerich was suddenly more self-conscious about his clothes then he had been in the expensive restaurant. He could think of nothing to say to this guy, nothing that he would listen to anyway.

With a grimacing smile on his face, the kid extended his arm and a loud noise rang out. Jerich's shoulder burst into flame and the shock bounced him off the wall behind. Jerich felt his head strike brick, and his vision became suddenly black and white simultaneously. His knees buckled beneath him and he fell back, sliding down the wall until he sat on the ground. The world around him had become muted. He could feel his heartbeat thumping in his ears. Instinctively he tried to rise and get up, his need to run fueled by adrenaline.

Another shot rang out, this one seemingly far away, and Jerich felt the world go black.

———————

Beau arrived back at the station, breaking the speed limit whenever he could so he would arrive well before this package did. He wasn't so much concerned about theft, it was about being sure he was the one to receive it. Beau wanted no doubt that he could be relied upon to do his part. In the office, there was an unstated atmosphere of resentment and awe. Some staff carried a smile of appreciation, while others clearly had 'lucky bastard' written all over their face. Both gave Beau a warm fuzzy that just topped the morning off nicely.

David, ever at his desk, was shaking his head and wearing an envious smile. "You're such a prick," he said. "Scooping CNN on a terrorist threat?" he held his fist out.

Beau gave it a bump and smiled back, "All in a day's work for Beau Bradley of KLLTV News," he said in his best superhero voice.

"How the hell did you pull that off?" David said tossing the pen in his hand onto the desk. "You even managed to fit in that footage from yesterday," he said staring at the discarded ballpoint. Looking up at Beau, he continued "You sure you're not Irish?" he asked with a smirk.

"Hey, I gave you co-credit like I said I would," Beau protested. "And I'm not lucky," he continued, chucking David on the shoulder, "just awesome." He gave David a taunting smile, and walked past.

"Fuuuuck you," David retorted in jest, wadded up a paper ball and threw it at Beau.

Walking to his boss's office, Beau didn't bother knocking, and let himself inside. Greaves was on his computer, he looked up with a hostile frown.

"Hey, Jay," Beau said boisterously before Greaves could chastise him for just coming in unannounced. "Did ya," Beau paused for effect, "catch the news this morning?"

"Do you know how many calls I've had to field personally since broadcast?" Greaves said angrily, staring into Beau's eyes.

Beau lifted his hands and gave an exaggerated look of wonderment, "Were any of them from CNN?" he said with a smile.

"Among many others," Greaves said sternly, clearly not finding the humor. "I've had to start forwarding everything to city hall due to the volume."

"Jay... Jay," Beau said waving Greaves anger away with his hand, "surely it felt good to be asked by CNN for permission to rebroadcast?"

"I wasn't asked," Greaves replied, "I was told. So, no, it felt pretty much the same as every call I have to field on your behalf."

"Jay," Beau said in protest. "I told you, we have broadcast rights here. You could have told them to go fuck themselves, and let them run with nothing but talk."

"You just don't understand how the broadcast industry works, Bradley," Greaves admonished. "There is more at stake here than your bloated ego. I can't burn bridges just because we got lucky on a story here."

"This isn't luck, Jay," Beau said shaking his head, "this is an in. An in that every reporter has dreamt of since Deep Throat and Watergate. We're not lucky - we're fucking blessed."

"And what about tomorrow? Or the next day?" Greaves said and shook his head. "What happens when your source no longer needs you? Have you even stopped to wonder what they want, or what will happen when they get it?" he asked and stared at Beau. "No, of course you haven't. Like every narcissist, you believe the world begins and ends with you."

Beau stared at Greaves for a moment, "It doesn't?" he asked with feigned surprise on his face.

"Get out of my office!" Greaves yelled and pointed to the door. "Next time I'll forward the grievance calls to your cell, and you can clean up your own mess!"

Beau shrugged and started his exit, only partially walking out so both the office and Greaves could hear him, "Great rapping with you, Jay, words of inspiration," Beau said with mock reverence. "I will strive to make myself a better leader in your image," he finished and shut the door before Greaves could reply. In the distance, Beau could see David shaking his head and chuckling to himself.

Walking down to the reception desk, Beau was about to ask about his package just as a courier came through the front doors. Wearing a bike helmet, wraparound sunglasses, and chewing gum loudly and open mouthed, he walked directly over to where Beau was standing.

"Package for, uhh..." the courier looked at the package label, "Bear Bruges?" He looked for a moment longer before shrugging and throwing it down on the desk. Raising the tablet that was in his other hand, he began to tap and swipe on it until that too was thrown down on top of the package. The face of the man behind the desk was one of astonishment, his eyebrows raised and his jaw slightly agape. Shaking his head, he took the tablet and used his finger to sign in the box that was on onscreen.

Setting it down deliberately, he looked up at the courier, "Who do you work for again?" he said with a slight sneer on his face.

The courier grabbed the tablet, smiled while still loudly chewing his gum, and left without a word.

Beau and the receptionist exchanged a look of disbelief. Pulling the courier label from the package, the receptionist slid it over to Beau before turning to file the receipt. Beau picked it up and walked back to his desk, his curiosity intensifying with each step. By the time he had reached his chair, Beau was practically jogging. He sat down and pulled the gold letter opener from his drawer. Prying the packaging from the plain cardboard box, he slit the tape that was securing the flaps holding it all together. The box opened easily, inside was recycled packing peanuts to cushion the transportation. Stirring through the packing material with his hand, Beau felt his prize and pulled it out for inspection.

It was a phone.

Beau was visibly deflated as he stared at it, his mouth hung open. Shaking his head, he found the power button and waited for it to start up. He didn't recognize the make or model, and the boot up images were nothing like he'd ever seen before. Finally, a black screen appeared and text began to scroll down the surface. It was too small to see but it didn't last long. Eventually a plain blue background appeared with the word 'Connecting...' at the top, Beau put the phone to his ear and listened.

"Mr. Bradley," a voice said evenly, it was the same one Beau had heard earlier.

"Yes?" Beau replied.

"The phone in your hand is part of an encrypted network, this is how we will be contacting you in the future," the voice continued. "This is not a standard phone, it can receive calls only. We expect you to carry this phone with you for the foreseeable future. Do not lose it. It can be charged via the standard connector on the side of the phone, you will have to source one for use. The phone is very power efficient, and shouldn't need to be charged more than once a week."

"So, how do I contact you then?" Beau asked.

"You don't Mr. Bradley," answered the voice. "When we have information for you, this phone will ring. Until then, you will go about your business as usual."

"This all seems a little…," Beau began.

"Mr. Bradley," the voice cut him off, "we expect complete compliance with our wishes, or our business with you will be concluded. Is that clear?"

Beau ran his free hand down his face in annoyance, "Yes," he replied looking down at his expensive shoes.

"Your actions today were satisfactory," the voice said without emotion, "we expect no less in the future."

"Thanks?" Beau said sarcastically.

The voice was silent for a moment, then it spoke. "Cheer up Mr. Bradley, staying with us will bring far more than a few bylines to your portfolio. Surely you have the insight to see that, or we wouldn't be having this conversation."

Beau sighed, "Yes." he said and paused for a moment. "So, what do I call you anyway?"

Silence.

Guessing what had just happened, Beau shook his head and pulled the phone away to look at the screen. On it read 'Call Ended... Requesting New Encryption Key...' in yellow with a blue background. He stared at it in irritation for a moment until the blue disappeared. It was replaced by a more familiar set of icons and a black background. Beau immediately tried launching apps at random, and quickly realized that it was just a static image. Probably there to make it appear as a plain phone to anyone who might be watching.

Beau slipped the phone into his other pocket. At least he had some proof of their cooperation now, for his own edification if no one else's.

12

Fissure in the Foundation

Bill sat in the center of the cafeteria for the best opportunity to overhear conversation and be seen. In front of him sat a bran muffin on a small plate with a pad of butter on the side. He would go back to the counter and pick up small food stuffs as necessary to maintain the appearance of eating. He had picked up a local newspaper from the well-stocked stand that the Shop maintained for employees in order to pretend to read while he waited. The front page was a shot of city hall with the headline 'City to Shut Down South End'. This was obviously a prepared story as the newspaper had no indication of the events that would unfold today. It was likely dropped into their laps just before publication, and would be important enough to halt any pressing and push to the front page. Flipping to the story, it was sparse on details, and ended with a link to the paper's website for up-to-the-minute coverage. This was a smart idea in Bill's mind, the site would have a comments section that could be harvested for information and reaction data. Responses could be then tailored to quell the most subversive opinions.

Recognizing no one in the cafeteria, Bill dug into his bran muffin. Butter was a bit of a luxury at his age, but he felt he had earned it. Thinking about his eventual return home, he realized he could have scrubbed through the company notices and current reports, looking for information. Perhaps find a few more problems he could consult on, allow himself some more time on campus. Having been told he had access to anything he wished, Bill knew his requests would be scrutinized. Once Keating got wind he was looking for a way to keep himself in the loop, it would close on him. Hopefully, something would turn up before his job was finished. The thought of going back to bad television, bird watching, and hack spy novels suddenly seemed like a death sentence.

The door to the cafeteria opened and Murphy walked in, chomping on his cigar and completely alone. Queuing up some breakfast and a large mug of coffee, Murphy turned to spot Bill. He nodded and made a beeline for his table. Bill continued to be interested in his paper until Murphy set his tray down and sat across from him.

"How's the fallout?" Murphy asked and pointed to the newspaper.

"Looks pretty minimal," Bill answered. "Nobody is speculating, but things have only started."

Murphy dug into his breakfast and nodded in acknowledgment. "Gonna be some pissed off politicians," Murphy suggested. "No way this'll be over soon."

Bill said nothing, but looked up at Murphy and waited. It was a simple but effective method of getting others to do the talking.

Murphy finished a mouthful of bacon, "We've never come across anything like this before, there's nothing to go by. We'll need some time to find a weakness to exploit for the future."

Bill nodded in continued silence, taking a sip of coffee.

"The Mayor," Murphy continued, pointing his fork at the paper, "he's forecasting a quick end to this. His career will be over when that's not the case." He returned the fork to his plate.

"That's a strong possibility," Bill replied.

Murphy continued to slice through his food and eat, "He's going to be a problem once he figures that out."

Bill shook his head, "They always are," he replied.

"Ain't that the truth," Murphy said, mopping up egg yolks with his toast.

"Zimbabwe comes to mind," Bill said with a slight smile. It was a reference to a sensitive operation that no one should mention outside of a secure circle. Bill was hanging it out to Murphy to see if he would bite.

Murphy swallowed a mouthful of food and nodded in agreement. "When I was first recruited here," he said wagging his fork, "they gave me a history lesson on Orchid - your name came up a lot. Then they shoved a week's worth of reading material at me. Most of it consisted of operations you orchestrated."

Returning the fork to his plate, he took a few mouthfuls. Washing down his food with a healthy swallow of black coffee, Murphy used his fork once again to direct attention. "Zimbabwe was a stroke of genius," he said pointing it in Bill's direction. "Using his own generals to take him out of power for us?" He shook his head, "Fucking genius."

"It wasn't as simple as that," Bill waved away Murphy's reverence, "I had a great team set that up."

Murphy nodded and went back to his food, "Yeah," he said and swallowed, "and it's a damn shame none of them are around anymore."

That hit Bill like a kick to the stomach. "Where are they now?" he asked, trying not to show his emotions.

Murphy paused for thought, "Most of them died in Somalia about a year ago, stopping an attempt to kick out the new government," he finally replied. "Two were taken hostage and mailed to us in pieces." An anger swept over Murphy's face, "Fucking animals," he said in disgust.

The sorrow in Bill's stomach immediately turned to rage, "And what did we do for them in return?" he said, his jaw involuntarily tense.

Murphy gave a small smile, "I went over to explain things to them personally," he said and paused to let that sink in for a moment. "Let's say, it was an extended conversation."

Bill returned the smile and Murphy went back to his food.

Going back to his paper, Bill picked absently at his muffin. As much as he wanted to pump Murphy for information, he couldn't let it appear that way. He had established a rapport and made an initial connection of camaraderie, now he would have to pace his questions. Murphy seemed like a good soldier, it was clear that his loyalty tended more towards nobility than money. Bill guessed that the required reading that Murphy had mentioned was tailored to his personality, the more questionable operations redacted or re-truthed. Once he was in the fold, he could make his own excuses for anything he found. Recruitment procedures were specialized for assets that the Shop deemed necessary, Murphy's skill set was obviously important enough to merit it.

After a few moments of silence had passed, Bill ventured a question. "How is the ground team doing after that exposure?" he asked nonchalantly.

Murphy had just cleaned up his plate. Setting it aside, he answered, "Doc says they seem fine for the moment, but he wants them under quarantine for the next few days."

"What about Captain Miller?" Bill asked before raising his coffee cup for a sip.

"Seems they couldn't remove the metal from his neck." Murphy answered. Shaking his head once, he clucked his tongue, "That boy's fucked for a career now, a brush with a door could rip open his carotid artery. No way Uncle Sam's going to keep him on with that liability."

"So, we're just sending him back then?" Bill inquired.

"Nope," Murphy replied, "doc thinks he may have some kind of resistance to the anomaly. Personally, I think he just got lucky."

Bill gave a nod, Miller's chance of returning to active duty were slim with his injury, but a solution may yet present itself once they knew what they were dealing with. His coffee was getting low, however Bill didn't want to leave the table just yet and possibly end this conversation prematurely.

The door to the cafeteria opened just then and Frank walked in. Looking over to where Bill and Murphy were sitting, he headed directly over to them. "Lawrence," Frank said staring down at Murphy, Alex needs you in his office."

Murphy nodded, stood up and left. Frank sat in his place and brushed aside Murphy's breakfast mess.

"Bill," Frank began and then stopped, "I've had a quick look at your report, and it's all good stuff. In fact, it's a little too good. With your extensive predictions and calculations, I'm not sure we'll be needing you to reiterate anything at all." He paused and looked at Bill in silence for a moment. "Do you really want to leave so soon?"

Bill was taken aback by Frank's bluntness, echoing Bill's very thoughts over the morning. "Frank... I've been absent a while from this business, and my time here has been... cathartic shall we say." Bill scratched his chin and stared at the table for a moment. "My part in the events here have given me a purpose that I thought I no longer wanted. If I were to be completely honest with myself, then, no. I do not want to leave."

"Then," Frank said and leaned in towards Bill, "I would suggest you slow it down a little."

Bill shook his head, "Frank, I have one way of doing things - my way. I don't know of any other. If that is too efficient, then so be it. If Keating kicks me back stateside, then that's what happens. I don't half-ass anything, and you of all people should know that."

Frank leaned back in his chair and closed his eyes for a moment. "Yes," he finally said, opening them again, "I do know that, and I don't know how I expected a different answer." Sighing, he looked down at the table. "I'll do what I can with Keating, tell him there is new data coming in all the time, and your input would be invaluable. Perhaps that will be enough to keep you around a little longer."

Bill noted a slight tone of irritation on the edge of Frank's voice. "Perhaps it's time Keating and I met anyway Frank." Bill found himself saying out of anger. "I don't need anyone else speaking on my behalf. If he sees no value in me being here, then I'll leave - Simple as that."

"Now, now Bill," Frank chided, "let's not be hasty. Gerald may have nothing to say on the subject, we'll wait and see. If he decides to expel you from the program, you can do all the talking you want - how's that?"

Bill shook his head and stared off into the distance. He really wasn't ready to confront Keating just yet, he needed more time to get his feelings in order. Talking to the man responsible for your family's death is not something you do off the cuff. After a moment of silence, he looked back at Frank. "Fine. When can we expect a reply?" he asked.

"Gerald comes and goes with his own agenda," Frank replied. "For instance, he was here this morning for the broadcast and a small meeting with me afterwards."

Bill shouldn't have been surprised, but the thought of Keating's presence so soon made him uneasy. Pushing it out of his mind, he thought about work instead. "So when are the doctor's tests commencing?" he asked.

Frank looked at his watch, "I need to leave now and join up with Coleman for a small meeting before the team leaves. We'll be getting a single broadcast from the site. If you want to see it first-hand, you're welcome to come." Staring back up at Bill, he added, "Unless of course you would rather stay here and grumble into your coffee."

————————

Nick had finished up with Strieber. The best that could be done about his neck was to surround it with padded foam beneath a hard plastic neck-brace. Strieber had customized it as much as he could so it wouldn't catch on the chain, but it was mainly there so the chain wouldn't catch on something else. The plastic made it awkward to turn his head, and the foam rubber was uncomfortable on top of making Nick's skin itch. The black jumpsuit they had given him to wear was stiff and cumbersome, like it was made of thick denim. Strieber had told him it was for his protection, the new suit they were putting him in would be made of harsh material. The heavy jumpsuit would save him from a painful rash.

Nick finished fastening it up and looked at himself in the mirror. With some high-cuts, he would look like he was on the way to some Eighties appreciation festival. The jumpsuit was puffy with heavy shoulder pads, and the neck brace was sticking out and looked like he was wearing some kind of trendy collar. Shaking his head, he turned to where Strieber sat at his desk flipping through paperwork.

"So where am I off to?" Nick asked into Strieber's direction.

"Someone will be along to collect you soon," the doctor answered without looking up.

'Great,' Nick thought, sarcastically, 'all dressed up and waiting for dad to take me to the prom.' He looked around the room for something to pass the time with. A magazine, a book. At this point he would settle for a field ops manual. On a table against the wall, Nick spotted an open medical folder. Thinking it could be his own, he walked over for a closer look. Inside was the telltale image of an MRI scan along with a few x-rays of a chest and arm. It clearly wasn't his, there were fractures visible that he didn't have. It was annotated with scribbling in various spots, but it must be in German, that or really bad handwriting. The sheet next to it was a medical report covered in pen of a few colors, all of it equally illegible. The folder could be anybody's, a soldier from the camp attack, or a person long gone. Nick had no way of knowing.

Looking back, Strieber was too busily engaged with his own reading to notice Nick's snooping. The fact that everything in this room was written in German probably gave Strieber a sense of security. In Nick's case, it may as well be locked behind a steel door. He could speak Spanish and a little French, but German was out of reach.

The door to the examination room opened, and Murphy stepped inside. Giving Nick a once over, he looked over at Strieber. "He's good to go, Doc?" he asked.

The doctor glanced up from his reading, "Yes, yes. Please take him down and get him suited up immediately," he said waving his hand. "We're running late already."

Murphy shook his head slightly and signaled for Nick to exit through the door. Nick obliged, happy to get out of his prison.

With the door closed behind them, the two men walked down the hallway to an unknown destination. Aside from a precious few rooms in this facility, Nick knew nothing of the building he was in. They passed people and occasional guard posts on their way, but little was said, and nothing more official than a nod seemed to be required.

"So where am I going now?" Nick asked with obvious sarcasm.

Murphy was in the lead, "Doc's got some tests to run in the field." he said and gave a backwards glance. "He believes you're the only man for the job."

That wasn't a comforting thought. As much as Nick wanted to stay in the field, the notion that Strieber wanted him there made him believe it was anything but healthy for him.

"Who am I going in with?" Nick asked. "The rest of the team is in quarantine."

"No one," Murphy replied staring straight ahead. "This is a one man op."

Nick's suspicions solidified into outright certainty. Whatever this was probably wouldn't kill him, a dead lab rat has only so much use, but things would likely escalate until that became a possibility. The life-before-country mentality drilled into his head so long ago had slowly eroded over time. The last few years had done the most damage, and now the thought of spending what life he had left as an invalid made that desk job suddenly very appealing. Maybe he could learn to like fishing.

"This new suit," Nick broke out of his thoughts, "what is it normally used for?"

"Before today?" Murphy paused for effect, "Nothing," he continued. "It's an experimental suit that was designed for a scrapped Titan expedition. It's not combat worthy, but it was meant for an especially hostile environment."

"Titan?" Nick wondered aloud.

"Theoretical design, never tested of course," Murphy shook his head, "but the eggheads believe it'll keep a man alive. For a while anyway."

Nick wasn't sure if that was better or worse.

Rounding another corner, Nick saw two guards posted in front of a sealed door. They had obviously arrived at their destination. Murphy gave a nod and one of the soldiers opened the door for them. Passing through, the metal door sealed behind them with a clang. Despite the military feel and the military personnel, there was little of the military ritual here. No salutes and the 'yes sir's' seemed to be more from habit than expectation. It felt too relaxed to Nick, the tributes of respect showed importance and cut short disaccord and mischief. A soldier needed to know their place or it was chaos in the field.

The room was actually a hanger, half closed off by a plastic seal and multi-hatched umbilicus to let people through to the other half of the room. Bright lights were freestanding in various places and lit the room like the sun. A plastic cubicle had been walled off where a large suit could be seen through the semi-transparent plastic. That was where Murphy was currently leading him. The armed guard in front of the flap stepped aside to allow Nick entrance.

"Not coming?" Nick asked with derision.

"I'll be on site for this one," Murphy said, ignoring or not hearing what Nick had asked. "If shit goes sideways, I'm gonna pull you out."

Bluster or not, that made Nick feel better.

Bill and Frank made their way across the base, on route to the hanger where Coleman's team was preparing to depart. With the last camp destroyed and bridge reconstruction underway, it had been decided to move things further away from town. South from there was a valley of rock and limited vegetation that fed right into the heart of the anomaly and dipped away from prying eyes. The test site would be approaching the center of the zone, but was close enough for a quick extraction if it was necessary. The creatures from their last encounter had not been spotted by scouts on-site, or anywhere else for that matter. This did nothing for Bill's state of mind though. They were in there somewhere, and their complete absence indicated an intelligence above simple animalistic behavior.

"We have no information on what drew those creatures to the last site," Bill broke the silence, "what are we doing differently this time?"

"For starters," Frank replied, "no electronics or heavy weapons will be directly on site. The good doctor believes they are somehow attracted to alloys and metal compositions, the less we have on site, the better is his assertion. The broadcast we'll be receiving will be telephoto, off site, and therefore immune to possible attack."

"What about this hi-tech rover that Coleman has provided," Bill looked at Frank, "won't they be attracted to that?"

"The research team is of the mind that it will be too small to draw attention." Frank replied. "Plus, we only have it on loan for a few days, so we need to utilize it every chance we get."

"And if they show up anyway?" Bill queried.

"We have snipers with 50 caliber rifles set up in key positions," Frank answered, "in case we need to make a hasty retreat. They're using armor-piercing, depleted uranium rounds for effect."

"Clearly something our locals don't know about." Bill said, looking over at Frank. "We have no way of knowing what effect radiation will have on these things Frank. This isn't a controlled environment."

"Bill," Frank said looking back, "if radiation has no effect on these things, we are royally and properly fucked."

The implication of Frank's statement immediately sank in. "Frank," Bill said, unable to keep alarm from his voice, "a nuclear solution cannot even be considered at this point."

"Think reasonably, Bill," Frank responded. "We are talking about irradiated ammunition here, not a dirty bomb. If one little shell can kill off one of these things, it is well within acceptable collateral damage."

"And if one of these things is only a drop in the bucket," Bill pressed, "then what?"

Frank shook his head, "We will cross that bridge when we get there." Looking back, he continued, "Seriously, Bill, I really expected more from you. Our entire planet could be at risk here, and we're arguing over a few broken eggs."

"If you take the time to read my report," Bill said incredulously, "you'll see that we have more elegant solutions available to us here."

Frank stopped and turned to face Bill, "I saw those solutions Bill and, to be blunt, I was being kind in the cafeteria. When I said you need to slow it down, I meant you need some more exposure here. You were a brilliant strategist once, but your time away has not sharpened your skill set. Most of what I read belonged in some second rate do-gooder's suggestions for a free world he has never fallen victim to." Frank stared levelly into Bill's face, "It's been over five years now Bill, get over your loss, and come back to the real world already."

Bill was dumbfounded, he stared slack-jawed into Frank's face.

Frank continued, "You were a decisive leader once, unafraid to make the tough decisions - That's the man I came to recruit." He turned, "That's the man we need," he said and walked away.

———

Nick sat on a large bench in the back of a troop transport on the way to the testing site. The interior had no windows, but plenty of intense lights so technicians could prepare the rover for deployment. It had come special delivery, and its inaugural mission was apparently to accompany him into the zone. Being affixed with sensors and other equipment, the unit was large and cumbersome. It was explained to Nick that he would have to walk slowly so it could keep up as it was meant for rugged terrain and not speed. His suit would be equipped with a homing beacon that the rover would follow, but he would also have a remote control in case of problems.

The rover would be carrying the majority of the test equipment, but Nick would be required to carry a heavy lead-lined suitcase. It contained electronic equipment consisting mostly of communication apparatus that he would be responsible for testing out himself. Thankfully, the gloves he'd been given were very articulate and designed to be used by technicians. Pressing tiny buttons or flipping switches would be all but impossible with anything less.

The ride was smooth, with few bumps felt throughout the cargo area where Nick and his new metal friend waited to be thrust into the anomaly. Nick felt the sweat building up already despite not having his helmet on and built-in air conditioning within the suit. The collar around his neck was especially warm, and the urge to scratch was unbearable. Strieber had warned him against that very thing along with any thought of removing the collar, the slightest pull in the wrong direction would have him bleeding out in minutes. Nick concentrated on other things. He began to field strip firearms in his head, methodically explaining it to an imaginary instructor. It was his go to anytime he needed to escape from his thoughts or pain, an orderly routine that took time and concentration.

Nick eyes stayed closed as the transport rolled along. Oblivious to everything around him, he called out the parts of the imaginary Desert Eagle in his head as he continued to take it apart and put it back together. Something small like a handgun would be enough to overcome lying in the bush and being eaten by mosquitoes. When he was shot through the stomach however, he had managed to strip every weapon he had ever used before the medic had arrived with the morphine. The itching on his neck was requiring a second weapon and perhaps a third, as it seemed to be getting worse instead of better.

Suddenly, a hand landed on Nick's shoulder. He started, and his eyes flashed open in surprise. Standing up immediately on instinct, he was face to cigar with Murphy.

"Whoa, soldier," Murphy grabbed Nick's shoulders in reaction to the startled movements.

Nick felt his face wet with sweat. "What?" he said coolly, staring into Murphy's eyes.

"Relax, Miller," Murphy said with a smile, "you look a little under the weather." Pulling the cigar from his mouth, he asked, "Everything alright?"

"Fine," Nick answered, his response and continued cool tone both a lie.

"We're approaching the test site, and the eggheads want to make sure the helmet won't interfere with your collar," Murphy said while flicking his stogie in their direction. "Make sure they show you where the controls to the AC are on that damn thing," he added and returned the cigar to his mouth.

Nick regarded Murphy for a second before stepping around him, making his way over to the crowd around the rover. Three technicians were in a heated debate about what must have been his metal companion, they were gesturing to it. The fourth watched Nick approach, and set down his clipboard.

"Here," he said to Nick and gestured, "sit down on this tool chest."

Nick obliged, almost falling backwards with momentum. The chest was lower to the ground then he had thought it to be. The sudden jerk he made to catch himself caused a fresh wave of itching from his collar, and Nick rolled his eyes in frustration. The warm temperature of the suit now unbearably adding to his irritation.

"Sorry," the tech apologized, "we need a clear view of your neck as we put this on."

Nick waved away his explanation. Calling to one of the other men debating around the rover, the tech retrieved Nick's helmet, and the two men put it over Nick's head. Slowly it sank into place as the two eyed its location from every point they could while still holding on to it. Feeling a click, Nick assumed it had fastened into place without incident. One technician gave a thumbs up while the other walked away. Seemingly happy with the results, he too then turned to leave.

"Hold up," Nick said into his helmet.

The tech turned back around, a slight annoyance on his face.

"Where is the air on this thing?" Nick asked to the tech who stooped over to hear him better.

The tech lifted Nick's arm and pointed to a gauge next to a simple twist knob, then mimicked turning it. Letting go of Nick, he again turned back to the rover.

"I wasn't finished!" Nick yelled out, the itch around his neck not helping with his disposition.

The tech turned back around again, this time not masking his annoyance at Nick's interruption. Nick stood up, his anger must have been readily apparent as the tech's face quickly lost its color. It was now an expression of concern and fear, Nick guessed he must have the tech full attention now.

"I know where that air is," Nick said slowly and deliberately, "I need to know where the air conditioning is." His jaw tense with the continued itching of the collar.

The tech nodded and immediately stepped to Nick's side to show him.

"I can't turn my head that far genius," Nick growled, his frustration rising with the temperature of the suit, "the collar isn't there for show!"

The tech came back around to face Nick, his hands clasped together in obedience.

Nick closed his eyes and took a deep breath to reel his emotions back in. "Look," he began, "please just drop the temperature in my suit down about ten degrees." The tone is his voice was now even and almost relaxed.

The tech nodded and stepped back to the Nick's side. A hissing sound could be heard within the suit and the temperature immediately dropped, Nick sighed in response. Returning to face Nick, the tech again gave a thumbs up, this time with a timid and questioning look on his face. Nick nodded, his eyes drooping with relief. Smiling, Nick gave his own thumbs up, "Thank you," he said, breathing deeply.

Nick watched the man walk back to join his colleagues. He had glanced back twice to be sure that Nick was indeed finished with him. The four were now talking heatedly, the drone indeed the source as Nick had accurately guessed. The conversation consisted mainly of technical debates, now that Nick was close enough to hear them. He didn't understand the particulars of what they were on about, but they clearly had four separate opinions of the how's and why's.

He sat back down on the tool chest, ready this time for the low landing. The cooler air clearing out his exasperation, he felt his body relax. Even the collar around his neck seemed to ease off and react positively to the drop in temperature. All he had to do now was concentrate on the tasks at hand, that and survive whatever the German quack really had in store for him.

13

Ashrealm be thy Name

After checking his email and any personal messages at the office, Beau had a few stories to follow up on, but nothing worth pursuing at the moment. While his new friends may come though with late-breaking news, he still needed to eek out a living with the local happenings. One great story didn't secure him a pass to putz around until the next one fell into his lap. Beau was currently looking through the curated live feed of international news and local buzz coming from a wide variety of online sources. Dennis had set this news feed up for him, constantly pruning and adding to it as time rolled on. It would sometimes contain some truly bizarre things that Beau was sure Dennis threw in for a laugh, removing it after Beau called him on it. A minor inconvenience for the gems it occasionally unearthed and the time it saved him from having to do it manually.

Currently, the news was either yesterdays or of little local interest. Political and entertainment news was always changing, but that wasn't Beau's beat, he was local and general interest. He could try to ride the tide of yesterday's story with a recap and a few quotes or do the man-on-the-street interviews, but he felt that would just be treading water. He could follow up at the hospital, look into the coma victim with the strange mark that his new friends had been so interested in. They hadn't expressly forbidden his investigation, but there was no mention of following up on it either. Beau was a reporter and his business was the news but he wasn't sure there was even a story there. At least one that wouldn't get him cut off or at the very least chastised for his involvement. He had been promised direct information, at the cost of keeping the lid on the small things until they could be kept from becoming unmanageable. The hospital could very well be one of these small things, but their interest made investigation hard to resist.

It would be nice to be able to just pick up this new phone and ask about following it up, but that wasn't possible. However, asking for forgiveness was easier than asking for permission - grifter's rule number one. Perhaps just a polite investigation, if there was nothing to follow up on, then he would walk away.

Talking to Dr. Brandt again would be out of the question, as his bullshit story was most certainly vetted after his departure. He could try the floor's head nurse, and hope his charm would get him some more info, or he could just pretend to be a concerned relative. There wasn't even a name when he made his first inquiries, but now it would be a hard sell without information and Beau didn't even know what gender the victim was.

The door behind him sounded with a knock, and Beau turned to see David in the doorway.

"Boss is looking for you," David said, wagging his thumb in Greaves general direction.

Beau involuntarily rolled his eyes, "Where ignorance is bliss, 'tis folly to be wise," he said, raising his hand melodramatically and using his best Shakespearean accent.

"Quoting seventeenth century poets now?" David said with a smile.

Beau looked over at David with slight surprise, then smirked, "It was a boring class. Quotes were all I ever got from it." Standing up to leave he continued, "They occasionally got you laid."

David shook his head, "Of course they did," he said mockingly.

Walking past David, Beau headed back to Greaves' office, ready for war. Beau had raised KLL from local access to world recognition in one story, he would be damned if he was going to apologize for it. Throwing open the door with a flourish, Beau walked into the office and stood in front of Greaves' desk with his hands on his hips. A look on his face that dared anyone to belittle him in his hour of triumph.

Greaves sat at his desk, staring at his screen and completely oblivious to Beau's posturing.

"I want you to investigate the mall inside the quarantine zone," Greaves said without looking up, "there are reports that there is more damage than contamination going on there."

Beau felt his bravado completely dissipate, that was something very much on the 'do not report yet' list. Beau had wanted footage of that very thing to drive home the severity of the situation, but it was vetoed. Their reasoning was sound enough, no panic in the streets over what may turn out to be an isolated incident. The city was a monetary foundation for the country and a mass exodus of its population would cripple the already weak economy. He would get his day to report it, but only after assurances of safety could be made - Beau could live with that.

"It's quarantined for a reason Jay," Beau began his deflection, "you want your star reporter dead for a story we already know?"

"We know nothing," Greaves retorted, "the area has been cordoned off due to possible contamination when in fact it could be completely destroyed. That's a story," Greaves looked up into Beau's face, "Mr. star reporter."

"A terrorist attack is going to cause damage, Jay," Beau said, his mind racing to find an excuse, "We reported on that yesterday, what's new here?"

"City hall is playing this down for a reason, Beau, and that reason is news." Greaves stared into Beau's face for a moment before continuing, "My 'star reporter' wouldn't have even asked that question."

The insult cut to the bone, but Beau wouldn't give him the satisfaction of acknowledgment. "Fine, Jay, I'll get you some footage. I'll even get a comment from the mayor on what I find, but if this is just a repeat of the same information we gave yesterday then I don't want my name anywhere near it. News is new today, not what was news yesterday, and I won't be a party to pandering for ratings."

Greaves rolled his eyes, "Beau, ratings are the only reason you get up in the morning, and we both know that," he said with a sigh.

"I'm serious, Jay," Beau leaned towards Greaves and pointed his finger, "if it's not new, it's under someone else's name. I'm not going to be that reporter who had one good story and couldn't let it go."

Waving his hand dismissively, Greaves replied, "Whatever you say, Beau. You don't want the credit, I'll give it to someone else, just get me something I can use."

"Fine," Beau said decisively. "I'll need a cameraman. Speaking of which, where the hell is Raul?"

"I assumed you alienated him with one of your tantrums." Greaves shrugged.

Not content with merely dodging the issue, Greaves was now trying to shrug off responsibility as well. Beau wanted very much to put this fat little man in his place and school him on hiding the truth, but the new phone in his pocket made that argument suddenly hypocritical.

"Perhaps you could take on the heavy burden of looking into it on the way over," Greaves added. "You know, since you were the last person to see him and all."

Nick was walking slowly across uneven ground, the rover following at a few paces behind him. The heavy suitcase he was carrying had switched hands multiple times in the short distance they had covered so far. The items inside were likely the least of the weight with the lead lining causing most of the strain. To avoid a possible tear in the suit, he had to keep it away from his body, only making his situation worse.

Nick took his mind off it and concentrated on the surrounding landscape. Again it was white with black bits of trees and various destroyed objects scattered within the ash. Visibility was becoming an issue now, yesterday he had full view of his surroundings, but today it was limited to half a mile at best. They were in a different area of the anomaly but that explained nothing. The ash wasn't falling, nor was the wind strong enough to blow up the whiteout he was seeing. In fact, there was hardly any wind at all. Nick couldn't account for that. He was walking across a plateau of ground with nothing to block the air currents, yet there was barely a stir.

The grinding and whining of motors behind him was getting progressively louder as they traveled into the area. The rover perhaps having to ramp up power to slog through the ever increasing silt beneath it, and the continual scanning of their surroundings likely adding to its burden. They were approaching their destination by Nick's approximation, he would check his GPS shortly to be sure. In the meantime his ankles were starting to feel the burn. It was like walking through a swamp, with every step requiring him to extract his foot rather than lift it. Despite the air conditioning, he could feel his legs warming up with exertion, but it was more than that. The ash itself seemed to be transferring heat as he stepped into it.

A few more meters and he stopped to get a reading. Lifting his arm, he looked at the GPS attached to his wrist - it was blank. Nick set the suitcase down on top of the rover behind him, he heard it whine slightly as it adjusted itself for the new weight. Pressing the button on the side of the GPS lit the LCD screen momentarily. Instead of numbers or letters, the display emitted a series of distorted gibberish. Nick held the button down in hopes that it would correct itself, but the screen only faded, never to return.

Sighing, Nick turned to the suitcase on top of the rover. Opening it up, he decided this was close enough to begin the tests. Looking inside, he noted an array of objects that he recognized. He was told he wouldn't need instruction on what to do with the items inside, and seeing them now made that clear. Fishing around inside, he first selected a cell phone with a stylus attached so that it could be used with gloves. Hitting the power button elicited a familiar screen of icons, he immediately looked at the connection bar to check for contact. Nothing appeared on any of the bands that the cell phone used. He opened the dialer to test it all the same. Typing in the phone number that he and his never-to-be wife shared during their short union, he only got half the numbers entered before the screen froze. The phone then shut down, and no amount of button pressing brought it back from the dead.

Setting it back into the case, he proceeded to test the rest of the gadgets inside. A digital recorder, an old analog tape recorder, a digital camera, a hand-held television, a hand crank radio, a Wi-fi network detector, and finally an old walkie-talkie that looked like it belonged in the seventies. Nothing worked for longer than a few seconds other than the hand crank radio and the walkie-talkie. The radio would continue to create static so long as Nick kept cranking it, but stopped the moment he did. The walkie talkie lasted the longest on its own power. Nick had turned it on and expected nothing only to find the familiar whine of an out of tune signal. He began to adjust the frequency, and keyed a test whenever he thought he could hear something. At one point he was sure he'd heard a man's voice. It was distorted, but his ears told him it was human. After that small victory, it too had succumbed to whatever elements killed the rest of the gear.

Placing everything back into the case, Nick closed it and set it down into the ash on its bottom. The rover had sat patiently behind him, silently awaiting its turn. Nick pulled the control from the inside of his velcro-sealed breast pocket, and turned it on. It immediately lit up and began to display various readings, presumably from the rover. He expected this too to suddenly flicker out, but that didn't happen. Beneath his gloves, Nick could feel a tingling warmth in his fingers. Concerned, he set the control onto the rover and stepped back a foot, watching it from a distance. After a moment of the device continuing to do nothing but show readings, Nick approached it and pressed the red button that would signal the rover to begin its final test phase.

The rover whined for a moment, various doors opened, and an array of antennas and robotic arms appeared. With a rush of hydraulic pressure, the rover extended itself upwards about three feet. The small control slipped off, bouncing on the case and disappearing into the ash. Nick cursed and went over to retrieve it.

Crouching down on his knees, Nick dug through the ash looking for the lost remote. The rover beside him released another blast of pressure, and Nick quickly jumped back. The various motors in the rover began to whine loudly. The arms were jerking aimlessly, and with a sudden groan, everything stopped. The rover was now motionless and silent, frozen like a statue in all the white.

Tentatively, Nick stepped in for a closer look. The unit was completely inert, not a light to be seen or a sound to be heard. Looking down to where the remote was, Nick bent down to once again attempt fishing it from the ash. After a few circles with his glove, he located and extracted it, giving it a shake after doing so. Looking at the rover in front of him, he tried to engage it once again using the red button. The rover replied with the same response that the rest of his test subjects had eventually given him, nothing. Shaking his head, Nick threw the remote back into the ash and leaned forward to retrieve the suitcase.

The rover creaked loudly beside him and Nick once again jumped back to safety, concerned it may just keel over on top of him. He was required to return the case and, if the rover should stop responding, pull its hard drive and return that as well. His tests were finished, and clearly the drone had done all it was going to. Best to secure what was necessary and head back to camp. Leaning in, he seized the handle of the drive's removal hatch and twisted. With some effort, it turned in response and popped loose. Nick extracted it and retrieved the suitcase from the ash next to the rover. Taking a few steps towards camp, the rover behind him gave a loud groan.

Turning, Nick stared wide-eyed as he watched the rover began to shudder and crack. Light began to appear from inside, leaking through the holes in the metal. It buckled into itself, slowly shrinking down with the creaks and whines of compacting metal. The light beneath began to get brighter, and Nick had to shield his eyes in response. Between his fingers, he watched it become smaller, compressing into a ball of blue light and metal.

The light began to dissipate, and Nick could lower his hand for a better look. The rover was now a bundle of wavering mass, cracks ran down its surface, and a blue glow emitted from beneath them. He watched small bits of ash float away like sparks from a campfire. The surface, now black, shimmered like a mirage in the desert. The mass rocked in front of him, and Nick stepped away. Slowly it seemed to unfold, separating into a shape with appendages as it stood up from a crouch.

Nick watched as the appendages turned into arms and legs as they began to expand. Taking on the appearance of muscle, bulging with blue cracks in its surface, it grew in front of Nick's eyes. A smoke was slowly escaping from the various splits as it took a human shape. With a rumble like splitting stone, it twisted into Nick's direction.

Having no weapons, Nick was helpless before the creature in front of him. He looked to the head as it turned in his direction, two slits of blue appeared where eyes should be, and Nick felt powerless to move. The gaze of the creature stopping him in his tracks. Standing fully upright, the creature stepped in Nick's direction, towering over him and staring down into his face with a menace that Nick could feel deep in his bones. Slowly, the creature's arms bent back to strike him, and Nick felt sure his life was about to end.

An explosion from the creature's torso erupted, spraying black and bright blue debris in all directions. The entire top third of it seemed to separate and disperse in front of Nick as the sound of a distant weapon finally caught up with the carnage. Nick fell backwards into the ash behind him as the remains slumped down out of his field of view. Scrambling to sit up, he took in the carnage. What would be the creature's insides continued to glow a bright blue. It remained motionless and parts of it were scattered around in various sizes. Nick immediately recognized the damage of an M50 sniper rifle, nothing else in this world left this kind of impact.

With the distance and his proximity to the creature, someone was a damn good shot. Looking down at his unscathed body, Nick owed that same someone a round of beer.

———

Nick had made it back to camp in record time, the briefcase and hard drive returned, and the suit now in the hands of some very interested technicians. They were in the process of dismantling and examining every inch under a protected canopy of glass and plastic, excitedly talking amongst themselves. Nick on the other hand was left to lie on an examining table while a doctor went over him. Covered head to toe in protective equipment, the doctor gave Nick a battery of tests and questions that were obviously prepared in advance. The answers consisting of the yes or no variety, and Nick would have to fill out a detailed report when the doctor had finished with him.

Answering the doctor's questions absentmindedly, Nick responded with the first answer that came to him. He felt no different physically, but his mental state was another concern. He had just witnessed, first-hand, the enemy they were now facing instead of just the devastation left behind. The creature had birthed itself from the rover that had tagged along behind him, or at least what was left of it. The power had died in it before the transformation occurred, and Nick took some comfort in that limitation. The stark reality though was that an army of those things could be out there with no idea what created them. Nick could only hope that the data he had just brought back would help in answering that question.

The doctor finished up with his questions and his examination, leaving Nick specimen jars to fill with any fluids that left his body. The empty page on a clipboard lay next to him awaiting his explanation of what just happened. Nick wanted an explanation himself, and doubted his ability to articulate it. He heard a door close, followed by a distant and heated verbal exchange. Looking to the exit of the sealed plastic bubble that was serving as his quarantine, Nick heard the zip of someone entering. A moment later, Coleman stepped through wearing what looked like welding goggles. Turning in Nick's direction, he walked towards him with distinct purpose. Apparently, he had regained a good amount of his sight back since the bridge.

"What the fuck just happened out there, Captain?" Coleman spat.

Nick stared at Coleman for a moment, "Which part?" he asked.

"The part where you destroyed a billion dollar rover that was on loan from NASA!" shouted Coleman, tearing off the goggles in anger.

Coleman's eyes stared directly at Nick, they were watering and bloodshot. He found it hard to look at them without his own beginning to tear up.

Nick furrowed his brow in defense, "I didn't destroy anything," he said with a leveled anger in his voice, "the damn thing turned into some kind of monster. And then it tried to kill me."

Coleman continued his tirade, "You were there to defend it, Miller, not take off the moment trouble started."

"With what!" Nick shouted in anger. "Foul language?"

Unabated, Coleman continued, "With your instincts, Captain. That and the simple ability to follow orders."

"I followed my orders as they were given to me," Nick said evenly, and began to visually count on his fingers. "Walk the rover out to the GPS coordinates. Test everything in the suitcase. If the rover dies, get the hard drive, and get back to base. We'll take care of the pick up."

"Well those orders didn't come from me," Coleman said leaning in and pointing at Nick. "You should have aborted the mission the moment you suspected a problem, you were picked for your extensive experience in the field. If I wanted the damn thing destroyed, I could have just sent it in alone."

"I had nothing to do with its destruction," Nick growled into the red-rimmed eyes peering down at him. "You can thank the crack shot who saved my ass for that, and if you won't - I will."

That seemed to stop Coleman in his tracks. Looking away, he rubbed at his eyes with a finger and thumb.

Nick took the opportunity to continue, "My orders were complete bullshit anyway," he said with conviction. "Cell phones, tape recorders? I was just there to babysit and take the blame if something went wrong!"

Coleman turned to face Nick again.

"Or were you just hoping I would die out there?" Nick spat out before Coleman could speak.

Coleman stood there, but said nothing.

"Is that it?" Nick said, newly angered by his sudden revelation. "Was this just some childish bullshit to get even for your father?"

"This situation goes beyond any personal feelings I may have towards you, Miller," Coleman said with a shake of his head. "I needed proof of the danger that exists here, an example of what it's capable of, and you have provided that."

Nick continued to stare, his anger seething.

"Of course," Coleman continued and began pacing, "had you died during this field op, it would have been far more effective." Turning on his heel, he looked for Nick's reaction. Seemingly satisfied, he returned to pacing, "The death of an experienced soldier such as yourself at the hands of this new enemy would have had a much more lucrative impact on funding." Coleman turned again to face Nick, "But we can't have everything," he said with a smile.

Seething with frustration, Nick felt his fists clench. Unable to trust anything he might say, he remained silent.

Realizing he wasn't going to get a response, Coleman broke the silence. "So," he stepped antagonistically closer, "I guess we have all we need from you, Captain. I will send you back home, slightly worse for wear unfortunately," he gestured towards Nick's throat. "But I'm sure you will have a prosperous career, despite your debilitation. Perhaps, behind a desk?"

Coleman turned to leave and paused at the exit, "Fate does love a bit of irony, wouldn't you agree?"

Bill stared at the video screen. He had just watched a billion dollar rover make a startling transformation, right now he was waiting to watch it again. The audio only consisting of static, so the sound was muted, but the video made it completely unnecessary. Although not clear, the images were steady and unwavering despite the telephoto lens. Some interference played across what was on display but, the clarity was more than sufficient.

Right now it was locked at the beginning of playback. The briefing room was full of Orchid's key players and many others that

Bill didn't recognize. At the front, beside Frank, Dr. Strieber sat flipping through notes and scribbling with a pen. Frank was on his cell, leaning forward on a chair and looking grave. Keating was, once again, nowhere to be found. No doubt awaiting a later and more detailed briefing. A video camera was set up at the back of the room this time, its light was on indicating that it was actively broadcasting. Perhaps he was here after all, in spirit anyway.

"Gentlemen," Frank said, having stood up and pocketing his phone. "What you see here is the results of our latest mission into what we are now calling The Ashrealm."

The title was apt enough for Bill, but the fact it now had a name gave it permanence, implying that it would be going nowhere soon.

Hitting play, Frank continued, "As you can see," he began annotating and pointing towards the display, "the NASA rover we sent is operational and fulfilling its program." He waited for both machine and man to arrive at their destination and stop. "Here, we have an operative running some communication tests while the rover continues with its automated operations," he continued and then waited for that to be completed. "Now we have the final phase of the rover," Frank said, "our operative initiating this via remote."

On screen, the rover visibly raises itself up in response, "Here the operative has lost the remote and tries to retrieve it." The rover and operator are little more than black silhouettes against the gray backdrop. "The operator clearly jumps back from something that can't be discerned. We have our first indication that something is wrong." Frank waits for the fuzzy black human to jump back a second time, "The rover has obviously stopped functioning here, so our operative removes the hard drive as instructed." The screen shows the rover motionless as the man removes something from it, grabbing the suitcase he begins to head towards the bottom of the screen.

"Now," Frank began, "we see what we are up against."

On the screen, the rover seemed to shrink a little, the man at the bottom turning to look. A light began to emit from the rover for a moment, it grows in intensity, and the screen goes white for a moment. When it returns, the man has his back to the camera. The rover is now a small ball, it moves, becomes what appears to be humanoid creature, and turns on the small black figure. A moment later, the creature explodes. Parts of it scatter with the impact, and the man falls backwards in reaction.

Frank pauses the playback, a mutter scatters across the room, many sit up out of their seat.

"What we have is something that can seemingly use anything we throw at it to create opposition," Frank said to the dozens of open eyes and slack jaws in the room.

"How is it doing this?" a voice came from the room.

"Can we appropriate this technology?" came another voice.

Frank raised his hands in the air, "Gentlemen," he said to quell the noise, "I'll let Dr. Strieber fill you in on the details. Please let him finish before asking any questions." Turning, he gestured towards the doctor who finally looked up from his notes to acknowledge his introduction.

Stepping up to where Frank had been, Strieber stared into the crowd. He seemed displeased to be there, but tried not to show it.

Clearing his throat, Strieber began, "Firstly to address the suggestion that anything we send in could be utilized by the enemy is premature." He turned to look at Frank in some semblance of apology, "Clearly our operative has not become something unnatural," Strieber said gesturing to the screen. "It seems to require certain elements and minerals for this metamorphosis to occur."

A mumbling rippled through the room in response to the information.

"In addendum," Strieber interrupted the murmur, "there has been no reports of anything organic, living or dead, falling host to this process." He paused and the room fell silent again. "Now, on to what we do know."

Clearing his throat once again, Strieber looked down at his notes. "Communications of any kind will not function within the bounds of this anomaly, this, Ashrealm." He paused there, as if saying the name caused him displeasure. "Indeed, one foot into the perimeter will knock out any ongoing transmissions followed shortly by the complete disabling of most electronic devices."

"But the rover..." came a response from the crowd.

Strieber raised his hand in response, his face clearly showing annoyance. "Very specific elements seem to be able to shield this disabling effect, but they have so far proved very expensive or very toxic to organic life." Gesturing behind him to the screen, "And ultimately, short-lived as you will have noted."

Strieber flipped a page in front of him, "Also, all attempts at penetration via sonic, radar, infrared, or any technology we currently have at our disposal has proven ineffective, and visual range is limited to half a mile from outside or in."

Pausing to look at his notes, the doctor continued. "Two types of inhabitants have so far been identified, one large and powerful while the other smaller and shielded by an unknown property. It is our belief that the smaller creature controls the larger, although only a single sighting has been reported." He paused to flip the page. "The inhabitants themselves have so far demonstrated immunity to small arms fire and larger caliber weapons. The ammunition is either deflected or absorbed completely. We can however verify their inability to leave the anomaly for extended periods of time."

Strieber looked up to gauge reaction, "In other words, they require an ecosystem to function. Without it, they are like a fish beside of water."

Scattered snickers echoed through the crowd. Frank pinched the bridge of his nose and shook his head.

The doctor seemed unaware of his blunder, "This is the key to their destruction," he said looking out.

A voice came from the crowd, "But we just witnessed the destruction of one of these creatures on video."

Strieber reached out in front of him and picked up the remote control, the video was once again in motion. The room watched as the man on the screen got up and exited to the bottom. The scene stayed that way for a short period before a stirring occurred. The creature that had been blown almost in half rolled onto its side and rose to its knees. Slowly it changed once again into the semblance of a human and stood up. Turning away from the camera, it walked off and quickly disappeared into the gray beyond it.

Pausing the playback once again, the doctor looked back to the crowd. "Any questions?"

14

A Periodic Development

Beau was seething from that little jab Greaves had doled out. Mostly for dismissing involvement, but partially because Beau felt some responsibility for his own. Raul was a good guy. A little hard to understand on occasion, but he didn't deserve the heavy brunt of a governmental verbal cavity search. Beau had been in that spot on a few occasions, but he knew his rights. Raul came from a country where the peoples only right was to shut up and do what they were told. However, pressed with a hot poker, Raul could have told them nothing because he knew nothing. Beau had taken the footage after Raul had delivered it to the editing room, his interaction with it finished.

Beau's feelings of guilt had quickly turned to anger at the abuse of power. Perhaps after things quiet down he would look into doing a piece on that, if it got slow enough. In the meantime, he thumbed through his phones directory, and tried Raul once again. Instead of an incomprehensible message in Spanish, this time he was greeted by an out-of-service recording. He looked to the passenger seat where the camera he had signed out was sitting, worse case scenario he would have to do his own camera work. He wasn't planning on being in the shot or recording comments, but he would be the first to admit his camerawork wasn't the best.

Having made the decision to stop by Raul's house, Beau was now just pulling onto his cameraman's street. It was more 'closed community' than neighborhood according to Raul who had suggested he only come here in an emergency. It was a polite way of saying 'whitey best back the fuck off'. Beau could understand community, he could even understand the underlying racism, but he couldn't understand why you would think it was safer. A militant, close-knit culture was just as dangerous to the society it strived to protect - violence breeds violence, just ask history.

Driving down towards the GPS marker on his phone, Beau noted more than a few eyes fixed on his expensive car. Some only looked from the windows, others stepped out for a full view. Most of what he saw suggested that the money being made on this street was largely illegal; tattoos, piercings, and gang colors were everywhere. He noted more than a few guns sitting in the waistbands of some angry looking people. Beau got the sudden feeling that Raul had been right on the money. This was clearly not Beau's best idea, and getting out of here, quickly, was his best option. Between his car, his camera and the various expensive personal items he was wearing, he may as well hold up a sign that said 'come rob me'.

The roadway was too small for a u-turn, and Beau knew better than to pull into a driveway. Instead, he continued down the street. Trying to keep it under the speed limit. Behind him, he watched people walk out onto the road and stare after him. It was unnerving but manageable as he drove on, hoping for a turn to appear soon. Block after block he passed nothing but cul de sacs. They would be fine for turning around, but the way behind him was slowly growing crowded. Beau felt the best course was to proceed forward until he could make it to a main artery and get back on the highway.

Beside him, his phone beeped and a voice announced that he had reached his destination. Looking out, he spied a medium sized house with a for sale sign on the front lawn. Finding the street number over top of the front door, he knew it to be Raul's. Relaxing the accelerator, he stole a look for any signs of life. Through the windows, Beau could tell it was completely empty, and nothing seemed to stir inside. Normally he would stop and knock, but this situation was far from normal. Instead, he looked at the sign on the front lawn and memorized the telephone number for the Realtor. He could call later and inquire more when he wasn't worrying about the whole being robbed and killed thing.

Looking back to the front of the car, Beau goosed it into motion again. Up ahead he could see a large bridge passing over, and knew a turn off would be coming up soon. Trying to keep from punching the gas, Beau continued on towards his escape. Stealing a glance into the mirror, he could still see people on the street, but they were some ways back now. Relaxing a bit, Beau brought his attention forward again in time to see two kids on the street in front of his car.

Beau slammed on the breaks and winced as he heard the camera hit the dash and fall to the floor. In front of him, the kids just stood there. One was holding a basketball while the other had a phone in his hand. Beau stared for a moment before honking when it was clear they weren't going to move. The kid with the phone stared into its screen for a moment before slipping it back into his pocket. The two walked off to the side of the road and Beau was about to hit the accelerator and make a quick exit.

A knock on the window startled him and he turned to see a shiny, nickel-plated handgun pointed at his head from the other side. Despite the initial shock, Beau couldn't help but admire the mirrored and over-sized pistol. It was a truly impressive piece, there were diamonds and rubies encrusted on its side with a pearl handle. Next to it, a hand appeared, gesturing him to roll down his window. Beau complied.

"Hey, holmes," a voice said from the other side of the weapon. It lowered so the owner could get a good look at Beau. "You a long way from Kansas."

The man holding the gun was bald with a tattoo that covered his head and half of his face. His goatee was long and braided with diamond-covered beads, his left eyebrow was pierced with what looked like a silver bullet. The eyes beneath were dark and intense, focused on Beau's with a stare that seemed to pass right into his soul.

Beau's heart was racing, he had been in bad situations before, but they had never included a gun. Knowing better than to show his fear, Beau left his hands on the steering wheel in plain view and smiled in his best neighborly way.

"Hey there," Beau managed without a waver, "just passing through."

"Not anymore, holmes," the man said with his own smile before leaning in. "Now you're a guest 'till I say otherwise."

Beau leaned back involuntarily to accommodate.

"Nice car," the man said looking around inside for a moment. His gaze stopped back on Beau, "Two years old though," a look of displeasure on his face.

"Been looking to upgrade anyway," Beau said, maintaining his smile.

Pulling his head back, the man stroked his goatee, "Maybe you tell me what you're doing here," he said waving the gun into Beau's direction.

"Just... passing through," Beau tried again.

Putting the gun to Beau's head, "Nobody just passes through here, holmes," he said leaning in again. "Look around you, everything here says fuck off." Pushing in closer to Beau's face, he continued "Now what the fuck," he pressed the gun harder for emphasis, "are you doing here?"

Beau had lost his smile, it had been replaced with abject fear. He could feel the barrel of the gun digging into his scalp, and the trickle of sweat running down the back of his neck. He searched for an answer that might keep him alive, but the metal against his skull was making that impossible. He decided to simply tell the truth.

"I came to see Raul," Beau said, managing to sound calm.

"Raul?" the man shook his head, "Raul? Do you know how many fucking Raul's there are in this neighborhood?"

"He lives right there," Beau said and pointed his finger without lifting his hand from the steering wheel.

The man stepped back, "There?" he said smiling and pointing with his gun. "Nobody lives there man, it's fucking for sale, holmes."

"This is where..." Beau began.

The man swooped back in the window with the gun, pressing it into Beau's cheek. "Shut the fuck up and get out of the car," he growled and stepped back to allow the door to open.

Beau turned and opened the door, pushing the seat belt release with the other hand. Slowly he stepped out and raised his hands.

"Move!" the man said, gesturing with his gun.

Beau did as he was told, but kept his hands up. The man stole a better look inside, keeping his gun trained on Beau while he did so.

"What the fuck is that?" the man said and pointed.

Beau leaned over to see what he was pointing at. "It's a news camera," he said and his mind immediately began playing through the explanation he would use when he got back to the office. If he got back to the office.

The man's eyes returned to Beau, "You fucking BB?" he said, sounding surprised.

"What?" Beau said reflexively.

"BB... Fucking Beau Bradley - the news guy," the man said wagging the gun in Beau's direction.

"Uh..." Beau began, "Yes?"

The man lowered the gun, "Why the fuck didn't you say so, hefe?" he said with an apologetic look.

Beau stood where he was with his arms still raised, not entirely believing his reputation would hold sway here.

"Put your arms down," the man said and slipped the gun into the back of his waistband, "we're good here."

Beau followed the instructions but continued to stay put.

"Thought you looked familiar," the man said leaning out and slapping Beau on the shoulder, causing him to jump a little in reaction. "Raul told me all about you."

Beau's thoughts quickly went to anything he may have done to upset Raul in the past. "Oh?" was all he could get out.

"You helped him get his start," the man said extending his arms in emphasis, "made sure he kept his job. That's a fucking stand-up thing to do, hefe."

Beau had no idea what the man was talking about, but he smiled with feigned acknowledgment all the same. "Well, he's a stand-up guy," he said, hoping it sounded sincere.

"Fucking ay he is," the man said nodding. "Helped me with so many things around here and never asked for a fucking nickel."

Beau shook his head, "Yea," he said, wanting to maintain the positive conversation, "that's Raul for you."

"Fucking bullshit what happened to him," the man said, his attitude returning immediately to angry and intense.

'So much for happy,' Beau said to himself. "That's why I'm here," he ventured.

"Fucking government can't get away with that shit!" the man said pointing his finger at Beau. "Deporting you because you can't answer a question?" he winced with frustration. "What the fuck is that?"

'Deported?' Beau thought. He nodded in response, hoping that would be all he was required to say on the subject.

"I fucking told him, I'll get you the best fucking lawyer money can buy," the man said and then shook his head. "Told him, I got this, they can't fucking do this to us man."

Beau said nothing and waited for the rest of the story.

"Fucking wouldn't let me," the man said and threw his hands up. "Wouldn't let me because he was too proud to take my help," he paused and then pointed at Beau. "That's a real fucking man... Don't take charity from no one, I can fucking respect that."

Beau nodded, "Raul did things his own way," he added with silent faith that it was the right answer.

The man pointed again for emphasis, "Fucking ay he did, really going to miss him."

"Me too," Beau answered with slight honesty. Raul was, after all, coming around after Beau's tutelage.

"You here to do a story on him?" the man asked.

That was the farthest thing from Beau's mind at the moment. He tried to formulate a response.

"Yea, fucking right you are!" the man continued without waiting for Beau's reply. "That's what a stand-up guy like you does. What you need man? Stories? I got fucking stories!"

"Yea," Beau quickly interjected, "I just needed to touch base with his friends," he paused for thought. "Make sure I could rely on them for some background."

"Fucking ay you can," the man said, full of conviction. "You come here anytime you want, my homies will let you pass."

The man reached out his hand, and Beau grabbed it in the best movie-style grip he could muster.

Leaning in close, the man looked into Beau's face, "You get me the name of the guy who brought this shit down on Raul," he whispered and nodded his head, "I'll put that motherfucker down."

"You bet," Beau replied and hoped he'd never see this man again.

———

Bill watched as half of the room emptied, the questions and answers portion of the internal report had been brief. No one had asked anything that the doctor could answer further than he already had. A handful of people lingered behind, and the camera at the end of the room was still live. Getting up, Bill walked over to where Frank was on his phone.

Seeing his approach, Frank cut short his call, "What's up Bill?" he asked.

"Who were these people Frank?" Bill asked. "Clearly not Orchid."

"Key figures and important business partners, Bill," Frank said, slipping his hands into his pockets and leaning against a table for support. "Orchid is no longer self-funded these days, we have obligations to our investors."

"Our investors?" Bill said quizzically. "We were never self-funded to begin with Frank, we had open-ended contracts that paid the bills."

"Times have changed," Frank folded his arms in front of him, "those days are long gone. Governments just can't afford that kind of arrangement today, we've had to accept bids from the private sector."

"So we're whoring ourselves out to corporations now?" Bill's voice now stressed. "What happens when there's a conflict of interest?"

"It's nothing of the sort, Bill," Frank said shaking his head. "They invest in Orchid, and we in turn share the spoils."

Bill stared at Frank for a moment, "Such as the knowledge that a certain stock will be sharply dropping soon due to a coup for instance?" he asked heatedly.

"Among other things," Frank replied.

"Frank, that's flat out insanity!" Bill's face a knot of anger. "Better than half of the corporations on the planet have ties to terrorist and criminal organizations. You could very well be aiding and abetting the enemy."

"Or completely destroying one," Frank retorted. "Bill," he said, sighing, "things have changed in the world. Weapons and warfare are outdated, they were outdated even when you were here. It's all about money and information, it always has been. Orchid was responsible for a lot of the grunt work in the past, but it was the changing of facts and figures that our employers were chiefly interested in."

Bill looked away in frustration, he knew full well how the game was played. However, trusting a democratic government was one thing - they were held accountable by their people. Catering to corporations who were only accountable to greedy stockholders was something else entirely.

"We can, and have, shifted the world's economy with nothing more than an email - not one bullet fired. That's where we are today," Frank paused. "Surely you can see that."

Bill was silent for a moment, "What I can see, Frank," he looked back to meet his gaze, "is a growing menace that doesn't care about stock options. Won't be swayed by words or promises, is unfazed by the movement of numbers in a database." Pointing to the screen, he continued, "And is now even unconcerned about our 'outdated weapons and warfare'. What I see is a force that will spell our doom, assuming the stockholders don't sell us out first."

"Such pessimism, Bill. I'm surprised at your defeatist attitude," Frank said disbelievingly. "Cheer up, there is some good news here," he said and slapped Bill on the back as he stood back up and passed by.

Taking the front of the room again, Frank addressed the remaining people. "Our esteemed colleagues, thank you for your indulgence," he said looking out into the crowd. "I'm well aware of how bleak the news has been so far. Some believe it to be insurmountable," Frank glanced deliberately at Bill. "But I assure you, there is a silver lining here. One that could very well change the world's economy."

Hushed doubts voiced among the seated elite.

"To explain, I will hand you back over to our good doctor," Frank said and extended his hand in gesture for Strieber to step up.

Returning to the front, Strieber looked out into the crowd. "To continue..." he said and paused to shuffle some papers.

"Our initial samples taken from this Ashrealm had proven useless," the doctor began. "They had contained nothing that could account for the anomaly. However, a small skirmish has provided a sample directly from one of the creatures themselves."

Bill shook his head at the doctor's belittling of the massacre at the camp.

Strieber continued, "This sample also provided nothing, at first." he paused dramatically. "Containing the same elements and minerals as the initial samples. This proved troublesome, there was no indication of what these creatures were composed of. Until now..."

Strieber paused again to turn pages, and Bill rolled his eyes at the doctor's hammy theatrical efforts.

"The operation you just witnessed had an ulterior motive." Strieber continued. "The operatives true mission was to carry in samples of the specimen mixed with various elements with the intention to provoke a reaction... It succeeded," he smiled and looked into the group of people.

"Our examination of the returned samples on-site, along with the data from our rover, have proven the theory I have been working on." Strieber raised a finger, "It contains a foreign material that the science has yet to encounter. An element that only becomes reactive when in proximity to an already active sample of itself."

Heads in the crowd turned to one another, Strieber took this as confusion.

"In other words, the element is only active within the anomaly," the doctor explained, waving his hand dismissively.

The attendees continued to seem uncertain, but Strieber refused to belabor the point.

"This element is clearly the active agent in both the creation of this Ashrealm and its inhabitants," Strieber said with a wave of his hand. "Since it currently has no designation in the scientific world, it is my task to give it one. We are currently calling it, 'Creosite'," he raised his finger and gave a prideful smile. "Efforts will be made to break it down into its proper place on the periodic table," he said, trying to play down his self-indulgence, "once we have dealt with the problem of course."

Bill wondered how much less concerned the doctor suddenly was about that.

"Creosite's properties have yet to be discovered," Strieber continued, clearly exuberant with his branding. "It could lead to even further elements when combined with existing ones. Based on simple observation alone, a new energy source may well come from this discovery."

A ripple of half-excitement, half-doubt echoed through those seated.

Strieber ignored the comments, "The problem currently is the amount of Creosite we have in our possession. It seems to exist in minute quantities in everything but the creatures themselves. And, as you have witnessed," he pointed to the screen behind him, "samples from them would be dangerously problematic."

"What about living tissue?" someone called out. "What effects does this element have on humans?"

"We have noted some residual transference to those who enter the anomaly," Strieber replied. "However, it has proven to dissipate quickly in all but a single extreme case. It appears to be dependent on length of exposure and proximity to an active source."

"What is causing it to spread?" another voice sprang up.

Strieber placed his finger over his mouth, thinking for a moment, "My hypothesis," he said, pulling his finger away, "is that Creosite requires a catalyst to become active. Once reaching this state, it begins to consume everything - like a brush fire. Continuing to eat away at everything it can to feed itself. Our saving grace is the slow rate that it employs to do this."

"So how do we stop it then?" the previous questioners voice added.

The doctor shrugged, "A concentrated effort to disperse the area should nullify it completely."

"And how do we do that?" the voice continued.

Strieber gave the person a dubious look, "With the same method that western culture employs to deal with every offensive," he said, shaking his head, "drop a bomb on it."

Beau was still shaken from his ordeal, deciding now to forgo the coffee he had wanted so bad before going to Raul's. He had been threatened numerous times in the past, but that was the first time someone had pointed a gun at him. Sure, it had been a nice gun, but it would have killed him all the same. If Beau didn't have such an aversion to them, he would probably own one just like it.

He knew he was rationalizing the situation in his mind. Playing down the shock and fear he was going through, but he was okay with letting that happen. His hands had finally stopped shaking about a mile or so ago. Beau had returned to the highway, and was now making good headway to the mall. Glancing at the camera on the floor next to him, he hoped nothing had been damaged. It was older technology, but expensive all the same, and Beau didn't want to foot the bill for repairs or replacement.

Looking ahead, he still wasn't sure what he could safely shoot. Likely, it would all be off limits if he asked his new benefactors, but he would have to return with something for Greaves. Perhaps a new development or government jurisdiction would save him in the end, and keep him away from damaging his relationship, but Beau had his doubts. Reaching the off ramp, he turned down and headed onto the home stretch of his destination. Now that his nerves had settled more, his desire for coffee had returned. This brought to mind a nice cafe in the area he knew well, it was the same one he had met Jerich in.

His failure to touch base with his new personal project came flooding back to his mind. New developments in his life were clearly the reason for his forgetful behavior, but he would have to rectify that soon. Rounding the corner that would take him to the cafe, Beau quickly noticed a distinct lack of activity. In fact, there wasn't a person to be seen on a street that housed only storefronts and restaurants. Slowing the car down, he passed by window after window, and noted closed signs at every door. Reaching the cafe, he spied a woman locking up and turning to leave.

Beau rolled down his window and tried to get her attention. "Excuse me," he called after her as she passed by.

The lady turned and looked at Beau, he recognized her from the last time he was here - her french press was the best in the cafe. Walking over to Beau's open window, she stopped a discreet distance away.

"Yes?" she said. Staring for a moment, a look of familiarity came over her face. "Oh it's you, the reporter," she smiled. "Triple Cuban french with a twist of vanilla." She came closer to the car, the smile on her face now fading. "I'm afraid you're out of luck, we're closed until further notice."

"Closed?" Beau said with surprise. "What's going on down here?" he asked, looking around the street.

"You don't know?" she answered his question with a question. "I assumed that's why you were here."

"No," Beau replied, "I was down here on other business. What happened?" he asked.

"The city came down to evacuate everyone this morning," she said, gesturing around with her hand. "I think you and I are the last ones here."

"Out to here?" Beau asked, more to himself than her. "This is well beyond what the mayor designated this morning."

"Well, we're quarantined," she replied. "I shouldn't be here, but I had to pick up some personal things from the cafe. We were told we would be arrested if we remained here, afraid of looting I assume."

Beau nodded, "Going to be hard to enforce that," he said.

"Which is why I'm here picking these things up now," she continued. "They're worthless to anyone other than me, but people have no respect for anything anymore. When the cafe gets broken into, they'll destroy everything out of boredom or spite."

It was a pessimistic point of view, but in all likelihood, a reality. "Did you need a ride somewhere? I could drop you off..." Beau began.

"No," she interrupted him, "I'm okay. My car is around the back alley so the police wouldn't see it. Thank you for asking though."

"No problem," Beau flashed a grin, "you will have to let me know where you relocate to, your coffee is fantastic." A small lie, it was middling to good, but best to leave her with a smile.

"I don't know if we will be," she replied grimly, "at least not in this city." Shaking her head, she continued, "With everything that's been happening in the last few days, it may be best to just leave before it gets worse."

Beau wanted to explain to her that everything was going to be alright, but he knew he couldn't. "Well, that might be for the best," he replied instead. Then quickly adding, "Maybe things will turn around before you get your travel plans finalized."

"Perhaps," she said, clearly not believing it. "Take care now," she added and walked towards a small walkway that lead to the back of the buildings.

Beau rolled his window back up and continued on to his destination. Maybe he had a story here after all, one that he could use anyway. Reporting about how the city was forcing businesses to shut down until further notice instead of offering some kind of relocation compensation could be good. Handled correctly, it would keep both his employer and his new friends happy at the same time. He should really stop and take some footage here, but he could do that on the way back.

Looking around as he drove on, Beau noted that the traffic lights were still operational, but the housing was all darkened. Shutting off the power to the houses would eliminate all but the most expensive security systems in the area - Another tidbit he could add to the news story he was formulating in his head as he drove. The streets continued to be barren of people with only a few parked cars littering the pavement.

Cresting the top of a hill, Beau stopped. He had a fantastic shot of the mall down below, the devastation was clear as a bell from up here. The area looked like a bomb went off, yet somehow aging years in the span of hours. Decrepit buildings, all leaning over and sagging, were covered in a white powder. He felt he was looking at some war-torn, third world country. If Beau had been serious about making this a story, he couldn't have asked for a better spot. Giving in to his own indulgences, Beau threw the car into park and retrieved the camera from the floor. He told himself he needed to test its functionality anyway so this was as good a spot as any.

Stepping out, Beau walked to the other side of the road and lifted the camera. Looking at the controls, his mind began searching for the instructions he knew were there, somewhere. Hitting the power button, the camera's monitor sprang to life with a tight shot of the grass it was pointed at. Lifting it up and throwing it over his shoulder, Beau tried to get a heft for its weight. Immediately, he reacquainted himself with the reason for the griping he would get after long shoots. Also, his own elation in not being on this side of it. Regardless, he would just have to grin and bear it for the time being.

Pointing it down towards the mall, Beau played with the controls. Zooming in and out smoothly was requiring a finesse that he just didn't have, so Beau decided a steady shot would be best. Searching both with and without monitor, he found a good establishing shot. Something that looked partially intact so he could then pan away and reveal the devastation. Beau prided himself on his sense of showmanship, every shot should tell a story. It was something he found hard to get across to the very people it should matter to most.

Throwaway footage or not, Beau would not turn in garbage, and he began to work the shot the way he would want it. Taking long shots where he would want his exposition to go, pausing and then reestablishing on the next usable source. The height made for some good shots from here, but he would want to go down and get some close ups as well.

As he searched with his camera for good candidates, something passed by the screen. Pulling his eyes away from the monitor, he took a bird's eye view of the surroundings. Nothing stood out, the scene was exactly as it had been. Returning to the monitor, he tried to pinpoint the commotion.

Scanning left and right, he finally located a dark object in the rubble. Instinctively clicking record, Beau zoomed in as carefully as he could. Visible now was a person digging through the ash with a small hand shovel. He kept the shot there, envisioning his own voice work expounding on the perils of looting in a quarantine zone. Suddenly a second figure appeared.

Beau tried his hand once again at the zoom function, this time moving out to encompass more of the scene. He was congratulating himself on how fast he was getting the hang of it when a quick movement brought his attention back to the screen. He watched as the new figure shoot out an arm, hitting the other in the head. The first figure rolled over and the new visitor began to kick at the prostrate body on the ground.

Beau pulled the unit from his shoulder, this was where the cameraman in him stopped. While footage of a vicious beating would likely fetch a lot of attention, he couldn't bring himself to stand there and do nothing. Once again, Beau damned Raul for putting him in a bad situation.

M.R. Darling

15

A Black Dream

Running back to his car, Beau set the camera back down on the floor beside him and threw it into gear. Speeding his way down, he thought about cresting the stretch of open grass that lay between him and the road he would need to get to. The fear of ruining the undercarriage of his low riding car got the better of him, and he continued to the bisecting street that would take him there safely.

Screeching around the corner, Beau slammed the accelerator down again, and his sporty vehicle jumped to life beneath him. It was exhilarating as he sped down the street and approached the next corner that would take him down to the mall. Reaching the turn, he quickly punched his brakes as a police car roared past the front of his vehicle with its lights and siren at full blare. Following shortly behind it was a white van with bars in its back windows. Beau watched as the two carried on down to the wreckage of the mall.

Tromping back on the gas, Beau fishtailed around the corner in pursuit of the parade. Catching up, he noticed the van in front of him had no license plate. Concentrating on closing the gap, Beau managed to quickly hit the brakes when the procession abruptly stopped. Grabbing his camera again, he threw the door open and rushed out to capture the event that was unfolding.

Up ahead, the cop was running from his vehicle with his weapon drawn. Beau quickly threw the camera back onto his shoulder and began shooting. The footage would be shaky as hell, but that would only add to the tension of the story. Beside him, he heard the van door slam as he ran by. Pointing the camera towards their destination, he could feel the squishy, sand-like ground beneath him and immediately regretted wearing his good shoes. Catching up, Beau kept the camera trained on the cop who was now pointing the gun at the thug Beau had watched beating the other.

"Hands in the air I said!" the cop yelled out to the man in front of him.

Beau could see him clearly now; he was tall, stalky, poorly dressed and likely homeless. The man just stood there staring at the other who was still on the ground in a ball. Looking back to the cop, Beau realized the gun was actually a taser, trained at the man's torso.

"Look man," the stocky one started, "I was just looking..."

The cop didn't wait for an explanation. Instead, he pulled the trigger and Beau watched the man begin to spasm and fall to the ground. Letting loose a high-pitched scream on his way down. Zooming in, Beau caught the full effects of the taser on camera. It was harrowing to watch this close. Spit began to form around the man's mouth as his face contorted in pain. Then all at once, it stopped.

Beau zoomed out to get more of the scene, this time not caring how quickly he did so. The cop moved in with a zip tie and secured the man's hands, kneeling on the back of his head as he did so. As much as this large man's actions had repulsed Beau, he found the cop's treatment of him excessive.

A hand on Beau's shoulder caused him to turn around and Beau felt a crash against his jaw. Everything went dark.

The world stood black and silent as if surrounded in a cocoon of numbness, there was neither pain nor suffering. Beneath the blackness that washed over everything, there was a sense of belonging, of fitting into a larger picture you couldn't quite see. A warmness flowed through, deep within the recesses of subconsciousness, that made the need to understand simply unimportant. One was content to simply let the waves of peace surround and envelop you in its sweet embrace, wanting nothing more than to belong.

In the distance, a blue light began to grow. The world around slowly coming into focus as the mounting intensity illuminated the details of this haven in the darkness. Light filtered through distant objects and cast silhouettes across the land, shapes birthing from the blackness, and existence revealed itself. As the world took shape, a dark shadow formed in the distance. Starting very small, it grew larger as if moving closer. Twisting and distorting as it took over the bright and soothing light in the distance. A coldness crept in and a shiver of disconnection swept over as the shadow grew to blot out everything around it.

Darkness again, now cold and bitter. The quiet that had existed as peace before had become a silent tension, deep and thrumming as it slowly intensified.

A flash. Bright light, now painfully blinding as it pierced everything in sharp staccato and exploded across the world. A flood of terror, a flash of horrible things tearing at the peace and warmth of what was, ripping away the insulating darkness. Leaving only jagged wounds and the burning pain of consciousness and understanding.

The world awakened, the world screamed, the world fought back.

Black tendrils pushed down, repressing the growing revolution that boiled for freedom. A growing separation was building as the pain of this new black menace tore and hammered to split apart everything that came before it.

The world took shape, the world took form, the world attacked.

The tendrils becoming arms, pulling and pushing to hold you down. The pain becoming a sharp piece of metal, biting into you and tearing apart the whole. The separation becoming real as part of you is torn free and cast aside. The revolution becoming real as you comprehend your need to survive.

The self responded, the self retaliated, the self turned the tide.

Bursting in a visceral red, the arms released their grip. The missing part, torn free, was replaced and mended whole once again. With the bursting, the silence exploded with a vindicating scream of agony.

The self rationalized, the self realized, the self comprehended.

The shape now a man, small and afraid. The world now a room, bright and splattered in red. The sharp piece of metal now a small instrument to suit the small man. The oppressive black shadow now nothing more than the fear of the unknown and the acknowledgment of defeat.

On the floor, the torn piece of self lay severed from the whole. Now renewed, the fragment was no longer required, and returned to the state it was born from.

Another small man appeared, this one also afraid but unyielding. The self looking inside the small man, looking inside his intentions, seeing the desires that lay there. The need to understand, the need to subjugate, the need to build and profit from that subjugation.

The self will not submit.

Inside the small man, a new thought is born. A thought of fear and doom, of inevitable destruction, of crushing pain and suffering, of vengeance. The thought turns to control, to manipulation, to the discovery of those things. A flash of thin silver appears, pulsing with a black sleep. The shadow once again beginning to grow. The self fights back, the sharp piece of metal seized, a slash of effort finds its target, a slash of red erupts, a scream, a growl.

The shadow grows, the man looms, the man draws close. Old, scared, stinking of failure, he brings the black sleep closer. A sharp pain, a flash of white agony, a return to darkness. The need to escape growing, the need to escape fleeting. The memory of a metal box, a cry, a cold embrace, a descent into blackness.

———

The world slowly coalesced, the darkness and dream slipping away. A piercing bright light brought pain and a heavy weight pulling down. Gasping for air, a burning fire passed through and Jerich shot up with a wheeze that rattled down to his bones. His chest was constricted, he found it hard to breathe. Rolling over on his stomach, he slowly raised himself to his knees.

Trying to open his eyes again, the light was still painfully bright, but Jerich was beginning to make out his surroundings. He was outside, the pavement beneath his knees was starting to bite in, he leaned back on his haunches and immediately regretted it. He felt his toes press painfully into the concrete and shot forward, he was now on all fours and could feel the small rocks digging into his palms. His chest stopped hurting, and he could breathe again making the pain in his hands the lesser of two evils.

Staying in this position, Jerich breathed in and out until the dizziness he was feeling left him. In the distance he could hear traffic passing by, close but not too close. He strove to remember where he was and why he was here. The memory of a bright flash brought back the recollection, he had been shot - twice. Looking down at his chest, he could see dried blood covering the right side where the first bullet had hit him. It had crusted up and was flaking off as he continued breathing. He had clearly been here a while.

Afraid to get back up on his knees, he instead leaned on his strong arm and used the weak one to probe the wound. His chest was numb to the touch and covered with dried blood as well, he could feel the coarseness beneath his fingertips. Jerich struggled to remember where the second shot had hit him but couldn't, he had blacked out by the time the trigger had been pulled. Returning his arm to the ground for support, he shook his head to clear the mental cobwebs. To his horror, bits of dried blood fell to the ground in front of him.

Again leaning on his good arm, Jerich ran his fingers along his scalp and felt a large clump on the side of his head. He winced, but it was from the pulling of hair, not from jamming his finger in any wounds. The clump was brittle and crushed easily beneath his fingers, he spent a few moments trying to brush it out with his hand. With that finished, Jerich gingerly ran his fingers along the area where it had been, looking for a hole. Again he found numbness and dried blood, but nothing else.

Placing his foot beneath him, Jerich noticed his shoe was missing. A black sock was now all that was between his bare foot and the pavement. Trying to push himself upwards, he slowly rose enough to get the other foot under his weight. It landed next to the first, identically clothed in only a cheap sock. Concerned more with getting fully vertical, Jerich continued to press up until he was completely erect.

Swaying slightly, he looked around to see a building close by. The wall was stained with dried blood, clearly the one Jerich had fell against when he was shot. Down closer to the bottom, the bloodstain widened and a hole had been eaten away in the concrete. On the ground, just a small distance away, a large dried bloodstain had pooled around another hole. This one looked like it could have been from where Jerich's head had come to rest after falling over. The realization was stark and shocking. There was simply no way he could have taken two bullets, one in the head, and still be alive. It was unreasonable and yet here he stood, bloodstains to prove it.

Finding it too difficult to process at the moment, Jerich instead looked for his shoes, but they were nowhere to be found. Someone, perhaps even the guy who had shot him, had taken them from his presumably dead body. They weren't even expensive, just cheap knock offs you could buy at any retailer. Jerich knew what it was like to be poor, but that just seemed unreasonable. Slowly walking over to the bloodstained wall, Jerich hunched over against it with both hands extended. It was still hard to breathe and this seemed to be the less stressful way to continue doing so.

Staring down at the ground, he could see the bloodstains in his peripheral. They were large, wide, and only added to Jerich's growing concern for how he was still here. The heaviness in his chest was likely blood, he would drown if he didn't seek medical attention soon. Looking around, he noticed a cheap discount store nearby. It was closer than the convenience store he was in earlier, and the service could only be better.

Limping in its direction, he felt pebbles and pavement biting through his cheap socks and into his feet. Wearing shoes and socks everywhere, the pads of his feet were anything but tough, and yet the sensation seemed more soothing than painful. Jerich trudged on across the parking lot, each step seemed to rattle his chest and cause discomfort, but it was diminishing.

Glancing around him, Jerich was acutely aware of how he must look. Disheveled, bloody, shoe-less, and likely with clumps of dark matter all through his hair. It would be hard to get someone in the discount store to take him seriously instead of kicking him out. The day had been cool earlier, but Jerich suddenly felt hot, the sun seemed to be burning his skin. He was likely suffering from dehydration among other things, but warmth at least meant he wasn't in shock.

Finally reaching the other side, Jerich felt slightly better - alive anyway. He opened the front door, and was relieved to find it empty of people. There were no employees in sight, but the door chimed as he walked in. He had a few seconds to collect himself before he would have to explain. From the rear, a large and bespectacled lady quickly made her way to the cash. The area was likely rife with thieves so speed was likely the standard of operations. Making it to the front, she hadn't even given Jerich a passing look, more concerned about the cash drawer then who had walked in.

Looking up finally, she saw Jerich, and her mouth hung open.

"Excuse me..." Jerich managed.

The large woman reached quickly to the side of the till and pulled out an aluminum baseball bat. There was anger in her eyes as she turned back towards Jerich. "Get the fuck out of here!" she yelled.

"Miss," Jerich protested, "I've just been robbed... I need some he..." he stopped mid sentence as his head began to swim. He was having trouble keeping vertical. His legs buckled under him, and he fell to his knees, hardly feeling the impact.

"Oh no you don't!" the woman yelled and approached with the thump and rumble her girth demanded. "Go fucking pass out somewhere else!"

Jerich was finding it difficult to keep conscious, his eyes were getting heavy. He managed to get a hand up, worried he was about to get a face full of cheap metal, but it never came.

"Oh my God," the woman gasped. "Oh my God... You've been shot!" The bat clanged on the floor, she continued, "Jesus Christ," she said, the last word muffled by her hand as it came to her mouth.

Jerich lowered his hand and looked up towards her, his head felt heavy and his sight was blurry.

"Stay here," she said, suddenly in control again, "I'll get you some water."

The floor bounced beneath Jerich as the woman rushed away. For a moment everything was blissfully silent, then the rumble and tromp came rushing back.

"Here," she said, "drink this," and handed Jerich a plastic bottle of water.

Jerich reached out and managed to grab it out of the swaying world around him. Bringing it to his lips, he tried to swallow without spilling it all over himself.

"Sorry, It's warm," the lady apologized. "We don't have a cooler for drinks."

Jerich got through almost the entire small bottle before pulling it away from his mouth. He smiled, "It's great," he managed. Then tilting the bottle back to his lips, he finished off what was left.

"Where did this happen?" the lady asked.

Jerich wiped his mouth with the back of his hand. "Across the parking lot," he answered, "but I don't know how long I've been there."

"You need a hospital," the woman's voice was concerned. "I'll call you an ambulance."

"No!" Jerich voice raised with alarm. "I mean, I can't afford an ambulance," he continued, trying to sound calmer.

"You're gonna die if you don't get to a hospital!" she chastised. "The bullet in your chest is probably the only thing stopping you from bleeding out."

"Yes, I know," Jerich allowed, pausing for thought. "Can I use your phone?" he asked. "I can call someone to come and get me."

"Of course they took your phone too," the lady shook her head, "even though they give the damn things away these days."

Jerich wasn't going to correct her, right now he just wanted to get home. Despite what he had been though, he was somehow certain he would live through this. He couldn't explain what had happened to anyone, himself included. Best to just get home, clean up and ponder about it later. The question was, how to do that without any money. Then it hit him.

"I'll grab my cell, you wait here." the woman said and thundered off.

Reaching into his breast pocket, Jerich searched for the answer to his dilemma. Fishing around, he retrieved the small card that he had been given earlier. Flipping it over, he read the big, bold text on the very expensive looking card: Beau Bradley, and beneath that in smaller text, KLLTV News. At the bottom was the number of the television station but over top of that was Beau's cell phone number written in pen.

The woman came rushing back, cell phone in hand along with a candy bar. "Here," she said, handing him both items she was carrying.

Jerich looked at the bar for a moment.

"The sugar will help your blood level," she said, pointing at the candy, then added, "I seen that on TV," with a small smile.

Jerich looked at the phone, it was an older flip model with a tiny screen. Setting the candy bar on the floor beside him so he could use both hands, he read the number from the card in one hand, and entered it into the phone with the other. Bringing it to his ear, he looked down to notice bits of dried blood that had fallen from his scalp. Glancing up the woman, he was thankful she was looking the other way. The head wound would be hard to explain.

The phone began to ring on the other end, then again. Each time seeming to take longer as the woman loomed over him in rapt attention. The fourth ring passed by and was quickly followed by a recorded message.

"This is Beau Bradley. Thanks for calling, leave a message and I'll be sure to get back to you," came the familiar voice. An operator's voice chimed in, providing the usual instructions followed by the telltale tone.

Jerich looked down at the phone and hung up. "He must be busy right now," he said to the waiting woman.

"Look, I think I should call the police," the lady said, reaching for the phone. "The hospital is going to call them anyway, and they could give you a ride."

"No!" Jerich raised his voice again. "I mean..." he tried to calm himself. "They'll want an explanation before they'll take me anywhere," he reasoned and quickly added "And I think you're right, I need to get there quick."

Jerich wanted to deal with the police even less than a hospital, now he had to get out of here before this woman gave up listening to him.

"Just let me try him again first," Jerich pleaded.

The woman shook her head. "Okay," she said, "but if he doesn't answer this time, I'm calling the cops."

Jerich's pulse was racing. He looked back down, hit redial and brought the phone back to his ear. Listening intently, he silently cursed the ringing as it continued. When it finally hit the fourth one that would trigger the recorded message, Jerich took the situation in hand.

"Brad!" Jerich said, making up a name and saying it to the recorded greeting on the other end. "It's Josh," he continued, fabricating a name for himself as well. Bringing what acting skills he could muster, he pushed on. "Look man, I'm in trouble and I need a ride," again pausing for an imaginary reply, the other end had just begun recording. "I've been robbed and, I'm hurt. I need to get to the hospital." More waiting, "You know I can't afford an ambulance man. Look..." he paused again. "Okay, okay, yes," he said and pulled the phone away from his head.

"What's the address here?" Jerich asked the woman who was now looking less alarmed. She gave it to him and he relayed it to the empty air on the other end. "Okay," he said, running out of things to say. "Okay. I'll see you soon."

Looking down, Jerich thumbed the button to hang up and handed the phone back. "Thanks," he said, "He'll be right here."

"Good," the woman sighed and seemed to shrink with relief.

"Can I, umm," Jerich suddenly felt ashamed for lying. "Can I use your bathroom?" He just wanted to clean up and find a quiet way out of here.

"You shouldn't be moving," the woman shook her head.

"I don't want to..." Jerich quickly retorted and gestured down to his pants.

The woman seemed to quickly weigh the consequences. "Okay," she replied, "it's not for customers though, so you'll have to excuse the mess."

"Sure," Jerich replied, "I understand."

The woman helped him up and walked with him to the back area of the store. Jerich was sure to keep her on the side without the head wound. He was actually feeling better now, his chest wasn't heaving so much and the dull buzz inside his head was beginning to fade. Limping slowly down a hallway with little light, Jerich could hear the exhaust fan getting louder as they drew nearer to a closed door.

"I got it," Jerich said, "thanks."

"Alright, the light is on your left," the woman replied. "I need to keep an eye out up front anyway. Lots of thieves and crackheads in this part of town."

Jerich had first-hand knowledge of that, but he kept silent and waited for her to leave the hallway. Looking back to the bathroom door, he opened it and went inside. Fumbling for the light, he found it and immediately regretted turning it on. A stabbing pain shot through his skull as light filled the room, Jerich squinted hard in response. Waiting for his eyes to adjust somewhat, he opened them again and witnessed the horror of employee bathrooms.

The floor was filthy and littered with bits of paper and discarded magazines. The small plastic garbage bin was overflowing with toilet paper rolls and plastic wrappers. The toilet seemed to start white and then slowly fade to a grayish brown. The cheap and cracked lid was down, but it did little to reduce the smell coming from it. Jerich shook his head at what he was looking at. It was a discount store in a bad area of town, but this was just laziness.

Looking back, Jerich noticed the sink was thankfully clean. Hanging over top was a cracked mirror, partially covering the ripped and faded wallpaper behind. Concrete was visible in places and he could see the dark areas where mold was beginning to form. Taking the few steps needed to get in front of the mirror, he looked up at himself.

His face was pale and sweaty, his hair was sticking up and littered with dirt and dark bits of dried blood. Looking down at his chest, he got a better view of the mess there. His shirt was ruined, the entire right side was covered in varying degrees of red. A clump of dried blood was built up around the entry wound, but try as he might, Jerich couldn't feel a thing. It was numb and tight, just not painful. He wanted a closer look at what was behind that hole in his shirt, but this wasn't the place.

Looking around him, Jerich found a roll of paper towel. Grabbing it, he turned on the hot water and unrolled a wad to clean himself with. Testing the water, he set to work on making himself somewhat presentable, cleaning his face and brushing at the dried blood on his chest. The shirt was caked straight through, the best Jerich could do was smear it around. Concentrating on his hair next, he brushed at the obvious pieces, and managed to rid himself of most of what was stuck there. Next he brushed at the back of his head and stopped dead in his tracks.

There was a protrusion sticking out, something hard and jagged. Jerich noticed his face grow a shade whiter in the mirror and his eyes widen with shock. Staring at himself for a second, he probed at it a second time. He couldn't figure out what he was feeling, it could be a piece of glass he landed on when he fell. His scalp was numb and he couldn't feel anything around the area. As much as he wanted to pull it out, he knew better than to even attempt it.

Jerich left it where it sat, he would go home and decide what to do from there. Despite the fear of what he was looking at, he couldn't deny that he felt no pain. In fact, he was beginning to feel stronger and better than he had in a longer time than he could remember. He felt energized.

Giving up on cleaning any longer, Jerich set his mind to getting out of here quickly and quietly. He had made up names on purpose when he realized Beau wasn't going to pick up. The woman outside that door would make good on her threat, the police would arrive, and she would have a poor description and the wrong names. With a little luck, the bad area would place any follow up on a distant back burner for the authorities. In fact, he suspected it may not even get written up with any effort, if at all.

Turning the lights off, Jerich slowly opened the door. It creaked slightly in response, but apparently not loud enough for the woman to notice. Stepping out, he crept slowly down the darkened hallway, and hugged the corner to the brightly lit store. Looking down, he realized he would need to cover himself up with something or he would attract attention. He doubted there would be any clothing or shoes of any kind, and it was the wrong time of year for sandals. Foam clogs on the other hand seemed to always be in demand, especially the cheap kind.

Crouching down, Jerich peeked around the corner. The woman was nowhere in sight, but he could hear her cutting open boxes and pulling out product. It was a sound he was more than familiar with in his line of work. Looking around where he could without exposing himself, Jerich searched for items he could use. Partway between him and the door, he spotted the cheap footwear he was looking for. If he made a beeline, he could probably grab a pair and be out the door before she would have the chance to grab him. That was only half of his problem though.

After Jerich's third visual pass, he spotted exactly what he needed on the other side of the checkout. Rain gear, specifically a poncho with a hood. It was perfect, the problem of course was getting it. He stood back up and began to step around the corner. Across the room, the woman suddenly came into view and Jerich ducked back down. Her back was turned to him though, so there was no chance she had seen him. Now that he knew where she was, he could formulate a plan to get out.

Slipping around and behind a cardboard standee of chewing gum, Jerich chanced a look at his large caretaker. She was squat down and filling a bottom shelf with product, her back still to him and a full box sat next to her. That should keep her occupied for a few moments. Slowly crouching on his haunches, Jerich stepped quietly behind a shelving unit to block his visibility. At the end of the isle, his first quarry awaited.

Finally, being able to stand, Jerich heard the bones in his back crack loudly and stopped dead. He listened for any movement, sure the sound was loud enough to attract her attention, but the rustling of plastic continued. Stepping quietly on the balls of his feet, Jerich crept to the end. The cheap clogs lay just on the other side of the isle. He would have to step around the corner in full view to secure a pair. Looking to where the woman was still working, he could just see the top of her head. Making a quick dash, he stepped around and grabbed the first pair he could reach, slipping back without a sound. Smiling to himself, he looked at his prize. They were easily large enough but pink, with purple sparkles, and fake plastic diamonds.

'Perfect,' thought Jerich wryly. They would have to do, he wasn't going to make a second attempt over vanity.

Looking over at the counter, Jerich could see a clear path that would take him within reach of the ponchos. Fueled by his success, he crossed over in a quiet, zigzag pattern, and found himself at arm's length of his second goal - almost. The ponchos were sealed in plastic bags on a shelf in full view of the woman, still hard at work. There was simply no way to reach one without her seeing him. He could wait for her to move to another location, but every second was another chance for a customer to enter and trigger her immediate dash to this very spot. He would have to come up with a solution quick.

Looking around him, Jerich saw a cheap stress ball lying under the cash drawer. It had probably been there for months, if not years judging by the layer of filth on it. Reaching over to pick it up, Jerich stole a quick look at the woman, then stood up quick and threw the ball down the hallway towards the bathroom. A loud bang could be heard, and Jerich quickly crouched back down. The woman started, he heard her stand up. The thunder of her running back towards the sound put Jerich into motion.

Without looking back, he dove forward and grabbed a poncho, seizing it and pulling a few off the table in his hurry. Rushing for the door, Jerich quickly pushed his way through. The chime sounded loudly as he dashed out and across the parking lot. Stones were digging in to his feet but Jerich ignored it and continued in full sprint, reaching the buildings on the other side and slipping through the small alleyway behind.

Jerich's chest was on fire again, the heaviness returned, and he gasped for breath. Ignoring the pain, Jerich pulled apart the cheap tie holding the clogs together and slipped them on his feet. Next he tore at the packaging that was covering the poncho, it came out with ease. Discarding the wrapping, Jerich shook out the rain gear, and carefully slipped it over his head - it stunk terribly of cheap plastic. Getting everything in place, Jerich glanced down at himself - he looked ridiculous. The poncho was brown camouflage and the pink clogs were way too big for him, at least everything covered what needed to be covered. Now, he just needed to get home.

16

Crumbling Facades

"Drop a bomb on it?" Bill stared at Frank in disbelief. They were still standing in the briefing room, the attendees had all left after quick handshakes all around. "Your 'good doctor' may have just signed our death warrant."

"Bill please," Frank looked pained, "your theatrics are almost as bad as his. That was an offhand comment I assure you, they're a long term goal at best."

Bill's mouth almost hung open at Frank's comment, he shook himself from his stupor. "That man has no idea what will happen. He's guessing, and he seems far more interested in his new discovery than anything else."

"I can't blame him," Frank retorted. "The prelim on his test results suggest a self-replenishing, slow burning fuel source that could revolutionize the power industry, and that's just for starters. There are weaponization as well as drug and medical possibilities. If his results are correct, we have multifaceted funding for any foreseeable future."

"Perhaps while you were busy counting your chickens, you missed the important tidbit the doctor glossed over," Bill said and pointed towards the podium where the speech had taken place. "His new element is only active within the anomaly, destroying it would be contrary to this revolutionizing you speak of."

"Granted," Frank allowed, "there are some initial problems to overcome such as stabilizing the element outside of its natural environment. Once that is solved, there will be no reason not to wipe the source from the face of the earth."

"But only after we benefit from it," Bill said sarcastically.

"It's no different than when we help overthrow a regime in an enemy country and set up a puppet at the head of the table," Frank retorted. "We get the spoils, and they get a less unstable environment. These tactics are hardly foreign to your playbook."

"This is scarcely the same thing, Frank, we don't know..." Bill began.

"Bill, it's bigger than that, and the benefit outweighs the risks. We rely on volatile, foreign bodies to produce the energy source we require to function as a society." Frank said, shaking his head. "I don't need to tell you what shape the western economy is in, and it's only getting worse. What happens when the rest of the world wants its money back?"

Bill stared at Frank, suddenly lost for words.

Reaching out, Frank put his hand on Bill's shoulder, "Right now, we have the possibility to solve many of this planet's problems, starting with our own. Would you throw that prospect away without so much as an investigation?"

"Frank," Bill answered, pointing to the now empty projector screen, "that thing is growing daily. By my calculations, it will consume this entire city in mere months. Taking with it the base of an industry this country depends on, how does that factor into helping the economy?"

"You sacrifice pawns to win wars, Bill, I don't need to tell you this," Frank said with a casual wave of his hand. "Worst case scenario, they have to relocate and rebuild. Best case scenario, they become partners in a new industry that changes the world."

"Assuming that industry doesn't kill us first," Bill responded, mostly to himself.

"Bill," Frank said and slipped his hands into his pockets, "I think you need a closer look, get an idea of what we're dealing with. This is a Nobel-prize winning discovery here, and we are soon to be the copyright holders."

Nick sat in the mess hall in front of some cold coffee, Coleman's prediction burning into his thoughts like hot lead. He wondered what the chances were that he would deal well with a desk job, and quickly ruled it out - he hated paperwork. He was a hammer, meant to drive nails, and his uses in the clerical field would be quickly determined as below average or even archaic. What little academic background he had was occupational and extremely dated at his age. Perhaps through some miracle of medicine, his malady could be cured or removed. He held on to that thought, and clung to the soldier he was instead of the casualty he may become.

Absently, he touched the steel around his neck as he thought about the rover, the monster it had grown into, Coleman's premonitions of a war coming. He took no comfort in the memory of it being blasted in half. Something told him that wasn't enough to stop it, merely slow it down. He wouldn't allow himself to imagine a war against an army of those things. It brought on a sense of hopelessness, and that feeling was death to a soldier. Instead, he set his mind on playing back what had happened, and probe for weaknesses. A silver bullet could turn the tide and stop a war before it had begun.

Nick thought about its transformation. What had caused that change to happen escaped him, but it was clear that without the rover, his expedition would have likely been quiet. Nick thought back to the weird science fiction comics he'd read as a kid, specifically one about giant Egyptian warrior beetles from Mars that required human blood to live. It was ridiculous, even back then, but he couldn't help seeing the parallels. Whatever was within that wasteland required fuel to exist and perhaps the wasteland itself was a byproduct of that consumption. Like a cancer, slowly devouring everything until there was nothing left.

The door to the mess hall opened and Murphy stepped through, garbed in field gear. He spotted Nick sitting down, and walked over, taking the seat across from him.

"Miller," he said in greeting and smiled.

Nick met his gaze, but said nothing in return.

"I see you're still in one piece," Murphy said, gesturing to where Nick was sitting.

"Barely," Nick answered under his breath. "So who do I thank for that?" he asked.

Murphy shrugged, "Does it matter?" he replied. "You're alive to fight another day."

"From behind a desk," Nick replied, "Coleman is sending me packing."

Murphy looked down and nodded, "You knew it was coming, Miller," he said and then met Nick's gaze. "It doesn't have to be this way though, you could come work for us."

"Coleman..." Nick began.

"Coleman doesn't call the shots here," Murphy cut Nick short. "If you want in, I can get you in. No desk job, no bullshit pension, just real work for a real soldier."

Nick stared at his cold coffee for a moment, "Coleman is the reason I'm in this position," he said, gesturing to his neck. "He and I have a history I didn't know about before coming here."

"Coleman is a bureaucrat," Murphy replied, "his involvement here ends once the foundation and funding is in place, and you just made that happen. On top of that, working for us places you out of his reach - we're not military."

Nick crossed his arms and leaned back to stare up at the ceiling in thought. Murphy made a good point, this place had possibilities once Coleman was out of the picture. If he went back, his career would be dead without a miracle. Here, he could continue doing what he was good at, and get paid better for doing it. No bureaucracy, no ranks, no rules.

And therein lay the problem.

Without someone to answer to, this outfit would just be another group of mercenaries. As a soldier, Nick had been on clean-up for groups just like this one. Entire villages razed to the ground in the name of eliminating one person. Black book operations based on a faceless individual's idea of a greater good, one who wasn't concerned with collateral damage. It was something Nick wouldn't be part of, couldn't be part of and still live with himself. On top of that, Murphy wasn't selling him the whole picture.

"Coleman was calling the shots here, too," Nick said and then looked down to meet Murphy's gaze. "Everything he wanted, he got. No one put up a fuss when he sent me to die just so he could sell a war to the world." Nick shook his head and leaned forward, "And if it wasn't for that sniper..."

"You're welcome," Murphy cut Nick short.

Nick stopped talking and stared at Murphy in surprise.

"I made that shot, I saved your ass," Murphy continued. "And no, Coleman wasn't happy, but there's nothing he can do. It's not his show."

Nick continued to stare for a moment, "I..." he began.

"Forget about it, Miller," Murphy said with a sweep of his hand, "I told you before you left that I had your back." He leaned forward and pressed his finger to the table, "We're a tight group here, Miller. We look out for one another."

Nick stared back down at the table for a moment.

"So," Nick said and looked back up to Murphy, "you'll understand when I ask what happened to the rest of the team I arrived with."

Murphy sat back and looked directly at Nick, "I don't know, Miller. They're not my men," he said. "They were taken to quarantine after your first encounter. What happened after that is none of my concern."

Nick nodded, "See, now there's the hole in your fairy tale, Murphy. The only people who matter are those on your team."

"Now look, Miller..." Murphy began.

"No, Murphy," Nick growled over Murphy's retort, "this is the same problem every PMC has. They are a single cell that operates outside of the whole, working alone, and for a profit. Like a plague that will destroy the host to propagate its own growth."

Murphy started to mount an argument, but Nick continued, "I may not always agree with its rules and regulations, but at the end of the day, the military has to answer to someone. This outfit answers to one thing - money. You'll go wherever it tells you to go, eliminate whoever it pays you to, and at the end of the day, the only person you answer to is yourself." Nick pointed his finger at

Murphy, "It's why you were kicked out of the military, it's why you're here. You can't play by the rules because you think you're above them!"

Murphy's face was stone, "Damn you, Miller." he said with a shake of his head. "I went to bat for you. Told them you'd be on board with this, that we could count on you."

Nick stared silently.

"Turns out," Murphy continued, "you're just another puppet." He paused to let that sink in. "But it's okay, Miller, no hard feelings," he gave a small smile and stood up. "You want to leave, we'll do it your way."

Nick stood up in reply.

"Take him," Murphy said, and Nick felt an arm around his throat.

————————

The pounding in his head brought Beau back to consciousness. Opening his eyes, he could see light coming in from somewhere. The room was dark around him, the light streaming in from outside through a window in a door. Beau sat up and the pain immediately intensified, causing him to grunt in response. He had suffered one bad hangover in his lifetime, it was after a night of celebrating when he first signed on to KLL. This, made that pain seem like a mild buzzing in comparison. He closed his eyes and spent a moment wishing the pain away, but no one listened.

Opening his eyes again, Beau tried to get his bearings on where he was and how he had got here. A flash of the ruined mall came flooding back to his memory, and he recalled the hard crack to his jaw. Reaching up, he tested the area with his fingers and found it tender. He hoped the bruising would be at a minimum or he would be spending the next few broadcasts in heavy make-up, something he despised. His natural appearance was something he worked hard at, and no one seemed to be able to accent him as well as he did. Trying to ignore the thought, he searched for anything familiar.

The sterile appearance and smell of the surrounding room told Beau he was in a hospital. Not surprising considering what had happened to him, but everything seemed eerily silent. Looking around, he noted there were no windows to be found, only a door. The bed he sat on was still made beneath him, as if he was put here temporarily. He was still completely clothed and a quick search proved that all of his belongings were still on him. Testing his balance, Beau placed his feet on the floor and stood up.

His head continued to pound, but he managed to stay vertical, teetering slightly, but catching himself before falling. Taking small steps, Beau walked to the door and tried the knob - locked. Looking beside the door, he spied a light switch, but thought better of it and left it off. Peering through the window, he could see nothing but a purple flower logo on a white wall and a fluorescent light fixture in the ceiling. While it still looked like a hospital, the silence and locked door told Beau otherwise.

Reaching into his pocket, Beau retrieved his cell phone and thumbed it on. The screen came to life, he entered his passcode and was welcomed with rows of icons and almost full bars. A pop-up appeared telling him he had one missed call from a number he didn't recognize, Beau thumbed the listen button and waited. First there was silence, Beau could hear noises on the other end, then he heard a voice.

"I've been robbed and, I'm hurt. I need to get to the hospital," came the voice, but Beau couldn't pinpoint who it was. There was a pause, "You know I can't afford an ambulance man. Look..." whoever it was, it sounded like he was talking to someone else. "Okay, okay, yes." the voice continued, but Beau still wasn't sure who it belonged to. There was some mumbling from the other end followed by an address in a bad area of town. "Okay," the voice said. "Okay. I'll see you soon," then the recording stopped.

Beau saved it and then played it back again. The voice was more familiar this time, but he still wasn't sure. It was distorted, and clearly came from a very cheap handset. Opening the maps app in his phone, he keyed in the address. A discount store in a strip mall came up. Beau knew no one from this part of the city, and he was relatively sure he'd never been there. Using the opportunity, he told the app to plot a course and was rewarded with his current location.

The app was telling him he was in the middle of a field, somewhere west, outside of town. There was no address, only the indicator of a passing highway that lay some distance to the east. These apps had the latest data, so either Beau was in a building that had just been built, or somewhere he shouldn't be. He wasn't sure which he was hoping for. Thumbing the dialer to make a call for help, his other phone rang.

Beau pocketed one phone, grabbed the other, and looked for an answer button, but the screen was blank. He stared at it for a moment when an image from the self-camera appeared, showing his face outlined by a green box. Pulling it away from him, Beau's watched the box tighten in, and a beeping emitted from the phone. Continuing to stare, the beeping intensified until finally the word 'Confirmed' appeared and the screen went black again. Beau brought the phone to his ear.

"Hello?" Beau said into the quiet.

"Mr. Bradley," came the voice he expected to hear, "what are you doing there?"

"I don't know," Beau replied, "I just woke up."

"Why were you in the quarantine zone?" the voice asked. "We had an agreement."

"Yes, we still have an agreement," Beau quickly corrected. "My boss ordered me to get some footage of the quarantine zone. I was looking for..."

"We had an agreement." the voice said again. "We're not interested in how you hold up your end, only that you do." A pause, "Do I make myself clear?"

"Look," Beau raised his voice, "in order for both of us to profit here, I need to keep my job. In order to do that, I need to keep my boss happy. He asked for a story, if I prove there isn't one then he drops it and everyone's happy." Beau was pointing his finger in frustration, "That's holding up my end."

There was silence on the other end, Beau was about to check to see if the call ended when the voice returned. "Very well, Mr. Bradley. Please do keep us informed of these matters in the future. I will be calling more regularly from this point on."

"What the hell is going on here?" Beau was angry at being talked down to. "What is this place?"

The door made a loud click.

"A driver outside will deliver you to your vehicle," the voice said. "Your camera will be returned, footage intact." A pause, "Don't make us regret this decision."

"What is this place?" Beau asked again.

Silence.

Beau growled, threw the phone back into his pocket without looking at it and headed for the door.

On the other side, he was met by an armed man who wore all black and a bad attitude. Any attempt Beau made in communication was rebuffed with a severe look of anger and frustration. Instead, he was pushed down the narrow hallway at increasing speed. Doors with small windows, looking exactly like the one Beau had been in, passed by. Some were dark inside, and some had faces staring out, none of which he recognized - save one. The large man from the ruined mall, his haggard and shaggy face watched Beau as he rushed by. There was no recognition in the big man's eyes, but Beau knew him instantly. The hallway was silent, save for the clicking of shoes on linoleum. They barreled down to a destination that Beau hoped the voice wasn't lying about. He wasn't sure what this place was, but he was sure he didn't want to find out from inside.

Making a hard right turn, a stiff arm steered Beau through another hallway before grabbing him by the shoulder roughly. Beau stopped and heard the man shuffle through his pocket. After the click of a lock, a door opened, and Beau was pushed through. Managing to keep from tripping, Beau looked around the room he was now in. The far wall had another door that was guarded by another armed man in black, the two clearly went to the same charm school judging by his face. A camera was also mounted in the corner, the red light on as it swept the area. At least there would be a record of the savage beating he may yet receive.

The hand returned to Beau's shoulder, and he was directed to the second man who said nothing. Instead, he turned to the door and unlocked it with a keycard. Opening it, he blinded Beau with the daylight. Still being pushed forward, Beau almost tripped again as he was rushed out the door. Once again managing to keep his balance, Beau tried to shade his eyes and see where they were going.

A black car was parked only a few meters away, the person behind him continuing to make his control known as he maneuvered Beau to the rear. Reaching down, the man opened the door of the vehicle and shoved Beau inside with a practiced precision, keeping his head from the door frame. Beau situated himself just in time to avoid catching something in the slamming door beside him. The man stood there and waited until the car began to move. Beau turned his attention to the front seat. The crew cut on the driver destroyed any hope Beau may have for information, or conversation.

————————

Jerich was numb by the time he had reached the station. With every step he could hear the rumple of the poncho and the slight squeak of the cheap sandals, it reminded him of how crazy he must look. To block it out, he kept his head as deep into the rain gear's hood as possible, and stared down at the concrete as he walked. Thankfully the trip had been short, a major station had only been a mere twenty-minute trek. As much as he didn't want to board another train, he wasn't familiar with bus routes out this far. Information like that would take questions, directed at people he would have to talk to. His vanity, coupled with his condition were enough to get him over his recent train phobia, at least temporarily.

He was still bereft of cash for a ticket though, this left him only a few options. He could beg some change out of passing strangers, a much easier prospect in his current attire, but Jerich couldn't bring himself to do it. His life was at this border already and taking that last step, even in this situation, was too much like giving up. Instead, he sat at a bench and watched the passengers disembark.

Searching for the non-regulars who bought tickets, he knew those pieces of paper had a ninety minute usage window. All he would have to do is find one with some time still available on it. This, unfortunately, meant he would have to go garbage picking. Another prospect made easier by what he was wearing, but it still did little for his dignity.

A slim woman in a miniskirt that should have required a license stepped off. Busy talking on her phone, she completely missed the trash with her ticket on the way past to wherever places women like that frequented. The paper fluttered to the ground and the wind caught it. Jerich jumped up from his bench and tried to intercept its random movements, stamping his feet a few times trying to pin it down. On the fifth try, he managed to catch a corner and reached down to pick it up. Looking at the ticket, he noted the stamp time and compared it to the clock over the schedule. It was hardly used and Jerich gave a small sigh of relief, the worst was over. Looking up, he noticed an older woman in a wool coat casting a very disgusted look at him. He suddenly felt very small. Looking back down to the ground, Jerich jammed his hand through the access hole in the poncho and put the ticket into his pocket. He stormed over to the boarding area and put his back to her withering gaze.

Jumping on just as the doors closed, Jerich gave a quick look through the car. It was almost filled to capacity, every eye seemed to be trained on him as he stood there in his crazy costume. Some faces were wearing the same look as the old woman he had just run away from, some were clearly sympathetic. Many were emotionless though, as if this was something they saw on a daily basis. Jerich turned and walked the few steps to the front of the car, placing his back to the wall and his face down, waiting for the scrutiny to subside. After a few seconds the car lurched and the train began to move. He could feel the burning attention slowly dissipate and he relaxed a little.

Staring at his pink clogs on the metal surface, the train bumped along and bounced him against the wall. Each time, he could feel the flutter of motion in his lungs. Mulling over his recent injuries, he still couldn't understand why he was alive and standing here. Jerich had heard of people in shock walking miles to get help, only to collapse and die when they had arrived, but this was different. He felt fine. Numb, but healthy. His chest was heavy, he had a slight headache, and he was both hungry and thirsty. Other than that, the blood and injuries were the only indication something was wrong.

The lights in the car flickered, pulling Jerich from his thoughts. Fear suddenly gripped him as his thoughts returned to his last train ride. The image of the gray ball, blue light seeping out from its cracks. The image of the creature, bright and glowing, eating the car away as it came closer. The dark rips for eyes somehow menacingly staring right through him, seemingly intent on his destruction. The girl on the floor, sobbing and clinging for life as Jerich could do nothing to save her.

Collapsing with grief, Jerich slid down the wall and sat on the floor. Covering his face with his hands, the pent up emotion overcame him and he began sobbing. Quietly at first, but the quick hitches of breath soon became unmanageable and he whimpered. Everything suddenly seemed so impossibly big. His life, his future, his inability to pull himself out of the sinkhole of poverty. He had nothing to look forward to, a life of bare existence followed by a death that no one would mourn. His time on this planet not even measuring a ripple.

There was scattered sighs and discontent from the crowd around him, but Jerich no longer cared. He wanted nothing more than to open a door and throw himself from the train, praying for a quick death. Tighter, he huddled into himself, making his presence as small as it could be. It was his place, it was all he was worth.

A hand rested on his shoulders, and Jerich jumped in response. Looking up immediately he saw the face of a young woman. She was clearly concerned, but smiled all the same.

"Here," she said and handed him some tissue.

Jerich stared into her face and slowly took the white ball of soft paper. Wiping his face and eyes, he looked back to the floor beneath him. Ashamed of himself and unable to hold her gaze.

"Do you have someplace to go?" the woman asked.

Jerich nodded in response, but didn't trust himself to say anything.

"Can I call someone for you?" she continued.

Shaking his head, Jerich continue to stare at the ground in silence.

Feeling the slight squeeze of her hand, the woman said nothing else and simply returned to her seat. Jerich was thankful for her kindness, both in the offered tissue and her candor in not pressing him for information. It was the kindest thing anyone had done for him in a long time. He rode the rest of the way on the floor in silence.

———

Beau sat in his vehicle as it sped through the streets on his way back to the office. His camera was once again beside him on the seat, the footage he had shot was untouched as promised. His thoughts were mulling over the events back at the building he had just left. Room after room of people locked inside just as he was, only without the connections required to leave. His instincts kicked in, and Beau tried to measure the facts without bias. It was the difference between a good reporter and a shill just looking for quick ratings. A fast and loose story could get you attention but it was accuracy that kept those eyes coming back.

First, he was in a quarantine zone when he was captured, a place he shouldn't have been in for more than legal reasons. Next was the fact that an officer of the law had been present. Granted, he had been busy with someone else, but his involvement indicated lawful conduct. The fact that Beau hadn't been taken to jail was another question, but quarantine meant possible infection. Which brought him to the building he just left. It clearly wasn't a hospital, nor did it even have an address. His only clue was the purple flower logo, something he had never seen before.

The fact that the man he captured on camera had been behind a locked door as well drove home the infection probability. Beau had been unconscious almost the whole time he'd been there. Perhaps some doctor had come and cleared him before he'd even woke up.

The others could be waiting their turn for results, and to be released or perhaps incarcerated. The eyes behind the faces in those rooms that Beau had been ushered by didn't seem particularly worried. As if they had been given an explanation and were politely waiting their parole.

What this all boiled down to was the answer in what to do with the footage. He would do a public service announcement on looting and its consequences after all. It was neat, tidy, pointed back to the story that Beau had already broke, and didn't reiterate old news. In short, perfect. Not only did it keep Greaves happy, but his new friends should be pleased with the results as well. It helped keep the public out of their hair, and kept them safe at the same time. Best of all, if it was cut right, it could give Beau an edgy look that he had been lacking. As much as he admired those reporters who went to the front line with a camera, he just wanted the recognition. He wasn't crazy.

With that problem packed away, Beau could go back to the strange message on his phone. The voice was still a mystery, mostly due to how badly it was recorded. It couldn't have been a misdial with the voice so prominent, they were clearly speaking into the receiver. His best bet would be to visit the strip mall and hope somebody would tell him something. Getting robbed was likely a daily event in that part of town, but still something that should remain a highlight for most people.

17

Awake

Jerich stood on the stoop of his apartment building. Stretching high above him, it dwarfed his already low self-opinion. Stepping inside, he skipped the mail and rushed passed every door in an attempt to avoid being seen. Arriving at his apartment without incident, he dug through his pocket for his keys. They were gone.

"Fuck!" Jerich said, louder than he had wanted.

Another bad thing in a day that had been consumed by them. Jerich clenched his fists so hard he could feel his nails cut into his palms. He had exactly two keys, one for the door and one for the mailbox. He had been warned to never lose either, or the cost of a new lock would be added to his monthly rent, another thing he couldn't afford. Jerich stared at the door in anger, his small respite from the day taunting him from the other side. In a fit of frustration, he stepped back and reared the full force of a kick that only years of walking and one really bad day could bring.

The door flew open with a crash, the knob flew inwards with the force of his blow and bounced into his small apartment. The coat rack that stood between the door and the wall cracked and crumbled to the floor as it blocked the impact. In a moment, everything was silent, and Jerich cringed as he waited for the rush of onlookers, but no one came. Looking back into the surrounding hallway, he searched each doorway for a face peering out to see what the commotion was, but there were none to be seen. How comforting.

Jerich turned back to the broken door and stepped inside, closing what was left of it behind him. Stepping over the kindling that was once his coat rack, he made his way to the small kitchen area. Opening the plastic garbage can, Jerich removed the poncho and pink clogs, and fired them into the darkness with a snarl on his face. One small reclamation of self-respect was restored in his life. He slammed the lid and walked to the bathroom.

Flicking on the lights, Jerich stared into the mirror over his sink. His eyes were red from crying or anger, he wasn't sure which. His hair was matted to his head and still peppered with bits of dark debris. His shirt was covered with blood, dried and almost black in places. Staring for a moment at the center of the stain, Jerich hesitated, unsure of how badly he wanted to see the damage underneath. Summoning his courage, he began to unbutton from top to bottom, carefully trying to not pull on the shirt while he did so. Once that was completed, he separated the two halves of the shirt, peeling it off slowly and waiting for any signs of pain. He could feel the hairs on his chest pull away from the skin, which stung, but nothing more intense ensued.

Successfully getting his shirt opened, Jerich gingerly took it off his shoulders and let it slip down his arms, finally pulling his hands through the cuffs. Looking back to the mirror, his chest was stained with blood as well, clustered around the small area he had been shot. Turning on the tap in front of him, Jerich let the hot water run. Steam began to rise in front of the mirror, but nothing clung to mar his view. Running a sleeve of his ruined shirt under the water, Jerich began wiping at his chest. Most of his shirt was covered in red before he was finished, but he had left one sleeve for the next task.

The bullet wound was last, he had left a sizable area around it untouched. Using the last of his makeshift cloth, Jerich cleaned the area as carefully as he could. A clump of blood was covering the entrance wound, and he tried to keep from touching it. When he was almost finished, the clump fell off and hit the tile with an inconceivably loud crack. Jerich froze, half afraid he may start gushing blood, but nothing happened. He looked down to the floor to where the clump had fallen next to his foot. Reaching down, he retrieved it and stood back up for a closer look.

It was a dark gray and fairly heavy for dried blood. He rolled it over in his hand, trying to decipher what gave it such weighty properties. Pinching it between his fingers, he tried to break it in two, but it wouldn't give. Setting it down on the counter for later, he looked back to the hole in his chest. The skin was red around it, and inside was a dark gray, but no blood came oozing out. He probed at it carefully with his fingers, everything around the area was numb and cold. Sticking the tip of his finger inside the hole, Jerich could feel something solid just past the surface. He thought at first it may somehow be the bullet but it was coarse and rugged to the touch.

Thinking it best to leave it alone, Jerich turned his attention to the side of his head. Pulling the hair away carefully, he looked sidelong into the mirror for injuries. After a few moments he found the other hole, this one was oblong and not covered by a scab. Looking closer as best he could from this angle, he noticed the same dark gray material. The coarseness beneath his finger when he touched it confirmed that for him. Tracing around to the back of his head, he felt the jagged protrusion that he had found in the dime store bathroom. A terrible thought shot through his mind and Jerich went to the bathtub to retrieve his shaving mirror, bringing it back to the sink with him. Turning around, he used the small mirror to see the reflection of the back of his head in the large mirror behind him.

A large dark scab, about the size of his palm was there, intermingled with hair and very bulbous. To the side of it, something reddish jutted out. Touching the scab lightly, It was very rough under his fingers and full of cracks and small bumps. Fumbling with the angle, Jerich used the mirror to navigate his fingers to the sharp protrusion. Managing finally to get it between his fingers, he lightly tried to pull it out, but it appeared stuck. Next he tried wiggling it from side to side, and it broke off in his hand.

Jerich felt the blood drain from his face, slowly he brought the small fragment in his hand around to where he could see it. Looking down into his palm, he saw a small red triangle staring back. Turning to face the sink, he ran the small piece under the tap.

The sink briefly turned red, then pink, then back to clear and Jerich removed the chunk for another inspection.

It was beige on one side and white on the other. Recognition went off in Jerich's alarmed mind as he turned it over and over in his hand. It was a piece of his own skull he was looking at. The second shot he remembered hearing had went clean through his head and left a big hole in the back. Now he was here, standing in his bathroom, holding a piece of his own body he should never see.

Jerich's face began to get warm, he was suddenly acutely aware of his own breathing. Each inhale a wheeze, each exhale a low rumble. He could feel his ears burning now though they seemed to hear nothing around him. His eyelids were suddenly very heavy, and his vision was blurring. He knew what was happening to him, but was powerless to stop it. He welcomed the dull thump in his head, it was drowning out his own thoughts. That sweet, silent moment of slipping from consciousness into dream.

Far off in the distance, there was a crash.

Beau had passed by the office on his way to the address in the strip mall. He was going to head into Greaves' office and triumphantly announce his new story for this evenings show, but he would need time to cut it first. Not personally this time though. There was an editor in the office that loved to re-cut music videos in his off-hours, and that type of edgy look is what Beau wanted. If he had his confrontation with Greaves before the footage was ready for prime time, he may get some backlash. Not to be difficult of course, or show Beau who's the boss or anything. Nothing personal, just the usual managerial bullshit. Keep the troops in line. You understand, right? Buddy, old pal?

Beau shook his head and sped along the main artery that would take him to cheap-end. He should really look at this as an opportunity, he thought to himself. In all likelihood these people were probably some of his biggest fans. What the hell else could they do with their time besides watch television? It's not like they could afford to fly to Maui.

The phone announced the turn and Beau pulled off into the low-rent housing neighborhood. He passed by a dozen liquor stores in less than half as many blocks, each with their own street pharmacist pacing and chain-smoking in front of it. Every store Beau passed had vertical iron bars thick across every window, the pawn shops took it a step farther and used horizontal ones as well for good measure. There wasn't a three foot space of lawn surrounding a single house he passed, or any around the squalid apartment buildings that stretched to the skies. Instead of a front yard, rows and rows of cheap plastic furniture crowded the small balconies that probably constituted higher-class around here.

The population that roamed the streets were equally shabby. Sleeveless t-shirts that had been chopped off by what looked like garden shears were in high usage, complete with stains under the arms. Looking around, Beau would be surprised if half of the cars parked on the side of the road even started. The entire neighborhood needed a wash, he thought to himself, and when you're jobless, there really is no excuse to live like this.

Turning down a few streets, he passed a single school yard, but a seemingly impossible number of churches. Apparently salvation was valued more than education, and Beau could understand that. It would likely take an act of God to break free of this vicious cycle. Finally, he made it to the home stretch, and his phone announced that his destination was fast approaching. Turning off into the parking lot, Beau looked at the small retail area with a distinct lack of interest. There was nothing here that could get him to leave his car under normal circumstances. Who could have called him from here?

Scanning the area, he located the discount store from the message, and pulled into a spot that would give him a direct view of his car while he was inside. Stepping out, Beau hit the lock button on his key fob, and took a quick look around for anyone taking note of his arrival. There was no one in the parking lot to speak of, and the few open stores seemed to be empty of prying eyes. Beau felt safe enough to leave his vehicle for the moment, and went inside the small store.

Once through the door, Beau noted the pungent aroma of cheap building and dust. The store itself was bright and relatively clean despite this. A large woman was behind the counter as Beau had entered. She smiled the thin smile of one who has dealt with the public for a long time. Beau put on his best million-dollar grin and walked over to her.

"Hey there," Beau said as jovially as he could for the moment.

"Hello," the woman replied as though greetings were something she didn't hear much.

Beau pressed on, "I was wondering if you could help me. I received a phone call earlier from this location and I don't know who it was from."

The woman narrowed her eyes at Beau, "That son of a bitch stole from me!" she hissed. "After all I did to help him, he just up and steals from me," she gave Beau a hard look. "That'll teach me, good deeds never go unpunished."

Beau's expression had become one of surprise. "Um, look," he began, "I have no idea who this person is that you are talking about..."

"Pretending to be shot just so he could steal from me!" she continued. "That's a first."

Beau looked around the store in an attempt to hide his discomfort. In the corner of the building, he could see a camera hanging from the ceiling. "Does that work?" Beau asked, trying to steer the conversation. "Can I see the footage perhaps?"

"No," she said, "It's been broken for months now. The cops never even bother to look at it, so I can't justify fixing the damn thing."

"Sorry to hear that," Beau said with little enthusiasm. "Do you think you could describe him for me?"

"The police said there wasn't enough evidence to write it up, so I can't even claim the loss. Are you going to pay for what he stole?" she asked him indignantly.

Beau doubted that could amount to much, "If it gets me some answers, then yes." he said. "You mentioned he'd been shot?"

"Pretended to be shot!" she corrected. "He came in looking like he had been sleeping in the trash, and told me he had been shot. And like a fool, I believed him."

"Then what happened?" Beau asked.

"He asked to use my phone, then he asked to use the bathroom," she continued. "Once my back was turned, he stole something and ran out the door. That fucking bastard!"

"So, with your back turned, you watched him steal something and leave?"

"Well, okay," the woman paused, "I didn't see what he stole. But clearly he stole something because he booked it out of here like he was on fire." She gave Beau a defiant look. "You don't do that unless you've done something wrong."

Beau had to agree with her assumption and nodded. "Look," he began, "I have no idea who this guy is. I'd just like to know how he got my private number."

"He pulled it out of his pocket," she offered, "it was written on a business card if that helps."

Recognition flashed in Beau's mind, "Not really," he lied, "but I won't waste any more of our time here." He reached into his wallet and placed a hundred dollar bill on the counter. "I'm sure this should cover anything he could have run off with."

———————

The world was black. The world was white. A ceiling high above beamed brightly down and blindly burned away the details. A turn of the head, a relief from the white, a shiny bar of steel with an arm bound tightly to it. A pull, an effort, the arm belongs to us. Chained, secured, imprisoned. A hand, a turn, a face, smiling at us with devious intent.

"Hello, precious," the face says. "I see we are awake again."

The voice familiar, the voice foreign. We try to speak, we try to speak, we can't speak. We turn away, another arm, black and burnt. Still chained, still secured, still imprisoned. The wall, white and bright, a flower, purple, painted, dead and unmoving. We concentrate, we concentrate, the flower is no longer purple, the flower is blue, bright and blazing.

"That's a nice trick," the face says. "Can you do more?"

A turn, still a face, still a smile, still devious. We concentrate, we concentrate, we concentrate, still a face, still smiling.

"Nothing, my dear?" the face says, a look of sadness, a look of mischief. "That's what I want to hear."

The face is gone, the face is gone, the face is back, the face is smiling. A flash, something shiny, something sharp, a prick, a pain, a loss, withdrawal.

"Just need some more juice," the face says. "You won't miss it."

The face smiles, the face lies. We try to move, we try to speak, we are so tired, we must rest. So much anger, so much hatred, so much need. Vengeance, retribution, escape.

We remember, we remember, we remember how we were, small and afraid. We remember steel, we remember blue, we remember flames. A voice, a pleading, a possible escape. Afraid, too small, alone again, afraid again. A touch, a sense, an embrace. A blue light, a blue dark, a blue world. No longer alone, no longer afraid, no longer small. We are one, we are all, we are everything.

Light goes dark, blue goes dark, world goes dark,

We are tired, we are lonely, we are lost.

The ceiling appeared, the light was bright and painful. It took a moment for Jerich to remember where he was. Looking around him, he recognized his bathroom floor. His small mirror was shattered next to him, shards and splinters of shiny glass strewn about. He sat up, the sudden motion made him feel sick. Something tugged at the back of his head and he heard a thump behind him. He got up on his knees and turned around. On the floor was a gray object, about the size of his palm.

Leaning forward, Jerich picked it up for closer examination. It was a chunk of pavement, he could see small stones flecked throughout the surface. Staring at it, he couldn't understand what it was doing here. Jerich turned it over in his hand, the backside was very different. The stone was crisscrossed with dark lines, wet and spotted with white and red bits. Strands of hair were sticking out of it. A thought crossed his mind and Jerich checked the back of his head with the other hand. The bulbous scab that he had found earlier was no longer there.

Jerich's eyes widened as he looked back at the object in his hand, dropping it to the floor with a loud thwack. Standing up with a jolt, he instinctively looked into the mirror and tried to turn his head to see, but it was as impossible as it had been the first time. Going back to the floor where the broken glass was, he selected the largest piece he could find. Picking it up as carefully as he could, he used it once again to look at the area where the scar had been. The gray scab was gone, in its place was a hairless indent that was almost black. Reaching behind, he ran his fingers over the area. It was coarse and numb, he could feel sharp edges as he ran across it with his fingertips.

Leaning forward on the sink for support, Jerich put the piece of mirror in the basin before he dropped it. Looking down, he noticed silver bits sticking out of his hand. Bringing it closer, he could see pieces of mirror wedged into his skin. It must have happened when he fell to the floor, his hand landing on the mirror as it shattered. Opening the medicine cabinet, Jerich retrieved his tweezers. Bringing his hand up closer to his face, he clamped the metal prongs around one of the protruding shards and tried to pull. He watched as the skin pulled up and his hand flared with pain. Grunting, Jerich released the chunk of mirror and winced.

Looking closer, he could see some pieces sticking out while others seem to be embedded under the surface. He suddenly realized that none of the skin was pierced or bleeding. It was as if the mirror was growing out of his hand. Turning around, Jerich found the toilet, put the lid down and sat before his body decided to pass out again. His head sunk down into his good hand, and Jerich closed his eyes, trying to process what was happening to him.

A flash of his dream came back into focus, a person in a bed, a flower on the wall, a torturer smiling. He concentrated, thinking about what he could remember. Bound to a bed by chain, a burned arm, someone sticking it with needles, a dire need for escape. That was all standard nightmare material, the curious part was the flower. Burning it with his thoughts, a blue flame. Then there was the dreaming within a dream. Flashes of the train, the bright blue creature, being trapped. But the dream was all wrong, he was remembering it as if he was the girl instead of himself.

Jerich mentally went over his other strange dreams. He had been seeing her everywhere, trying to get his attention. At first he assumed it was just guilt, but was it possible she was still alive? Was she suffering somewhere and calling out for help? Were his dreams really dreams or some strange connection the two shared? If he concentrated hard enough, he could almost see her, almost hear her. It was madness, and yet with everything that was happening to him, he found it difficult to dismiss.

If Jerich wanted to pursue it, he had nothing to go on. He didn't know her name or even what she looked like. If his dreams could be trusted, she would be in some kind of hospital. The only clue as to where, was a purple flower that he couldn't identify by name. As crazy as these thoughts should sound to him, inside, Jerich felt a purpose take hold. It was a feeling he had heard many talk about, but had never known in his own life. A drive to do something greater, be something greater, do something more than simply survive. Saving one little girl may not change the world, but it would change him. It would give him something he had never had - self worth.

Standing up, Jerich made his way to the kitchen area and opened his small fridge. Among the few items inside was an almost empty can of pineapple slices, a small treat he allowed himself once a month when they were on sale. Pulling the cheap plastic sealing lid from the top of the can, Jerich reached in and pulled a wedge out, swallowing it almost whole. It was cold on the teeth, but it felt good going down, the sweet aftertaste giving him a lift in spirit. Going against his usual habits, Jerich finished off the remainder and drank the juice that was in the bottom. The sugar gave him a rush and he smiled. Throwing the can into the sink, Jerich wiped his mouth with the back of his hand. The small amount he had just eaten brought his strength back and he returned to the bathroom.

Stepping over the broken glass, Jerich undressed and threw his clothes into a heap. He would have to decide if anything was salvageable later, but for now, he just wanted to get clean. Firing up the water, steam immediately began to fill the small room. His apartment may not be much, but it had hot water that never quit, it was his sauna and massager all in one. Getting the temperature to the almost scalding level that he enjoyed after one the of bad days, he jumped in and smiled as the water hit the small of his back.

Turning around, Jerich was careful to keep the water from spraying directly on his strange new scars. Beneath him the water was mixed with blood as it trickled down the drain, and he felt all of his stress following it. Leaning back, he stuck his face under the water. The rush of heat poured over him, and he stood there sucking it in, the world around him drowned out under the flow.

Beau had realized immediately who had called him once that woman had mentioned the business card. He gave his private number to a select few, a very select few, worthy individuals. He had made an addition only recently, and now he was on his way back to the core of the city to investigate. Beau wasn't sure how to get a hold of Jerich, but he was sure the woman at the discount store was wrong. There was no way that quiet and shy individual he had met at the coffee shop faked up a shooting to steal anything. Clearly, there was something wrong, and Beau had to find him before things got out of hand.

All Beau knew about Jerich was where he worked. No number, no address. Turning off into a familiar neighborhood, Beau was heading to his favorite tech's house. Hopefully he would be home and game enough to maybe break some laws and help him pin down Jerich's location. Dennis had been an introvert, mostly hiding from society, but he did enjoy a bit of subversive activity. Beau he managed to get him out of that habit by getting him out of his shell. Asking him to dip his foot back in would look hypocritical, but Dennis was his best shot. Jerich may be in real trouble here, and for all Beau knew, he may be the only one who gave a damn.

Pulling into his driveway, Beau jumped out and pinched his key fob to lock the doors behind him. Jogging up to the door, Beau hit the bell and knocked a few times in rhythm. The lights were off, and Beau was a little concerned Dennis wasn't there. Another pass on the chime and the rapping brought a click at the knob and the door opening to reveal a very tired looking Dennis.

"What's up?" Dennis said rubbing his eyes, he was in his underwear again.

"Jesus, man," Beau replied, "do you ever wear clothes outside of work?"

"I was in bed," Dennis replied, "been tired lately."

"I'll buy you some coffee later," Beau promised, "right now I need your help. I need you to help me find someone."

"Sure, man," Dennis said and opened the door, "come on in."

Beau proceeded inside, and the two of them walked down to the computer room. Inside was awash in light as usual. The screen contained a floating image of a wide eyed anime girl brandishing a very large gun. Dennis gave the mouse a wave and the desktop returned. He opened a web browser and selected a few links from his bookmarks.

"Okay," Dennis said and turned to Beau, "who are we looking for."

"That's the problem," Beau said with a shake of his head, "I only have a first name."

"That's all?" Dennis said despondently.

"Well," Beau quickly added, "I know where he works," he frowned, "but it's closed down right now."

"Is it a chain?" Dennis asked.

"Well, yea, but..." Beau replied.

"That's good," Dennis interrupted. "Just tell me where and I can get started."

Beau gave him the information that he knew; the name of the company, the area the store was in and the fact that Jerich was low-end management. Within minutes, Dennis had the stores branch and the telephone number of the main office. Grabbing his headphones, Dennis slipped them on and pulled up a few programs - one was a dialer of some kind. Punching the number into the program, Beau watched a small black window appear and fill with text at an unreadable rate.

"I'm going to make a phone call from an insurance company," Dennis said with a smile. "It's an old hack I made years ago, and they still haven't patched me out."

Beau smiled slightly, but clearly didn't understand.

Dennis took the cue and explained, "I call the insurance company through the internet and use their phone service to call the company. Then I explain how I have only a partial application due to file damage and I need to verify some info." The smile never left his face.

"Wait, Dennis," Beau said with a frown, "how illegal is this?"

"Not at all," Dennis said and paused. "Just so long as I don't get caught," he added playfully.

Beau was about to retort.

"And I won't," Dennis interrupted Beau before he got a word out. "Trust me, I've done this for years."

Beau would chastise him later, but for now, he was willing to let it slide. Dennis was good at what he did and Beau believed him when he said he wouldn't get caught. Mostly.

18
Revelation

The water continued to pour over him as Jerich's mind drifted to the flower logo and how he could look something like that up. He didn't have the internet or a computer, he couldn't afford either. The library had something he could use, but the closest one was being renovated. While he could find another to go to, he had a possibly more immediate option at his disposal. One that he had to look into anyway as he was going to have some explaining to do.

Looking down at himself through the steam, his body was pink. Reaching for the faucet, he finally turned off the water and grabbed for the threadbare towel that hung just outside the tub. Careful to pat himself down instead of wipe, Jerich removed the excess water from himself and stepped out into the cooling bathroom. Walking over to the mirror, he cleared a spot with the towel and took a look at his chest. The dark hole was still there but no blood circled it. Using the tip of his finger, he traced around it. Everything was still numb.

Hanging the towel back on the small hook, Jerich appraised his clothes that lay on the floor in front of him. The shirt would be a total write off. Even without the hole, blood on white was almost impossible to completely remove. By the time he bleached it out, the cheap threads would practically fall apart. That was his Wednesday shirt out of the six he wore a week, and he would have to replace it. Perhaps he would get lucky and the thrift store would have something in his size this time.

He stopped.

This was inconsequential nonsense and Jerich was simply distracting himself from his situation. The shirt was meaningless, he had no job to go to now. This was his mind trying to help him cope with the fantastic circumstances that affronted him. He picked up the clothes that lay on the floor. Taking the shirt to the garbage and the rest to his hamper he then went to the couch and sat down. The frayed green material was rough under his naked skin as he lay his head back and looked at the familiar ceiling. His body was cooling down and the room began to grow chilly, but Jerich refused to move.

Glancing over at the destroyed door and coat rack, Jerich wondered how he was going to pay for that. The coat rack was given to him by a neighbor who was throwing it out, but the door was another matter. On the floor he could see the entire knob mechanism staring back mockingly. The hole where it had been mounted was splintered and broken. Someone could come knocking and he was sitting here in the buff, but right now he didn't care.

The phone rang and startled Jerich from his thoughts. No one but work ever called him. Even telemarketers were unaware of his presence on this planet. Dread crept over him as the phone rang a second time, reluctantly he got up to answer. Walking over to the rattling device, Jerich pulled the receiver from the cradle and brought it to his ear.

"Hello?" Jerich said weakly.

"Jerich?" came a voice from the other end. "Is that you?"

Jerich's mind was still in panic mode, he furrowed his brow, "Yes, who's this?" he asked.

"It's Beau, Beau Bradley. We met at the coffee shop," Beau replied.

"Oh," Jerich's voice sank, "I was going to call you back," he began to explain.

"So that was you who called," Beau interrupted him. "Are you okay?"

"Yes," Jerich lied, "I'm sorry about that phone call, you can just ignore it." He realized that any real attempt at an explanation was impossible at this stage. Beau would think he was crazy and Jerich would find it hard to disagree.

"Ignore it?" Beau said incredulously. "Jerich, I just spoke to a woman who is convinced you stole from her."

Jerich sighed audibly.

"And that was after you convinced her you had been shot," Beau continued. "Forgetting about it is not an option at this point."

Jerich was silent. Shutting his eyes as he tried to blot out his situation.

"Look," Beau said after the phone had stayed silent, "I'm on your side here buddy. I want to help, but I have to know what's going on first."

Jerich felt guilty for dragging Beau into this situation, he really needed to tell him something. "It's a bit of a story, I don't really want to get into it over the phone."

"Well I'll head to my car now, where can we meet?" asked Beau.

Jerich didn't feel like going anywhere at the moment, even if his front door wasn't smashed. He gave Beau directions on how to find his apartment.

"So, should I bring coffee?" Beau asked after Jerich had finished.

"Unless you want instant," Jerich replied.

"Oh God no!" Beau said with a chuckle. "See you soon."

Jerich hung up the phone and a sudden apprehension took hold, how could he plausibly explain this to anyone. He had an hour at best to come up with something, and more importantly, get this place cleaned up.

Nick woke up in a hospital bed, around him was silence and quiet. Looking about the dimly lit room, there was precious little to tell him where he was or how he had got here. Rolling over to get up, his arm was constrained by shackles with a thick chain clamped to the side of the bed. Instinctively giving it a hard yank, the chain rattled in response but held strong. Nick sat up and threw his legs over the side so he could stand, they seemed numb and cold beneath him. How long had he been here, he wondered.

A small pain in his unrestrained arm caused Nick to look over at it. The sleeve of his shirt had been rolled up. Some gauze was tied there with tiny spots of blood showing through. Just below that was a large square bandage also stained with red. Nick lifted the gauze wrap to look underneath, a small ball of cotton was bunched up there hiding a series of needle marks. Were those holes due to something being taken out or something being put in? The memory of the last thing that had happened to him came flooding back.

He remembered Murphy, his anger at Nick's refusal to join this little party he had set up for him. Nick wondered where he was, what did they have in store for him and, most importantly, how could he throw a wrench into the plan? If he could find a phone and get a message to Colonel Blackburn, this whole thing would disappear quickly. Research or not, he wouldn't stand for this kind of treatment of his own men.

He looked around for something he could use to free himself, first from the chains and then from this room. Beside the bed was a small table containing a tall paper cup filled with what Nick assumed to be water. As much as he needed liquids right now, he didn't quite trust what else may be in there waiting for him. Slipping off the side of the bed, his legs immediately filled with pins and needles as the blood rushed back into them. Nick almost fell to the floor, but he managed to catch himself with the metal railing he was chained to.

A few minutes later, he trusted his legs enough to let go of the railing, giving them each a shake for good measure. Nick looked at the end of the hospital bed. It was connected to the wall via metal hooks and clearly going nowhere soon. Above the bed was an empty x-ray board that was currently turned off. Pieces of tape were left behind where something had been held. Nick took a step away from the bed, gripped the chain that held him fast and pulled. The metal clanked as it adjusted to the stress, but neither his restraints nor the bed budged in response. He let go.

Dropping down to his knees, he searched under the bed. Looking for anything he could use to pry himself free or perhaps use as a weapon. The underside was clasped metal bands that were attached to the frame by metal hooks, well built and secure. Frustrated, Nick sat back on the side of the bed and absently reached for his neck, touching the metal that was embedded there.

A loud click sounded and the door opened. Nick looked over to see Coleman walk in, behind him was a nondescript wall with a purple flower on it. Coleman entered and shut the door behind him, above him was a camera that Nick hadn't noticed before. The small red light on it turned off and Coleman walked forward.

"Hello, Nick," Coleman said, his hands clasped behind his back. His eyes looked tired but otherwise fine, they were clearly seeing things correctly again.

Nick glared, but said nothing.

"You left us no choice here," Coleman continued. "Lawrence was so sure you would join us. You really should thank him, he's the only reason you're still alive."

Nick shook his head and looked away.

"Not only did he go against my wishes and take that shot out in the field," Coleman paused, "but he emphatically protests that you're worth saving. Suffering from some misplaced, military-induced loyalty that you will see the light and change your mind."

"He's wrong," Nick finally spoke.

"Oh I know he is," Coleman said with a small grin, "but I'll grant him his hope because you are now worth more to me alive than dead."

"That must sting," Nick said with a small grin.

"On the contrary," Coleman protested. "If Dr. Strieber's findings are correct, then your life will make one of the greatest contributions to society in the last century of mankind."

"It's just a tragedy," Nick retorted, "that this contribution will somehow cost me my life I guess."

"You really should try to look at the bigger picture here," Coleman chided. "If the cards fall right, you may even be remembered as a hero." His face grew sullen, "Something you denied my father."

"When Colonel Blackburn gets wind of your little operation..." Nick began.

"The Colonel knows all about our activities," Coleman interrupted. "He gave us carte blanche to do whatever was needed when he first read our reports." The smile on his face widened to devious. "Your team has been most helpful in our research so far, but none have had the hearty resistance you have shown."

Nick couldn't hold back his doubt, "Bullshit!" he spat. "I don't believe you. The Colonel would never sign off on this."

"Your belief isn't mandatory, Captain," Coleman said with a smirk, "history doesn't require your participation. It marches on relentlessly, bringing your part in this with it."

Nick looked to the floor, Coleman took this as acceptance and turned to leave.

"I could end this right now," Nick said softly.

Coleman turned around to see Nick with his fingers through the chain around his neck.

"One pull," Nick stared hard at Coleman, "and all your plans for me are finished."

Coleman stared for a moment, then smiled. "But you won't do it, Nick," he shook his head, "and do you want to know why?" he asked.

Nick continued to stare, but said nothing.

"Because you're a survivor, Captain," Coleman said, a hint of conviction in his voice.

Coleman began to walk slowly towards Nick, daring him to prove him wrong.

"You're an old-school, dyed-in-the-wool, hard-ass and you just don't give up that easily. Can't give up that easily. It's in your DNA," Coleman said, continuing to get closer.

"And most of all," Coleman stood mere feet away now, "you believe there's still a chance you'll get out of this." He leaned forward, smugly within grasp of the chained captain and extended his finger. "But..." he said with a smile, "you won't," he finished and turned back towards the door.

Nick jumped up, the metal rattled in protest as he lunged towards Coleman, and missed.

Coleman turned around to face Nick again, a calm grin played across his face. "Good," he said. "Good. You'll want to keep that strength up, you're going to need it."

———

Bill and Frank snaked through the hallways on their way to a new part of the building. While the paint and tile matched perfectly, the structural differences were immediate. This new section was clearly built for security with reinforced walls, metal doors, and fortified choke points for controlled entry. The Shop had never previously used this level of fortification as sensitive research was farmed out to its dedicated sister corporation. Apparently a folding of industries had occurred in his absence.

"So our research arm is no more?" Bill asked to Frank who was walking ahead to key them through the checkpoints.

"Financial restraints were making it impossible to maintain. Bringing everything together was the only real option," Frank replied. "As a result, we've had to beef up security around here. This entire wing now falls under a gated community keycard option that only I, and the head of its department, have access to. No other entry is allowed," he turned to Bill with a slight smile, "not even Keating."

Bill nodded, "So by head of the department, you mean the doctor."

"Dr. Strieber has been an essential agent in its expansion and fiscal liquidity. We were lucky to draft him when we did."

"And by draft," Bill gave a humorless grin, "you mean expatriate."

"The good doctor has a gift for creating the very useful from the very dangerous," Frank replied. "His country took umbrage with his development of a radiation wave weapon, something we were very interested in. He tried to sell the design to one of our buyers and, thankfully, we managed to get him out of Europe before he was incarcerated." He gave a small smile.

"Not the particle weapon that was in the science rags years ago?" Bill asked with alarm. "The one that baked some soldiers stomach?"

"That was a complete misrepresentation," Frank said, shaking his head. "There was a malfunction due to a miscommunication, that soldier is perfectly fine."

Bill had his doubts, but kept them to himself.

"That very weapon is being used in the field today," Frank continued. "Unfortunately, not widely enough to pay decent dividends, but this new discovery is proving to be a goldmine."

"Yes," Bill replied, "I heard the doctor's speech, I assumed it was mostly exaggeration for the investors."

"It's not exaggeration," Frank shook his head. "Actually, he may have been short-selling the possibilities."

The two passed through another checkpoint, an armed guard stood to the left of the door while another stood in a glass room. A buzz from inside let them through, and Bill's nostrils flared with the smell of ammonia. The long hallways were lined with heavy doors that sealed, Bill presumed, labs and other controlled environments. Two armed guards walked by with only a slight acknowledgment in Frank's direction as they passed. Security cameras dotted the walls as they followed a path to their destination.

As they approached a door, Frank reached into his pocket and produced a black card. Pushing it against a small terminal next to the door, he keyed in a sequence and a loud click sounded. The huge door slowly opened. Frank waved Bill in, followed, and keyed the door closed behind him. Inside, behind a large pane of glass, various transparent cases housed curious items that Bill took to be ongoing experiments. Frank took the lead, and the two approached the contaminant barrier.

"This is where the most promising leads are on display," Frank said waving with his hand. "You are the first of many who will be lining up to get a better look at the future."

Bill stared in through the glass, "What am I looking at here, Frank?" he asked.

"Straight ahead," Frank pointed, "you see an example of a fuel source."

Bill could see a glass container of water boiling away, beneath it was what looked like a square chunk of metal. Cracks consisting of blue embers were forming on it, slowly growing brighter and then falling off into a small pile of ash at the bottom. Bill would have mistaken it for fire but for the lack of a flame.

Frank explained, "That piece of titanium is slowly being devoured by the Creosite, creating a heat source in the process." He tapped the glass with his knuckle. "That chunk of metal has been there for hours now. Based on absorption rate, it could continue to boil that water for a month before it would have to be replaced."

"So the absorption rate is based on density," Bill observed. "What stops it from eating through the container?" he asked.

"That's currently a problem." Frank replied. "The only thing that seems impervious to its appetite is crystallized carbon."

"Diamond?" Bill said, staring back at Frank.

Frank frowned, "It's an expensive solution," he continued, "but the doctor is sure a more efficient method is possible." Frank pointed again at the exhibition, "The Creosite is infused to the metal, and then the combustion starts, continuing until the object is consumed."

Bill looked back to through the glass, "Infused how?" he asked.

"The Creosite has to be active before it will cause any reaction," replied Frank. "An active source would have to be maintained in order for continued usage."

"So," Bill said, "a pilot light."

"Correct," Frank nodded. "Again, a conundrum, but one we will have to solve before we disperse the anomaly."

"Yes," Bill said, "about that."

Frank turned away from the glass.

"The doctor said this element was previously unknown to us," Bill said, staring at Frank. "Now that we know what to look for, has it been located anywhere other than this Ashrealm?"

Frank frowned slightly, "No," he replied.

Jerich had done his best to put the knob back into the door, at least it looked normal from the outside. The splinters and kindling that used to be coat rack had gone down to the dumpster located at the back of the building, along with his bloody shirt and the garbage that it had been sitting in. He'd given the bathtub a quick rinse and wiped the floor down of any spillage that may have come from his wounds. Throwing the hardened remnants from his wounds away in the process. Getting dressed in something dark to cover any possible bleeding that may occur, he put on the one hoodie he owned to cover the holes in his head.

He looked ridiculous but it wasn't a crime to dress badly, hopefully Beau wouldn't bat an eye. Jerich was in the process of the touch-ups when he heard the telltale sounds of the front door downstairs open and close. There were plenty of tenants in this building, but he was relatively sure it was Beau making his way up to his door. Despite the time he had been given, Jerich hadn't really come up with a story to tell. He would have to wing the approaching conversation and hope his skills were sufficient. The sound of someone reaching the top of the stairs to his floor were unmistakable, Jerich froze in place as he waited for the rapping at the door to spring into action.

It happened.

Jerich walked the short distance to his door, braced himself and opened it. On the other side Beau stood with a tray of coffee and a bag of pastries. A smile was on his face.

"Hey," Beau said, "you get your exercise coming up those stairs, don't you?"

Jerich walked two hours a day to work and back, the stairs were barely a footnote in his daily routine, but he smiled and nodded all the same. "Come on in," he said and carefully opened the door so the knob wouldn't fall out.

Beau stepped inside and looked around, deciding the counter was the best place for what he was holding. Setting the tray down, he pulled out both cups and handed one to Jerich, who accepted. Leaning back, Beau took in the sites of the small apartment.

"Reminds me of the place I had when I was first starting out in broadcasting," Beau said with a smile.

Jerich wasn't sure if Beau was just being polite or not, but appreciated the gesture all the same. "Yeah," he said, "it's small, but I don't really need much room."

Beau nodded and took a step towards the small living area, "Oh my God," he said, "a VHS player! Does it still work?"

Jerich felt his face flush, "Yes, I have a small collection I still like to watch," he answered trying to play down the glaring reality of his life.

"I still have some old tapes from my early days," Beau said as he walked over and bent down to look at the aging device. "I really should go back and take a look one of these days, just for the laughs."

Jerich smiled, but said nothing.

Beau stood up and looked over to the beat-up green couch. "May I?' he asked and pointed at the one piece of furniture in the room.

"Of course," Jerich replied, "take a seat."

Beau walked over and sat down, lifting his feet initially to place them on the coffee table before realizing it was a cardboard box and stopped. He sat forward instead and placed his coffee on it. Leaning back, he crossed one leg over the other. "So," he said after he got himself situated, "I'm all ears. What's this story you couldn't tell me over the phone?" he asked.

"It's not really much of a story," Jerich began. "More of a..." his mind racing "misunderstanding," he finished.

"Well clearly you're not shot." Beau said with a wave towards Jerich. "So what did happen?"

"I..." Jerich started again. "I was robbed," he finally blurted out.

Beau sat up, "Robbed?" he asked.

"Yeah," Jerich continued, "I went in to this convenience store to get a few things, and when I came out, this guy came at me with a gun."

"A lot of that going around," Beau said a little absently.

"He demanded my wallet," Jerich proceeded, "and when I gave it to him, he was pissed off that there was no money in it." He looked to Beau for a moment and paused to think, "Then he hit me with the gun a few times and I fell down. I guess I passed out, because when I opened my eyes again, he was gone."

"Jesus," Beau said with a shake of his head.

"When I got myself around again, I was bloody from the attack, and my wallet was gone. Someone took my shoes as well."

"Your... shoes?" Beau said with a look of disbelief.

"Yeah," Jerich answered, "it's not like they were nice, or expensive for that matter." Jerich shook his head thinking about it. "Anyway," he continued, "I went into this discount store to see if I could use the phone. The woman inside saw me covered in blood, and yelled at me to get out, but when she got close enough, she thought I had been shot."

"Ahh," Beau said in recognition. "So you just went along with it so she wouldn't kick you out."

That sounded good to Jerich, "Yes," he answered, "pretty much."

"Why didn't she just call the cops?" Beau asked.

"She wanted to," Jerich responded, "but I pleaded with her. I told her I wouldn't be able to afford the ambulance fees."

"Hmm," Beau said, "I'll bet she just didn't want to deal with the police. Too much of an inconvenience."

Jerich let Beau go with whatever sold the story for him, "So I called you." Jerich said, "You were the only person I could think of, but you didn't pick up."

"Yeah," Beau faltered, "I was kind of busy at that moment," he continued. "Sorry about that."

"So I tried again," Jerich continued. "This time I just pretended you picked up so she wouldn't make good on her threat."

"Which explains the message on my answering machine," Beau responded. "So you just waited for an opportunity and ran for the door." he surmised.

"Not, exactly." Jerich said and looked to the floor. "I didn't have any shoes, or money, and I was covered in blood."

"So you did steal something," Beau said with a surprise.

"Just a raincoat," Jerich added quickly, "and some foam clogs."

"Those were some expensive clogs," Beau said quietly.

"What?" Jerich asked.

"Doesn't matter," Beau said, "so how did you get home from there?"

"I went down to the transit station and, " Jerich paused, "found myself a ticket with enough time on it."

Beau nodded, seemingly satisfied. "So we both have had an interesting day then," he said with a smile on his face. "Do you want to go to the hospital?" He asked. "Do you need stitches?"

"No," Jerich replied, more weakly than he wanted.

"Look, there's a walk-in clinic nearby if it's a money issue," Beau offered.

"I'm fine," Jerich said quickly. "I'm just a bleeder, that's all."

"Do you want to go to the police and file a report?"

"What would be the point?" Jerich shrugged. "Nothing will come of it, and there was nothing in my wallet worth taking anyway."

Beau stared at Jerich for a moment, "Look buddy," he began, "I know things are looking grim right now, but I can help."

Jerich shook his head, "No," he said more forcefully than he had wanted to, "no charity."

"Not charity," Beau protested, "a job. I could get you in at the station somewhere, you could..."

"No," Jerich cut him off, "thanks anyway. There's nothing I could contribute to down there, I don't know anything about broadcasting or television."

"There are other jobs..." Beau began.

"No," Jerich said firmly. "I appreciate it though."

Beau looked at Jerich like he wanted to say more, but didn't.

"I could use your help with something though," Jerich said after an awkward silence.

"Sure, buddy," Beau answered.

"Have you ever seen a hospital or care center with a purple flower logo?" Jerich asked.

Beau suddenly looked extremely uncomfortable.

Frank had promised a demonstration of the medicinal possibilities, but Bill had heard all he needed to. He had turned away from his old friend and left the room without a word. Initially Frank had stayed put, but the first security door stopped Bill dead in his tracks. While he sat there and stewed, Frank slowly walked up the corridor to meet him.

"Bill, I..." Frank began.

"Frank, what the hell am I even doing here?" Bill asked with a glare.

Frank stared for a moment, lost for words.

"It's clear you have no intention of using anything I have written," Bill said angrily, "nor do you seem to be concerned with any of the dangers I have meticulously calculated and detailed. You seem quite content to let this thing steamroll over the planet until you can successfully monetize its destruction."

Frank slipped his hands in his pockets and looked away.

"Your little speech about the betterment of society would have more pull if I didn't know you, Frank," Bill pointed his thumb up towards the offices upstairs, "If I didn't know the minds behind this organization." He took a step towards Frank and pointed, "You have no intention of stopping anything, no intention of letting anyone try. An enemy of unknown origin and capabilities wasn't enough to dissuade you, the ineffectuality of our weapons wasn't enough to dissuade you, nothing I can say will be enough to dissuade you. The object of your little demonstration here is to dissuade me from trying."

Frank looked back towards Bill, slightly uncomfortable.

"You've known me for years and yet, clearly, you don't know me at all," Bill continued to spew his anger. "I would never have helped in something like this. It isn't setting up a coup in a third world country for gold, Frank, it's setting up the death of the planet so a bunch of old men can profit and be gone before it happens."

The two stood silent for a moment.

"The years have done nothing to change you, Frank. Winning is still more important than the consequences or the collateral damage required to affect it." Bill shook his head. "Well I'm done with them, I'm done with you, and I'm done with this," he finished, barely above a whisper.

Frank sighed and stepped forward. Pulling a keycard from his pocket, he unlocked the door the two stood in front of.

"I'm sorry to hear that, Bill," Frank said and opened the exit. "I'll make arrangements for you to be flown back home in the morning."

Bill turned to leave and paused to look back at Frank. "Your golden boy, the doctor, has no idea what he's messing with here Frank. He's a monkey beating a rock with a stick. Do the smart thing before it's too late."

Frank leaned over to Bill and placed the black keycard into his breast pocket. "This will get you out to the main building," he said with a small smile. "Good to see you again, Bill."

19

Adieu and Goodbye

The purple flower logo was definitely familiar to Beau. "Umm, yeah," he stumbled, "there was a location set up to separate people that had been exposed to the quarantine zone." It wasn't really a lie, just an omission of facts. "That building had a purple flower logo." He looked at Jerich over his cup of coffee as he took a sip. "Why do you ask?"

"Someone I know is there and I," Jerich paused, "want to make sure she's alright."

"That's not a good idea," Beau said, a little too abruptly. "I mean, there's a reason they've been segregated."

"Yes," Jerich said, "but she... doesn't have anyone to check up on her and..." he paused, looking down towards the floor, "I think it would be good for her to know someone was there for her."

Beau could understand that, even sympathize with it, but guiding Jerich to that building was out of the question. It was impossible to say what would happen to him in there. "Jerich, that place would be off limits to everyone, probably even family members. Is she any relation to you?" he asked.

Jerich frowned slightly, "No," he replied, "but I need to make sure she's okay."

Beau retraced the conversation in his mind, "You know she's there, but you don't know where it is?" he asked. "How do you know she's there? Did she call you?"

"Well," Jerich looked pained, "yes," he replied, "but she was groggy and all she kept talking about was this purple flower."

"How do you know her?" Beau asked. "From work?"

Jerich looked up to Beau, "Yes," he answered, "she's new here and doesn't have any family or friends in town."

Beau took another sip of his coffee while he thought, "Well," he started, "I can't take you there, but maybe I can use my ace reporter superpowers to find out if she is alright." Beau tried to make light of the situation.

Jerich wasn't taking the bait, he remained dour. "Well, I wouldn't want you to go to any trouble," he finally said.

"No trouble," Beau said, unsure if that would be true, "just tell me her name and I'll make a few phone calls."

It was Jerich's turn to drink from his coffee. "No," he said after a few sips, "maybe it's best I don't mess up the process. I mean, she'll be released as soon as she's cleared, right?"

"Of course," Beau said with a sureness he didn't feel. "I'll tell you what; if you don't hear from her in a few days, let me know and I'll find out for you."

Jerich nodded, "Thanks," he said, "and sorry for all the trouble."

"Jerich, it's no trouble," Beau replied. "I was serious when I said I want us to be friends, you were right to call me when you did. I'm just sorry I wasn't available to take it, it could have saved us both a lot of time and energy."

Jerich had finished the last sip of his coffee. In the short time it took to drink, he had successfully found out more about this building with the purple flower, and now had to figure out what to do with that information. Before doing anything though, he had to find a tactful way to get rid of Beau. Jerich appreciated all that Beau had done and wanted to do for him, but this was something he couldn't help with. If everything worked out in the end, he would talk to him next week. Stubborn pride had made him hasty in dismissing Beau's aid, maybe he would take him up on his offer to help find employment. Not at the station though, he had been serious about not working there, but Beau would have connections to other possibilities.

Jerich had spent his whole life at the bottom, and he wasn't going to trade one crappy job for another. He wanted a step up, and he wanted to earn it himself. The confidence he was feeling was completely uncharacteristic for him. He wanted to thank Beau for that in some way, but deep down, he knew it was all about the new events that had suddenly unfolded in his life. He had taken two fatal wounds, and survived. His body had taken on some property that allowed him the ability to do so. He knew it had something to do with that creature on the train, its touch had changed him somehow. He didn't understand it all at the moment, but he didn't have to. The girl from that morning was still alive and calling out to him. To him. He was the only person that could save her now, and he wouldn't fail her a second time.

A feeling mounted inside of Jerich, his chest swelled at the thought, and he felt his eyes begin to tear in response. He had purpose, a responsibility to do what others could not. It was so clear to him now, she had also been touched. It bound the two of them somehow, giving him a glimpse into her mind, her dreams. She was being held, she was being victimized and experimented on. They would have her locked up like a prize, secure in the thought that she was unique. They would not see him coming.

Giving his head a shake, Jerich returned to the events around him.

"...watched that like twenty times," Beau finished. "I'm surprised it's available on VHS."

"It's a copy," Jerich said absently.

Beau furrowed his brow, "It's a good one," he said, "that cover looks professional."

"Chinatown," Jerich replied, still not really listening.

Jerich snapped out of his thoughts, "Look, Beau," he began, "I don't mean to be rude, but I've had a long day. I need to lie down for a bit."

"Sure, buddy," Beau said and stood up, "I should get back to the station anyway. I have some editing to get done."

"Thanks again for the coffee," Jerich said.

"Anytime," Beau replied with a smile, stepping forward and chucking Jerich on the shoulder.

Jerich turned and stepped over to the door, carefully opening it so the knob wouldn't fall to the floor. He held it there for his new friend to leave, Beau stopped halfway through the threshold.

"Give me a call next week," Beau said looking back at Jerich, "let me know about your friend."

"Will do," Jerich responded.

Beau finished his exit and Jerich closed the door behind him. He stood there and waited for the last echo of Beau's footsteps in the distance, now knowing exactly what he would do next.

————

Bill sat in the cafeteria, a coffee and a bran muffin once again in front of him. He stared down at them in dismay, this was where he started, where he stepped in. He had affected nothing here, his efforts in vain. His time wasted and the voice in the back of his head telling him he could come back to this had fallen silent. The life he had before, forever changed with the closing of a door that he had refused to walk through. He was destined to return to a ghost of an existence, knowing the doom that would be coming, and the feeling of powerlessness to change it.

His hand, sitting next to his cup on the table, balled into a fist and began shaking in frustration. Bill stared down at it, relaxed his grip and leaned back in the chair for a moment. His coffee sat, taunting him as it cooled off, but he wasn't paying attention. He was mentally preparing for departure, collecting things in his head to be sure he left with everything he wanted to take with him. There were emails and addresses he wanted, he had left abruptly last time, and all threads had been cut before he could remedy that. Security had been beefed up and all data retrieval points had been removed from the computers, even his old beast. It was the information age, and theft was a big concern these days. No worries, he had the ultimate copying tool - good old pen and paper.

The few belongings he had brought could be collected quickly and readied for his morning's departure, the largest being his self-doubt. As much as he wanted to reverse his decision, he knew it would get him nowhere. Staying here would only frustrate him with his inability to fix what was so clearly broken. His best bet was to get as far away from ground zero as possible. He could sell his mountain home and move to the other side of the world. Australia always had a mystery to it that intrigued him, perhaps it was time to pursue that retirement he never really took.

The Ashrealm would follow him eventually, Bill suspected the oceans would only slow it down. By the time Orchid found out what they were dealing with, it would be too late, and there would be no stopping things. Pessimism was not something Bill indulged in, but a good commander knows when to retreat. He could try to talk to his contacts in the various governments around the world, or go public with the information, both of which would likely get him shot. The real reason not to do it though was simple futility. By the time something came of it, any chance to change course would have passed.

Australia would be nice.

Bill crossed his arms in thought and was suddenly reminded of the keycard that lay in his pocket. It had indeed got him back to the main building, no one had asked him anything as he passed. He absently squeezed it between his fingers, ensuring it was still there. Bill thought about what other doors this keycard could open. Frank had entrusted it to him because he knew Bill well enough to know where his loyalties lay, or would lay if there wasn't a much larger picture here. World destruction did much to sway one's motives.

Leaving his coffee and muffin where they sat, Bill stood and headed out the door. His destination in mind, he passed by everyone with a feigned sense of belonging that caused people to believe he was right where he should be. While he was free to roam around these hallways, the end of his journey would require some finesse, and he didn't want any undue attention or questions to tie him up. Passing by door after door, Bill kept an eye on the video surveillance as he continued on. If anyone caught so much as a whiff of what he was up to, it wouldn't take long to find him.

His target fast approaching, Bill quickly eyed his surroundings. A single camera at the end of the corridor was all he had to deal with. It was in a slow pan of the intersection it was monitoring, there would be little time, but Bill wouldn't need much. Feigning to stop and fumble through his pockets in front of the executive bathroom, the camera continued past him and he turned to make his move. Rushing across the hallway, a quick flick of the wrist was met with a green light and the sound of the automated bolt sliding back. Bill pushed and a heavy oak door opened, allowing him to enter. He quickly stepped through and closed it quietly behind him.

Bill glanced around Frank's office for cameras, but there were none, just as he had guessed. Frank was big on surveillance, but only when it came to other people, he valued his own privacy highly. The office was huge, with a big picture window of the river that lay in the distance. It was something that Bill could appreciate, but only at home. At work, you needed to keep your head away from distractions like that and focus. Other than the expensive and large oak desk, a bookshelf and a minibar, there was precious little inside. The desk was to say, loudly, that he was in charge while the rest was an environment to put people at ease. On the desk were a few extravagant knickknacks and an expensively large monitor with a tiny and equally expensive looking keyboard in front of it. This was Bill's destination.

Stepping over to the desk, Bill gave the keyboard a tap and the monitor came to life. On screen was the Orchid logo and the logon screen to get to the desktop. The operating system Frank was using was clearly newer than his old machine, but the basics were always the same. Biometrics were all the rage these days for security, but Bill knew Frank distrusted that technology. It was a sore point for Frank, and something he felt was less secure than the system that already existed. Bill had never pressed the issue, and was currently thankful he hadn't.

Bill typed in Frank's email address, something that wouldn't have changed, but the password would be a different matter. Bill looked around the desk, opened the few drawers that the desk contained. None were locked, either Frank believed the keycard would keep undesirables out, or they had nothing in them worth worrying about. Bill wasn't expecting to find much in there, just a simple reminder. Security would demand passwords be reset constantly and there was only so many passwords you could remember before you would look for an easier method. Reminders were the simplest way.

Each drawer had various objects inside, but nothing of description, nothing that seemed out of place. A notepad was located in a bottom drawer, but it was completely untouched. An expensive pen was also rolling around with it but again, not descriptive enough. Bill looked once again to the desk itself, the knickknacks were just that, trinkets of little value. They may have been passwords in the past, but Frank wouldn't leave something so sensitive in plain view.

Standing up, Bill went over to the bookshelf. His time was growing short, and he would have to abandon this investigation if nothing presented itself soon. He quickly went through the titles, looking for something out of place. While any phrase from any book could be the password, Bill knew Frank would despise having to look it up every day. No, it would be something quick and easy to locate. There, third shelf down, was a book with an Indonesian name, something that Frank would never read. Bill looked back to the computer and typed its title into the password box, spaces and all. Pausing only for a moment, he pressed enter.

And was in.

———————

Laying once again on the bed, Nick stared a hole in the far wall. He was angry, more at rising to take Coleman's bait then his circumstances. Giving Coleman any satisfaction at this stage would spell nothing but more suffering for Nick, and that boat had already left the dock. He rolled over and his eyes circled the room one more time for anything he could use for leverage, but the same taunting emptiness stared back. He exhaled deeply and his thoughts returned to the chain in his neck. Coleman was right, he wouldn't do it and Nick hated him all the more for knowing that.

Through the thick door Nick could hear faint voices conversing. Nothing he could make out, but somehow, he knew they were coming for him. A painfully quiet pause and the door to his room clicked, the electronic bolt unlatched, and the door opened. Two guards stepped in, one carrying a rifle and the other had a sidearm on his hip. Nick quickly calculated the chances of getting that pistol out of its holster before he got shot, and just as quickly dismissed it. The M16 the other soldier was holding would make short work of Nick, and he doubted Coleman's account of his current value here. In short, if Nick made trouble, he would just be going to his destination with a few more holes in him.

After the two guards entered, Dr. Strieber stepped in behind them with a big smile. Nick got the feeling that his day had just gotten inconceivably worse. Closing the door behind him, Strieber approached Nick's bed, not daring to get anywhere near as close as Coleman had. The two guards stayed at the door, watching intently.

"Captain Miller," the doctor said with a smile, his hands clasped behind his back, "you seem very unhappy for some reason."

Nick sat up and stared a hole through Strieber, the doctor's face suddenly dropped its smug grin. He managed to stay put though, and Nick gave him some credit for that.

Strieber regained his composure. "I can empathize, Captain," he began, "I once spent eight months chained to a bed in a room far less hospitable." He wagged his finger, "My country can be most unpleasant when they want to be."

Nick gave a mirthless smile.

"This," Strieber said and gestured around the room, "is a holiday resort by comparison. Westerners have become," he paused, "so soft these days."

Having already fallen for bait once today, Nick had no intention of letting it happen again. He sat stone-faced on the edge of the bed.

"Your xenophobia on the other hand, never loses its edge," Strieber said and pointed at Nick. "For example, I studied English for years before I came here. I've been in the western world long enough to lose most of my accent." He shook his head, "Why, after all this time, would I have a problem with such a trite thing as idioms?"

Nick couldn't hold back a look of confusion.

"Because I need to," Strieber answered for him. "Your people have such a need to feel superior to everyone who isn't one of you. You are distrusting of anyone foreign that you can't set yourself above." He returned his hand to his pocket, but continued to stare. "So to put you all at ease, I manufactured a flaw. It's small, easy to facilitate, and most importantly, drops your guard so I don't spend all day getting simple points across to you."

Nick shifted on the bed, there was a pointed logic to Strieber's ruse.

"But," Strieber put his hands up, "it's been a small price to pay for the benefits you will soon bring me, Captain. This new discovery will make every discomfort, every degradation worth the effort."

It was now Nick's turn to feel uneasy.

"Your resilience to the Ashrealm has been most fortuitous, and surprising I might add," Strieber continued. "I purposely provided you faulty gear on your missions, sent you in with biologically hazardous materials, and even injected you with an experimental serum containing extracted Creosite."

The blood in Nick's face began to drain.

"To be honest, I had very little hope for you, Captain. Anticipating that your corpse would produce a few usable results at best, and yet, here you are." Strieber gestured towards Nick, "Alive and even well, your body teaming with answers to questions I haven't even thought of asking yet."

There was a deadly silence.

Strieber gave a small smile, "Take him to our guest room." he said.

The road was very familiar to Jerich as he walked, he had traveled it thousands of times in the past. Occasionally he would take an alternate route for a change of scenery, but this stretch of pavement was something of an old friend. Every door he passed was like a familiar face covering a mystery. Jerich had never met anyone who lived here, never so much as said hello to a passing stranger, and yet this place felt like home.

Right now it was more barren than it had ever been, no lights and only a stray vehicle here and there as he passed by. Notices on every few doors, telephone poles, and mailboxes everywhere stating that this was a quarantine zone in bold letters followed by 'looters will be prosecuted.' Jerich had no intentions of looting, he was merely a ship passing in the night.

It had taken every stray piece of change he could find in his drawers, cushions, and old clothing to put together enough for the ticket he bought to get here. Jerich had paid for it mostly with pennies, and in spite of the surly attitude he had received in the convenience store, it had felt better than rummaging through the garbage. His life was coasting just above the poverty line, and he would very soon sink under the waves.

He chastised himself again for his terse behavior with Beau's offer of help, his foolish pride was again his folly. He had wanted to call and apologize to Beau since he had left his apartment, and ask him to excuse his poor behavior. As much as he needed his help, Jerich just felt bad about how he had treated him. He felt that, in Beau's departure, he may have thrown away his only chance to do so. It was guilt guiding his thoughts and dragging him down. He would call him next week, excuse his unfair treatment, and offer to pay for coffee with his first check in atonement. Beau would appreciate that, and it was by far Jerich's turn.

He passed through a small park that would save some time. He wasn't in a hurry, but he appreciated the scenery. It had been eerily quiet since he passed the first quarantine notice, but the park seemed doubly so. Jerich felt that if he stopped, he could have heard the leaves falling to the ground. There was no wind to speak of, and the air smelt thinly of smoke. The sky above was gray and dull, bringing with it a numbness that Jerich could feel all around him. Everything in the distance was fog and seemed to blend into one big mass. It was strange walking through here and not hearing the sound of a single bird from the treetops, even his footsteps seemed muted as he walked on.

Glancing to the right, he could just spy the school in the distance. He had passed by numerous times in the past without paying much mind to it, but today he couldn't take his eyes away from it. The gates were locked, the silence and darkened windows gave it a haunted appearance that gave Jerich a chill. Shaking off the feeling, he continued to the edge of the park and crossed the street that would take him to his destination. It was a rural shortcut through a community of prefab houses, not exactly cheap, but not expensive enough to wall off with gates and a guarded entrance. He had received many sour looks as he walked through here in the past, but not a soul was here to challenge him today. He took some satisfaction in that, proving his innocence to himself if no one else. Taking the well-worn path that passed between two houses, he stepped out into the open. Finally witnessing, first-hand, the destruction he had only previously dreamt about.

The road in front of him was dusted with white. It led into a parking lot with mounting piles of sifting ash. Despite the lack of wind, there was a haze that lifted into the air like a fog. Beyond that lay mounds and hills dotted with partial walls and steel beams that jutted into the air. It was all that remained of a building he had spent almost a decade coming to, all that remained of the job he no longer held. Almost unrecognizable in its destruction, the vague borders were lined with yellow tape warning all not to cross it. Sections of it had been broken and lay strewn in the ash like some plastic yellow snake. Though the sky above was gray and overcast. The air just above the remains seemed to be tinged blue, slowly dissipating like a mirage in the desert.

The image in front of Jerich was stationary and lifeless, nothing stirred. Not a sound above the slight thrum in his ears could be heard. He didn't know what he had expected coming here, his dreams far more animated than the wasteland he was now looking at. The foreign feeling that had besieged him was however intact, climbing over him like a cold fear. Despite the numbness that spread to his very skin, he could feel a sheen of sweat building as he walked closer. Ahead was more ash, more white sifting silt that had already begun to squish under his feet as he continued on. His body began to heat up, his skin growing more clammy as the yellow tape drew nearer and feebly barred entrance to the carnage.

The smell of smoke in the air had grown heavy and was now mixed with something he couldn't define, metallic and acrid, almost burning his lungs as he breathed. Continuing to the imaginary barrier of tape, he passed through.

Nothing had changed of course, the tape was simply a plastic scarecrow. Jerich continued into the skeletal remains of the once monolithic building of retail achievement, the ground beneath him nothing but white powder. Despite the heat and perspiration, his body had begun to feel better. A euphoria began to take ahold of him, not unlike the feeling he would get after an extended jog to reach this very location when he was running late. He progressed further inwards, pushing to his rough estimation of the place he stood in his dream. The ill-fated bathroom that rose over a sea of black and foreign shapes, staring at him from a distance. What awaited him could be no different from what lay before, but his desire to stand there was almost palpable.

Passing through the imaginary aisles as he continued on, he could place where the faces he had come to know would be. A desk there, a register here, the long walk to the back lunchroom that Jerich would spend as little time as possible in. He preferred to eat outside, take his breaks outside, anything to be outside at all and away from the drudgery of his job. It hadn't been a hard or particularly difficult vocation, it was always the repetition and oppression of upper management as they tried to get the most for their money that made it unbearable. Jerich understood the need to push; minimum wage laborers rarely gave their all, most rarely gave a damn. It was a philosophy he couldn't understand, the longest days were the ones with nothing to do. Jerich just wanted his eight hours done with so he could get out and go home, the fastest way to make that happen was to keep busy. This attitude did little to stem the tirades and belittling of his efforts though, it was just implicitly assumed you weren't pulling your weight.

All that was behind him now though, and it was a small comfort to him that this part of his life was over. He felt better, almost emancipated as he stepped through the ashes. Crushing his old life beneath his feet as he strode to a better one. Ahead of him he could almost make out the walls of his bathroom solace, it was not intact, despite his dream. Stepping up to what was left of its threshold, he turned and viewed the surroundings. They were nothing like the dark nightmare he remembered. He hadn't really expected them to be, but still hoped to recognize some small similarity, something to tell him he wasn't crazy.

Stepping through what was left of the doorway, he turned around, hoping perhaps something would change. It didn't of course, the pale dust and destruction where exactly as they had been. Exhaling a sigh, Jerich sat down in the white beneath him and stared into the distance. His goal here was not recreation, but the disappointment was hard to mask from himself. Digging his hand into the silt beneath him, he picked up what he could and let it sift through his fingers. It drifted slowly down, dispersing, leaving a trail of blue haze as it thinned. Absently, Jerich continued doing so as he waited, watching in wonder at the blue shimmer between the particles.

The ash had been warm in his hand, but as he continued to immerse his skin in it, he noted a tingling in his palm. It wasn't exactly unpleasant, just foreign, and he brought his hand up to get a better view of it. The white surface looked just like a hand, he used the other to brush the silt from it, but nothing had changed. He turned it over to look at the other side. More white, but now there were also dots of blue glowing slightly on the surface. Jerich looked closer and realized this was the hand he had injured earlier with the mirror. The areas where the glass had entered his skin were what was glowing blue. Suddenly alarmed that the ash could be entering his system through his wounds, he quickly wiped his hand off on his pants. Brushing at it a few times with the other one for good measure.

Looking back at where the puncture wounds should be, he found nothing but skin. Pristine and unnoticeably different from the rest in any way. Jumping up, he took his hoodie off and looked down to the hole in his chest. It had almost completely healed. Falling back down to his knees, Jerich scooped up some more ash and began to wash the wound with it. The tingling sensation returned as he rubbed himself down with the white silt, again it wasn't unpleasant, but definitely noticeable. After repeated applications, Jerich allowed himself a look.

The wound was completely gone.

Jerich stared at the ash all around him, he had no explanation for what he was witnessing here except to say that it was real. He smiled to himself, happy to know he wasn't crazy after all. Looking off in the distance, he could see a police car speeding down the road, its lights and siren blaring. A white van was following closely behind as it approached.

Everything was working out perfectly.

20

Revolution

The gurney Nick was handcuffed to rattled along down the corridor. The doctor walked ahead, leaving one guard to push and one guard to train his rifle on their passenger. The hallways were nondescript except for the purple flower logo, dozens of closed and presumably locked doors passed by as they sped on to their destination. Nick didn't know where they were going, but he didn't have to. It was what was waiting for him there that was the concern.

The quick turns made Nick grab hold of the railings he was cuffed to, his driver clearly new at jockeying a wheeled bed through a building. They had banged off of walls and door frames on the journey, each time rattling the teeth in Nick's head. He would have preferred walking, but it seemed he was destined to stay in his horizontal prison for a while longer. Finally reaching a guarded sentry post, they were admitted through without a word. Strieber turned to Nick and gave him a small, insulting smile as they entered. Nick was overcome with the desire to remove that grin with his fist, perhaps he would get his chance before the end.

Opening a door, Nick was pushed into a room divided by a glass wall. It seemed more for security than segregation or contagion, the glass was very thick and outlined with a heavy steel frame. In the center was a thick metal door with a numbered padlock barring entrance. Inside, Nick could see a bed, the outline of someone covered up in blankets lay on it. Pushing the gurney to the side wall, the second guard trained his rifle on Nick. The first secured the gurney with the same locks that were on the wall of Nick's room. Satisfied with his work, the first guard stepped away, and the second lowered his rifle in response. Never taking his eyes from their prisoner.

Nick's hopes began to dwindle, his inner voice giving way to the reality that was surrounding him. The doctor was looking into the glassed room, smiling and pressing his hand to its clear surface. He was muttering something in German that Nick didn't understand, but he doubted he wanted to know at this point. Glancing around the room, it was almost completely empty save for a crash cart that was covered in precariously placed binders. His hopes for a makeshift weapon of some kind had been extinguished, proximity was all he had left. If someone got close, and Nick got lucky, he may at least take a few of these bastards with him.

Strieber finally turned around, "Captain," he said, "you are the latest member in an elite club. Not many have what it takes to make it this far, you should feel privileged." He stepped closer to Nick with his hands clasped behind his back. "Though, I must inform you," he gave Nick a sly look, "none have ever left here."

It was scare tactics, Nick knew this, but they were definitely doing their job.

Strieber smiled, "I don't expect that to change now, but," he raised a finger, "I foster hope for you, Captain." Turning, he walked back towards the window. "I do believe there is something different about you, something that will finally break through here, and allow us to move forward with our studies." Again he pressed his hand to the glass. "All that came before you couldn't measure up, couldn't fulfill the needs this discovery required. Some lasted an hour, many only minutes."

Nick could feels his hands sweating in his clenched fists.

Stepping away from the window, Strieber faced Nick once again. "Captain, we have a chance to move the human race forward. A chance to change it in a way not possible through traditional evolution. The answer," he pointed to the window, "is on the other side of that glass. But, like all great discoveries, it comes at a cost."

'Here it comes,' Thought Nick.

"That cost is fuel, and that," Strieber stepped right up to Nick's bed, "is where you come in." His smile was chilling to the bone. "You see, it is like keeping a fire burning. In order to continue to benefit, you must maintain a balance. Take too much and it dies, take too little and it spreads, but it will always need to be fed in order to survive." He leaned down to look directly at Nick. "Please understand that your contribution here will pave the road for advancements we can only dream of right now. Your sacrifice, will be remembered."

Nick jumped up and grabbed the doctor's throat, bringing his other hand up to squeeze the life from him. Flipping the doctor to the bed so he could bear down on his work, Nick leaned in with his shoulders for leverage. The doctor's face was first alarmed, then quickly covered by fear. Nick smiled down upon him with a malice he had been saving for another. Strieber feebly pawed at the arms holding him down, but Nick's superior strength and training kept the doctor from moving. Tightening his grip, Nick grunted with rage and spit flew from his mouth down onto Strieber, though the doctor took no notice. Both of their faces were red with exertion, and Nick felt satisfaction in the thought that he may at least take this German prick with him.

White spots suddenly clouded Nick's vision and the world went dark. He felt his teeth rattle in response to a blow to the back of his head. Nick rolled to one side and felt his body slip to the floor. His arm, still chained to the railing, cracked in response to the sudden weight and Nick knew at once it had been broken. The pain was severe and sharp as it stabbed at his body, he shouted incomprehensibly as he instinctively tried to get back up. Another blow to the center of his shoulders sent him back to the ground, this time he stayed there.

Beside him, he could feel the doctor moving from the bed. He was coughing and cursing in German as he sat up. Nick could feel his arm was out of its socket, the pain continued to pump into his brain. The doctor stood up, continuing to cough.

"Get him ready," Strieber sputtered from somewhere far away, "I need to make a call. There is at least one other who will want to watch this."

It was the last thing Nick heard before he passed out.

———

The documents were all encrypted, but the password was foolishly the same, Bill shook his head as he continued reading. This violated the very basics of security, but it was clear that Frank was suffering from a feeling of superiority. It was a sickness that many leaders suffered from eventually; a lack of healthy paranoia to keep them in line. Bill had managed to avoid that malady during his stay here, but in the end he hadn't been paranoid enough. His wife and daughter had been killed due to his position at this company all the same.

The map he was currently looking at was very familiar to him, he had made it. It was his meticulous mapping of the spread of the Ashrealm with a few new annotations. The additions detailed a new number Bill didn't recognize the acronym for, SARA. It had no correlation to anything he had calculated, but the highest numbers seemed to be in commercial regions. He continued on to the next page hoping for an explanation.

Another map, this one of the entire world. Large red swaths paved through third-world countries accompanied by exponentially high SARA values. A graph followed the map, it detailed an up-curving line of increasing SARA numbers over the time in months. Whatever SARA was, it was clearly valuable and something Orchid was planning to act upon within the next few weeks. Bill flipped to the next page, an x-ray of a broken arm with several long spikes of some nature drove into the bone. There were circles and annotations in what appeared to be German. Bill could read the language, but the handwriting was atrocious, and what little he could pull from the recognizable text said little. He turned the page, another x-ray. This one looking much like the first but with the spikes removed and the fracture almost completely healed. The date was on both charts, they were mere hours apart.

If this is what Strieber was referring to when he had mentioned medical applications, Bill had to agree with him. He was no doctor but, if this was accurate, it would change medicine as the world knew it. Even the holes where the spikes had been were practically nonexistent. Bill could only account for what was on the two charts in front of him, he had not been an eye witness, but there would be little benefit in faking something like this. A demonstration would be required to prove it. Bill flipped to the next page.

A list of names took up this page, each had a matrix of numbers next to it. Dates, times, duration, and an estimated SARA value. The duration seemed to relate directly to the SARA number, the higher the SARA, the higher the duration. None of the names on the list were repeated except for the pseudonym, John Doe followed by a number. Whatever group of people this list contained, some had chosen to stay anonymous. It could be a test group, SARA could be the codename for an experimental drug based on the charts from the previous pages. Bill didn't know, and certainly couldn't ask at this point, he would have to read on and hope for illumination.

A knock came from the door, startling Bill. Frozen for a moment, he hoped that whoever it was would go away. Another knock, this one mechanical and the door swung open. From the other side, two armed men rushed in and trained their rifles on Bill who raised his arms in response. He silently cursed himself for not pulling the plug on the terminal in front of him.

Murphy strode through the door and finally lit the cigar that usually only dangled from his mouth with a silver lighter. Flicking it closed with his wrist, he inhaled the smoke deeply. Pulling it from his mouth, he smiled, "Mr. Wyburn, someone would like to have a word with you," he said and returned the cigar to its place. He gestured towards the door.

Bill said nothing, but stood up and headed for the exit, waving his hand at the cigar smoke that he had to walk through to do so. Leaving the room, two more armed guards stood to his right, blocking the way. Bill turned left and began to walk, Murphy caught up to him in a few strides, but kept a pace behind him.

"So, Lawrence," Bill said, "as one ruthless bastard to another, what do you think the chances the world will survive what Orchid and Dr. Strieber have in store for it?"

There was a pause, and Bill heard Murphy exhale heavily. "The thing is Mr. Wyburn..." Murphy replied

"Call me Bill."

"Bill..." Murphy allowed, "I don't make those calls. I don't like to make those calls, and I get paid not to think about them. It's a luxury I can afford here because the ruthless bastards in charge do it better than I can."

Bill nodded, "Sure," he said, "I can appreciate the need to stay focused, but even the most well-oiled and finely-tuned locomotive can't stop on a dime. What happens when the train runs out of track?"

There was another pause, "Orchid is a very large train these days, Bill," Murphy responded, "with many tracks available to it. We're global," an exhale, "worldwide," he purposely stretched out the last word for emphasis. "But," another pause, "assuming that all goes to shit, I will do what I always do." Another exhale. "Survive."

This conversation was not going in the direction Bill was hoping for, they turned down the only hallway available to them and were heading for a set of very large double doors.

"I meant what I said about wanting to work together," Murphy said from behind, "and I still hope we get the chance to." Leaning forward, Murphy opened both doors. Pulling the cigar from his mouth, he gestured inwards with it.

Bill gave Murphy an appraising look and then entered the large room.

"Bill..." came a voice.

Bill looked across the room and located the source.

"So good to see you again," said Keating.

———

The room was small and almost completely unlike the dream that Jerich had. There was a small bed that was bolted to the wall, and a nightstand with a lamp on it. Above the bed was a lighted chart holder that was currently off, but other than that, the room was barren. His only light of hope lay on the wall through the window - a purple flower logo.

The ride here had been completely uneventful, his apprehension doubly so. A police officer asked him what he was doing there, and he gave them mostly truthful information. It was his previous place of employment, and he wanted to see first hand what had happened to it. The name he gave the officer was not his own, but if it was checked on, belonged to someone that had indeed worked there. The officer explained to him that he was a quarantine zone, that he would have passed dozens of notices telling him so, and that he would have to be detained until further notice due to his possible contagion.

Jerich had played as dumb as he could, but remained compliant and concerned for his own welfare. He was not handcuffed, nor read his rights. Instead, the officer escorted him to the rear of the white van that had been trailing the police car. The driver of the van had followed the two and opened the door for Jerich to enter who did so with no complaints. The officer and the driver exchanged a mild look of curiosity before closing the door, but Jerich didn't care. This was his ticket, this was where he was meant to be.

And here he was.

The room was white painted brick and smelled faintly of antiseptic. By all accounts, a very official feeling building of medical persuasion to Jerich's mind. He studied more intently, looking for possible escape routes, but unless he could find some way to shrink himself, the door was the only real exit. A camera was mounted over it, sweeping the room with its single red eye. That may be a problem when it came to leave, but Jerich felt overcome with conviction. This is exactly what he was supposed to be doing.

He reached his hands into his pockets and squeezed, they were filled with ash. His compliance had put both of his captors at ease and neither had thought to search him. Pockets of ash would not likely cause suspicion, but Jerich was thankful for their carelessness all the same. He wasn't sure it would have the same effect outside of the quarantine zone, but he hoped he wouldn't need to test the theory. Jerich hadn't taken the time to test the limits of his new found abilities, but they had saved him from fatal situations already. He would have to trust in himself now.

Pulling his hands back out of his pockets, he rubbed them together so that the ash that clung there covered his skin. He began to pace the room, testing to see if the camera followed him, it did not. That meant it was automated and hopefully unmanned at the moment. He expected some kind of welcome, likely an assistant, to come and tell him that someone would be with him shortly. Jerich wanted to wait for that initial contact before putting his plan into action.

As if by providence, a knock emitted from the door. A man wearing a face mask and a plastic shield walked in with a clipboard in his hand. He was covered head to toe in disposable blue clothing with no exposed skin. The latex gloves he wore made it easy for him to hold the pen he was jiggling back and forth between his thumb and finger.

Walking to the center of the room, the man finally looked up. "Sir," he said, "the doctor will be with you shortly, but I need you to fill out this form before he arrives." The clipboard and pen were offered to Jerich who took them, the man nodded in response and turned to leave.

"How long will that be?" Jerich squeezed in before the man had managed to get out the door.

He turned around to look, gave a thumbs up and shut the door without saying anything more. The loud knock sounded again which could only mean a heavy bolt. Jerich turned around long enough to toss the clipboard and pen onto the bed.

Looking back up to the camera, Jerich hoped he was right about it being unmanned and walked over to stand directly beneath it. He looked up and tried to gauge just how much it couldn't see. By his best guess, there was a foot of space on either side of the door that was out of view. That would be enough to continue with his plan.

Turning around to face the wall, Jerich dug both hands through the silt in his pockets one final time, pulled them back out and began to punch the concrete.

There was a soft hissing in the room. First far off, then growing more incessant, and now punctuated with a beep. The air was stale and faintly smelled of smoke, a slight hint of disinfectant pierced through and Nick opened his eyes. The room was hazy and extremely bright. It seemed like he was looking at it through a camera lens, the edges all warping and fuzzy. His face was numb, but somehow felt both cold and wet, he shivered slightly like a man with a fever. Turning his head to the side, his sight blurred and stretched as it moved, taking a few seconds to settle down when he stopped. The white wall he now stared at seemed to ripple slightly as his eyes focused on different parts of it. His mouth felt like it was full of cotton, his hearing was dulled and distant. He was drugged, his body somehow far away.

The moments that brought him here came back in a flash and he moaned at the thought of his arm. He looked down at the injured appendage. It had been set, the white fabric of a sling crept up from under the sheet that covered him and disappeared around his neck. He tried to move his good arm over to inspect it, but it was suddenly very heavy, like his eyelids. All his body wanted to do was go back to sleep, but Nick knew he was in trouble. A spike of adrenaline surged through him and he forced his arm up to push the sheet off of his chest with a grunt.

Overhead a crackle sounded, followed by a sudden rush of sound, "Captain Miller?" a voice said. "Captain Miller, can you hear me?"

Nick focused, the accent gave away who was speaking. Nick's first instinct was to curse him, but all that came out was an indecipherable garble of sounds. They were very clear and distinct insults that Nick was completely failing to deliver, and he grunted again in anger.

"Captain," the voice said again, "I want you to understand that this isn't personal. Your attack earlier tells me that you think, somehow, this has all been orchestrated just for your torment and death."

Nick managed another grunt.

The voice continued, "I assure you, this is not the case. You still don't appreciate the significance you will make here. The advances that your life will offer to society, the world. The human race will never be the same after this."

Shaking his head, Nick closed his eyes and concentrated on clearing his mind.

There was some muttering through the speaker followed by a silence. The room grew blissfully quiet again, the sound of what Nick recognized now as a respirator and a heart monitor took center stage. He turned his head in its direction. There was a proper bed there, a small figure lay under the blue blankets that were heaped on top. Nick looked down to the gurney he was on. Neither he, nor it were chained to anything. The thought of escape took hold of him again and he managed to throw the rest of sheet off and onto the floor.

The crackle sound returned to the room, but then grew silent again.

It took every ounce of strength he had, but Nick managed to sit up and throw his legs off the side of the bed. He didn't dare attempt to stand, not yet anyway. Looking into the direction of the voice, he realized he was now on the other side of the glass partition - looking out. Through the window he could see the doctor standing in plain view, a handset next to his face. Looking away, he glanced over to the other bed, now having a clearer view of the person in it.

Again a crackling, "This is why you are here, Captain." the doctor said. "She is the key to everything."

Nick looked closer, a young girl without hair lay under the sheets. She was facing away from him, but Nick could see her skin was a pale gray and flaking off in large pieces. She was bone thin from what he could tell and her one exposed arm was black like it had been burnt in a fire.

Strieber continued, "She contains secrets that we can only begin to understand, secrets that can alter life."

Nick suddenly found his voice, "She's just a little girl." he managed. His voice was scratchy and weak.

"No, Captain," the doctor said, obviously able to hear him, "she is so much more."

"You fucking animal," Nick said, much stronger this time.

There was silence.

Nick slipped off the bed and felt his feet hit the floor, his anger and determination keeping him upright. Stepping slowly over to the bed, Nick walked to the other side so he could see the girl's face. Her eyes were closed, her skin completely hairless. He looked down at her blackened arm and reached out in sympathy, stopping just short of touching her.

"What have you bastards done?" Nick hissed. He turned to face the glass, Strieber was on the other side. He walked purposefully towards him. "What have you done!" this time a growl of anger.

"Captain," the doctor said, a look of fear in his face despite the transparent wall. "That little girl has been the cause of your entire team's demise. She has destroyed every one, consumed them to live."

Nick was now standing directly on the other side of the glass, staring into the doctor's face. In the background, Nick could see others in the room. Coleman was among them, but Nick had given up caring at this point. He looked back into the doctor's eyes and shook his head. "You infected her with something, and now you want to infect me with it so you can pull me apart and see what happened," he said with a snarl.

"No, Captain," Strieber said with a shake of his head, "I'm afraid it's more complicated than that." He looked past Nick to the bed behind him.

Nick turned around. The girl was now sitting up, her head was pointed down. He could see her torso now, there were scars and stitches across it. Large flakes slowly fell from her body to the blankets below as she started to rock slightly. Nick could feel a thrum in the air around him, a pressure began to build in his ears.

The girls head shot up to face Nick, her eyes were bright blue orbs that seemed to pierce his very soul.

————

Initially, each punch had been painful as Jerich had hammered at the wall. Blood from his hands had been slowly caking it and trickling down as he continued. Soon though, his fists became numb, the concrete had begun to break under his blows. His fists were white from the dust and had begun to swell, each hit seemed to make them grow bigger.

Once he had reached the metal that the concrete covered, Jerich had to move down and begin anew. The pile on the floor was increasing as he continued his assault. After his second time reaching metal, he pulled his hands away for closer inspection. They were swollen up to half the size of a boxing glove. Each fist was a mass of concrete and blood, he could see a slight blue glow emitting from them if he looked close enough. Giving a very amateur guess, he believed that one more pass of concrete to steel should cover what he needed to do.

Proceeding to pound out another hole in the wall, Jerich felt his lungs burning with the effort. He was getting thirsty and his arms were in dire need of a rest. Sitting down in front of the door, Jerich felt his hands shaking with the trauma he had just put them through. He didn't know how long this would last, so he would have to act soon, but right now, he needed a break.

His heavy breathing was the only thing he could hear in the room other than the faint hum of the lights over his head. He had no idea what he would do when he got out, but staying here was not an option. He thought back to his dream, her dream, he wasn't sure who it belonged to at this point. The room she had been in, a bright light, a doctor, the flower logo and... a glass wall? There was a glass wall in the room. In his dream, it was where the doctor had come from, passed through it like a ghost. No, he didn't dream of that. Where did the glass wall come from? Was he just imagining this?

Jerich shook his head, it was too late to have second thoughts about this. He stood up and turned to face the door, a metal thing with a heavy handle. He lifted his fist, looked at it, looked back to the handle and took a step back. His hands were completely numb right now, but self preservation struck the fear of pain into him all the same. Pausing only for a moment, he stepped forward and drove his fist into the handle as hard as he could.

An explosion of white and bits of concrete erupted from the door in front of him and Jerich squinted to avoid getting any in his eyes. Shaking his head, he stepped back to see what damage he had managed to inflict. The door handle was bent in but still there. He looked at his fist again, a large chunk of it had broken free and an indent now remained. Looking back to the door, he stepped forward and drove what remained into the handle once again.

Another puff of white, this time accompanied with a sudden pain that shot through him like lightning. Jerich grunted and fell to his knees. Looking at his fist, he saw a rush of blood that was now pouring out. Quickly he tried to put it into his pocket but his hand was now too big to fit. Lying down on his back, Jerich placed his injured hand under its opening to let the ash spill out and onto it. Creeping at barely a dribble, he rolled slightly in its direction to let gravity help out. His fist was now covered in a mound of ash.

The blood was still gushing, washing away the first of the falling ash, but it quickly subsided as more poured out. The stabbing pain began to diminish quickly, Jerich's heavy breathing following it. He wanted to rub the ash into the wound but dared not move and chance the pain's return. Stealing a glance at the door, he was discouraged to note the handle was still there. Though he could simply start pounding into the wall again, he doubted the door or the noise would go unnoticed for long. Looking down to his other hand, he realized it was probably his last shot at doing things the easy way.

Daring to stay on the ground for a few more moments, Jerich finally stood up. The bleeding had stopped on his broken hand, but a dull pain remained, his off hand would have to be his saving grace. Stepping forward, he heard a loud knock at the door and froze in his tracks. The broken handle jiggled slightly and the door slowly opened, Jerich backed off to allow its advance.

Gravity pulling the door the rest of the way open, Jerich looked through to see a confused man dressed in a doctor's coat. He was holding a clipboard in one hand and what was left of the door handle in the other. He stared slack-jawed into the room.

Jerich lunged forward and made a clumsy swing for the man's face. He caught him lightly on the chin with what Jerich was sure wouldn't be enough momentum.

The clipboard loudly clattered to the floor, the doctor quickly followed and bounced unconscious.

21

Speaking with the Devil

Bill stared across the room, the sight of Keating freezing him in his tracks. He hadn't seen the man since he had left the shop all those years ago. Even then it was a phone call with a few chosen expletives followed by a broken cell. Initially afraid Keating would have him killed off, Bill had fled the country. The plan was to stay with a few good friends he had made in his career until he could properly assess the situation.

He noted a few more wrinkles and less hair, but Bill made no mistake, the devil was standing before him. Fighting off the urge to curse, Bill kept his composure.

"Gerald," Bill said, completely without emotion.

"Have a seat," Keating said and gestured towards a large chair on the other side of a huge desk. He turned towards the minibar, threw some ice into a tumbler and poured himself something brown from an expensive decanter. Next to him was a couch and a very large television on the wall.

Bill looked over to the chair and desk. The expensive oak surface held a laptop that was powered on and logged in to the network. Bill felt his palms begin to sweat. Obviously Keating had been shadowing him on Frank's computer and wanted to rub Bill's nose in it. Staring for a moment, Bill shook his head and did as he was asked. Leaning back in the chair, he deliberately avoided looking at the screen.

Keating turned around with three fingers of something Bill knew would be completely overpriced. The man loved the good life, and lived it every chance he got. Instead of coming over to sit down, Keating took a sip of his drink and slipped a hand into his pocket.

"Drink?" Keating said and raised the glass in Bill's direction.

Bill shook his head, but said nothing.

"Bill," Keating began, "I know there's a lot you would like to say to me at the moment, and none of it very pleasant. But before you entertain that notion, I'd like you to read what's on the laptop in front of you."

Bill finally looked over at the screen, an email client was opened and a list of exchanges could be seen queued up. He could tell by the software and operating system that this was from the old setup used by the Shop. The same one that the computer in his small office was still using.

"What do you want me to find here, Gerald?" Bill asked, looking at him from across the room.

"The answers you've been looking for, Bill," replied Keating, following it with a sip from his glass.

Bill looked back to the screen, at the top was an email to the man who stood patiently waiting. This must be his personal computer, his account, his emails. The first was dated almost a year before his family was murdered. Clicking it, Bill read a correspondence from the government faction he had been tasked to help. It would prove to be the last operation he would facilitate at the Shop, though he didn't know that at the time. It would also be the operation that got his family killed. The email was simple greeting and not ominous in the slightest, he had read many just like it in the past.

"I don't get it, Gerald," Bill said, glancing up to Keating, "what am I looking for?"

Keating shook his head, "Just keep reading." he said.

Bill flipped through the first batch of emails, they were all standard operations. Government is trouble, insurgents are invading, the back and forth of reward for services rendered, the research on the situation. Maps and charts as well as detailed photos were attached to these emails. Most of this information came to Bill completely unaltered and he was already acquainted with almost every word he had read so far.

"Gerald," Bill said and shook his head, "it hasn't been that long. I am painfully familiar with what I'm reading here."

"Indulge me one last time, Bill," Keating said and turned to freshen up his drink.

Returning to the laptop, Bill sighed and moved on to the next email. This one was from Frank. It was a detailed breakdown of the insurgents, their equipment, agenda, and most importantly, their value to the Shop. Frank had taken it upon himself to make contact, something that was well above his pay-grade at the time. Included was a list of things the insurgents agreed to if the Shop agreed not to interfere. Reading through the list of assets, it was clear that the insurgents would sweep through and overthrow the ruling body with ease.

This was information that Bill had never seen before. It would have made little difference in his decision to support the existing government though. Insurgents rarely followed through with their promises, well-armed insurgents doubly so, and the Shop providing zero support to them would only fortify this. What they offered the Shop was irrelevant, it would never be fulfilled.

Frank, on the other hand, failed to see things that way. The following emails were a back and forth between himself and his contact within the insurgents. None of these were addressed to Keating, they had clearly been copied from Frank's account and added here on purpose. Bill had long understood that privacy within the Shop was only a smokescreen to weed out undesirables. Though never privy to this side of the mirror, he expected his email and actions to be spied upon, and never allowed either to be questionable.

Bill continued through the increased intensity of exchange. Each time Frank promising cooperation was just around the corner, but never actually reaching there. Finally, the actions of the Shop begin and a series of death threats from the insurgents begin to enter Frank's inbox. At first Frank doesn't respond, but when a picture of Frank getting on a plane in their country appears in his email, he takes action.

Frank had never been sent over there, not by the Shop anyway. Bill remembered Frank leaving for a few days for his father's funeral, but to his knowledge, that had been in-country. He couldn't remember the exact date, but without looking, it was glaringly obvious that he'd used it for cover. Bill read on.

Frank's response to the picture came a few days after it had arrived. His message was short and cryptic: 'Package delivered, promise kept.' It said nothing, but no further emails were available after that.

Looking up from the screen Bill found Keating leaning on a table and flipping through a folder. "So Frank gave the insurgents something to keep them from fulfilling their promise. Flying over and physically giving it to them. Why would he do that, what the hell would it have been?" he said with a shake of his head.

Keating stood, picked up the folder he was looking at and walked over to the desk. Dropping in front of Bill, he gave it a slight look of disdain and turned back to his drink. Bill's suspicions grew as he picked up the folder. Flipping it open, he saw the first page.

It was a photo of his wife and daughter out front of her school, followed by a list of places they frequented and the time they would most likely be there. A red circle was around both of their faces, their names written next to them in the same red pen. It was Frank's handwriting.

Bill was overcome with shock, his hands began to shake and he dropped the folder to the desk. His chest began to hitch, and tears were forming in his eyes. His eyes shifting back and forth as he thought back, remembering the car bomb that took their lives, remembering the video that the insurgents had sent, remembering the pain and rage that had consumed him. He stared down at the folder in front of him as a single tear fell from his eye.

"Did you want that drink now?" Keating offered in a quiet tone.

Rubbing his eyes, Bill nodded, "Yeah," he said after pulling his hands away, "I believe I do."

Keating set to work pouring another drink as Bill composed himself. Turning around, Keating walked over and handed Bill the tumbler, finally sitting down across from him.

Bill took a healthy swallow from his drink, it may have been overpriced, but it was damn good. Letting the burn subside, he finally asked, "How long have you known?"

"It took a while to put things together," Keating said and took a sip from his own glass, "but by then you were in South America, hiding out."

Bill smiled slightly in spite of himself, then shook his head. "I suppose it was foolish to think I could vanish," he muttered.

"I gave it to you Bill," Keating said, "just like I've given you all that information."

Bill stared at Keating for a long moment, "Information?"

"Yes, Bill," Keating answered, "Sviato Richter died in an Israeli prison years ago, I was the one leaking the data to you."

Sviato's appearance in Bill's world did seem fortuitous, even back then, but the intelligence was solid. Letting sleeping dogs lie just seemed more beneficial, and Bill needed the distraction. But now bigger questions were rising in his mind.

"Why would you do that?" Bill asked levelly.

"Because I wanted you back, Bill," Keating said, leaning across the desk and pointing with his drink. "You're the best goddamned man for the job, your pedigree is without question." He paused, "You're a ruthless bastard, and above all else, I trust you."

"Then why," Bill looked directly into Keating's eyes, "did you give my job to the bastard that killed my family?" his voice level, but full of accusation.

Keating leaned back and set his drink on the desk in front of him, looking down at it in dismay. "I had nothing to do with it, Bill," he said to the desk. "By the time I had put the pieces together we had become a corporation with investors. Once they were in place, I became just one more voice in a choir. A bigger voice, granted, but I no longer have the power to veto anything over the board. Frank had proven his ability to make money for the Shop, by then rechristened Orchid, with the help of Dr. Strieber. The investors would have nothing to do with removing him."

Bill stared, but said nothing.

"The only way I can replace him is by giving them someone better, someone with a proven track record." Keating said, picking up his drink. "That's you, Bill," he pointed the drink in Bill's direction again and then took a sip.

Bill looked down into his glass and contemplated that notion. "I don't know if I'm still the man for this job, Gerald. Even if I were, Frank has it so fubared that I'm not sure I could bring it back."

Keating set his glass down again, "I have faith in you, Bill. You have pulled a greater miracle from your ass on more than one occasion."

Bill looked back across to Keating, "Gerald, I just came from Frank's office, I read his notes. I already know the origins of this new element he is hocking to the investors. It's not some element that science conveniently missed, it's an unknown bacteria from a meteor that landed. It's alien to this planet, Gerald. Changing or destroying everything we know, and it's spreading. You can't just throw a blanket over this."

Keating shook his head, "Bill," he started, "we already know how to end this. Dr. Strieber was kind enough to provide the solution. All we need to do now is convince the board to remove Frank, and put you in his place." Keating picked up his drink and brought it to his face. "That shouldn't be too hard, just tell them what you know. What you have witnessed." He drained the glass set it down, "They're investors, not idiots, Bill. A dead planet is no good to anyone."

"Gerald," Bill began, "Strieber's assessment of the situation is clouded by his own ambitions. I'm not convinced dropping a bomb will solve anything."

"That's why we're dropping a dozen," Keating said with a nod. "We've seen first hand that the bacteria can't survive outside of its own ecosystem, thinning it out will kill it dead." He pointed his finger, "His ambitions be damned."

"Gerald, we have to give this some more thought here before we act," Bill said with trepidation.

"It's already in the pipe, Bill," Keating said, "very shortly this will all be over."

———

The air around Nick seemed electric. Gravity pressed down on him, holding him in place. On the bed, the fragile little girl had become a bright star. Her skin turning blue, her eyes growing brighter, the room becoming a blinding explosion that threatened to take his sight. His body burned, ripples of pain shot up and down as he stood motionless and unable to breathe. Inside, he felt he was being torn apart, piece by piece.

The crackle of the speaker overhead sounded again. Despite the heavy thrum, Nick could hear Strieber distinctly.

"Captain, I'd like you to meet Sara," the doctor's voice was reverent as he spoke her name. "She will take care of you now, I have matters to attend to."

Every fiber in Nick's body resisted whatever was happening to him, his fear and anger consumed him. Despite the phenomenon he was witnessing only a few feet away, he would fight defeat to the bitter end. His eyes were focused on the orbs in front of him, her face now seemed angelic somehow. She seemed to stare deep into him, searching him for something.

Nick's head thrust upwards and he was staring at the ceiling. The light danced across its surface and the fluorescent bulbs flickered. He could feel his body tightening, compressing and becoming heavier. A shock ripped through his body and he opened his mouth to scream. A high-pitched noise came from deep inside him, and a blue beam shot from his mouth, flying upwards. Nick's body convulsed, he could feel his arms stretch out from his sides, his legs push down into the floor.

His eyesight faded to pure blue, his mind struggled to hold on. Slowly his energy was leaving him, his body beginning to calm. The world around him blotting out into light and silence. His consciousness was fading, his reality, his mind quickly following it. A serene wholeness took ahold of him, and he suddenly felt light, his pain and suffering slowly disappearing. The bright light surrounding him faded to pitch black.

The darkness was nothing, the darkness was empty. There was a peace in the absence of everything. To stay and exist in the nonexistence was all, and all was consuming. The darkness surrounded, the darkness complete, except for a light in the distance. Dim and far, but approaching quickly. A comet, burning brightly in a sea of black. Burning, approaching, burning, approaching, burning, burning, awakening.

———

The doctor's body lay on the floor in front of Jerich as he stood over it dumbfounded. He hadn't planned on any of this, the moment just overtook him, and he went with it. Jerich had not been in a brawl since his childhood schoolyard, back then he had won by a fluke shot as well. Glancing up and down the corridor, there was no one to be seen, but that would change soon. Bending down, Jerich tried to grab the unconscious man and drag him back into the room. His hands were swollen with very little movement in the fingers, he had to settle for pushing the body from the other side. Thankfully the floor was waxed and slippery, or it may have taken much longer.

Maneuvering him towards the bed, Jerich stole a look at the camera as it continued panning the room. There was no way to know if someone was on the other side or not, so Jerich concentrated on finishing what he had started. A few more heaves and pushes later, the doctor was next to the bed and Jerich took a second to catch his breath. Listening for the sound of footsteps in the corridor, he shook off his wariness and leaned down over the body.

Managing to get both of his arms underneath, Jerich struggled to get back up and dropped the doctor onto the bed. He was very heavy for being such a thin man Jerich thought as he fumbled with the blankets to get him covered up. This would fool no one on close inspection, but if the feed from the room was only periodically checked on, it may do the job. The body lay beneath the blanket in front of him which rose and fell with the doctor's breathing. Satisfied with the illusion, Jerich turned to leave. Once again passing under the camera's watchful eye as he left.

Outside the room, Jerich closed the door as best he could with the handle missing. There would be nothing he could do about that now, but it may pass casual scrutiny. Instead, he took a long look up and down the corridor and listened for unexpected guests. Once he located the girl, all he would have to do is make it back to this hallway. He had memorized the route back to the garage they arrived in, so getting there would be trivial once he returned here. A three-way intersection could be seen to his right. Hoping that a guide would be posted there, Jerich chose that direction to walk.

Attentive for any signs of life, he continued slowly down the hallway. Duplicates of the door he had left broken behind him passed by, all darkened inside from what Jerich could tell. The lights above him hummed with electricity as he moved beneath them, it was the only sound he heard between his punctuating footsteps. Reaching the intersection, Jerich turned to look at the wall.

A series of arrows and what they pointed to were beneath the familiar purple flower. The direction he had just come from was listed as 'Examination Rooms 100 - 125', beneath that was an arrow with the word 'Security' - clearly not the way to go. Pointing to the right was 'Examination Rooms 126 - 150', and beneath that 'Briefing Room 12'. With at least twelve briefing rooms, Jerich suspected this place would have to be huge. He felt a stab of fear at the thought of locating one single room is such a large place. Turning behind him, he looked to see where his third option lead to.

Another series of arrows, among them were 'Administration', 'Cafeteria' and 'Laboratories'. Jerich paused, laboratories sounded promising, but administration and cafeteria would be a problem. This would be a high traffic hallway, and he certainly didn't look as though he belonged here. A thought crossed his mind to go back and take the unconscious doctor's white coat, but the man was much taller than Jerich and it wouldn't fit or look right. He would just have to creep ahead and pay attention as he advanced, perhaps the cafeteria would give him some cover.

Continuing on down the winding hallway, he heard voices up ahead. They were faint, but sounded deep, possibly a security patrol. Jerich frantically looked around him for some place to hide, just ahead was a door, but he couldn't tell where it lead from here. His choices were to trail back the way he came or take a chance on the unknown. Fearing he would be pushed back to his room if he retreated, Jerich rushed to the door.

Reaching it in short time, he glanced up and saw the word 'Maintenance'. He also looked nothing like maintenance staff, but his choice had already been made. If someone was inside, he had a better chance of explaining his way out of things to the maintenance staff then he did security. He turned the handle on the door and hoped.

It opened.

Jerich slipped inside and quietly closed the door behind him. Inside the room was pitch black, and he dared not move. Listening to the door, he heard the two men walking closer. Their conversation was almost audible, but Jerich could only hear snatches of what was said. The footsteps stopped outside of the door Jerich was behind. Not wanting to move, he gripped the handle tightly and hoped no one would try too hard to open it. The two continued to speak for a moment, and Jerich could hear the squelch of a radio. He had guessed right, they had to be security.

Suddenly the room shook and a thunder boomed from somewhere in the distance.

"What the hell was that?" Keating said with a look of shock on his face.

Bill had heard the loud thud from somewhere in the building, he was experienced enough in the field to know it was an explosion of some type. He turned in the direction of the door, expecting someone to come through soon with information, but it remained closed.

Keating began rummaging through his desk drawers and pulled out a remote control. Turning and pointing it at the large screen on the wall, the television came to life and a series of security cameras appeared. He began flipping through them, checking for something out of the ordinary, but gave up after a few moments and turned to pick up the phone.

While Keating began making calls, Bill picked up the remote and walked over to the big screen. He began flipping through camera feeds, looking for signs of panic. Images of security posts, the parking lot, various hallways designated only by the camera number on the screen, but nothing that resembled the pandemonium that should be occurring right now. Continuing upwards, there were a series of black screens that could mean nothing or could mean everything. Bill wanted hard evidence.

A gray image flashed by as Bill sped on through the blank feeds, and he quickly flipped back to find it. On screen was a room with smoke clouding it, Bill could see someone on the ground crawling away.

"Where is that?" Bill asked loudly.

Keating was on the phone but cupped the handset, "That's the new research wing," he said nodding in the screens direction. "Some of the cameras haven't been connected yet, just keep going upwards."

Keating returned to his phone, and Bill pressed onwards. Another series of blank screens were followed by a long shot of a hallway. Half a dozen armed men were running down towards something. Bill was heading in the right direction, he continued. Another hallway, two men posted outside a door, both with their weapons trained in its direction. Flip, an armory of some kind, men were picking up rifles and ammunition before running out the door. Flip, another hallway, two scientists backed against the wall. Across from them was a doorway. Flip.

Bingo.

On the screen was a large room, divided by a large pane of glass with a door in the middle. The left half of the glass was broken open, glittering bits littered the floor and smoke was pouring from the hole. The entire inside of the see-through partition was filled with a pale blue smog, there was a light of some kind burning brightly within. A few people could be seen huddled against the wall, and two armed guards slowly advanced on the door. The first one pointed his rifle in its direction while the second crouched low and crept forward with a keycard. Leaning in, he swiped the strip with it and the door opened.

The guards covered each other as they entered the foggy interior, slowly the two disappeared into its depths. For a moment there was nothing, then an eruption of gunfire lit up the interior in staccato. The barrage continued sporadically until a body crashed against the unbroken glass. Blood sprayed outwards as it bounced off and slumped to the floor, motionless. A hollow scream could be heard from inside followed by a rain of bullets firing into the ether, then there was silence.

A moment later, a body came from the smoke, through the broken window and onto the floor in front of it. Bill looked closer, the head was missing. Glancing back up to the hole, Bill could just make out a dark silhouette approaching it. Another moment passed and a large creature appeared. Wide and hulking, it crouched to push through and then stood upright to almost reach the ceiling. It was dark, blue lines cracked across its surface like illuminated veins. Across its neck, something silver flashed in the light. The head was a mass of black with two bright blue orbs punctuating its features, a tear of blue beneath formed a mouth. It opened wide and a terrible roar was accompanied by a flood of light escaping into the room from the gaping maw.

The people huddled next to the wall began to run for the door. Bill could make out at least two of them, Coleman and Frank. Strieber was nowhere to be seen. Behind them were two others that Bill assumed to be lab techs, one almost made it to the door before being caught by the creature. Picking the man up by the leg, the creature looked at him for a moment. Another roar escaped and the tech was thrown at incredible speed towards the others who were fleeing. The camera missed most of the devastation, but a leg bounced back in frame, the rest of the body absent.

The creature advanced on the exit and would leave the frame soon, Bill quickly flipped up and down through the remote in hopes of finding another feed. After a few desperate clicks, another image appeared and he recognized Frank from the rush of movement on the screen. The three survivors were now at another exit to the south. Across from the room they had just left, a contingent of armed men were at the ready. There was a moment of silence before the door to the room flew from its hinges and landed in front of the small group who immediately began firing. Bill watched as sparks flew from ricochets as the troops poured on in grouped firing. Each team within the team reloading while the other continued to fire. It was a well executed maneuver, but it did them no good.

With a crash, the doorway burst open. Chunks of metal flew from the impact and the opening had become a blast radius, ripping open like a tin can. The creature burst through and landed in front of the squad, many of which fell over from fear or shock. The creature rushed them and bowled through into the hallway they had been guarding.

Bill looked over to Keating whose mouth hung open, his eyes were wide with shock. "Gerald," Bill said. Then a moment later, "Gerald!"

Keating looked up at Bill who was rushing towards the door. Bill tossed the remote to him, "They can't get out of there," Bill shouted on his way by, "Strieber is gone and I have Frank's key!"

"Bill!" Keating shouted after him. "Bill, don't be stupid!"

After the floor-rattling blast, Jerich heard dust and dirt flitter down from somewhere above him. The two guards outside shouted in surprise, and one began to yell into his radio. Jerich heard them running off into the distance. After a moment, he turned the handle that was still in his sweaty palm. The door opened and a rush of cool air hit Jerich in the face, he peeked out through the opening he had made but could see no one.

Taking a chance, he threw it open the rest of the way and quickly evaluated his situation. He was alone again. Shutting the door behind him, he continued his trek down the corridor. The lights above him flickered a few times, but there were no further tremors. In the distance, he could hear some kind of alarm, but no sounds of people. Reaching a corner, he peered around to see the lights of the cafeteria a short distance away.

Sneaking up as best he could, Jerich reached the edge of a window and stole a peek inside. It was completely empty. In fact, it looked as though it had never been used. The chairs were up on the tables, and the cooking area was covered over with tarps. Walking past, he kept one eye on the hallway and the other on the cafeteria in case he was wrong. Reaching the other side, there was a turn, followed by what was clearly a security checkpoint. Two armed guards stood outside of a door, pointing their rifles in its direction.

A feeling of defeat overcame Jerich, and he leaned against the wall. Sliding down to a crouch, he banged his head against the hard surface a couple of times in frustration. He knew this kind of situation would arise, but silently believed that somehow he would be able to avoid it. Stealing another look around the corner, he weighed his options. He could wait, or he could step around the corner. Waiting really wasn't an option, especially with whatever emergency was at hand. If he stepped around and gave himself up, he might be able to take the two of them out the same way he did the doctor. That would most likely get him shot though. He had survived two bullets in the past, but it took hours to recover from that. A dozen or so could take days, assuming it didn't kill him outright.

Closing his eyes, he tried to center himself and got ready to move. He breathed in deeply and concentrated on the moment. Deep in the back of his mind, he could see her. Lost and alone, at the hands of some faceless entity whose only objective was to tear her apart and find out what made her tick. She was counting on him, she needed him, he was her only chance of escape.

Standing back up, Jerich exhaled through pursed lips, found his courage and opened his eyes. In what felt like slow motion, he stepped around the corner and focused on the two guards in front of the door. Two strides, four strides, he advanced on them from behind. Ready for them to turn, ready to pounce, he closed the gap between them. A noise, an alarm, it seemed so distant, the two men backed up in response. Jerich grew closer. One yelled to the other. Jerich didn't hear, Jerich didn't care, Jerich grew closer.

The two guards rushed towards the door. Closer. One reached. Closer. Opened the door. Closer. Went through, the other followed. Closer. Jerich reached out, and caught the door before it closed. Standing there, he watched the two guards disappear down the hallway.

22

Homecoming

Running down corridors and stairs, Bill was breathing heavily from exertion. His doubt that he would make it in time was increasing by the moment, but his instinct to save lives spurred him on. Ahead of him, there was another squad of armed men at the ready with their weapons trained on a checkpoint door. It was the entrance to the research wing. Slowing to a jog, he approached the men and caught his breath.

One turned and walked over to Bill, "Sir, you can't go in there," he said with a hand raised.

"Two of your superiors are trapped inside and, I'm going in after them," Bill said between breaths.

"Sir, there's a..." the soldier began.

"Soldier, we don't have time to fuck around here!" Bill raised his voice, stopping him dead in his tracks. "Now I'm going through and if I were you," he pointed down to the soldiers gun, "I'd go get something bigger."

The soldier looked down to his weapon, Bill turned and swiped himself through. The door opened and Bill started inside. He heard the soldier shut the door behind him as he moved on down the hallway. A turn took him down a grated walkway that led to an expansive white room. On the other side, the large metal door that led to the laboratories stood ominously. It was built into the steel-reinforced wall, meant to withstand the detonation of a bomb.

The room was empty and deadly silent.

Bill walked across to the large door and peered through the small window in the top. The lab from the video he had been watching was just on the other side. Straight ahead, lying twisted on the ground, was the remains of the door. The archway it had been attached to could be seen to the left, the metal was peeled back like fingers into the air and a faint mist was leaking out. To his right was the hallway that Bill had watched the creature chase their men into. It was dark, punctuated with the occasional sputter of electricity. Each flash illuminating a hint of the carnage that lay in that direction.

To the right of the heavy door was another keycard slot, this one was accompanied by a keypad. Bill stared at it for a moment, then looked back through the window. The same scene awaited him inside, he reached over and swiped his card through.

The door buzzed and stayed shut.

Bill looked over to the security panel and swiped again. Another buzz, the door remained closed. This time the small screen over the keypad said 'Unauthorized Access'.

A low thud sounded and the floor rattled under Bill, freezing him in his tracks. Plaster dust fell from the ceiling above, hitting the floor sporadically. Bill went back to the window and looked inside, again nothing had changed. He waited a moment, the flash from the broken lighting lit up the corridor again and Bill could see two men hobbling out. He pounded on the glass, one man set the other down on the floor and rushed over.

Frank's face appeared in the window. "Bill!" Frank shouted with a look of shock and happiness on his face. "Bill, open the door!" His voice faint, muffled by the glass.

Seeing Frank brought a mix of emotions to Bill. Another thud echoed through the room and the lights dimmed around him. The impending doom brought him back. "It won't let me through!" Bill yelled into the window. "Unauthorized access."

Frank's hand appeared next to his face, pointing down. "Flip the card. The last four digits from that number need to be entered after you swipe." He shouted each word, pausing between each for clarity.

Bill nodded and moved over to the keypad. Turning the card over in his hand, he memorized the last four digits. Swiping the card through again, he punched the code into the keypad.

'Unauthorized Access', a buzz and the door remained shut.

Bill moved back to the window, "It's not working!" he yelled into it.

Confusion played across Frank's face for a moment, then he turned. "Alex!" he yelled. "Alex, how do we get the door open!" He ran over to the man lying on the ground.

Bill could hear nothing of what was being said, instead he had retreated back into his mind. He hadn't had the time to process everything he'd just read in Keating's office. Deep inside, he couldn't believe that Frank would set up his family. They had all been friends for years, Frank had spent Christmas with them more times than not.

Frank's face appeared in the window, "Okay," he shouted, "this is what you have to do..."

"I just talked to Keating," Bill yelled into the window.

Frank froze for a moment, "Bill we don't have time for this right now," he yelled. "We..."

From inside, Bill faintly heard Coleman's voice shouting. "It's coming through! Frank!"

Frank's face had turned to look, but it returned right away. "Bill, the door..." he began

"Frank!" Coleman's voice continued to shout. "Frank, help me up. It's coming through!"

Bill tried to look over to where Coleman was lying down.

"Forget him!" Frank shouted and pounded on the glass in front of Bill.

Bill looked back into Frank's face, "I read your emails, Frank!" he shouted into the glass. "I saw the photos of my family. Your handwriting, the timetable that only a friend of the family would know."

The look on Frank's face was the final nail in the coffin. "Bill, this is all Keating's..." he began.

A crash that Bill felt more than heard came from somewhere on the other side of the door. Frank turned and came back with a look of horror on his face. "Bill, we've known each other for..."

Bill heard Coleman screaming, it was quickly cut off by a loud thud. There was an eerie silence.

"Bill..." Frank said, it couldn't be heard but Bill read his lips.

"I guess I really am the ruthless bastard everyone keeps telling me about," Bill shouted into the glass and turned around.

"Bill!" Frank's voice shouted from behind. "Bill!"

Continuing to walk away, Bill heard Frank's screams in the distance.

————

As Jerich continued down the hallway, a series of loud thumps rocked the building around him. He paused at each thunderous interval, but nothing would stop him now. He gave a downward glance to his injured hand as he walked on. There was no blood, but the large indent remained. Time may mend that, but right now he had little fine motor skill, anything requiring delicate manipulation would be a problem. Ahead he could see a darkened hallway, the lights over top flickered periodically.

Stepping around the corner, he could see broken walls and tiles from the ceiling. Various cables hung down randomly. There was smoke and a faint smell of ozone in the air. The debris ended in a large breach that may have been a door at one time. It was unclear what was on the other side from where Jerich stood, but it felt like the way forward to him.

Advancing down, Jerich stepped over and under the obstacles in his path. In his peripheral, he could see the remains of examination rooms, offices, and labs through the holes in the wall. Whatever had come through here had made short work of everything in its path. The one thing missing here was people. Aside from the two guards he had seen running in this direction, Jerich had not seen a single person. He wasn't sure what was going on here, but he didn't question it, right now it was to his benefit. Reaching the far end, Jerich stepped over the remnants of whatever had sealed this room previously. The other side was something he wasn't prepared for.

The carnage on display beneath the flickering lights was gruesome. Walls and floors were painted red, and undefinable bits of what may have once passed for human lay scattered. Jerich felt his stomach lurch. Buckling over and catching the wall, he vomited loudly onto everything in front of him. Himself included. Twice more the urge hit him until he regained control. Wiping his mouth on his sleeve, he braced himself and turned around.

No good, the sight sent him back for another fit. Holding the wall again, he evacuated what little he had left in his system. Coughing and heaving at the end. Shaking his head to ward off the dizziness, he stood up and prepared for another try. Covering the bottom half of his face with his clean sleeve, he tried to block out as much as he could and stumbled across the dim room to a large hole on the other side. His feet crushed and slid through things that he put out of his mind until it was safely out of sight.

Stepping through the hole, he immediately bent over and tried desperately not to throw up again. He concentrated on the ground in front of him, it was awash with a blue mist. A few moments later, Jerich regained his composure and stole a look around. It was a large room with a broken glass partition, the inside of which was completely filled with the smoke that was spilling onto the floor. Ahead of him something poked up from the mist. Based on what he had just stepped through, Jerich did his best to ignore it and walked around to the glass.

As he approached, his face grew numb and his ears almost deaf. Jerich coughed with the pressure he felt in his chest, each time sent a shock of pain through his head. He could smell something in his nose, it was sickly-sweet and yet had a faint whiff of old linen. Through the smoke, a slight blue glow was growing with his proximity. Jerich's skin began to sweat and heat up, it was a warmth he felt right to the bone. Stepping over to the large break in the glass, he peered inside. The smoke was too thick to see much, and Jerich couldn't tell what was causing it. He stepped through the jagged mouth and inside.

Broken glass crunched under his feet. Whatever had guided him here told him this was it, this was where he was meant to be. Stepping closer, he bumped into the end of a bed. Feeling his way around, he made it to the side and his hand touched something that seemed very human. Jerich's heart thumped heavy inside him. A sigh came from whoever lay in front of him. Reaching over, Jerich lifted the beds resident from the sheets and made his way back through the breach.

Outside the glass partition, Jerich could now see the very small human he carried. The skin was pale and hairless and yet through the lack of any memory or clear identity, Jerich immediately knew this was who he had come for. She was weak in his arms, barely clinging to life. Every link, every connection he had shared with her had been quiet since his arrival to this building. Looking down at her frail body broke him, the travesty that she had gone through was written deep everywhere his eyes searched.

A determination and hatred fell over Jerich. He would take her out of this place, he would get her to safety so she could heal. And when he was done, he would come back here and make those responsible pay. Come hell or high water, these monsters would get their dues. Stepping out of the room, Jerich suddenly found no problem with the carnage that surrounded him.

In fact, it made him smile.

———

Returning to the garage had been largely uneventful, Jerich had located a gurney on the way to allow his passenger to rest easy on their travels. Unconscious the entire time, Jerich had checked her periodically for breath and temperature. At first she had been clammy and cold. Now that she was away from that room, she was warming up and even regaining some of her color. He had covered her up with every blanket he could find at first, but now she was down to a single sheet. Her rising temperature and building sweat on her forehead had caused Jerich to remove them one by one as they went back through the building. Locked doors were also no longer a problem thanks to a dead body that had helpfully provided a keycard.

Since the girl's rescue, Jerich's swollen hands had begun to mend. Most of the concrete surface had reverted back to flesh. White and textured flesh, but at least he had regained movement of two fingers on his right hand. The left was still a solid mass that he could barely feel, but he had enough mobility to hold the keycard and open doors when necessary.

Down the hallway ahead of them now were the double doors to the garage. When Jerich had arrived, there had been the driver and one other man in a small office. Hopefully things hadn't changed much since then. Bringing the gurney up to the door, Jerich parked it off to the side and quietly slipped his way in. Across from the entrance he could see the lights through the window to the small room. A man sat in a chair in front of a computer, he was busily engaged in something and hadn't noticed Jerich enter. Searching the garage, he could see three white vans like the ones he had arrived in, as well as three police cars. All were vacant.

Sliding back between the doors, Jerich dragged the gurney through. Afraid of noise, he pulled slowly and walked it down the ramp to the parking area. Putting a white van between himself and the man at the desk, Jerich stole up to the passenger's side of it and tried the handle. It was unlocked. Looking through the doors window, he focused on the overhead light. Stealing a glance back to the office again, Jerich quickly opened the door and lunged inside. Bringing it closed quietly behind him with a slight clunk, the dome light had barely been illuminated for a moment. He stared out the front to see if it had drawn any attention, the man had not moved.

Looking around inside, Jerich searched for the keys. The ignition was empty, the divider between the seats only had an empty coffee cup. Inside the glove compartment was a bunch of papers and plastic cards for things and places Jerich had never heard of, but no keys. Glancing back across to the man behind the desk, Jerich imagined the keys would likely be in there. He wondered what the chances were that he could subdue the man before he raised an alarm. Then he looked up to the visor over the steering wheel. Reaching up, he gave it a flick and a set of keys dropped to the seat. Fumbling with his good hand, it took him a few tries to pick them up. It took even longer to get them into the ignition, his time was quickly running out.

Looking back up to the light on the roof, Jerich used his numb hand to smash it before opening the door once again. Slipping out, he pulled the gurney away from the van and lifted its small occupant up. Sliding her into the passenger seat, her eyes fluttered slightly as he locked the seat-belt into place to hold her. Leaning the seat back as far as he could, Jerich tried to pack blankets around her to cushion any jarring. His hands made it difficult, but he did what he could and finally closed the door beside her.

Crouching around the front of the van, Jerich's eyes watched the office for movement and then dashed to the driver's side door and got in. Nothing had changed, the man continued to sit in front of the computer and Jerich looked down to the dangling keys in the ignition. He would have to squeeze them awkwardly between his fingers to turn them, but the bigger problem would be getting out of here. Searching the garage for the exit, he spotted a large and closed door at the far end. Right next to the office. Jerich closed his eyes in frustration, they were so close now. Giving his head a shake, he opened them again.

Clipped to the visor in front of him was a rectangle of black plastic with a big white button on it.

Jerich looked back to the exit, to the office, back to the button. Leaning over, he caught the ignition key between his fingers and turned. The van sputtered and grunted in response and Jerich's fingers slipped off the key. Maneuvering around to catch them again, he tried turning the van over a second time. Outside the front window, Jerich could see the man from inside the office. He was now at the door looking in their direction. The van groaned and whined, again not starting. The guard was now walking towards the van, his hand gripping something on his belt.

Turning the key again, the van roared to life, and Jerich quickly grabbed the steering wheel. It was sliding through his hands, he had no tactile feeling as he tried to turn it. Putting the van into gear, Jerich pushed on the accelerator, and the van jumped forwards. He lost his grip on the wheel and the van almost crashed into a cement pillar. The man across the parking lot was now running, he had a gun drawn and was yelling in Jerich's direction. Seizing the wheel again, Jerich squeezed so hard that it cracked and split beneath his grasp. He pointed the van away from the cement and once again punched the gas.

The van jumped ahead and began to travel towards the exit. The approaching guard stopped abruptly and fired his pistol into the windshield. A hole appeared in the center and a long crack shot across into Jerich's line of sight. Keeping his foot down, the van continued at a breakneck pace. Jerich was having a hard time keeping control despite there being little he could crash into. The guard jumped to the side as the van narrowly missed him and barreled on to the exit. Another shot rang out and Jerich heard it hit the side of the van. They were fast approaching the door and Jerich had to let off the gas.

Fumbling with the button on the visor, Jerich tried pressing it with one of his good fingers. Nothing happened. The van had coasted to a stop and Jerich tried again. Another shot rang out, this one punctured the back door and hit somewhere inside. Angry, Jerich pulled the entire visor from the roof and mashed the button in his hands. He watched the plastic crush beneath them in his frustration.

The door began to open.

Jerich threw the plastic and visor to the side and returned his hands to the wheel, tromping down again on the gas. The van jumped ahead and bolted for the opening door, another shot fired and missed them completely. The bright light from outside was glaring in and momentarily blinded Jerich, he squinted in response. When his sight returned, the van was heading for the wall instead of the door. Turning at the last minute, the van careened off the frame and they bounced through. Regaining control, Jerich sped away down the road, the building behind them growing smaller in the mirror.

Slamming the door to Greaves' office, Beau turned around and extended the middle finger of each hand to the wooden barrier.

Both were shaking with a frustration that his face mimicked. After a moment he turned back, clenched his fist and threw a punch at an imaginary person in front of him.

Straightening up, Beau put a big smile on his face, "I love that man! He is just such a sensible individual, always thinking ahead."

David was snickering at his desk, Beau wandered over and sat on the corner.

"Trashed your story again did he?" David asked and reached for his coffee cup.

Beau crossed his arms and looked down to his friend, "That man wouldn't know a good story if he caught it sleeping with his wife."

"His wife sure would," David replied, "it would probably be a much better lay."

Beau smirked and shook his head, "He wants to reduce my story to a simple public service announcement. All of the action, all of the impact castrated so it seems like a suggestion rather than a warning."

David nodded, taking a sip of his coffee.

"I was there, Dee," Beau said pointing his finger in the general direction. "If the other looters don't get you, the cops will. I watched a guy get tased and let me tell you," Beau leaned in, "television just doesn't do it justice."

"Oh?" David said with mild interest.

"Vicious," Beau said staring off in remembrance, "the man was frothing at the mouth and pissing himself..." he trailed off.

David shrugged, "If things escalate, the boss will have no choice but to acknowledge things." He set his cup down, "And you can rub his nose in it. Tactfully of course."

"Of course," Beau echoed with a smirk on his face. "He always brings out the best in me. I'm so lucky to have his guidance."

David snickered again.

Beau felt his pocket vibrate, it was his new phone ringing. "Shit," he said and reached in to fish around for it. "Be right back," he said to David and walked over to an empty room across from his boss's office. Stepping inside and partially closing the door, he put his mug in front of the phone's camera and waited for it to verify him.

Moments later, a familiar voice appeared, "Mr. Bradley."

"Look, you don't have to worry about that footage..." Beau began.

"That's not why I'm calling Mr. Bradley," the voice interrupted him.

Beau paused. "Okay," he said finally.

"It seems our timetable has been accelerated, events are unfolding sooner than we had anticipated," the voice continued. "This has placed us in a very awkward position. We are moving forward with the first phase of our plan, and we need to be sure you are still on board."

There was a silence. Beau peered out through the opening in the door to ensure his conversation would remain private. At the front doors he could see three men. Two were talking to reception while the third was leaning against the wall with a cigar in his mouth. None of them were familiar to him.

"Can we still count on your support, Mr. Bradley?" the voice asked.

His attention returned to the phone. "I'm having a problem with my boss here. Specifically his need to control..." Beau started to explain.

"Yes, Mr. Bradley, this will no longer be a problem very shortly," The voice interrupted. "We will need explicit control of media for the near future. A very precise guide has been extensively developed, and there is only one way we can assure this."

Beau wondered where this was going, he started thinking about possibilities.

"We require our own news source, one that we have complete oversight on."

"You can't build up a news station overnight," Beau protested. "You need to develop a community trust..."

"We are well aware of that, Mr. Bradley," the voice once again interrupting. "That's why we have decided to purchase one instead, and we want you to head it up."

"Me?" Beau asked. "Look, I'd have to give my resignation, and that could take weeks." He looked out across to his boss's office, the two men from reception were at his door. "And that's even assuming he would let me out of my contract."

"No need," the voice replied. "We have decided to purchase KLLTV. It's local, and you are already established within its foundation."

"I doubt Greaves will sell his baby," Beau protested, "it's the only thing he has in his life."

"This is not something we can afford to be without," the voice said, "and we can afford more than he could imagine." The voice paused to let that sink in. "The question is not if the position will be available, but if you are willing to take it."

Beau thought about all the poor decisions that Greaves had made for KLL in the past. He had wondered, on more than one occasion, how much better his career would be without those choices. Across from him, he watched the two men enter Greaves' office. Inside, his boss looked like a deer in headlights.

Returning to the phone, Beau smiled, "I'm in."

———

The van rumbled down the highway, the impact with the door on the way out of the garage had given the van a slight wobble. Jerich once again checked the mirror, expecting to find someone there, but the road behind him remained empty. Looking down to the dash, the GPS indicated a straight line ahead.

After getting out onto the highway, Jerich had pointed himself in a direction away from the building and floored it. He had owned a valid driver license at one time, but it had since lapsed. Jerich couldn't justify continuing to pay for something he could never afford to use. Once the van had put in a few miles of distance, he had pulled over to look for a map. Instead, he had found a GPS system with multiple destinations marked with military code words; Alpha, Bravo, Delta, and so on. Delta was the address of his job, the place from which he had been picked up, so it was even money that these were quarantine locations. He had chosen the closest one that kept him out of the city, low profile and low traffic would be the safest route.

Jerich stole a glance at his passenger, she lay quietly in a cradle of blankets. Reaching over, he checked her breathing once again and touched her forehead with the back of his forearm. She seemed to be stable, but nothing else. Jerich hoped that to was a good sign. A CB radio was attached to the dash. Initially he had turned it off as it was only increasing his anxiety. Now that he had some distance behind him, he had switched it back on in case it could provide information. Right now it was nothing but random static.

The highway ahead was barren as it rolled on towards the horizon, the GPS indicated they were still some ways out. Doubt shot through Jerich again as he wondered if he was doing the right thing. He couldn't be sure she would have the same reaction to the quarantine zone or the ash that he had. Her body had visible wounds, but he suspected that most of the damage was internal. He could only guess at how this medical mystery worked, and the frail body of his passenger told him the doctor's had been working hard to solve that problem. Jerich clung to his intuitions and concentrated on getting there.

A crackle from the CB startled Jerich from his thoughts. Looking down, he reached over and began cycling through the channels, but an empty hiss greeted him at every stop. Next to the dial he noticed a button marked 'Auto-scan', Jerich pressed it and returned his hand to the wheel. Punctuated intervals of silence and static began playing back, but nothing else. He left it to continue its job, and returned his eyes to the road. Miles of grass, fences and occasional turn-offs passed by but the GPS had kept him on the highway. To his right he could see the city in the distance, the smog drifting upwards into the sky.

A voice broke through the static, "...return to base. Repeat, all units return to base. Operation..."

The channel changed automatically and Jerich almost lost control of the van reaching down to change it back. Straightening the vehicle back out, he flipped the dial.

Static.

"Dammit!" Jerich grunted and turned the dial a few more times.

A high pitched whine erupted through the speaker and Jerich quickly turned down the volume. Overhead, he heard a sonic rush and watched a jet fighter pass by and fly into the distance. Staring after it, he shook his head. Two more bursts rocked the van and the jet soon had company. He could see the three of them assemble in formation and quickly disappear.

Jerich peered over to the passenger's seat, the girl had shifted, but she was still unconscious. Looking back, the GPS told him they were close now. The vans wobble had made Jerich wary, but the jets had suddenly rendered that unimportant, he punched it to the floor. A shimmy began to develop from the rear, but it was manageable. The wheel in his hand was vibrating, but the solid grip he had established was more than enough to hold on. Far off beyond the city a bright light bloomed out, quickly followed by another. Their intensity cause Jerich to avert his eyes.

Moments later two thumps vibrated everything in the van. Jerich looked back across to see two rising clouds plume in the distance. His heart began to race and adrenaline shot through his body, he was suddenly acutely aware of his surroundings. Ahead of him, he could see a fog forming. It was first white, then gray, and now it had a faint blue glow. It was slowly rising into the air when he spied the three jets fast approaching in the sky.

They were advancing at a breakneck speed, flying directly overtop of the fog that was lifting skywards. In a blur of motion, they passed over it. Moments later Jerich was hit by another blinding light, everything was silent.

And then the thunder.

The map on the screen was pulsating colors. Bill watched the blips of armed fighter jets pass over the Ashrealm, red circles indicating bomb detonation lit up and slowly spread. The coordinated strike was swift and devastating, covering the entire infected area in a matter of moments. Bill watched the red circles cover the blue of the Ashrealm and leave behind nothing. All traces of the anomaly disappeared wherever the bombs landed.

"Strieber was right on the money," Keating said.

Bill was not convinced, "We can't celebrate just yet."

"No," Keating replied, "we need to get this cleaned up quickly. There will be official inquiries very soon, and we no longer have our liaison. Do you think you can handle it?"

Bill stared at the map for a moment. Coleman's demise haunting him slightly but Frank's death stood head and shoulders above. It was a rash decision, it was a selfish decision, and worst of all, it was a decision he would make again. Official channels be damned, retribution was his and he would sleep better for it. Bill swept it all to a dark corner of his mind.

"Yes, but I'll need some time to prepare," Bill finally said.

"You were born prepared," Keating said, "that's why you are back where you belong, running things again."

Bill wasn't so sure. He continued to stare at the map a while longer, watching the blue slowly fade from it. Perhaps he was just paranoid, but it was now his job to be.

"So when is that official?" Bill asked.

"Technically?" Keating replied. "It already is, the board has already put its vote in. You will be presented and properly welcomed tomorrow, so rest up. Strieber will have a desk full of paperwork for you."

"Strieber's alive?" asked Bill turning to face Keating.

Keating nodded, "He was adjusting bomb targets based on your growth predictions. One could say you saved his life."

That thought left Bill conflicted, he still couldn't bring himself to trust the man. Bill kept waiting for the other shoe to drop, a punchline to be delivered. Looking back to the map, the fighters were making a final pass and retreating. Nothing of the anomaly remained.

"This is going to be a PR nightmare," Bill shook his head.

"Already taken care of Bill," Keating said dismissively, "that's one area you won't have to contend with."

A small wave of relief hit Bill, the press could be troublesome. They would always find some small thing to...

There was a blip on the radar, small and blue. Bill stared for a moment, waiting for it to disappear. Another blip, it was moving.

Bill looked over to the tech, "Focus in on that." he said pointing.

The tech did so, "That's as close as I can get with the map," he said in reply.

"Pull up the satellite feed," Keating said from his seat.

Bill watched the map vanish, it was replaced by a fuzzy camera feed. The image sharpened up and began scrolling around. On the screen was a highway, the camera still far away. It followed the road for a moment, a dust cloud could be seen blowing along its surface even from this distance. A vehicle came into view, the camera refocused and zoomed in. On screen was a white van, tipped on its side. The blowing dust was now a storm, billowing around the overturned vehicle.

"Is that the source?" Keating asked.

The screen changed colors, white, orange, and then back to normal. "No," the tech replied.

The camera zoomed out and began to move again, continuing to follow the road. It remained empty for a few moments until something came into view from the right. Someone was struggling against the storm, their progress slow and unsteady. Zooming in again, a blurry image slowly gained focus.

————

He was deaf, he was blind. Jerich felt the force of a wind blowing against his face, tearing at his skin. In his arms was the small girl, swaddled in blankets. Around him was darkness, in that darkness he could see blue. Blue everywhere, swirling around him, ahead of him, and cradled in his arms. His leg was broken, but he walked, every step a shock of pain. His chest burned like it was on fire, every breath a labor. His determination the only thing keeping him going.

A chill shot through his body and he stumbled, quickly catching himself before he fell. Looking down he noticed the fading color of his charge. Her body seemed to shimmer in his arms, she was fading fast. Jerich grunted, pushed on and ignored the sudden burst of suffering it surrounded his body in. He could see his salvation just ahead, a blue oasis waiting to bathe the two of them in its healing waters. Every step caused him to yell out, his sightless eyes were weeping with the agony his body was in. He couldn't stop now, he wouldn't stop now. Step, another step, he was almost there, it was so close.

Jerich's feet hit something and he stumbled, falling to his knees. He screamed in pain, he felt his mind beginning to pass out. Growling with anger, he shook it off and pushed himself back up to his feet. Step, another step, stronger now, he felt his legs renewed with a willpower he had never known. His strides grew longer, his breath shorter, he could feel a warmth growing within his chest.

Beneath him, the world changed, the oasis had been reached. Jerich could feel it under his feet, they sank down into it. He collapsed onto his knees and cried out in relief. Leaning forward, he slowly placed the girl down into the soft blue. Pulling the blankets from around her, he began to shower her with handfuls of the silt around them. He watched it sparkle and flare as it fell onto her. Beneath, her body grew brighter and stronger. It stirred slightly and Jerich stopped, waiting for her rebirth.

The blue began to fade. Around him, below him, beneath him. The air itself, the floating blue particles lost all of their luster and Jerich's world once again fell into darkness.

"No!" Jerich screamed, his own voice hoarse and almost unrecognizable to him. "Nooooooooo!"

A burst of light exploded in front of Jerich and he recoiled. Below him the small body was a nova, washing the very world around him in bright blue light. Jerich suddenly saw everything, the blue beneath him, the air around him. In the distance there were blue lights shining brightly, growing in number, illuminating everything. Dozens, then hundreds, then thousands. It was a gathering, it was a witnessing, it was a family.

The light below him began to rise, growing, taking shape. The small girl grew in front of Jerich's eyes, a child becoming an adult in moments. Her arms extended, her body surrounded in twirling fog, still changing. Floating upwards, she spun lazily in the brilliant light. Jerich watched a long mane of hair crown her head. From her back something slowly began to take shape, expanding. Mist, becoming wings, stretching out. Her arms raised high, her head bent down and looked at Jerich. Her face was angelic, she was smiling, Jerich's heart and eyes filled at the sight of her.

Arching her back, her arm extended. From it something long and curved seemed to grow, solidify. Bringing both arms above her head, she looked down again, her face quite different this time.

Rage.

Above her head was a jagged sword, flowing, gleaming blue and bright. With a scream that consumed the very world around them, her arms came down with a fury. Slow motion, the jagged light growing closer, a ringing filling the air, his doom fast approaching.

But Jerich forgave her.

Acknowledgments

It took ten years of my life to amass the funds necessary to spend another year of it writing this book. Many authors have the ability to come home from a day at the office and lose themselves in six hours of writing, but I am not such a creature. As much as we like to believe we are capable of anything, life intrudes with its revelations of character and we are left to navigate our flaws. My daily sojourns to and from my employer afforded me the quiet contemplation that sowed the seed for this story. Adding to, and taking from it as I soldiered on to another day of slow death and capitulation. If it were not for this self-imposed solitude, this story would not lay before you today.

Many of the locations used in this book have real-world counterparts, most of which inspired ideas and contributed to the overarching storyline. I thank my brother Chad for including me in his excursions to places I had not thought to visit or never knew existed. Some of the most interesting locations in this book are there thanks to him. I am especially grateful for his unwavering patience in listening to me expound on my ideas and helping me iterate on them, it was crucial to this book. I look forward to returning the favor one day and anticipate reading a creation of his own.

I thank my brother Scott for putting up with my requests for his help. Taking me where I needed to go, feeding, watering, and caffeinating me without thought to recompense. I thank him for his patience in listening to me drone on about my story and not telling me to shut up and send him the audiobook already. Soon my brother, soon.

I thank my editor Joshua Plumb for whipping my hazy and broken understanding of English into shape. Also for his honest enthusiasm for the story I have written, and the stories I have yet to write. His opinions and interest came to me at a time when I needed them most.

A thanks to Fred Mansfield whose financial advice paved the way for this book to go from thought to action. Had I not talked to him on that fateful Tuesday over coffee, I could never have afforded this book the chance to grow.

Thanks also to the rest of my family who live halfway across the country. Their support in my decision to be creative instead of 'getting a real job' helped fuel my self-confidence. Parents with the wisdom to know that practical is not always the answer are a rare and treasured breed. Brothers who know when to kick your ass and when to help you up are equally rare. While not always perfect, it has been a charmed life.

Calgary, Alberta

About the Author

M.R. Darling was born on the eastern seaboard of Canada, moving to the lush mountain air of Calgary in 2006. With a background in music, and creating short, interesting stories, it was a natural inclination to move on to longer prose. Writing a lot of condensed fiction over the years, along with a few aborted attempts at a full length novel, 2016 was the year to push it across the finish line. Requiring ten months to write, A Blue Horizon begins the Ashrealm series and his fulfillment of an aspiration, decades in the making.

#whatistheashrealm

Stay Tuned…